Ruth Fawcett

Ruth Fawcett

Honor in the Heart

A Novel

Ambrosia Press
Cleveland

This is a work of fiction. The personalities, actions, and viewpoints of the characters are not the author's, but their own, within their fictional context. Any resemblance to actual persons, living or dead, is purely coincidental.

HONOR IN THE HEART
Published by Ambrosia Press

Copyright 2004 by Ruth Fawcett
Cover art copyright 2004 by Pamela Dills
Library of Congress Number 2003093162

All rights reserved. No part of this book may be reproduced or transmitted in any form or by any means, electronic or mechanical, including recording, photocopying, or by any information storage and retrieval system, without the written permission of the publisher.

Printed in the United States of America. For information address: Ambrosia Press, 2 Waban Road, Suite 3, Willowick, Ohio 44095

Hardcover ISBN 0-9729346-3-4
Paperback ISBN 0-9729346-4-2

FIRST EDITION

ACKNOWLEDGMENTS

My deepest appreciation for their considerable support goes to many special people: to my beloved husband, Bill, for his constant encouragement and a get-away flat; to my wonderful children, April, John, and Jennifer, for their patience, emotional sustenance, and, in some cases, critical reading; to my steadfast sons-in-law, Philip and Richard, for their interest and friendship. I owe a great debt to artist- niece, Pamela Dills, for her generosity, patience, and talent in designing and developing the cover art.

I am grateful for my many friends and former colleagues at George Washington School for their encouragement and anticipation.

I am especially indebted to dear friends: literary soul mate and truth sister, Roberta Smearman, for her advice, perspective, humor, and patient listening; my forever mentor, Arlene Fenton, for her ongoing interest, encouragement, and skilled critical reading; Mary Bruss, Karin and Dan Garland for their interest, encouragement, and generous listening. I salute every charter member of the Royal Order of Wools (both absent and present) for their constant love and enthusiasm for life which have inspired me over the years.

For technical information on polymers, I thank Global Products by DuPont Engineering for their website: www.dupont.com/enggpolymers/english/products/index.html.

Statistics related to homelessness, American business and culture are quoted with gratitude from Ben H. Bagdikian's article, "A Secret in the News: The USA Now Has a Permanent Poor" (The Homeless Grapevine, Issue 48, July-August, 2001, pp.12, 14-15).

To my sister, Marianne Numinen, my first strong linguistic role model, who cannot possibly know the extent of her influence on my love of words.

To educators and school families everywhere, with utmost respect for the beauty and nobility of their important work.

CHAPTER ONE—HOPE

Hope Fleming awoke before the alarm, riveted with memories. *One by one I watched them die. I felt them die. I mourned for all of them, every last one. They had meant so much to me, comforted me when I needed it, helped me stay sane, kept me focused.*

She threw back the covers and swung her legs to the floor. *I'm through with mourning now. Those dreams are dead. I aim to take my place among the living. Forge new connections. Restoreth my soul.*

Anticipating that this day would mark the beginning of an experience that would change her life, though unaware how profoundly, she rose from her bed in the dark bedroom, bristling with energy. Pulling on her butter-colored velour robe, she skipped down the shadowy stairs.

That holly bush is dying, Hope thought as she finished her breakfast tea on the dim sun porch. She loved the predawn morning. She treasured the Victorian green wicker furniture she had chosen so carefully for the enclosed porch. While it was similar to Mary Margarethe Baldwin's veranda furniture she had fallen in love with as a teenager, Hope would not let herself think of Mary Baldwin. Hope had paid for the furniture with her first salary from part-time university teaching. She had insisted on a full-sized sofa with thick cushions so Michael and she could take naps on the porch, which was laughable since neither had been nappers. The watery pink peonies on the white duck cushions beckoned her. She felt sad to think that no one in the family had ever lain on that sofa although she had achieved the inviting visual effect she sought. For a brief moment Hope wanted to stretch out on those gorgeous cushions. She breathed deeply, her lungs filling with lavender, no longer in bloom but still subtly fragrant. She could hear the steel wind chimes softly singing in the breeze from the open glass door. She heard the rustle of a small animal in the wooded ravine and saw a shadowy form skitter past.

She walked to the wind chimes and touched the cool steel, remembering that thirteen-year-old George had given them to her their first Christmas without

Michael, when they were both in their determined-to-be-brave-and-carry-on mode. Hope's eyes scanned the porch lovingly. She could see two-year-old George, unruly blonde hair framing his chubby apple cheeks, playing with his cars on the floor while she marked term papers spread in stacks over the sofa.

Looking again at the holly bushes, Hope noted that the male holly bush looked dead. *Doesn't that just figure. The male bush, Hope. Yet another male has let you down.* She worried that there would be no red berries on the female bushes this Christmas. She made a mental note to replace the male holly bush soon. *I have no one to help me do that.*

She slid open the glass door and reached out to pluck a small, brown leaf from the dry bush, wondering why she had not noticed its poor condition sooner. She turned the sharp-edged, lifeless leaf in her hand. Hope wondered if she were capable of removing the sick bush and planting a new one on her own. That's one of the disadvantages of being single, she thought; but she welcomed the challenge.

She felt guilty admitting how much she enjoyed single life. She hadn't always enjoyed it. Not when Michael and she had first separated after months of bitter arguing, and she was struggling to keep things at home on an even keel for thirteen-year-old George and herself. But once their emotions calmed down and they began to accept the situation, she and George, each too wounded to risk expending the smallest bit of emotion, had settled into a predictable routine. That was until George began to realize what it meant not to have his father at home. Thinking now of George's suddenly missing his father, Hope could feel his desperation. She could see herself and George driving home from the championship soccer game, which his team had lost miserably. A soft rain had begun to fall and she had turned on the heater against a damp chill. She resented the fact that she had to go to that game, all the games, in Michael's place. George blamed the loss on his several bad plays.

"It's only a game," she had said gently, trying to stop his self-condemning remarks that stabbed her heart sharply. She couldn't bear to see him that way after all the pain he had suffered from the divorce. She resented Michael's selfish refusal to attend George's games once the marriage was dead. She knew he wanted to punish her.

"It's not just a game!" George had shouted with unexpected intensity. "You don't understand. I wish Dad had come; he knows." George met Hope's gaze with cold eyes. She could see those icy blue eyes, looking oddly amiss on his sweet baby face.

"Well he didn't!" Hope surprised herself, retaliating that way.

"It's your fault! You drove him away!" George's voice rose. Hope, suddenly sweltering, turned off the car heater and braced herself for the next assault. "You didn't take care of him. You——"

"I didn't take care of him? He didn't take care of me! He's a mean person." Hope seemed to have no control. She hated herself for arguing with her son, but the angry words kept coming. She realized the car was starting to edge into the next lane and swerved the steering wheel too sharply. She looked around nervously for a police car.

"Wives are supposed to make a nice home. Fuss over their husbands. You didn't even act glad to see Dad. You were always in your study." George sat stiffly, facing straight ahead, trying not to cry. But Hope could see big, shiny tears spilling down his cheeks onto his damp black soccer jersey which hung oversized on his tall, muscular frame. At fourteen he looked like a child in a man's body. She fought back tears as she thought about the incident. She refused to think she might still be healing.

Neither he nor his father had enjoyed home-cooked meals, preferring take-out food, going to restaurants, or just snacking. But they both liked to guilt her when work at the college kept her way past dinner, and she made no pretense of providing any kind of supper for them. In fact, she would often come home exhausted, take a hot bath, eat a quick bowl of cereal, and fall into bed. She had to fight feelings of inadequacy on those occasions but had always rationalized by thinking that they were both capable of getting themselves a meal. She realized that her cavalier attitude toward providing their meals became unacceptable only when there were other issues in the forefront. In fact, her weak commitment to cooking had long been a family joke they all frequently had laughed about, hadn't they?

Hope now understood that the act of cooking for one's family could be symbolic, an act of love. The realization that she could have been oblivious to her family's needs was too painful to bear. Pain shadowed every memory she had of her life with Michael.

They had been so in love. When had it all gone sour? Not that there weren't early signs, those dark moods. Why hadn't she listened to her own doubts about marrying him? She was doing just fine on her own. She had her degree from Vassar and a job offer. She ignored her sister, Frances, who had been quite vocal about her disapproval of Michael, calling him "Dr. Jekyll's third cousin." *I've never told Frances how right she was. It was his meanness more than his business fiascoes—it was always his meanness.*

When George went away to college, Hope had welcomed the solace of a quiet house. She enjoyed greater energy when she no longer had to endure George's resentment and did not have to think about what she should have done differently in her relationships with George and Michael.

The porch grew lighter. She saw approaching sunrise through the eastern window. "I must get to school," Hope said aloud to the empty porch. She took a deep breath of lavender and lifted her cup and saucer.

Her heart racing with anticipation, Hope rose, carried the teacup to the kitchen, and climbed the stairs. She dressed carefully in a tailored red wool dress. Hope loved the feel, the smell of wool, of good woolen clothing. She had selected the dress to fit the image she wanted to convey to everyone she would encounter in her new post. She wanted instant respect and admiration and had learned early on that people who were well dressed seemed to be treated with more importance than those who were not.

Hope removed the red wool dress gently from its padded hanger and slipped it on. Another reason she had chosen the dress was because she already owned just the right shoes to go with it: red and saddle tan, lowish-heeled spectator pumps. She slid her feet gingerly into the leather pumps, noting what good condition they were in despite numerous wearings. All that methodical cleaning, storing with shoetrees, and polishing had paid off, she congratulated herself. She had a fleeting glimpse of elderly Mary Baldwin removing trees from expensive Italian pumps while nineteen-year-old Hope waited to drive her to the bank. She felt grateful to Mary for teaching her so much about fine living. Hope swallowed hard. With nervous fingers she removed the self-belt and added a thin, saddle tan leather one.

She did not want to think about Mary Baldwin. She unbuttoned the collar and inserted a subdued animal-print scarf, tying it to be barely visible at the neckline. Checking herself in the full-length mirror, Hope felt warm with excitement; she saw a capable professional woman. *I look as much in authority as any male administrator would.* She smiled. *As important as any blue-blooded aristocrat.*

Perhaps being too carefully dressed will put parents off, Hope suddenly worried, recalling how many casually dressed staff, faculty members, and parents she had met these last few weeks before school started. *Cotton shorts and shapeless T-shirts have been the uniform of the day. Am I the one who's out of step here? Can't wait to see how everyone dresses once school is in session. If I end up in T-shirts, I'll find cashmere ones.*

She did not understand how otherwise attractive people, or even more so, unattractive, could be so casual about their appearance. For as long as she could remember Hope had been driven to be, not just neatly dressed, but tastefully and stylishly dressed. She could still hear her mother gently remarking, "It doesn't matter how many times people see you in the same outfit as long as you wear it well and it's something good," quoting articles from fashion magazines she fervently read each month. It seemed strange the way Hope had learned her good taste from her mother, not by example but from her careful coaching. The clothes Hope would wear on any given occasion meant as much to her as the occasion, itself, if not more. Dressing a certain way became somehow vital to her self-esteem. Hope knew she dressed to please herself and would not—could not—change now.   She ignored a shallow feeling in the pit of her stomach. *People like to have reasons to criticize a new official; let them criticize my dress if they want, better that than my performance.*

*

Hope smelled acceleration fumes and heard a swoosh of tires as a black minivan swerved around her, hurrying to beat her onto the freeway ramp. Hope frowned, reminded of Boris's van. When she noticed the bumper sticker: *Protect wildlife; throw a party,* she knew it was Boris's.   She thought of his youthful exuberance and his excitement at a job offer in a tight market for teaching positions. He had impressed her with his sincerity and the way his love for children came through again and again as he described his plans, bristling with provisions for active learning. Reminding herself that those traits cannot be taught to a novice teacher, she, once again, justified having recommended him for hiring.

Hope had spoken frankly to Brian, her supervisor, about the need to add male teachers to the largely female faculty. "These kids need male role-models. Many of them live with Mother only. They have hungry hearts for male companionship. Some have fathers in the home, but they're seldom there. Families have such busy lives today. And at times we need an adult male in the lav or clinic. You know, sensitive emergencies or a need for assistance." She had reluctantly admitted that some defiant students submitted more readily to a male figure. She loathed admitting that but knew it was true. Brian had agreed. But Hope preferred not to think that gender had driven her choice of Boris. His commitment to teaching and his creativity were strong attributes.

The black minivan turned into the driveway and, tires squealing, stopped in the space nearest the entrance door of Poore Pond Elementary School. Hope ignored the question: *Why wouldn't Boris think to save that space for the principal?* and reminded herself that she had much work to do to teach him proprieties. It thrilled her though to see him arrive so early for work. She parked under one of the several large, leafy maple trees surrounding the school. She stepped out of her car and took a deep breath of the crisp, autumn air, feeling chilly in her light wool dress. Boris, gathering armloads of instructional materials from the back of his van, waved and smiled at her. He gave sizzling energy to organizing them for a one-trip transport. She took a moment to admire the red-brick building with its stately white-columned front portico. The aged trees and traditional flower beds gave a look of stability to the school, built to look older than its true age.

The school's history intrigued Hope. Philanthropist Harold Poore had deeded the land to the school board with stipulation that it be used for the site of a school named after him. Mr. Poore had dictated the classic building design as well. It had taken considerable tact and effort to get him to agree to locate the school as far away as possible from the pond included with the property, Brian had explained. Mr. Poore had envisioned the beauty of the Jeffersonian building facing a water-lilied, cat-tailed pond; but school-board members persuaded him to forego the pond in favor of student safety.

I love this school, the entire setting. She climbed out of her car. *Though different in design, it has the same stately look as Mary Baldwin's manor house. It was made for me.*

"You're looking smart today, Boris." Hope could not bring herself to call him Bo as he had requested. She smiled, noticing his crisp, tan cotton blazer, pressed black pants, and good black loafers. "You're sending the right message to your students."

"Thank you, Hope. How long will the assembly run this morning?" Boris asked, making strong eye contact, his jaw set. He skillfully opened the door for her, managing to keep a grip on his books, bags, and posters. Holding the door, he greeted Millie Blackwell, who walked in behind them, loaded down as he was.

"Good morning, Millie. All those materials. You'll be ready for anything." Hope smiled at her. Turning to Boris, she said, "Twenty to thirty minutes."

"That'll give me time to run my copies," he said with authority.

"I require teachers to stay with their classes in the assembly," Hope looked directly at him. The freckles on his face seemed to deepen, but he did not blush. "Right." Boris dropped his eyes. " I can copy later—or maybe now if the copier is free." He sprinted down to his classroom, calling out cheerfully to a teacher across the hall. *He feels he must always be seen as in charge. Male ego or lack of confidence?*

Hope stopped at the kindergarten room, expecting to see a visual feast for five-year-olds. What she saw delighted her. She had been confident that Melanie Armstrong, the new teacher she had found—discovered really—would outdo herself. She stepped into a veritable laboratory for the most curious of young learners: an inviting book corner featuring books of all sizes, a few big books standing open ; a carpet woven with large, primary-colored letters and numerals; and a child-sized rocker. Melanie had included a tape player for books-with-tapes atop a miniature red enamel table with matching chair. Activity centers dotted the room, all dressed with enticing posters and small manipulatives to attract the most reluctant kindergartners. "That Melanie," Hope heard herself say. "What a find." She left the room, thrilled for the tiny students who would grow in this inviting classroom.

Silently Hope prayed that all Poore Pond teachers would open the school year with equal dedication and enthusiasm for satiating the hungry, young minds of their students. She gave thanks that she had decided on an education major in addition to English literature. *Immersion in an elementary school is much more exciting than analyzing the work of dead poets and authors.* Hope found the workshop nature of the classrooms with visual aids and colorful bulletin boards more appealing than stark instructional rooms in hallowed college buildings. The teachers, too, were different, much more open and sharing. Many of them were secure enough to ask for help with teaching techniques, and that impressed her. *Little of that in academia.*

Hope admired the polished corridor floor and noticed the courtyard door near the office standing open. She could smell the musky odor of early chrysanthemums and freshly turned soil. She walked into the beckoning courtyard, delighting in the carefully trimmed ivy, the swept walkways, and the tended soil. She crossed to the small pond, seeing the waxy green water plants on the dark, shiny water and Japanese koi, swimming serenely, orange blurs beneath the film of water. She thought again of Boris's question about the assembly. Does Boris have a real commitment to his students? she worried. Had she erred in choosing a male teacher? A young, inexperienced male teacher? He was about the age of her son, George, who didn't seem to be committed to anything, she thought, breaking her own rule against indulging in bitterness. Boris had completed his degree, hadn't he? And he had cared enough to seek a position in his field. He showed enthusiasm for his work; he'd worked in his room on his own time every day the past two weeks as many of the veteran teachers had. The most enthusiasm she had seen from George was his passion for blaming her when his father left.

Hope choked back the emotion rising in her throat. *Where does George live? How is he? Is he safe? It's been four years. Why does he feel no obligation to contact me?* She decided she would try again to reach Michael. Perhaps he had heard from their son.

Hope unlocked her office door and felt a rush of stale air. She put her briefcase on the desk and reached over it to open the window, the earthy smells of the courtyard pouring in. Hope surveyed her tiny office, a cubicle really, the large window facing the courtyard its one redeeming feature. A worn but still attractive tall oak bookshelf stood against the wall, waiting to be noticed. Hope smiled at it and made a mental note to thank Ray for bringing it from the storage room so promptly. She would transfer onto it piles of papers filling the desktop and half the table. She loathed the untidiness, but each pile represented a priority task. Her eyes landed on the yellow card filled with a to-do list for today, August twenty-eighth:

-Ring Mr. Bradford (teacher change)
-Ring PTA
-Give Bella list of bus changes
-Review emergency plan
-Check teacher signs at entrance doors
-Staff birthdays
-Scope building w/ Ray
-Outdoor sign

I forgot to check the outdoor sign, Hope thought as she perused the three new-student registration forms and yesterday's note to ring her supervisor ASAP. She made a mental note to place the new students, then go check the sign, then ring Brian, who probably would not be in his office yet.

Two of three late-registering students could not be assigned to a teacher until Hope had further information about the learning disability of one and medical diagnosis of the other. She began sorting papers from a pile, scoffing at a tip she had read about handling each sheet of paper only once. *Act on it, file it, delegate it, or trash it*, she remembered, rolling her eyes at the new registration forms waiting in limbo on her desk.

Still awaiting return calls from new students' former schools, Hope hurried to find Ray and join him for a quick inspection of the building and grounds. She knew it was essential that the fifty-year-old building and its vast grounds looked absolutely clean, well maintained, and safe, especially the front entrance and playing fields. She also knew that Ray would feel slighted if she showed no interest in the work he and his crew had done to prepare the school for today. Well-polished floors shone up at her throughout the school, emitting a clean, waxy odor. Hope could hear the happy voices and laughter of safety-patrol students in the service closet, readying their equipment for a new school year. She stood for a moment and savored their sweet voices, their enthusiasm.

"Good morning, Ray." Hope found his wiry figure untangling rope on the flagpole. "Are we ready for countdown?" Without looking up, Ray continued working the rope with deft fingers and concentration as if she had not spoken. His thick, grey-brown hair too low on his collar, stared back at her. She could hear the cluster of keys jangling rhythmically from his waist, underscoring his silence as he worked the rope. Her eyes scoured the front entrance for clean windows, swept sidewalks, and washed floor mats as she denied a feeling of annoyance. The glistening window glass shone, unstreaked, in the bright morning sun. An increasing wind scattered the clean walk with monkeyballs from a nearby tree. Hope wished she had put on her jacket.

"Good morning," Ray finally returned, still not making eye contact, keeping his stiff back to her.

"Let's do our walk-through now," Hope said with a smile. "The building looks great, from what I've seen."

"As soon as I lay out the flag for the student helpers," Ray said with authority as he headed down to the boiler room.

"Meet you in the upper common room, then—five minutes," Hope added, continuing to smile at Ray's indifferent back.

"Good morning, Dr. Fleming," two safety-patrol students, looking official in shoulder belts with big, silver badges and carrying neon-colored signs, called to Hope as she walked back inside the building.

"Good morning, Jessica, Betsy," Hope smiled back. "You are right on the job and responsible! Did you get the slickers and flags organized?" The girls shook their pony-tailed heads and walked away laughing.

Hope wished Ray could show such friendliness. He certainly has an independent attitude today, she noted. She pondered reasons why Ray behaved that way. *He probably just needs more time to adjust to the new principal. And to the new principal's gender.* She immediately felt ashamed of her mental sarcasm. She vowed to stick to her original strategy: stay calm, warm-but-business-like, and in charge.

Bella blocked the door to Hope's office, insisting she explain the bus changes. After Hope described the last-minute requests for busing to different locations, Bella told her that Brian had called twice. "He was upset that you hadn't called him yet," she asserted, mottled-blonde pageboy hair swinging as she rushed to answer the telephone.

Resenting Bella's use of the word *upset*, Hope dialed the familiar number. As it rang, Dave, the PE teacher, looking neat in khaki shorts and white polo shirt, popped in to say, "<u>Parents</u> needs an <u>e</u> on the outdoor sign. Three parents and twenty-some students have told me." Hope gave Dave a wave and a nod just as Brian answered the phone.

"So how's it going?" Brian's easy drawl spilled out of the phone. "Is your sign up to date? Bus duty posts covered? I need your assembly schedule."

At that moment Dave burst in again from bus duty, a big grin on his weathered face. "You forgot the line-point sign for the new teacher's class. Shall I hand letter one for now?" Dave brushed his windblown coarse, dark hair back off his forehead with his fingers. He dashed out, taking the paper and marker that Bella, ever the efficient secretary, extended to him.

"A man on the phone insists on talking to the principal. Sounds scary," Bella said softly, mouthing her words exaggeratedly when she noticed the phone in Hope's ear.

"I have another call, Brian. I'll fax you a copy of the teacher survey I'm designing. This afternoon. For sure."

Scary? There she goes again, Hope noted. Bella used *upset,* then *scary.* She obviously likes provocative words. Has she done that all along and I only just noticed?

Mr. Patel, in a rich, foreign voice, expressed concern that none of his daughter's friends shared her classroom assignment and that she had the less-popular teacher. Hope assured him that Shruti's high ability warranted placement in an enriched class, with a more challenging course of study. She emphasized the opportunity for her to make new friends while enjoying intellectual stimulation. "I regret that you could not attend last-week's meeting on the enriched class," Hope said. She invited him to come in and speak to her about it. Mr. Patel agreed happily to a meeting date.

It was 11:00 o'clock before Hope had a moment to reflect on her first day of school as new principal at Poore Pond Elementary. Waving at those who noticed her, she closed the office window against excited cries of a class of third graders exploring the courtyard with their teacher. She had not expected the hectic morning since she had spent the previous weeks meticulously preparing for opening day. She assured herself that she would have the afternoon to work on Brian's survey and tie up other loose ends.

Enticing smells of Mexican pizza wafted through the office from the servery. *I'll just grab a quick lunch.* Hope's stomach rumbled noisily as if her 5:00 A.M. breakfast had been days ago.

"Miss Moran needs you, Dr. Fleming," a freshly scrubbed student, looking proud of his mission, announced at her door. "James refuses to come out of the bathroom."

Hope hurried down the hall, keeping a leisurely pace so as not to arouse alarm. *I must not lay a hand on him—too easily misconstrued.* She lamented the fact that there would not be a social worker on staff for two more weeks. *I'm scheduled for crisis intervention training next month, should have taken that summer session Brian recommended.*

The door to the boys' lavatory was propped open with a tall waste can. Every light blazed on.

"Are you in there, James?" Hope looked down the wall of open urinals to the closed door of the second private stall. She could see small, curled feet in white athletic shoes and knocked on the door. "James? It's Dr. Fleming. You remember me, don't you, from the assembly today?"

"Yes," James' voice was barely audible.

"Are you all right?" She waited. "James, I need you to come out now." Still she waited. After what seemed to be five minutes, she heard the latch slide. The door opened, revealing a small boy, his fist wringing a knot of wet T-shirt above the hiked-up waist of khaki pants. His face was resolute as he scrubbed the top of his dark hair with his other hand.

She took his hand, then stopped short of a puddle of water. "How did that happen, James?" she asked, pulling a length of paper towels off the roll.

"I spilled it," he said in a flat voice, dropping his chin. Hope handed him a wad of paper towel; and together, they stooped and mopped up the water.

Hope coaxed an explanation from him that he had tried to stretch his too-short shirt, and included harsh accusations against his father. *Could his father really have treated him that way? Is this a case for Children's Services? Verbal, not physical abuse.? I need more information.*

CHAPTER TWO—RAY

Ray carefully laid out the school's American flag so the student helpers could easily find it. He did not like them to have to run around looking for him when they had so much to do before the last bell. *Another new year.* Ray sighed. With strong, broad hands he stroked the freshly painted surface of his work table around the folded flag and realized how he loved the opening of a new school year. That was when being plant supervisor felt really fulfilling, the promise of a brand new year for so many people: teachers and other staff, parents and kids. And he set the scene for it all. He looked admiringly at the clean, resurfaced cement of his boiler room floor and out into the hall at the shining, waxed tiles. A smile broke across his weathered face, small featured but with imposing dark eyes under bushy brows. He savored the rich aroma of oil-based paint mixed with silicone wax that permeated the building. He knew that in a matter of days the paint and wax smell would be replaced by a new one, the odor of hundreds of sweaty young bodies coming in from their recess games with damp, dusty hair and wilted socks. The air in the school would be full of high-pitched voices making recess plans and calling shrill remarks to one another. Glancing at the clock, Ray wondered why the students had not yet come for the flag.

Hope's waiting for me upstairs, he reminded himself. But he deliberately stopped to rearrange two boxes of books on the four wheeler. As he climbed the stairs, Ray spotted the red wire bin holding assorted game balls and immediately thought of former principal, Keith Broski. He had missed him all summer and remembered fondly the casual way Keith ran the building. Ray had told him he was tired of chasing balls and needed a container for the wriggly things. Keith had given him a catalog the same day, and Ray had chosen the sturdy bin. Ray liked the way it looked: up to date, colorful, and strong.

Things were different now with Hope here.

"There you are, Ray," Hope smiled. "I would not have thought this common room could look so clean. I can see how hard you and Marty worked on the floor."

It's really shiny; did you use the wax I told you about, the Glascote?" She looked him right in the eye.

"We did," Ray replied, dropping his eyes. "Took forever to dry."

"Well, it looks wonderful," Hope insisted. "It was worth the extra time." She kicked at a small bit of red tape embedded under the wax but did not comment on it. She could feel Ray watching her red-and-tan shoe work insinuatingly at the tape. "What is this bit? Stuck fast, was it?" Hope looked at Ray's flushed face, redness covering his neck and the hairy patch of chest showing through his open collar.

Ray cleared his throat. "No." He laughed nervously. "It's just, well, — I sort of left it there on purpose." Hope looked curiously at him. "It's sort of a reminder of a student we had. He's dead now. Batten Disease. Quite a character." Hope could see emotion in Ray's eyes.

"I'm sorry to hear that." Hope's voice showed concern. "What was his name? How old was he?"

"Fourth grade when he got sick. Fifth when we lost him. He was a character." A smile crossed Ray's solemn face. Hope's curiosity grew. "Bucky Ames. He liked to help Keith and me—Keith Broski, the former principal—retape the game lines every year. Keith and I'd laugh about Bucky's taping work." Ray covered his cough with his fist. "He took it so seriously. But he was so uncoordinated." Ray chuckled.

"I can still see Bucky. He was a skinny kid. His squeaky voice—he had this squeaky voice kids get— explaining why he taped outlines of **two** pitchers' boxes for kickball practice. 'The second one's for kids who can't pitch, Mr. Supe.' Bucky always called me Mr. Supe."

Hope, obviously anxious to get on with the run-through, could see the fondness in Ray's face. She shifted her weight to the other foot. Her eyes scanned the large room.

" 'Mr. Supe,' " Ray continued his story. " 'They stink,' Bucky said. 'But you still havta give them their turn, my dad says.' I can see him standing in his home-plate box. That elfish face, smiling like a toothpaste ad." Ray looked at Hope, modeling Bucky's wide smile. She smiled back, enjoying the rare moment.

"So you left that small trace of your young friend embedded in this gymnasium floor for posterity?" Hope looked at Ray with kind eyes.

"I guess so," Ray dropped his eyes. He squatted to touch the red patch.

"You obviously used two coats to get that deep shine." Hope resumed her inspection.

"Yes, but I hate to think about stripping this wax next summer," Ray whined, rising. "It's tough." He lifted an oversized dust mop from the floor.

Ignoring Ray's remark, Hope instructed, "Let's move the lectern to the center, Ray. And the speaker in front of it." She nodded toward a stack of folding chairs near the wall, "Open those chairs, enough for all the teachers," she continued. "Thanks again, Ray. Everything looks great, just the way it should."

Ray watched Hope walk away, her heels tapping on the stairs, and took his time getting back to work. He could hear soothing New Age music coming from a nearby classroom.

Hope Fleming is shades different from Keith Broski. Keith never cared, didn't even know what kind of wax I used. He agreed with me that teachers should get their own chairs for assemblies. Heck, some of them didn't even use chairs, preferred to stand, police the kids.

Yep, Hope Fleming is no Keith Broski. And I might as well get used to it. But I don't have to make it easy for her.

CHAPTER THREE—Ian and Helsi

"When is Dylan supposed to take that bloody test?" Ian bellowed up the shallow stairway to his wife, Helsi, the wood-frame colonial house nearly vibrating from the sound waves.

"Friday morning," Helsi called, projecting her soft voice down the stairs as best she could.

"Lovely! Isn't that just like our brilliant headmistress? Testing a five-year-old at the end of the week. Never mind that he's worn out by Friday. Heck, I'm worn out by Friday, after working all week!"

"Dylan will be six by Friday. His birthday's Thursday, remember." Helsi smiled as she entered the kitchen, looking girlish in her jeans and red T-shirt. "Remember, Ian, his birthday is Thursday. Anyway, I set the time. Dr. Fleming asked me when would be convenient for me to bring him. Rachel's in preschool then. Makes it easier for me to take Dylan. I can go right over to Poore Pond from Earlylearn. Saves you leaving work." Helsi carried a gallon milk jug to the refrigerator.

"I want to take him. It's a big test. Want to make sure his frame of mind is right. It's just ridiculous that he's in kindergarten again, smart as he is." Ian opened his bulging brown paper lunch bag and checked the contents.

"Ian, be realistic. What do you think this test will show that the test in July didn't? And here we go, putting Dylan through all that hard work and stress all over again."

"That test was a farce. That what's-his-face head doctor at the school board office said Dylan wouldn't stay on task. Well, of course he wouldn't stay on task. Giving him blocks and patterns to play with. Dylan thought it was playtime for sure. He didn't take it seriously. This time Dad's going to see that he understands: it may seem like play, but it's work, important work that'll get him into his rightful grade. He's going to first grade and this test better by golly show that's where he needs to be."

"And what if it doesn't?"

"It will. Dylan didn't know what was happening. Dragging him to that big, unfriendly building downtown. Just to play blocks with adults, yet. No children there. He didn't know. This time the test will be at the school. Dylan will see that he needs to work hard for the teachers. Like the other kids. He wants to be like the others."

"He will work hard. Worked hard last time, tried his best. Didn't want to disappoint you. But if he can't do it, he can't do it. Putting him through the same thing all over again. For what? For naught. He's a child. Six years old! And we're making him feel like a failure already! Shame on us!" Helsi's lip quivered as she spoke, and her eyes went cold as she stared at her husband.

Helsi stiffened as Ian put his big arms around her small shoulders. She could feel the sharpness of his starched work shirt. "Don't you worry, Helsi. Dylan's going to be all right. I won't let him get too stressed. That's why I want to take him Friday." Ian's strong arms and the deodorized smell of his just-showered skin engulfed her. Helsi, feeling a familiar reassurance in their embrace, softened and hugged her husband back.

"I'll call Dr. Fleming and change the day, if you like," Helsi said, brightening as she pulled away from Ian. "Monday? Is that better? For Dylan?"

"Let's just leave it at Friday. Dylan can go to bed earlier Thursday night. No sense giving Dr. Poore Pond a reason to be down on Dylan." Ian gave his wife a quick kiss on the cheek and went out the kitchen door, pulling a nylon windbreaker over his regulation blues.

As Helsi cleared the bare-wood breakfast table, she thought about the birthday celebration she was planning for Dylan: a special dinner, his favorite shepherd's pie with sausages instead of minced beef, and a three-layer chocolate cake with his name in yellow candy letters. And a trip to the video store to rent his own choice of movie. She wanted him to have a wonderful birthday; and now that it would fall the day before his grueling test, she wanted it even more. Why does he have to go through that ordeal again, she thought, running the dishwater hotter and faster than usual without realizing it. She knew he would feel bad about himself all over again.

Helsi flinched as she put her hands into the scalding water. Adding cold, she recalled Dylan's question to her the day after he took the first test on that late July day. They were sitting near the big window shaded by the locust tree, a soft breeze floating through the open window. She was reading his alphabet book with him, enjoying the touch of his small, sweet body folded into her lap. When they came to the page with the letter _d_, they talked about the mythical dodo bird in the illustration. "The dodo bird didn't pass his test, did he, Mom?" Dylan had asked with sweet innocence on his face. "Rob says I'm a dodo 'cause I didn't pass my test." Helsi had hugged him closely and reassured him that he was not a dodo.

"Rob thinks he has to tease you because he's your brother," she had said, knowing that Rob would find a new way to tease him when he failed this next test. She knew that teasing was Rob's way of appreciating the fact that Dylan shared Rob's own struggles with school.

Slowly washed and rinsed each dish. Feeling the slippery soapsuds as they rinsed away with the hot water, she recalled how she and Ian had worked with

Rob on letter sounds every day that summer so he would not have to repeat kindergarten. She could still see eleven-year-old Sean and ten-year-old Lucy flashing letter cards to Rob. She smiled as she recalled hearing them utter "aaaaaa" and "bbbbbb" in Rob's small, eager face, helping their little brother learn to recognize letters and their sounds. The entire family had seemed desperate to keep Rob from repeating kindergarten. And with everyone's help, Rob had squeaked by into first grade.

Why weren't they rallying now to help Dylan pass, Helsi wondered. Could they see the same limitations in Dylan that she secretly suspected? Or were they just bored with the prospect of going through the whole tedious process all over again? *It's just as well. Dylan is not Robbie. I know he needs some other kind of help, but what? It falls on me to find the answer. I will—I must find a way to help Dylan.*

CHAPTER FOUR—Hope

"Dylan really is a lovely boy," Carol Davis commented to Hope as they walked to the office to await his arrival for scheduled achievement testing. "Our colleagues in Pupil Services kept saying how great his attitude was when they tested him at Central Office last July."

"He is," Hope agreed. "And he tries so hard to please his father. I know you will get the best from him on the test, Carol. From what I've seen, you know how to put children at ease quickly." Hope stopped at the door of the music room and watched Carmen Ricci leading a class of fourth graders in two-part harmony, admiring the intense participation of each student. What an outstanding music teacher Carmen is, she thought. No one can accuse her of merely tolerating the less-talented students; she gets every child to participate.

Hope and Carol continued down the hall. "Wouldn't it be wonderful if your tests showed him at first-grade level? Solve so many problems."

"Fat chance of that from what Sue says about his classroom work, not to mention the July test results. By the way, Sue is worried about seeing Mr. Bradford at Parents' Night."

"Why is that?"

"He scares her. He's so big and burly. And with his loud voice. She says she tries to joke with him, and it falls flat every time."

"His bark is worse than his bite," Hope quipped. "You should see him with Dylan and Robbie, how his face softens when he sees them." Carol nodded with understanding.

"But that's not the case with Mr. Brewer, James' father. He's a tense man. His face seems to harden as soon as he sees James. Do you know the family, Carol?"

"I know that they went through a recent divorce. A bitter one. They're in the throes of a custody battle. And from what I've heard, James is angry, keeps insisting he wants to live with his mother. Tells her Dad is mean to him. I suppose that would make any father furious. Don't know if it's true. Why, what's happening to James?"

"This morning he went into the lav as soon as he got off the bus. Wouldn't come out. He's dug in his heels like that three or four times this year. He's in Pam's class. I was able finally to coax him into the workroom. It turns out he is embarrassed by the clothes Dad made him wear to school today. Or at least, that's what he says. Says the pants are too baggy and the shirt is too short," Hope explained.

"Are they?" Carol asked. "If they are, I'd be embarrassed, too."

"Well, a little, but they're not much different from what a lot of children wear. He was seething with anger, so I can't help but think he has a deeper issue than clothes he doesn't like." Hope opened the glass office door for Carol. " Anyway, Pam lent him her new school sweatshirt that was still in the bag. She's sensitive to those kinds of child problems. I'm glad he is in her—"

Just then Bella announced in her most formal voice, "Mr. Bradford is here for Dylan's appointment, Dr. Fleming." Hope invited an unsmiling Ian Bradford into her office.

"No need for pleasantries, Doc." We're just here for Dylan's test, so let's get on with it." Remnants of his garlicky breakfast hung in the confined air of the tiny office.

"Mr. Bradford, this is Mrs. Davis, our school psychologist. Mrs. Davis, this is Ian Bradford, Dylan's father, also Robbie's, and Sean and Lucy's, for that matter. How are you today, Dylan? You know Mrs. Davis, don't you? You've seen her around school, helping children. And didn't she come to your class to talk about friends. Friendship?"

Dylan dropped his eyes, nodding slightly. Ian met Carol's extended hand with a weak handshake and indifferent eyes. She then shook hands with Dylan, who returned Carol's smile shyly with downcast face.

"Thank you for bringing Dylan today, Mr.Bradford," Hope smiled and extended her hand.

Ian ignored Hope's hand and walked out of the office muttering, "Where do we go for this?" Carol led him down the hall, Dylan slowly stiff-stepping behind them.

"Good morning, Hope," Ali Cantrell smiled and walked into Hope's tiny office, closing the door softly. "Do you have a minute?"

"Of course," Hope said, drawing up a chair for the first-grade teacher and swiveling her desk chair to face her.

"I'm just trying to head off a situation," Ali explained. "I know you agreed to one night for Parents' Night instead of the two that we used to have. Everybody likes that........Hope."

Hope was still thinking about Ian's blatant rudeness toward her and ways she might win him over, for Dylan's sake as well as hers. "I'm sorry, Ali. I'm listening now."

"As I was saying, some teachers are objecting to the two assemblies. Mary Jane said they did that at her old school and it was a disaster. Teachers got stuck in their classrooms with high-maintenance parents from the first shift. They couldn't gracefully leave. Didn't make the second-shift assembly. It was awkward."

"I understand." Hope smiled. "You would prefer a single assembly. Is that right?" She was conscious of how much she enjoyed talking to Ali with her sunny, blonde freshness and her apt choice of words.

"I guess so. Not me necessarily. But there is this undercurrent. Lounge talk. Some of the inexperienced teachers getting their backs up. I just want to head that off. Nobody wins then." Impatience filled Ali's eyes.

"Well, there's still time to rethink it. I'll see what I can do, Ali. Thank you for the heads up." Hope stood as she left, appreciating her mature understanding of human nature, a maturity well beyond her thirty-some years.

Bella handed Hope two messages: one from Brian, one from George. "He said his name was George Fleming," she said with raised eyebrows.

"Bella, did George say he would call back?"

"Nothing at all about that. I told him you were in a meeting with a teacher. He said to tell you he called."

"If George calls again, Bella, please interrupt me or find me. Keep him on hold, please. I have no way of reaching him. George is my son….." Hope's voice trailed off. She forced herself to look her secretary straight in the eye although she wanted to drop her eyes to hide the emotion she felt.

"Will do," Bella retorted, looking hard at Hope as if trying to see what she was thinking. *Or was I just imagining that?*

Hope was scooping the last bite of low-fat yogurt from its carton when Bella buzzed her for permission to send in parent Mrs. Tarantino. She quickly blotted her mouth with a napkin and swiped a lipstick over her lips, trying mentally to put a face to the name. She heard a gentle knock at the door and opened it to an attractive woman with a bright smile, relieved to recognize her from New-Student Orientation.

"Come in, Mrs. Tarantino." They shook hands warmly. "Please sit down," Hope invited, pulling out a chair from the small, round conference table. She was grateful for the vase of pink roses a student had brought this morning to thank Hope for counseling her about a small social problem with a classmate. They gave a touch of beauty to the otherwise austere office and perfumed the air, heavy with the chemical smell of copier toner from the over-used photocopier in the outer office. Hope sat down opposite her visitor.

"How's the school year going for Anthony? Does he like fourth grade? Hope remembered meeting the entire family at orientation. Both Mr. and Mrs. Tarantino and Anthony had come with such positive attitudes.

"Well, as a matter of fact, that's why I'm here," Mrs. Tarantino, a small woman with shiny black hair, spoke in a pleasant voice. "You know we've been very pleased with the school and the teacher...and you, of course, the way you run things. Anthony has made several friends and likes Mr. Kushner.

"That's good to hear, Mrs. Tarantino." Hope returned her smile.

"But we do have a problem with another child in the class. You see, Anthony's father and I are divorced—over three years now so Anthony's mostly used to it. But unfortunately, his father's new stepson is in Anthony's class. That child has been through a struggle. His mother up and leaving his own dad so suddenly like that. And now a new stepdad already. It's hard. Well anyway, he says cruel things to Anthony about his stepfather, Anthony's dad. He comes home upset, cries when he tells me about it." Mrs. Tarantino's eyes clouded. Hope looked at the pink roses. She inhaled their sweet fragrance. "Can you do anything about this, Dr. Fleming, or do we just have to stick it out?"

"What is this child's name?" Hope asked in a resolute voice.

"Tommy Grant. He's a tall, muscular boy...shaggy brown hair. Wears that army jacket all the time." Hope recalled seeing him in the lunch line. She had asked him to remove that very jacket until recess time. "He needs help— or something. I don't want him to get in trouble. I just want him to stop badgering Anthony." Hope was moved by Mrs. Tarantino's compassion.

"No, he will not be in trouble, not yet. But he will be if he continues to harass Anthony. It's just the first month of school, so our best move may be to transfer him to another class. Given the sensitive nature of their relationship, it makes no sense to have them thrown together like this."

What if Tommy's parents object to the move? Hope wished she could take back her words.

"Tell me, Mrs. Tarantino. Would you be agreeable to Anthony's transferring to another class if Tommy's parents object?"

"Ummm,.I don't know. It doesn't seem fair. He hasn't done anything wrong. I'd have to talk to Anthony about it," she frowned.

"Well, I will look into it. I'll talk to all parties."

"Thank you, Dr. Fleming. I would really appreciate it. Can I tell Anthony?"

"Not yet, Mrs. Tarantino. As I said, I have to talk to the teachers, Tommy's parents. It will take a few days. It's too bad we did not have this information ahead of time; we could have prevented this." Hope smiled to soften her pointed remark.

"I thought of that, too," Mrs. Tarantino's eyes went cold. "But I did not know that this was where Tommy went to school." She offered her hand and Hope shook it warmly, then walked her through the outer office, waving as she left.

"Mrs. Jackson is on the phone, Hope. She wants to know why we had outdoor recess yesterday. Wants to know if we're going out today. What should I say? I know there was a maintenance truck on the playground yesterday." Bella, in typical fashion, was forming her own answer to Mrs. Jackson.

"I'll speak to her," Hope said.

"Good morning, Mrs. Jackson," Hope said, trying to project a smile in her voice. Thank you for your interest in our recesses. What is your concern?"

Hope sat down with a sigh after talking with Mrs. Jackson. She gazed into the courtyard and saw Terence-the-Turtle the second he dove into the pond, making the tiniest ripple in the dark water. She could hear the lilting sound of the wind chimes hanging in Melanie's classroom window opposite the office. She thought about Mrs. Jackson's concern for her children. Teachers had told Hope how for years she had walked them into school every morning. She came in each year on photo day to comb their hair. She went through their book bags with them every day at dismissal. The teachers joked about her narrow life and how she was fostering learned helplessness. *Learned helplessness, a prime example of how we educators love our jargon.*

It reminded her of some of the things Michael used to do for George when he was in primary grades. Sometimes Michael would go late into work just so he could drive George to school with his project. Michael liked to carry projects into George's classroom for him. Of course, George loved having his father's attention that way when he was in early grades. But at other times George would beg Michael to come to school for a parent breakfast or other function, and Michael would adamantly refuse. *That must have been confusing for George. Why didn't I point that out to Michael when it was going on? What was the matter with me? I did so little to protect him from his father's dark moods.*

She could see George as a child, small with sturdy legs and thick dirty-blonde hair perpetually in his eyes. Hope choked down the emotion that was rising in her throat. She looked around her office, noticing for the first time how impersonal it was. Why, *I don't even have a photo of George on my desk,* she discovered. *What kind of mother am I? I must bring in a framed photo of my son.*

"Well hello, Hope," Brian answered his phone cheerfully. "How is everything at Poor Pool, I mean Putrid Pond Pedagogical?"

"Everything is fine here, Brian. We are trying to keep parents and teachers happy, for the most part. And the children as well. Maybe we should call ourselves Perfect Pond School," she joked. "What can I do for you today? Oh no, did I just use my p.r. voice with you?"

"There is something you can do for me, actually. I need your plan for raising test scores at The Pond."

"Oh is that overdue, Brian? The teachers and I are still working on it."

"Overdue? Nothing's ever overdue, Hope. You know that. In our business? I still remember getting pulled a thousand different ways when I was principal. What's the holdup?"

"The teachers. They were looking for ways to make the task more efficient. We've found one. We've parceled out the sections. We meet next Thursday to finalize it."

Can you wait until then for our finished plan, Brian?" Hope asked, knowing that Brian would find a way to accommodate her. He always did.

"Friday's courier will be fine, Hope. I'll expect Poore Pond's typical quality work. You've got some really capable, dedicated teachers there; have you discovered that?"

Yes, I have," Hope replied with enthusiasm, feeling gratitude for those teachers and for her understanding supervisor. *I hope we can complete the plan at Thursday's meeting,* Hope worried as she hung up the phone.

Hope turned to the yellow index card, her to-do list, screaming at her from the desk. A small envelope with HOPE F. penciled in careful manuscript stared up at her from the desk. The manuscript looked as if a student with meticulous handwriting had written it, but she doubted that a student would use her first name.

Or a parent. The teachers would, but they didn't bother with envelopes unless they sent a really confidential message, which they seldom did. Hope wondered if this could be some sort of formal teacher complaint about the two assemblies for Parents' Night. *I have had no time to focus on Ali's comments, let alone come to a solution. Why wouldn't they give me the courtesy of a little time to get back to them?* Then it occurred to Hope that, given the nature of it, Ali was unlikely to have told anyone about their conversation. But still, she seemed paralyzed to open the envelope.

Hope turned toward the window into the courtyard. She looked at the birdfeeder Ray had erected for her soon after she came on board. It was a welcome-to-Poore-Pond gift from the parent group who had surprised Hope by knowing how she dabbled in bird watching.

Mary Baldwin had introduced her to it, impressing the young Hope with her ability to identify many species of birds with only a glimpse. Hope thought then that bird watching was a pastime for the elderly and was surprised by her own emerging interest. She certainly did not consider herself elderly. Fighting back the memory of Mary Baldwin, she forced herself to focus eyes and mind on the bird feeder.

A small yellow-breasted finch pecked away at the birdseed Ray and his student helpers had placed there only this morning.

She had watched the two second-grade boys in their jeans and T-shirts, one proudly climbing the stepladder while the other handed up the birdseed importantly. She had watched Ray hold the ladder securely for the boy, his face reflecting warm feelings. She saw Ray's lips move in conversation, smiles all around. She was struck by the tenderness Ray showed them. He did not seem to hurry them or criticize the way they worked. Both boys had been in her office several times already this year for disrupting class and defying the playground supervisors. "Those little rascaljammers," Hope spoke aloud to herself. "Just look at them, being good citizens for Ray." She had turned away then, not wanting to invade Ray's privacy, or the children's.

Hope's attention went back to the finch who continued to peck, prancing from one side of the feeder to the other in little jerks between bites.

Hope opened the sealed envelope slowly; a brief note stated:

Hope-
It can't wait until our monthly meeting. Can we talk tomorrow morning at 7:30 before everything starts up? Ray

Feeling both relief and irritation, Hope pondered Ray's words. *Could he be* having *serious health problems? Or his mother?* Hope knew that she would have to meet with Ray tomorrow morning even though it meant canceling her plans to get her car in for service.

Just as the get-ready-for-dismissal bell rang, a student bus monitor came to Hope's door, speaking as authoritatively as her ten-year-old experience would permit, "Dr. Fleming, the driver of bus fifty-five needs you now. There's a car blocking the bus lane, and she can't get the bus in."

"I know I know!" the large woman with a bush of steel-grey hair, behind the wheel of the car blurted before Hope had a chance to speak. "I'm not supposed to be here. But how the heck was I supposed to know that? My first time here in years. Picking up my grandchildren."

"There's a sign, over there," Hope motioned toward the sign. "I'm sorry you missed it. Now you'll have to wait until those buses ahead of you pull out."

"You mean until they're all loaded?" The woman's fleshy face looked as if she had just been asked to perform brain surgery. She glared at Hope.

"You said you're here to pick up a student?" Hope asked as pleasantly as she could, trying not to inhale the flurry of engine fumes in the air.

"Two kids. The Richters. Sharon and Sam. Nobody told me how impossible it would be to get near this school. Wait till I see my daughter. You the new principal? Why don't you do something about this system? It isn't even a system; it's total confusion. What happened to Mr. Bloski? He was here when my kids went here. He never allowed anything like this to go on."

Hope could feel heat rising in her chest. "Just stay where you are. I'll go find your children. Don't try to pull out." Hope turned and collided with a child.

"Excuse me. Oh Sam, it's you. Where's your sister?"

"Here I am," Sharon ran to the car. The children got in and their grandmother charged out behind the exhaust clouds of departing buses just as another line of yellow buses roared into the drive, led by number fifty-five, whose driver adolescently rolled her eyes.

"Well, I'm sure that's the last time the Richter's grandmother will get caught in the bus line," Hope said to the dry autumn air. She could not deny the fact that the woman did have a point and promised herself she would think later about reorganizing buses and dismissal. She chuckled when she realized she had inherited this "system" from Keith Broski, "Mr. Bloski" as she had referred to him in loyal terms.

I wonder if I will one day become an institution at Poore Pond the way Keith is now. What makes certain leaders loved by everyone? Stepping on people's toes just goes with the territory when you're running a school. Is it simply a case of everybody loves you after you're gone?

Hope, back at her desk, began reading class groups of interim reports teachers had prepared to send home; so parents could see how their children were progressing at this midpoint in the grading period. She felt pleased with the care they had taken to use neat, legible handwriting and correct spelling.

But then she came across the word *disorganized* used incorrectly on one of Marsha Klements' reports. She printed *unorganized* on a one-inch post-it note and stuck it next to the error. On other reports Marsha had written *Too much socializing during study time is having a negative affect on his work* and *Her poor attitude effects her openness to learning.* Again, she attached post-it notes with corrections. She reached for her *Harbrace Grammar Handbook,* leafed through it to the page on troublesome pairs. She rose and headed out to the copier, nearly colliding with a tall, pleasant-faced man.

"Have a minute?" Mr. Barnes poked his head through Hope's open door.

"Sure I do." Hope set the stack of interim reports face down on her desk and extended her hand. "How are you, Mr. Barnes?"

"Fine. Fine. Just brought Barry back from his dental appointment, for Juggling Club."

"Yes, I read your note about his early release today." Hope smiled at the pleasant-looking man in his spanking-clean, gas-company uniform.

"I just want to ask you if you could use some paper. Scrap paper from my wife's work." He hovered near the door as if to expedite the conversation.

"Can you just tell me sizes, thicknesses, that sort of thing? I don't want to look a gift horse in the mouth, so to speak; but I shouldn't waste your time or mine if it's not usable for us." She picked up a pencil and small pad.

"Mostly standard-sized paper—what is that, 8 x 11? Regular white letter-type paper and some colored. A few boxes of thick, cardboard-like kind, my wife calls it index, I believe. I could drop it off if you're interested."

"We are very interested, Mr. Barnes. And it's good of you to take the time to do this for us." She jotted down his name and a note about the paper.

"Oh, no problem. They were just going to throw it out. I said, 'if you guys could use it, I'll get it there.'" He backed a few steps.

"Will you send in the name of your wife's company; that is, if it's okay to acknowledge the donation in our newsletter. Let me know. And thank you. Are you off to work now?"

"Yes, I've been gone long enough. Thank you. Bye." He walked briskly away.

He looks snappy in that uniform. I'd like to get Ray and Marty and Rosie into something along those lines. For that matter, I'd like to see the children in school dress as well.

Perhaps I'll mention it to Ray at our meeting tomorrow. Hope felt an embryo of anxiety forming in her stomach.

CHAPTER FIVE—Ray

"Good morning, Ray. Bring your coffee in with you; that's fine. I'll join you with my tea." Hope moved her stoneware mug from the desk to the round table. The spicy aroma of the tea suddenly reminded her of George. He had bought her the fat, round, blue mug with a crude outline of the earth on it, had given it to her when he was eleven or twelve to congratulate her on a new administrative position. He was so proud of the cup and its small, electric hot pad which, along with a packet of spice tea, constituted a set called Global Warming. Hope remembered how intense George had been at that time about protecting the environment. He had constantly policed the recycling at their house, sometimes to the point of annoyance.

Ray coughed lightly. Hope looked at him and sat down next to him at the round table.

"You may as well start, Ray; this is your meeting."

"I know you're busy, Hope, but... Things can't continue like this," Ray said forcefully, looking at her through grim eyes.

"Like what, Ray?" *This meeting is not about family problems. Is this a control tactic, calling this meeting?* She deliberately kept her voice neutral and calm.

"All this nonsense, letting the teachers and parents run things." Ray ran his fingers around the inside collar of his denim shirt.

"I don't understand, Ray. What do you mean?"

"Letting the teachers and parents always have their way, never mind how much extra work it causes for Rosie and Marty and me. We're already short handed." Hope could see the tension in Ray's mouth and braced herself for his next bullet.

"Letting the teachers and parents have their way about what, Ray?" Hope was careful to look directly into Ray's eyes as she leaned toward him. She could see a patch of red moving up his neck.

Ray cleared his throat. "Well, one long parents' night, for starters. How are we supposed to clean anything with the building full of parents and kids running around. Kids aren't even supposed to come. But nobody stops them."

"Are you saying then, that when there were two Parents' Nights, nobody brought their children?" Ray looked angrily at Hope and she wanted to take back the spiteful words.

"No, I'm not saying that," Ray's voice was rising. "I'm just saying that when we had two evenings, we could clean half the building one night and the other half the next. We're so short of time now, and people; it's hard to get all our work done. Then, we have extra activities; we get so behind it's ridiculous. Heck, the schools in Montrose, down the road, same size as us, have two more full-time custodians." Ray sighed and shook his head.

"I understand," Hope said without looking at Ray. She was confused about how Ray's crew could clean half the building when parents were visiting both nights. Which half? How? But she could see that Ray had become defensive.

"That's not all," Ray continued, looking at the small scrap of paper in his hands. Hope glanced at it and saw that it was covered with notes. "Just this week there was a morning meeting in the library. Nobody told me. I always vacuum the library in the morning. Scout groups and parent groups meet in there at night, leave the place a mess. We're finding ants. Teachers are letting kids have sticky drinks in the classroom. They spill all over the place, attracting ants. The spills get sticky and our dust mops catch on them. I thought we had a rule that water was the only beverage allowed." Ray stopped to take a breath.

"Wha—"

"And now Marty and Rosie are telling me that parents are coming after school. In droves. They want to get books and things their child forgot to bring home. Takes a lot of time to unlock doors and wait for them every night. And the pets. The rabbits and hamsters — gerbils are getting ridiculous. Teachers let the kids clean up after them and they don't do a good job. It's not the kids' fault. So it falls on us. Everything's falling apart." Ray dropped his voice and his eyes. He seemed relieved to have gotten out all his issues. He sat back and looked at Hope.

"You've certainly given me a lot of points to consider, Ray. Thank you for being so candid. Of course, I don't want extra work to fall unnecessarily on you. Or Rosie. Or Marty. Let me make sure I'm clear. You object to—"

"Me and Rosie and Marty object," Ray inserted.

"You, Rosie, and Marty object to: a single parents' night, drinks in the classroom, admitting droves of parents after school, classroom pets. Is that right?"

"And not being told in advance about meetings," Ray added, sitting up straighter and looking directly at her.

Hope recalled the week's schedule she had put in Ray's box, three copies. "Ray, again, thank you for coming to me with these issues rather than letting them fester. I will consider each one and look at ways to help everybody get their work done as effectively as possible. I will get back to you." Hope stood. Ray stood and walked out.

"So, you're in trouble with the principal," Bella chided Ray as he approached her desk.

"Not exactly. I just needed to see her, you know." Ray resented Bella's remark and wondered if she had overheard any of his conversation with Hope. "Anyway, don't you have better things to do than keep track of me?"

"What could be better than that?" Bella returned, laughing.

"You're right, Bella. Nothing could be better than keeping track of a handsome chap like me." Ray smiled.

"Have a good morning, Handsome," Bella laughed again.

"You have a good morning, yourself." Ray headed down the hall. *Bella really is a lot of fun. I wish I could kid around with Hope like that; but she is all business, hard as nails. Well, anyway, I told her what I thought about things. No sense letting her think everythings's peachy keen. She needs to work on her management.* He continued down the corridor to the boiler room.

She'll get back to me. She'll consider each one and look at ways to help everybody. Sure she will. He needed the release these sarcastic thoughts gave him. *Oh well, it doesn't matter. The important thing is I let her know I have rights, too. My opinion matters. If she wants to be all business, I can be all business, too.*

Ray could hear young voices laughing and talking in his boiler room. "Mr. Sellers should be here by now. We'll ask him why there's a shoe on his desk." More giggles erupted.

"Well, good morning, Samantha and Eric." Knowing he had not laid out the flag for them, he asked, "Did you turn that flag into a shoe with your magic wand?"

"No," Samantha and Eric spoke in unison.

"But that's a nice shoe, just my size. Could you conjure up another one?" Samantha laughed.

"If I do, I'll change both to my size," Ray teased.

"Where is the flag?" Eric asked. "It's not lost again, is it?" Ray went to the locker for the neatly folded flag and handed it to Eric. "Thanks, Mr. Sellers. I didn't mean you lost the flag. Remember when David Franks put it in the wrong locker, and we thought it was lost? That's what I was thinking." Eric seemed anxious to clear up any question of disrespect.

"Oh I do, Eric. I also remember how we scoured the building looking for it until Mr. Broski suggested we check the other lockers. Remember?"

"Yes, I do," Eric smiled. "Mr. Broski was all right." He looked off as if trying to remember his former principal accurately. "But so is Dr. Fleming. I like the way she had a special training meeting for all the school helpers."

"I know. Like we're real workers in a business or something," Samantha piped, laughing.

Ray watched the students walk away, anxious to do their job. He admired the way they were so responsible, taking even the lowest job seriously. He thought of their remarks about Dr. Fleming. It surprised him that they appreciated the way she was so business-like. He hadn't thought anybody would like that, especially kids.

Ray thought again of his meeting with Hope. Maybe he had said too much. Complained about too many things. He regretted bringing Rosie and Marty into it.

He wished he had not acted so hastily, calling for the meeting and listing those issues. He had to admit that most of them had gone on for some time, before Hope became principal. The truth was, they were just part of school life. He had worked in other schools where the same things went on, had talked to other plant supervisors, too. Poore Pond was no different from other schools. He should not have overreacted. He wondered why he had done that. Now he would have to stay late and catch Rosie and Marty tonight. Cover himself in case Hope actually did keep her word and talk to them before she got back to him. *Come to think of it, Hope Fleming would be just the type to follow through.*

Ray hated having to stay late today. He'd have to phone his mother and tell her he'd be late taking her to the grocery store. *She won't like it and I'll hear about it.*

"Come on, Ray, what's on your mind?" Rosie, taking a new pencil sharpener out of its box, looked impatient, in stark contrast to her affable auburn pixie haircut so suitable with her elfin face.

"Yeah, Ray, lay it on us." Marty stretched a fresh cover onto a large dust mop.

"Sit down. Please. Just give me a minute." Ray, thinking a casual tone was best, sat on his desk. Marty sat in a worn oak swivel desk chair opposite him; his sinewy shoulders looked one with the wooden chair arms. Rosie kept standing. "The thing is, I need to tell you I had a meeting with Hope today." He paused, wanting to make sure he put the right slant on this.

"And?" Rosie was growing more impatient. "Do we really have to know this?"

"Hold on, Rosie." Yes, you do have to know this because I spoke for you. I told Hope that we—you, Marty, and I—were upset about some things.

"Geez, Ray. I've gotten off on the right foot with Hope. She likes me. It takes a while to get in good with a new principal." Marty set down the dust mop.

"What are **we** upset about?" Sarcasm dripped from Rosie's words.

"Well, I told Hope you didn't like parents coming in after school to get things from classrooms. You know, when their kids forget homework and books?" Ray was feeling uncomfortable; he had to remind himself that he was the plant supervisor and his judgment counted. "You know what a pain it is to have to leave what you're doing and unlock the classroom door, then wait while they dig around for things. The kids never know where anything is. But you have to wait to make sure everything is in order when they leave. It's aggravating." Ray was feeling authoritarian now.

"What else are we upset about?" Rosie blinked her large brown eyes emphatically.

"Messes in the classrooms. Pets, spills, they attract ants. You know how those classrooms are getting. The teachers let the kids clean up and they don't do a good job. There's no excuse for it."

"Good grief, Ray, This is a school for gosh sakes. If the teachers and the kids cleaned the classrooms, we'd be out of a job. Are you finished now? Can we go?" Rosie slid toward the door.

"Ray's right," Marty inserted. "This clean dust mop I just put on will be sticky before the night's over. It's a problem." He engrossed himself in refolding the sleeve of his black T-shirt, further exposing his fine muscles. Ray gave him an appreciative glance.

"One more thing. Hope's probably going to ask you about these issues. She said she would look into each one and get back to me. I need your support here." Ray looked them in the eye, first one, then the other. "Oh, I also told her we demand advance notice of meetings. They affect our cleaning schedule."

Rosie pulled a paper out of her box on the wall and thrust it into Ray's face as she walked out. Ray looked at the memo from Hope with a two-week meeting schedule.

"These women sure do stick together," Ray muttered. He remembered that he was keeping his mother waiting and hurried out.

Are they going to support me with Hope? Or will they just make light of it all and make me look like a fool?

CHAPTER SIX—Ian and Helsi

"This meeting better not be long," Ian Bradford complained to his wife, seated next to him on a bench in the school lobby. "If they'd get started on time, we could get it over with. That looks like Miss Davis coming down the hall. She's the one who gave Dylan the test. I guess she was nice enough to Dylan, from what I could tell."

"Dylan really liked her," Helsi smiled at Carol Davis who looked casually professional in navy blazer and open-collared blue oxford shirt. Helsi praised herself for wearing a grey wool coat sweater instead of her usual zip-front sweatshirt with the black knit pants.

"Hello, Mr. and Mrs. Bradford." Carol smiled back. " Are you ready to begin? The team is waiting in the conference room."

"Hello," Helsi said brightly. She waited for Ian to greet the psychologist, but he was busy loosening the necktie on his regulation blue shirt. Helsi was glad Ian was required to wear a tie to work, thought it made him look important.

Six educators were seated around the long table. Helsi recognized all of them, their faces, at least, if she did not know their names: Dr. Fleming dressed in her classy style; Dylan's kindergarten teacher, Miss Fox, her thick, curly black hair tied-back in that earth-mother way; Miss Maher, Sean's former reading-lab teacher, looking very twenty-ish in brown velour mini-skirt and skyscraper platform shoes; grey-haired Mrs. Wheaton, Lucy's former first-grade teacher, in a tailored black wool military-style dress; the denim-jumpered special education teacher who had been at a meeting for Robbie; and the quiet, red-blonde-haired speech teacher who was seeing Robbie this year. They all stood and smiled when Helsi and Ian walked in with Mrs. Davis.

After a chorus of 'good mornings' with quick introductions and handshakes all around, Hope Fleming invited everyone to help themselves to coffee and then be seated. Helsi brought two cups to the table despite Ian's insisting he wasn't having any. Concentrating on his scowl, Ian pushed the cup aside. Hope explained the purpose of the meeting and that it would be led by Mrs. Davis.

"Thank you, Dr. Fleming. First, I want to thank you, Mr. and Mrs. Bradford, for taking the time to attend this meeting. We consider you a vital part of this team, here to discuss the best educational setting for Dylan. Also, I want to say that you are making a powerful statement to your son by taking the time to come here today. I know you are busy and that you, Mr. Bradford, have taken time off work to be here." Carol smiled widely at both of them.

"Let's get on with it so I can get back to work," Ian barked.

"Of course." Carol pulled a three-page report from her folder, handing copies to everyone. "I do want to say that Dylan was a very cooperative child during the testing. He tried his best to follow my directions carefully, and he had a pleasant attitude the entire time." Mrs. Bradford smiled warmly; Mr. Bradford glared.

Carol went over the narrative in her report and read the test results aloud clearly, explaining the task required by each subtest and the significance of Dylan's scores on each one. She related them to kindergarten and first-grade expectations. "As you can see, Dylan scored below first-grade level in every area except spatial relationships. He was able to answer all the questions about the arrangement of objects. Some of those questions are a bit abstract, but Dylan answered them. In fact, when I asked him which was closer to the barn, the garden or the horse, he chuckled and said, 'The horse. Not the garden, Silly. The horse would eat it when he goes to the barn'."

Grateful for the comic relief, everyone laughed, even Ian, although he tried hard to keep a straight face. "He was showing some abstract reasoning ability and vocabulary development as well," Carol added, looking directly at Ian, challenging him to smile.

"So, are you saying that Dylan can do more than your tests show? That he's just not a good test taker?" Ian had regained his resentful expression.

"No, I'm not saying that." Carol's silky voice was kind. "What I am saying is that while Ian's skills are well below first grade, he does have some strengths that should help him learn."

"Well, surely those strengths would help him learn, whether he's in first grade or kindergarten." Ian spread his big hands above the table for emphasis. Hope could feel the tension mount again. She looked at Helsi's face, full of despair.

"Generally speaking, Mr. Bradford. But let's ask Mrs. Wheaton to explain the curricular demands of first grade. We want to focus on what is best for Dylan," Carol smiled at Jan Wheaton.

Jan Wheaton began in a precise voice that matched the tone of her military-style dress. She outlined the reading program in which beginning first graders must be able to recognize letters and their sounds as they go on to word recognition, word families, rhyming words, and sentences." Every member of the team could feel Ian Bradford's restless movements as she spoke. "It is unfair to place a child in the position of trying to take the next developmental step in learning to read when he has not mastered basic letter/sounds," Jan Wheaton continued in her clear, neutral voice. Hope looked again at Helsi Bradford; her mouth was now firmly set, her face white. "We want to set the child up for success, not failure. Children develop these skills at diff—"

"It seems to me you teachers just try to make your job easier. You insist that children already know what it's your job to teach them; and if they don't know it, you want to hold them back. Never mind that you ruin their self-image, put them behind all their friends for the rest of their life!" Mr. Bradford's voice cracked and his face grew red. He gulped cold coffee from his rejected cup and rose to his feet nervously.

"That's enough, Ian!" Helsi Bradford stood and faced her husband squarely. "The report shows that Dylan ....is a little slow in his ability. Mrs. Davis' test results showed plain as day what she said: his IQ is below average, not a lot, but a little. He needs more time—"

"One test? One test shows he's a little slow? That's all you have to hear to let them hold him back? Put him behind for the rest of his life? That's what they wanted to do with Robbie and he's doing fine now in third grade." Ian's face was full of pain.

"Let me finish, please." Helsi put her hand on Ian's arm. "You're a good husband and a good father, Ian Bradford. But I am not going to sit back while you bully this school into throwing Dylan to the wolves. If he is not ready for first grade, he's not ready. It's simple as that. Has nothing to do with you or me or how smart we are or aren't. It's just how Dylan is. You heard Mrs. Wheaton say—try to say—that children learn at different rates. If Dylan needs more time in kindergarten, I'm here to see that he gets it." She sat down heavily, completely spent.

Tension was thick. Team members exchanged strained glances. Nobody spoke. Ian placed his cup on the table and stormed out. Helsi made a quick apology and ran after her husband. She had a vague sense of rendering the meeting silent as she left, but was conscious only of getting to her husband quickly.

The double exit doors swooshed shut behind her.

"I hope Dylan gets to stay in my class," Miss Fox's clear, young voice broke the silence. "He's comfortable with me and with the other students."

"Mr. Bradford needs to understand that Dylan is not Robbie," Miss Maher stated in a matter-of-fact voice.

"Good for Mrs. Bradford for speaking out like that. I could see how hard it was for her," speech teacher Maddy Marenko noted, surprising everyone with her uncharacteristic audacity. "I know what a terrible time she had persuading him to let Robbie come to speech class. Robbie's making good progress now."

Carol Davis offered her opinion. "Mr. Bradford is frustrated. He cares so much about his kids' education."

"You can be sure we have not heard the last of this." Hope stood, the others following. "Thank you all for meeting with us today. You were warm, yet professional."

"You're right, Carol," Hope said as they walked to the office together. "Mr. Bradford is frustrated. He does care deeply about his family. It was embarrassing for him, suffering his wife's berating like that, in front of us."

"That's how I see it, too." Carol agreed. "And how about Mrs. Bradford? Didn't you just want to cheer for her spunk?" They both laughed.

"She's obviously more in touch with Dylan's needs than her husband is. And more desperate." Hope waved Carol on as they reached her office door.

                                        *

The drive home was tense. Helsi tried to reason with Ian.

"No. No. They're not going to do this to Dylan. Not as long as there's breath in my body."

Alarmed by his scarlet face, Helsi fell silent.

CHAPTER SEVEN—Hope

Hope opened her office door. "Bella, please do not disturb me unless there is an urgent matter or Brian—or George rings." She closed her door quietly. She regretted the turn the Bradford meeting had taken. It pained her to see Ian and Helsi; indeed, any parent, humiliate themselves like that. *The parental bond is so powerful. It holds our emotions hostage.*

Hope sat down at her desk. She felt mentally overloaded with human issues. She noticed atop her urgent pile of papers, the sketchy list of Ray's issues and did not want to face them. She sighed and looked out at the courtyard where Ali guided her class in taking water samples from the pond. The children, filling plastic beakers and test tubes, chattered excitedly. Their teacher, just as excited, sat on the grass, directing the science lesson. Hope wanted to join the class. *That is one of the real pleasures of running a school. Watching children experience the joy of learning with a teacher who is equally enthralled.*

Reluctantly, Hope tore her eyes from the class in the courtyard and picked up the list. *What do these issues say about me? And what do they say about Ray? What about Jack and Rosie? 'Things are falling apart,' Ray had said. Are they? If Ray is thinking that, Ray and Rosie and Jack, perhaps others are, too. And it's only the second month of school. I must speak to Rosie and Jack, feel them out.*

Hope took out a legal pad and began writing down Ray's issues in detail, leaving space for her own comments. She could still see Ray looking tense until after he'd had his say. *Obviously, it was not easy for him to confront me. The stakes must have seemed really high to him.*

Well, the one parents' night is a done deal. Since it is crucial that parents' night serve the parents and the teachers; thus, the children well, the teachers need to feel comfortable with procedures. Hope knew that the whole point of parents' night was to build positive teacher-parent relationships that would foster parental support, ultimately helping the children feel positive about their school, too. *Can't risk the possibility of teachers' poor attitudes coloring their exchanges with parents, can we?*

Hope looked at the list again: *parents stopping after school, sticky drinks in classrooms, pets.* "I need more information on these," she said aloud.

Hope looked up as the door opened slowly. "George is on the phone," Bella whispered, peeking around the half-opened door, her eyes dramatically wide.

"I'll take the call, Bella, thank you." Hope felt her blood rushing. She took a deep breath.

"Good morning, George Dear. It's wonderful to hear your voice." Hope heard silence except for her pounding heart. She waited for George's strong voice to supplant the traffic sounds droning through the telephone line.

"Hello—Mother." George spoke tentatively, using the term for her he had always reserved for serious discussions. "What kind of school is that? Poor what?" Hope had a sense of his struggling to find words.

"Elementary school, George. It's an elementary school. For five-to-ten-year-olds. Poore Pond Elementary School. " Hope's voice began to crack. Her throat was unbearably dry, her chest hot. She took deep breaths, steeling herself not to give away the overwhelming emotion she felt. "How are you, George, really? Where are you? What are you doing with yourself?" Hope had planned when George called, to let him do the talking. But she could not stop herself from blurting out her most primal concerns.

"I'm — okay, Mother."

That serious term again. "Where are you living, Dear?" Hope reached for a pen and pad of paper.

"Well, I'm a city guy, I guess you could say." George forced a chuckle.

"What city, George? Don't tell me you're right in Columbus."

"As a matter of fact, I am."

"Give me your address, George. And phone number." Hope's pen was poised to write.

"I don't remember it, M—"

"You don't remember your address!" she interrupted. Hope had visions of George with a neurological problem. Or a brain injury. Some terrible condition. Her heart raced.

"No. I only just moved. I've been moving a lot. Can't seem to keep my address straight. It's not important. How's Dad? Have you seen him?"

"I was about to ask you that." Hope's heart sank at the thought of George's having had no contact with either parent. "Are you working, then? What are you doing? Do you have a phone?"

"I'm—uh—kind of doing research. Urban studies, urban renewal, that sort of thing. I don't have a phone yet."

"May I have your work number then?" Hope tried to hide her desperation.

"I don't think so, Mom." Fear began to seep into Hope's veins.

"Well I wouldn't abuse it, George. I want it only in case of emergency." She was surprised by feelings of anger. "It's been four years, George, for Heaven's sake. You're my son and we have not seen each other for four-r-r-r years. I don't think it's too much to ask to have your phone number."

"I've got to go, Mother. Congratulations on your new post. I'll call again."
"Tonight. Call me at home tonight." Hope heard the line go dead. The dial
tone sounded rudely. Hope stared in disbelief at the receiver. Her entire body
ached for one more word with her son. She longed to see him. *How difficult
would it be to find him if he's only thirty minutes away, right in our city, two suburbs
from here? Urban research. I could look in the telephone directory for companies,
foundations that study those things.* "George had decided to major in city planning,
" she said aloud. "At least that was his latest plan before he dropped out of school."
Perhaps he went back and finished his degree. Hope allowed herself a moment of
optimism. *I could contact local colleges and universities, couldn't I? Is it a matter
of public record who has had degrees conferred? I believe it is.*
   "Are we having outdoor recess?" Bella peered around the half-opened door.
   "I will check the playground." Hope glanced at the clock. "How did it get to
be 11:05 already?" she muttered. "Who wants to know?"
   "One of the volunteers called from the library. Said she'd get her daughter's
jacket from the car if they're going outside. I'll tell her to check the recess board
in five minutes."
   Hope walked briskly toward the rear doors. She could hear the hustle of five-and-
six-year-olds getting ready for lunch in primary-wing classrooms. She thought about
trying to locate George's employer after work tonight if she could get away early
enough, before institutions closed. She would check the telephone directory. As
distasteful as it was, she would call Michael. George may have phoned his father from
time to time even if he had not seen him. *Michael probably knows where he works.*
   She looked at the outdoor thermometer and posted *Outdoor Recess - Wear
Jackets*-strips on the recess signboard. The cooks were filling sectioned trays
from metal chafing dishes, the servery awash in appetizing smells of over-warmed
vegetables and baked chicken. She hurried to supervise the first-lunch line of
smiling, squirming, chattering students waiting to get lunch trays.
   "David Crowe, Justin McCullough, Susan Stern—I know that face. Don't tell
me don't tell me. Give me think time—Tiffany, no Taylor—Pruett. Your sister is
Tiffany. Right?" Hope moved child by child down the lunch line.
   "How do you remember everybody's name, Dr. Fleming?" a small, dark-haired
girl, looking smart in black velour pants and red argyle vest asked confidently.
   "I practice, just as I'm doing now. Bobby Clark, Kevin Smith—I know your
last name is Curtis; what's the first letter of you first name?"
   "Eric."
   "Eric Curtis. I knew that. And your sister is Ellen."
   "What's my middle name?"
   "I don't do middle names," Hope smiled. "Samantha Smith, Carol Brock,
Melissa Faye, Tommy Grant, Cheryl—Cheryl—I know it. I know it."
   "Cheryl Anne Fortuna!" A petite child with blonde braids cried through a
giggle.
   "Cheryl Fortuna. I should have known that; I know your face. Your father
just returned from work in Germany, didn't he? I will get it right next time."

Hope smelled toasty french fries and realized she was hungry. She noticed the catsup line stretching into the center of the corridor, blocking students coming through with lunch trays. "Hug the wall, please. Hug the wall." Hope herded the motley line of students toward the wall. Two students, intermediate-grade boys in blue jeans and football jerseys, wearing big smiles, pretended to embrace the wall. "That's a figure of speech. Do you know what a figure of speech is?"

"A saying. It means something else," Anastasia said excitedly, her long wavy hair rippling around her lovely, dark-eyed face.

"Something else besides what?" Hope asked, obviously enjoying herself. "Can you give me an example?"

"Uhhh——" Anastasia, brown eyes shining toward the ceiling, took a moment. "Hold your horses!" she exclaimed proudly.

"What a good example, Anastasia. What does hold your horses mean?"

"Wait a minute, have a little patience." Anastasia said unhesitatingly.

"So tell me what *hug the wall* means." Hope smiled, making eye contact with all the children in the line.

"It means stand against it," John said in a deep but quiet voice. His spiked red hair framed his broad face neatly.

"Thank you, John. And why do I want you to hug the wall?"

"So kids can get through with their trays," Anastasia beamed.

"You children know so much. I can't imagine what else we need to teach you."

This teachers' lounge could use some sprucing up. Hope sat in the empty lounge enjoying cold cranberry juice. She could envision decorative mirrors on the barracks-like concrete-block walls and several round tables to replace the one long rectangular one. She decided to try to improve the appearance of the room this summer, as a surprise to the staff.

"Dr. Fleming, are you in there?" Bella's voice resonated through the wall speaker.

"Yes, I am," replied Hope, raising her voice more than necessary.

"Brian Glover is on the phone. Says it's urgent."

"I'll take it in my office, Bella. Just tell Brian I'll need a few minutes." She gulped the last of the juice and hurried down the hall.

"Hi, Hope. Does the name Ian Bradford mean anything to you?" Hope hesitated. Obviously, he had called her supervisor; she wondered what he had told Brian.

"Of course," Hope continued in her most neutral voice. "We met just this morning to present results of his son's evaluation. He was not happy. You already know that, I'm sure, since he phoned you."

"Not happy is an understatement. The man was devastated, Hope. I'm surprised you didn't pick up on that, with your sensitivity."

"Actually, he stormed out of the meeting after his wife sided with us. I was going to phone him after he'd had time to cool down."

"What's his kid's—is it Donovan?"

"It's Dylan. What's his problem?"

"Exactly."

"He's showing barely low-average IQ and no readiness skills as yet. Mr. Bradford seems to think we just don't want to work with him. But to put Dylan in first grade will only further frustrate him. Lower his self-esteem. We could lose him motivation-wise."

"I understand. But you know as well as I do, Hope, that if the parent does not support the retention, it doesn't work. Heck, we don't even know if it works anyway."

"Oh, come on, Brian. Surely you know of particular children who have repeated a grade, especially kindergarten, or first—even second and have gone on to do average work. Don't you? I certainly do." Hope felt uneasy about where this was leading.

"I suppose I do. But in this case, what are the odds? Dad is devastated. I won't tell you what he said about Poore Pond. I told him that his son would go to first grade—on Monday. You do have space, don't you?"

"I have space in three classes, Brian." Hope's voice trailed off. "Did you tell Ian that I would call him? How did you leave it?"

"I told him you would call him with the teacher's name and room number. You can do that, can't you?"

"Oh please, Brian. Of course I can. I just wish decisions on what's best for a child's education could be left to us educators, that's all."

"Thanks, Hope. Keep me posted."

"I will, Brian. Thank you for your assistance." Hope replaced the phone carefully. Not wanting to focus on anything else at the moment, she took unnecessary time to fit the receiver into its cradle precisely. Her heart sank. *Everyone on the team worked so hard on this one.*

She pulled out her binder to check class lists. The three first grades with space seemed to be equally suitable for Dylan in terms of the distribution of high, middle, and low-achieving students as well as ratio of boys to girls. But she knew that Jan Wheaton's kind-but-firm style would probably keep him on track although Trudy Cooper would give him the large amounts of one-to-one instruction he would need. *She'd have Ian on the floor cutting out shapes every Tuesday.* Also, Jeff Masters, being a naturally nurturing teacher, could help Dylan maintain self esteem. *And he does bring in many parent volunteers to work with individual children. Jeff could good-ole-boy Ian until he softened.* Hope pondered each option. "I'll make the decision by tomorrow," she said to herself, knowing she needed to let the world turn at least once in order to have a clear mind.

Later that evening Hope stood at her kitchen sink, enjoying the crisp autumn air through the open window. She watched the pointy leaves of the hanging spider plant buffeting against the cupboard. Rinsing the dishes from her fried-egg supper, she thought again of Dylan Bradford. How could she make a clear decision on the correct teacher assignment for a placement in which she did not believe? To which she was utterly opposed? She felt such loathing for the politics of education. Of life, actually. *It's all politics. Running a school is highly political. Marriage is political; parenting is political. Life is just a string of situations, all political. Has anyone ever died from politicitis? Hah!*

The telephone rang sharply. Hope was thrilled to hear George's mature voice greeting her. She tried to keep him on the line, but he was anxious to go, obviously returning the call only to respect her request. They agreed to meet for lunch on Saturday at a neighborhood restaurant they had frequented as a family when George was a child. Hope felt encouraged; George had cared enough to call back as she had asked. She could hardly wait the three more days until Saturday.

Hope sat on her bed in her nightgown, lotioning her hands. *What a day this has been.* Now that there were concrete plans to see George, she felt able to face the difficulties of the day. She felt calmer. Hope had always found satisfaction in recalling the day's events. Resorting to her lifelong habit, she mentally listed: the heartbreaking Bradford meeting, Ray's niggling list of issues, George's frustrating first call, Brian's lack of support for the team's decision. She noted that human nature was very much in the forefront today. *Human nature is fascinating.* She had to admit she could see everyone's side in each situation. She was struck by the irony of it all. *When I finally escaped from Michael's obsessive control, I vowed never again to let myself be controlled by a man. Now I'm jumping through the hoops of four men!* She collapsed into robust, deep-in-the-belly laughter.

But the final event in the day was so refreshing: George's second call. "He actually agreed to see me," she cheered to the empty bedroom.

The doorbell rang sharply, frightening Hope. She peered out the upstairs window and saw a police car in the driveway below. Anxiety engulfed her. She descended the stairs slowly, grasping the banister to keep her weak knees from collapsing. She switched on the outside light, revealing the officer's imposing figure through the lace curtain.

"Who is it?" she called through the locked door, trying desperately to keep her voice from shaking.

"Police. Looking for Hope Minster. I have important documents for her."

Hope froze. No one had called her by her maiden name for years. Mary Baldwin's face filled her mind's eye. Hope wanted to tell the officer there was no Hope Minster here. She swallowed hard.

"Open the door, Miss!" The officer's voice boomed with authority.

Hope slid the chain and opened the door as far as the chain would permit.

"I'm Hope Minster." Hope said, her low voice full of defeat.

The officer thrust a thick envelope through the door. "These are for you, Hope Minster." He turned on his heel and left abruptly.

Hope could barely relock the door, her fingers shook so violently. She collapsed on the hall bench. Her hands trembled; the envelope slid to the floor. She began to gasp for air. She put her head between her knees. She wanted to tear out her hair. Raising her head, she peered down at the envelope and saw a return address in engraved black script: Dempsey, Dempsey, and French Law Firm.

"God, help me," she cried. "I'm so sorry, Mary. I should not have betrayed you." Hope began to sob violently. "I was young then, Mary, what did I know?" she called to the ceiling, sobbing uncontrollably.

Finally the sobbing stopped. The release restored Hope. She picked up the envelope and went to the kitchen, putting a kettle of water on the stove. She took out a milky white Spode china cup and saucer and a silver teaspoon. She filled a ball-shaped tea diffuser with green tea leaves and waited for the water to boil, the imposing envelope staring at her from the counter.

Sipping the hot tea, Hope tore open the envelope. She unfolded the pages-thick packet with the law firm's logo at the top of the cover page. The document was legal notice that Michael was putting Hope's house up for sale, exercising his right to do so in the event of financial reverses. It specified that Hope must make the house available for showing to prospective buyers and that she would have 30 days after a sale closed to vacate the premises. Tears of relief flowed down her cheeks, and she cried softly. If only she could erase the memory of what she'd done to Mary Baldwin. She was just a child. She had so little. And Mary had so much. It wasn't fair. She had really been a help to Mary, too. Made her life easier. How could anyone not forgive her? Did she have to be persecuted all her days for one childish mistake?

Hope refilled her teacup with boiling water and waited for it to brew, making a mental note to return Frances' call tomorrow. She remembered her appointment with George. She removed the diffuser from the cup and carried it upstairs. Perhaps I should take George a small gift, she thought as she settled into bed after another drink of tea. His favorite dark chocolate nut clusters. Or a nice leather organizer. Something to signify the celebratory nature of their meeting.

Emotionally spent, Hope drifted off to sleep, dreaming of a handsome, successful George on an impressive career track.

CHAPTER EIGHT—RAY

Ray watched a pretty, young mother in cropped black pants and a bright lime shirt, trying to placate her small son who was tantrumming in the parking lot. She carried two bagfuls of groceries along with a huge black handbag swinging out of tandem with the groceries, and could not grab hold of him. Ray was thinking he should lend her a hand when the child rose to his feet and followed his mother diligently to the car, his miniature shirttails swinging in the breeze. "Probably a single mother," he murmured, wondering what she said to get him to obey.

The after-four-o'clock sun felt unusually intense. He lowered the window in his blue minivan and thought of the single mothers he saw at school. Sometimes the more desperate ones asked him to help start their stalled cars, often worn-out models that had barely made it into the parking lot. A few had asked him directly if he would require their children to do cleaning chores around the school as punishment for low grades or not completing homework. One had even given him permission to spank her unruly son when he acted up in the lunchroom. Ray agreed with Hope that it was not his place to discipline students, other than the occasional reprimand; but he always felt sorry for the mothers, trying to do everything for their children on their own. He often longed to get involved in their lives outside school, help them raise their children, shoulder part of their burden. The poor kids were the losers; but the mothers lost, too. Ray never understood how fathers could leave those wives and children high and dry like that.

Ray watched a squirrel climb a tree in the shady yard next door to the supermarket. He could hear children's voices as they played field hockey somewhere behind the shopping strip and wondered if they were Poore Pond students. He thought of his meeting with Rosie and Marty, anxiety growing in his stomach. He resented Rosie's lack of respect. *She should have, well, kowtowed to me a little; I am her direct supervisor.* Marty hadn't really seen his side either, although he did support Ray about sticky spills ruining clean dust-mop heads.

Ray cursed aloud. *It's all Hope's fault. How much longer can I keep working with her?* He thought about bidding on a job opening at the high school. But he knew those smart-mouthed teenagers would drive him crazy with their attitude and outlandish dress. They reminded him too much of himself at that age, lost and rebelling against everything. He would miss the elementary children, their sweetness and the way they tried to please adults. *Heck, they think I'm as important as the principal.*

Ray looked at his watch and wondered how much longer it would take his mother to finish shopping. She had been stone quiet on the drive to the market, letting him know his lateness had offended her. But Ray knew she would talk to him again after gossiping with friends and acquaintances as she shopped. She always came out of the store bursting with news and opinions. Ray understood why she looked forward to shopping day and suddenly realized it was really a social outing for her. Shopping and church were her only weekly social activities, he reminded himself. She has such an outgoing personality, he noted, and a lot of love to give. She often gave sweets to the neighborhood children as rewards for their fetching her newspaper or mail or oversized garbage cans. Ray knew she just wanted them to have the treats but felt that their parents would be less likely to object if they earned them. She liked talking with them, and giving them tasks gave her more to talk about and kept them there longer. It's too bad she has no grandchildren to love. *Why, I wouldn't mind myself, little nieces and nephews coming over to the house from time to time. We could go to their ballgames and school programs. I'd be Uncle Ray.*

"Fat chance of that happening," Ray poohed his cheeks. He thought of his sister, Claire, his only living sibling. Claire was four years older than Ray, divorced, childless, and bitter, with no prospects of remarriage that he could see.

Caroline Sellers shuffled out of the market, leaning heavily on the metal cart she pushed. Ray pulled up next to her and climbed out to load the groceries. He held his mother's elbow to guide her toward the van, giving her broad, flat buttocks a hoist to make the high step. She breathed heavily, then gave him a cheerful thank-you. As he loaded groceries into the rear of the van, he could barely hear her babbling nonstop about a conversation she had had in the store; but he knew she would repeat it, every word.

"What time is Claire coming?" Ray asked, settling into the driver's seat and buckling his seatbelt.

"I asked her to come for dinner," Caroline said, "but she refused. Said she'd be late, just to save her something . She works too hard at that office. I bought fresh bleu cheese for your salad, Rayley." She beamed at Ray who continued to look straight ahead. He hated it when she called him Rayley. It made him feel like a child. But he had given up trying to talk her out of it; it always led to a big discussion about how much he meant to her, how grateful she was that he stuck by her, how lost she would be if he moved out of the house. "Why I'd have to go to the county home," she'd say in a pitiful voice.

"What time is Aunt Patsy coming, Ma?"

"For dinner, about 6:30. And she's always on time, right to the minute, she is. Been that way ever since she was a kid." Caroline's voice was full of pride in her younger sister. Ray winced; he knew she was throwing up to him, his lateness today. Anxiety stabbed him low in the stomach.

Caroline began an account of the gossip she'd heard about cashier Marge Lewis's fifth marriage, tiresomely relating every word of the conversation that generated it. Ray could not stop his mind from wandering. He hoped Claire would be extra late. He looked forward to some time alone with Aunt Patsy before she arrived. His sister had a way of charging in, complaining, demanding attention, and sucking all the energy out of the room. Ray knew that their so-called meeting to plan Caroline's birthday celebration would be just a matter of Claire's telling them what they would do.

*

Ray, his mother, and aunt sat at the red-stained maple table, enjoying a pleasant pork-chop-and-sauerkraut dinner and light conversation. Aunt Patsy always had funny stories to tell about her work at the hospital where she coordinated volunteers. And he had noticed, even as a child, how Caroline and Patsy got so giggly when they were together. It reminded him of teen-aged girls, how they were always giggling and teen-aged boys never knew what was so funny. They laughed themselves silly over Aunt Patsy's stories and were still laughing after the dishes were cleared. It was good to laugh like that. Claire's plate of dinner was left warming in the oven, and they moved into the small living room.

Heavy footsteps sounded on the porch and in rushed Claire, carrying several bundles and bags. Her dark brunette hair, Ray's hair—waves and all—hung damply in her eyes. Ray stopped short in his tale about the fourth-grader who had accidentally thrown his retainer in the lunch garbage and expected Ray to dig around in all that slop to retrieve it for him. It was one of his favorite stories and he didn't get to finish it. Aunt Patsy would have loved it. Aunt Patsy stood to receive Claire's off-center hug. Claire then hugged her mother and asked how she felt. "Hey, Ray," she said to her brother, cuffing him on the shoulder.

Caroline moved into the kitchen and set Claire's plate of warm food on the table. She laid a folded, thick paper napkin on the table with knife, fork, and spoon correctly placed. "Sit down and eat, Claire. You must be famished. I have your favorite: pork and sauerkraut."

"Thanks, Mom. Come sit with me, Aunt Patsy," Claire invited. After offering coffee to everyone, Caroline joined them at the table.

Ray pressed the on button on the television remote control. He flicked to world news and sighed. He wanted to block out the conversation in the kitchen. Already he could feel the changed atmosphere inside the house as if negative thoughts were weighting the ions in the air. He took a deep breath, trying to relax again. He wished Aunt Patsy had stayed in the living room with him. He missed her easy manner, now obliterated by Claire's arrogance. He tried to remember when Claire had started having that effect on him. Was it while they were still in high school? He could remember having fun with her in elementary school. They would ride bikes to the city park and swim or hit tennis balls together. Claire wasn't a bossy older sister then. They liked each other. When had it all changed? Was it after their father died when Claire was a freshman at community college? That's when she really started attacking him. "When is your responsibility gene going to kick in?" she liked to say.

"Ray, whatever were you thinking?" Claire appeared as if magically, beside his chair. "Not taking Mom to the pharmacy today when she has only one more dose of her medication left?" Claire's grimace made her normally translucent skin go blotchy. She stood over Ray, her arms folded rigidly on her ample chest.

"What are you talking about?" Ray kept his voice flat and did not look at her.

"I'm talking about Mom's heart medicine. She has only one more dose left which she will take tonight. That leaves her with none for tomorrow morning." Claire spoke slowly in her deliberate, patronizing voice, a technique she had mastered and could turn on at will when she wanted to berate Ray.

"It's the first I've heard of it," Ray said, still not looking at his sister.

"Aren't you the son who lives at home?" Hands on her hips, she stared through Ray's face. He turned and glared at her. "Aren't you the one who agreed to look after Mom?" Ray felt his chest burning. His dry throat made it difficult to swallow. "So given that responsibility and agreeing to it, don't you think you should have asked her if she needed to get medication? Especially since you ran errands today anyway. What were you thinking? Don't answer that. It's obvious you weren't thinking." She stormed out of the room.

Ray stood. He wanted to punch something. He stepped out onto the front porch. He breathed in the cool autumn air, enjoying the chilly feeling on his jacket-less arms. He looked up at the bright full moon and was cheered by it. He could hear the neighbor's television blaring through unopened windows. Looking up and down the Norman Rockwellian street, he was struck by the warmth of the lighted post and porch lamps. Apparently, all the households were complying with police requests to keep outdoor lights burning since there had been a rash of small burglaries in the area. He wished people would always keep lights on at night. It made the street look friendlier, definitely safer. He waved back to the teen-aged girl across the street, hanging out an upstairs window, telephone pressed to her ear. He watched her brother take his bicycle from the driveway and park it on the wide front porch.

Ray heard the front door creak open and turned to see Aunt Patsy. "Want to go for a walk, Ray? It's such a lovely night. Will you look at that moon."

"Oh—okay. I'll just get my jacket." He went into the house and came immediately out, pulling on a khaki twill windbreaker. "Is the party all planned?"

"Just about," Aunt Patsy smiled at him. She led the way down the steps. "The day is decided. And part of the menu. They don't need me for the rest of it. You know Claire has such good ideas. And your mother knows what she likes." They set off down the sidewalk. "Boy, this street is lit up like opening night." Aunt Patsy giggled. Ray told her about the police request for well-lighted streets.

Aunt Patsy took his arm. "Don't mind what Claire says, Ray. She has a lot on her mind. Her job and all. Trying to pay off those debts Jack left her. She got a raw deal from that short marriage. I know you take good care of your mother. She knows it, too. Everybody can see it." She patted his arm. "Want to go around the block?" she asked as they reached the corner.

"Might as well." Ray could see that the side street was well lighted, too. He enjoyed the Americana feel of the little street and the warmth of Aunt Patsy's arm in his.

"Looks like these people have lighted up, too." Aunt Patsy laughed. "Looks like a Christmas card, doesn't it? Without snow."

"Except for those jack-o-lanterns," Ray laughed.

They walked on in silence for a few moments, feeling a soft breeze on their faces. "Remember when you and Rory used to spend a week with me in the summer? We'd go for walks in that woods near my house. Rory always wanted to walk when the moon was bright." She could feel his body tense up. "I don't mean to open an old wound, Ray." She leaned toward him.

"I know I know. It's just that—it's painful to think about Rory, what happened to him." Ray felt emotion rising in his throat.

"We don't ever want to forget Rory, Ray. Forget that he lived. He was such a bright little presence."

"Please, Aunt Patsy," Ray's voice cracked. "It's my fault Rory's not here. I live with that every day of my life." His eyes were dry, but his voice was full of tears.

"Stop that, Ray." It was never your fault. It was nobody's fault. It just happened. An accident. How were you to know he would fall off the swing set that way? How could anybody know? "

"But it was my job. I was supposed to be watching him. I let him fall."

"For gosh sakes, Ray. You were ten years old. Anyway, you called for help right away, did the best thing. Caroline could have been standing right there and it still would have happened. The whole family could have watched it happen. Rory was a fearless little kid, a daredevil." She stopped in the middle of the sidewalk and hugged him.

Ray could feel his tears dampening her wool sweater. He hated letting go like this. Especially in front of Aunt Patsy, who thought so well of him. He didn't want her to see his weak side. But he let himself fold into her embrace, relishing how enormously comforting it felt. He couldn't remember when he had last been hugged, by anyone. It seemed like minutes that they stood on the sidewalk hugging before resuming their walk. They both worked hard to keep a conversation going, on safer topics.

"I may have to look for another job," Ray heard himself say.

"Why is that, Ray?" Aunt Patsy looked concerned.

Ray told her about Hope and how seriously she took her position as principal. Aunt Patsy quietly listened, nodding now and then, saying, "Um-huh," and looking into his face. Her rapt attention spurred him on, and he found himself describing small incidents that had taken place from Hope's first days at Poore Pond. When he told her about his disappointing meeting with Rosie and Marty, he sensed he may have said too much.

"Ray, Honey," Aunt Patsy's voice shimmered with warmth, reminding Ray of how he had always loved her soothing voice as a child. It made him feel cherished and safe. "May I offer you a word of advice? She smiled into his face.

"I wouldn't say yes to anyone else on that, Aunt Patsy. But you, yes. Give me all the advice you have." Ray smiled back. He was feeling relaxed again.

"Well, Honey. I just think that maybe you should look at your attitude for a moment. You've heard that saying, 'Attitude is everything,' haven't you? Do you think you could've been having a bit of an attitude with this Hope? You know, you've always worked for men since you started with the school district. Maybe you are just going through an adjustment period, working for a woman for the first time."

"Me? Attitude?" Ray's heart dropped. He could not believe his beloved Aunt Patsy was accusing him of this. He didn't want to look at her.

"Oh, we all have attitude at one time or another, Ray. It can get to be a bad habit. That may be why Sylvia broke your engagement. You said so yourself."

"W—" Ray tried to butt in. Aunt Patsy forged on.

"It looks to me as if you are letting a bad attitude get the best of you, trying to do a job on this Hope, show her a thing or two, put her in her place. And you're trying to get your colleagues to help you." Aunt Patsy was unrelenting. Ray had never seen her come on so strongly.

"Now wait a minute," Ray stopped, held up his hands, the backs facing Aunt Patsy. He felt hot in his windbreaker. His muscles tightened so, he wanted to run and flail his limbs. He began to walk very fast, Aunt Patsy nearly running to keep pace. He needed to shout at her, but he had no words. He could feel the silence between them, emphasizing the pain they both felt.

Attitude? Sylvia left because of my bad attitude? The problems with Hope are just a matter of my bad attitude? What's wrong with Aunt Patsy? She used to be so understanding. Now she's judging me. I don't get it? What's changed?

Ray glanced at Aunt Patsy's face, worried that she could sense his thoughts. He noticed that she was no longer holding his arm. *This can't be happening. I don't want to lose Aunt Patsy's love.* Ray bent his elbow and pulled her arm through it, unable to meet her gaze. They walked several blocks in silence, the wind picking up noticeably. Then they turned onto Crescent Street and saw the Seller's grey bungalow, porch light blazing.

"Is that Claire getting into her car," Aunt Patsy forced the emotion out of her voice. "Let's hurry. I want to get the rest of the deal on Caroline's party." She pulled Ray along at a fast clip. It felt good to run off the tension between them.

Aunt Patsy ran to Claire, who answered her questions quickly before getting into the car and driving away. A shivering Caroline watched from the porch. Ray adjusted the chain on the porch swing.

Aunt Patsy stepped onto the porch to hug her sister. "I'll see you Sunday. We'll have a wild birthday celebration." She laughed heartily, Caroline joining her. She faced Ray and hugged him long and hard. "You take care now." She looked deeply into his injured eyes. "I know you will give the whole matter more thought, Ray. You'll sort it out. You always knew how to do that." She smiled her old, doting smile.

"Bye, Aunt Patsy. Thanks for—I'll see you Sunday." Ray dropped his eyes. "I'm going to watch *Millionaire* in my room tonight, Mom. I'm tired." Ray ambled through the small living room where his mother was positioned in front of the blaring television.

"It's early, Ray," Caroline's disappointment rang in her voice. "But I know how hard Miz Fleming makes you work at school. Go ahead, get your rest. Don't you worry about her either. Sounds like the type who'll be promoted out of there soon. All that raw ambition. She sounds like an uptown girl to me. Then they'll bring in a man."

Ray winced. *When did I tell her anything about Hope.* After Aunt Patsy's reaction, he was sorry he'd ever mentioned his principal.

Lying between the cool sheets, Ray reviewed Aunt Patsy's remarks, still feeling the sting. He wondered how long she had thought those things about him, that he had a bad attitude. He felt a loss of something monumental. He had always counted on her good opinion of him. It kept him centered. All the changes at Poore Pond, caring for Mom, Claire's insults making him feel like the family black sheep; Aunt Patsy was his buffer against all that. He could not believe that she was now turning on him. Ray lay there, feeling tense. But a few minutes of watching Regis Philbin and the would-be wealthy contestants tranquilized him into deep sleep.

*

Ray vacuumed Hope's office first thing the next morning in compliance with her request that it not be done the night before. Dust forms again during the night, she had told him, and her asthma forces her to avoid allergens where possible.

Ray inadvertently knocked an object off the edge of Hope's desk. He retrieved it from the floor. Relieved that it was intact, he noticed that it was a silver-framed photo of a handsome young man. He could see Hope's pale blue eyes in the face. This must be her son, he thought. Hope with children of her own? Ray could not see it. But then again, she does get on well with the students, he had to admit. Always knows just what to say to them. Ray remembered the incident with those kids from Boris Mathews' class last week. Mathews, without clearing it through Hope or Ray, had stationed them at the return-tray rack in the lunchroom to monitor younger children returning their used trays. The students confused kindergartners by changing procedures; and the line was bottle-necking, slowing up the flow of outgoing as well as incoming students.

Hope noticed the confusion and sorted it all out. She told the students she was sure Mr. Mathews wanted them to gather ideas for improving the procedure first, which their stint at the rack today would help them do. Then they could monitor the younger students under their new plan when it was ready. Ray couldn't help but admire the way she'd handled it, putting a quick end to the problem without undermining their teacher and making the students feel important. He had to give her that. Now that he thought about it, he could see her with her own son.

"Good morning, Ray," Hope startled Ray, and he whirled around.

"Good morning." Ray noticed the overstuffed briefcase Hope placed on the table.

"Thank you for vacuuming, Ray. It smells fresh now." Ray wound the vacuum cord in a neat figure eight.

"I have a proposal for you, Ray." Hope waited for Ray to finish winding the cord.

"What is that?" Ray instinctively braced himself to resist, stay in control of the situation.

"I want to ask you to speak to the teachers at their faculty meeting on Wednesday."

"I —don't —think —so." Ray gave a slow, negative nod.

"It may help them see your side on these issues of spills and pets in classrooms. They always have good ideas; they'll come up with their own ways to help. I'm sure of it. Especially if you help them understand the pressure you, Rosie, and Marty face each day." Hope smiled, her eyes seeking Ray's eyes.

"Oh, did you talk to them about that?" Ray's stomach tightened. He had to force himself to give Hope eye contact.

"Yes, I did." Ray waited for Hope to comment on what Rosie and Marty had told her. "Getting back to your speaking at the faculty meeting, Ray; think about it, please. You have several days to decide. Let me know by Monday. How's your mother doing? Did you tell her how much we enjoyed the corn chowder she sent in? She really is a good cook. I'm a bit envious."

"She's fine. She keeps busy cooking. I did tell her how everyone here scarfed up her corn chowder. She was proud. She loves to cook; that's mostly what she does, cooks and worries. Worries about my sister. Now she's worried about her niece. Millie—maybe I didn't tell you— Millie Blackwell is my first cousin."

"Our Millie Blackwell? The third-grade teacher here at Poore Pond?"

"Right. You probably should know, Millie just found out she has breast cancer. The doctor gave her test results a couple days ago. Well, I 'm sure Millie will tell you herself. Maybe I should not have jumped the gun. Should've let Millie tell you when she's ready."

"I hate hearing this, Ray. Is she scheduled for radiation?"

"Radiation and chemo, as far as I know. I'm sure she'll tell you." Ray regretted having spoken out of turn, wanted to get out of Hope's office.

"You're right, Ray. We'll let Millie tell me in her own good time. It's as if you never said a word. Is she your cousin on your mother's side?"

"No, on my dad's side. She was Dad's favorite niece. His twin brother's daughter." Ray backed toward the door.

"I see." Hope opened her bulging briefcase. "I'm sorry about Millie, Ray. She is a fine person. And an outstanding teacher. Let me know about the meeting."

CHAPTER NINE —IAN AND HELSI

Helsi, in black sweatpants and Ian's olive fleece pullover, dug angrily at the hard soil, uncovering brown tulip bulbs which she placed in a plastic basket. She looked at her watch and thought of Dylan at school. It was time for lunch recess, and he would be sitting in Ms. Kurowski's office while his classmates played outside. Mrs. Cooper had probably given him workbook pages that he could not read, to complete. Dylan would be squirming in his chair, looking out the window, trying to make the time pass. A twenty-five-minute recess is an eternity to a six-year-old. Bella Kurowski would remind him to get busy on his work; Helsi had heard her do that with other sentenced students when she had stopped in the office with medical forms or lunch money. Helsi did not like the way Bella tried to make the children feel bad. "Shame on you. Not finishing your work," she would say. "Your father is working hard at the fire station for you. Your mother is working hard at home for you, washing your clothes, cleaning your house, cooking your dinner. You need to do your job here at school for them." It bothered Helsi the way Bella made it her business and got so personal with the children. How in the world did she think that would help the situation? And why did Dr. Fleming permit it?

A strong breeze swept across the garden. Helsi removed her suede glove to brush hair out of her eyes. She looked at the garden in its autumnal state, wanting to savor the remaining green leaves and dry-stemmed chrysanthemums before snow blanketed the entire patch. As much as Helsi loved the crisp autumn air, she dreaded the encroaching winter. *All those mittens, scarves, and boots to manage; kids stuck in the house.*

Helsi pulled her glove back on and dug again at the bulbs. She was disappointed that so many of them looked small and puny, not fit to produce again next spring.

Helsi had to fight the urge to go to school and sign Dylan out for early release to protect him from that ordeal in the office. Dylan was required to sit out second recess this afternoon as well. Maybe she should go sign him out now.

Helsi knew that Dylan needed some sort of punishment for not doing his work and talking back to Mrs. Cooper when she reprimanded him. *But why does it have to be taking away his recesses? He needs to get outside and run, breathe fresh air. He's an active boy. Couldn't he have a job to do, clean up litter on the playground perhaps? Something not as tedious or humiliating as sitting in the office, forced to listen to Bella's berating him.*

Mrs. Cooper had seemed understanding. She made Helsi feel, from the start, that she would give Dylan extra attention to help him catch up with the other first graders. She seemed worried about his self-esteem, too. Her voice was kind when she phoned yesterday to tell Helsi that she had to give Dylan a consequence. He had talked out repeatedly in class, disturbing other children during seatwork time. Or he had left his desk and wandered around the room. Anything but do his work. Trudy Cooper knew she had given Dylan the benefit of every doubt for too long. Helsi could not disagree. Dylan must follow the rules.

Helsi wanted to phone Ian just to talk to him about Dylan's recess detentions. But she had not told him of the incident for fear he would kick up a big fuss with Dr. Fleming and Mrs. Cooper and hurt Dylan's chances even more. Helsi dug up five or six more bulbs before she heard the kitchen phone ring. She dropped the trowel on the grass and ran inside.

"Hello. Helsi Bradford."

"Hello, Mrs. Bradford." Helsi recognized Hope Fleming's clear, articulate voice. "I'm sorry I have to give you this news, but Dylan is acting out today. He has defied Mrs. Cooper and now he's defying me. I'm afraid I have to ask you to come and pick him up. An emergency removal."

"What happened?" Helsi could feel her heart racing.

"It seems he hit another child while the class was signing out library books. Then he defied the teacher when she sent him to the office. Refused to go. Just stood rooted to the floor with his head down. He refused to come to the office with me until I threatened to phone you."

"But why did he hit the child? Had the child done anything to him?" Helsi tried to keep the anger out of her voice.

"As far as we know, the child did nothing to provoke it. He was ahead of Dylan in line and turned around only when he felt Dylan's fist in his back. They were right in front of the librarian's desk at the time; and she saw no action on the part of the other child, the alleged victim."

Alleged victim? Why is she using that word? Dylan's not a criminal; he's only a little boy. Helsi could barely control her anger. "I don't believe Dylan would strike out like that, for no reason."

"I was surprised myself. And equally surprised that he would defy Mrs. Cooper. He seems to have a trust level with her. I was shocked that he defied me; Dylan and I have had a good relationship. I know him as a good little citizen here at Poore Pond, for the most part. But he is clearly out of control today and needs to be removed. Are you able to come or shall I phone Mr. Bradford?"

"No, I will come. Don't phone Mr. Bradford. Just give me a few minutes to wake Rachel from her nap." Helsi dropped the phone. She retrieved it and heard a dial tone, then replaced it in the receiver.

Helsi did not want to wake Rachel who slept peacefully in her small room, a pink-and-white quilt snuggled over her and her dingy teddy. She gathered both child and teddy in her arms and carried them to the car, her shoulder bag swinging against Rachel's leg as she walked.

Rachel, now wide awake, asked, "Where are we going? You broke my nap, Mommy."

"To school to pick up your brother. He has to come home."

"Robbie? Is he sick? Rachel's small voice went shrill.

"Dylan. He just has to come home." Helsi worried about telling Ian. She would have to tell him the whole story now. He would be angry. Here we go again, she thought, resenting him for going to Hope's supervisor to get Dylan placed in first grade.

Rachel continued asking questions and chattering about squirrels and dogs she saw out the window. "Rachel Honey, please, not now. Mommy has to think about some important things." Helsi could feel Rachel's curious gaze on her. She knew she was letting her down. But she had to think of how to tell Ian. What words to use to soften the incident.

Helsi, Rachel in tow, stepped through blowing leaves to Poore Pond School's front entrance. She made her way through a class of students scattered in pairs on the lobby floor, drawing outlines of one another's bodies on large butcher paper. She had to prod a fascinated Rachel on through to the office. Bella directed Helsi to Hope's office where the principal stood next to Dylan, perched forlornly on the edge of a chair, his downcast chin resting on his small hand. Helsi's first impulse was to hug him, but she knew he had to see her disapproval of his behavior.

"Good afternoon, Mrs. Bradford. Thank you for coming to help Dylan." Hope spoke in a soft voice but did not smile. "He has made several bad choices today. He's not allowed to hurt children. Or ignore his teacher and principal."

"Of course, he isn't. He knows better than that." Helsi stooped down face-to-face with Dylan. "I'm surprised at you, Dylan Wallace." He did not look at her. "Why did you hit that boy? He'd done nothing to you." Helsi felt flooded with embarrassment. She wanted to shake Dylan. She longed to hug him. The second-recess bell sounded, and Dylan looked up.

"He hurt my feelings," Dylan chirped and dropped his eyes again.

"What did he say to you, Dylan?" Hope frowned and stepped closer to Dylan.

"Tell us what happened, Dylan." Helsi put her hand on his shoulder and his eyes met hers.

"He called me a dummy. Dummy Dyl—," Dylan lost heart and left his words dangling.

"When did he call you that?" Hope wanted to believe him.

"Where were you?" Helsi felt encouraged. Dylan swallowed hard.

"Seatwork time—asked him a word. He said everybody knows that word, Dummy Dylan." Helsi felt heat rising in her chest.

"Did you tell Mrs. Cooper, Dylan?" Hope kept her voice soft but firm. Dylan shook his head no. "You should have reported it to Mrs. Cooper at the time. She would have taken care of it." She looked at Helsi with tender eyes. "Mrs. Cooper and I will speak to Ryan. But you mustn't take matters into your own hands. You know that's a school rule."

A few minutes later Helsi was driving home, both children in the back seat and an official-looking envelope stuck in the outside pocket of her purse. Helsi had only glanced at the letter when Hope gave it to her. It was addressed to Mr. and Mrs. Bradford and contained only a few sentences. "Your son....emergency removal...repeatedly disregarding rules." She did not want to look at the letter again. Ian would be furious. *This whole thing was his fault. Insisting the boy go on to first grade when he's not up to it. But Ian would never see it that way.* Helsi knew he'd blame the school.

Helsi heard Rachel chattering incessantly in the back seat. She glanced around at a silent Dylan, looking out the window. He turned to her with vacant eyes. She choked back tears, then looked innocently at a cursing oncoming driver who swerved sharply to avoid hitting her van as it edged over the centerline.

Even that near miss could not keep Helsi's attention from dwelling on Dylan's predicament. Hope had walked her out to the car. After Helsi belted Rachel and Dylan into the back seat and closed the door, Hope had spoken privately to Helsi. "I know Dylan did not mean to break the rules today," she had said, slightly above a whisper. Helsi agreed with every point Hope made. Dylan is frustrated and rightly so. He knows he can't do the work the other kids are doing. His self-image is suffering. He should not have further consequences at home. Helsi felt relieved when she said that this emergency removal will be the end of it. She wanted to hug Hope when she looked deeply into her eyes and said, "Dylan needs our help." She appreciated Hope's promise to put him with a volunteer tutor, but she had little faith that it would help.

Realizing too late that the traffic light was red, Helsi slammed on her brakes and screeched past the stop line, just short of the intersection. An oncoming, left-turning driver shook her head sarcastically as she barely had room to make the turn. Rachel giggled at the sensation the force of the sudden stop caused in her stomach. A surly Dylan snapped, "That's not funny, Stupid. We almost got hit." Helsi, sharply reminded of her precious cargo, vowed to keep her mind on driving. She would think about Dylan later.

When Ian called to say he'd pulled equipment-cleaning duty and would not be home for dinner, Helsi was relieved. She hoped he would arrive after the children's bedtime, so she would not have to face his wrath over Dylan's emergency removal. And the recess detentions. She had not told Ian about those. She was sure Dylan would have to make up the one he missed this afternoon.

Helsi, standing at the ironing board in the wide archway between the kitchen and living room, ironed shirts and watched a television movie about a wife abuser.

The intensity of the drama kept her from thinking about Ian and his reaction to Dylan's troubles. Whenever her mind returned to the matter, she became so full of anxiety she could not think clearly.

Ian's heavy van pulled into the driveway. Helsi immediately wished she had decided the best way to tell Ian the news, what words to use that would be the least inflammatory. Her stomach tightened. Heat rose in her chest. She heard Ian opening the back door and concentrated on ironing the shirtsleeve meticulously.

"Hi, Luv," Ian, smelling of sweat and disinfectant, gave her a quick peck. He removed his navy windbreaker and hung it on the hook by the door. "What's going on? Anything new happen today? How're the kids?"

"Fine," Helsi said in a flat voice. "They're all tucked in." She could not look at her husband.

"How did Dylan do with his homework? Did you do the flashcards with him?"

Ian opened the refrigerator and took out a block of cheddar cheese and a can of beer.

"Same as usual." Helsi, concentrating on her ironing technique, did not look at him. She was grateful she did not have to lie; she had reviewed the flashcards with Dylan just after dinner.

"Dad?" a small voice came from the stairway. Helsi shuddered and went to the kitchen drawer to get Ian a knife.

"Hey, Sport. How's it going? Come down and say good night to your dad," Ian set cheese and beer on the small table in front of the sofa and held out his arms to Dylan, who walked into them hungrily. Ian hugged him completely and they both laughed. Ian lifted the boy, looking waifish in knee-length pajama bottoms that hung unevenly around his spindly legs, onto his lap. "What kind of day did you have, Dylan?" Dylan looked self-consciously at his mother. Helsi saw him swallow hard.

"You must have had a great recess; it was such a gorgeous day today."

Dylan, eyes pleading, looked at Helsi. She knew the moment of reckoning had come. "Tell your father what happened, Dylan." She busied herself buttoning the finished shirt onto a hanger, walking slowly to hang it on the doorframe.

"What's this all about?" Ian's face grew tense. He set Dylan next to him on the sofa and began to slice the cheese. He offered Dylan a piece. The boy took it and nibbled disinterestedly. Tension filled the room. Helsi could see Dylan's face cloud over.

"Say good night to your father, Son." Helsi took Dylan's arm and led him to the stairs.

"Wait a minute. What's going on here? I want to know what's going on with my son." Ian's voice rose. "Dylan." Dylan's eyes sought Helsi's. She put a finger to her lips and shook her head no to Ian.

"It's too late for Dylan. I'll be right down. I'll tell you all about it." She could see the anger in Ian's eyes, but he did not protest. She led Dylan up the stairs. She tucked him into his bed, telling him not to worry. She would explain everything to his father. Robbie, in the next bed, rolled over. Helsi sat down on the bed. She pushed up his pajama top and began to rub Dylan's back, so small and narrow it made him look utterly vulnerable. She wanted to rub the tension right out of his boyish body.

Ian took a sleeve of crackers from a box in the kitchen cupboard and carried it to the sofa. He sliced an inch of yellow cheddar cheese and placed it on the cracker. He looked toward the stairs and wondered what was going on with his son. Was that witchy principal on Dylan's case again, complaining that he couldn't do the work? He's hardly had time to get used to his new teacher; what does she expect? Just thinking about the way Hope Fleming ran that school made him angry. Robbie had problems, too, but Keith Broski saw to it that he passed kindergarten. None of this mumbo-jumbo about test scores and developmental levels. Keith just made the teachers give Robbie what he needed. And Robbie passed first grade. Maybe he wasn't a star student, but he passed. Dylan will do the same. He has to. He has to. There was no way he was going to see his son endure the teasing he had endured. His father wasn't there to fight for him when the Sisters made him repeat first grade.

He could see himself now as a boy, big for his age, tall and slender with a baby face, looking like a fourth or fifth grader. He was a real target for all the class bullies who'd gone on to second grade. He could hear Sister telling the whole class that Ian just needed more time. He could never forget the bullies' favorite taunt: Ian-More-Time, Just-Needs-S'More-Time, and how they made good use of it. They chanted when it was his turn to kick. Or bat. Or take the marker in a relay. *I've spent my lifetime trying to forget the sound of that chanting. I can't let the same thing happen to Dylan. At least I was a good athlete and could show them up. Dylan's so small and frail looking; why, they'd cut him to bits. He couldn't stand up to them.* Ian stretched his shoulders to shake the image of a skinny Dylan trying weakly to fight against older, bigger bullies. He could not bear it.

He felt so tired. He popped the cheese cracker into his mouth and sliced another bit of cheese. He gulped the beer and wondered what was taking Helsi so long. He found himself hoping she had fallen asleep upstairs. He was too tired to fight another battle tonight, so spent he hadn't the energy to get angry.

Dylan finally relaxed. Although he drifted to sleep soon after she started the back rub, Helsi continued rubbing. Words swirled in her head: Dylan... disrespectful...lashed out...taunted...frustrated...in over his head. She couldn't seem to find words soft enough to keep Ian from getting angry. She took another deep breath and went downstairs. She saw Ian chewing slowly and deliberately on the cheese, trying to stay calm. Her heart went out to him, knowing his anger would get the best of him when he heard the full story.

Helsi picked up a red plaid dress of Lucy's, her favorite, and began ironing it. She could see Lucy in the dress, going eagerly to school and felt grateful that she was a good student who learned easily. She could feel Ian's deliberate silence, waiting for her explanation, almost as if he were as reluctant as she to begin the discussion. "Dylan lost his recesses for a few days," she blurted, ironing furiously.

Ian stopped chewing and jerked his face toward her. Their eyes locked. Helsi could see his chest heave. He suddenly looked tired, older. "What has he done?" He picked up the remote and switched off the television.

"Talked back to Mrs. Cooper. She called to tell me. She was scolding him for not finishing his work." Helsi tried to read Ian's face, but it was set. She buttoned the ironed dress onto a hanger and hung it on the doorframe, now crowded with crisp-looking garments. "She had just helped him through part of it, felt sure he could finish it on his own. He told her to get off his case, just like that. In front of the whole class. That was disrespectful."

Ian looked at his wife with blank eyes. His lack of response frightened her, but she forged on, convinced that he may as well hear the whole story now. She began to iron Robbie's khaki pants. "Losing recess made no impression on Dylan. He hit another kid in the back in the library. He did say that kid had called him a dummy earlier. So he felt he had good reason. So Dr. Fleming called me again."

"What'd she do, expel him? I wouldn't put it past her. The woman's as cold as they come." Ian's calm voice confused Helsi. He took the last drink of beer and carried the can to the trash. He rewrapped the cheese and stood at the refrigerator, looking at his wife.

"She called it an emergency removal. I had to pick him up."

"Oh great. He hits a kid and gets a day off from school. What's that supposed to teach him?" Ian opened the refrigerator and traded the cheese for a bowl of black grapes.

Helsi felt anxious. "Do you want me to make you a ham sandwich, Ian?"

"No, I'll just eat these grapes. They have seeds?" Spitting seeds into his palm, he carried the bowl to the sofa. "So what does Doc want now, more of Dylan's blood?"

"No. She said the emergency removal would be the end of it. Doesn't want us to punish him at home. Thinks he's frustrated. Says he needs our help."

Ian switched on the television and focused his attention on cable news. Helsi did not know what to think. Such disinterest in Dylan's behavior worried her. He had no more to say in the matter, not even the following morning when the children left for school. Helsi reminded Dylan that he was to follow the rules and must not be disrespectful. She reminded him of his make-up recess detention. But Ian added nothing. He just waved his son goodbye. He left for work soon after the children left.

Helsi moved about the house, making beds, emptying waste cans, tidying up. She was irritated when she saw wood shavings in a pile on the floor near Dylan's bed. She wondered how they got there. The block of wood she saw on the table between the twin beds answered her question. She picked it up and turned it over in her hand. The corners had been whittled off, forming rounded edges. She saw faint pencil marks on the wood. Looking more closely, she could just make out a sort of animal shape drawn on the wood. Dylan must be carving something, she thought, wondering what knife he had used. She thought of Sean's scout knife but knew how protective he was of it. She wanted to think that he had shared it kindly with Dylan. Working with his hands would help him cope with his problems at school, she thought. He needed more projects like carving, things he was good at to give him pleasure, build his confidence. He had more than his share of failures at school. She placed the wood block back on the table and brushed the shavings into a small pile with her hands, then went to get a damp paper towel to lift them.

A loud clap of thunder sounded suddenly and a fierce rain pelted the windows. Helsi closed the boys' window and ran into the girls' room to close theirs. She was glad to see the rain; it meant that Dylan would be missing indoor recess and knew that that would be less painful for him than missing outdoor recess. She went into Sean's room to close his window, not noticing the absence of the red-handled pocket knife from the bookshelf where Sean had kept it since it had been awarded to him two years earlier. She took a bath towel to sponge beads of water off the curtains, hoping that they were not already water stained.

Helsi felt a slight sense of relief this morning, had felt it since she first woke. She attributed it to the calm way Ian had reacted to her news about Dylan. Was this a new Ian or was he simply too exhausted to face another school problem? She had always loved him for involving himself in the children's lives. Was he now leaving it all up to her?

She wrung the towel in the bathtub and smoothed it on the rod to dry. She dropped Sean's pillows on the floor and pulled the blue sheets up smoothly, folding them down at the top. She replaced the pillows neatly. Part of her wanted Ian to leave school issues up to her; he had always had the final say in those matters, not always to her liking. But part of her wanted him to stay involved, to share the burden, in case Dylan's problems took a long time to solve.

Helsi stopped vacuuming when she noticed it was time to pick up Rachel at preschool. She left the vacuum cleaner standing in the living room, hurrying so Rachel and her teacher would not be kept waiting.

Helsi and Rachel had a pleasant lunch of tuna sandwiches on toast and orange sections. Rachel liked to dig the sections out after Helsi had quartered the orange and curled back the peel to make it easy for her. She always ate nearly the entire orange that way. After lunch they snuggled under a small blanket on the sofa where they read an *Arthur* story together. Before they finished, Rachel fell fast asleep.

Helsi eased herself off the sofa and covered Rachel warmly. She removed clothes from the dryer and stood folding them, wondering again about the change in Ian. *What did it mean? Had he lost interest in dealing with family matters? Was he just burned out on kid problems? Was something amiss at the fire station, some serious threat to his job?* Helsi knew she was treading on dangerous ground, dwelling on issues, worrying, thinking the worst. She had gotten herself into a depressed state in the past thinking that way. She was determined not to let that happen again.

Maybe I'll give myself a little break while the house is quiet. She went to her bedroom for the novel she was reading. Back in the living room, she kicked off her shoes and curled up cozily at Rachel's feet, sharing the soft blanket.

The telephone rang repeatedly. Helsi, surprised she had slept, ran to answer it before it woke Rachel. She finally located the stray cordless phone on the dryer. The conversation took only seconds. Helsi pressed the off button on the phone and sat down heavily. She had to call Ian. Dr. Fleming said they both must come to school for a hearing with Dylan. Dylan was in serious trouble for bringing a knife to school.

*

Helsi spotted Ian's blue van parked illegally in the bus lane in front of Poore Pond School. She debated whether or not to suggest he move it. The wind whipped dry leaves at her legs as she walked into the school. She felt gratitude to her neighbor, Eileen Sploche, for agreeing to watch Rachel so she would not have to bring her along. This meeting would be too much tension for a four-year-old. For a six-year-old, too, Helsi told herself, her heart bleeding for Dylan.

Ian stepped away from the wall just inside the front door as Helsi entered. He touched her arm and she felt the tightness of his muscles in his touch. Together they walked toward the office, Although their bodies touched but barely, each drew strength from the other's nearness.

Dr. Fleming, her face blank, greeted them in the outer office. She led them into her office where Dylan sat next to a tall gentleman in a suit and tie. Hope introduced Brian Glover, Assistant Superintendent. There were just enough chairs for the five of them, and they all crowded around the small conference table. Hope thanked the Bradfords for coming in Dylan's behalf and explained the school district's Zero Tolerance Policy for weapons at school. Helsi was disappointed that Hope displayed none of the warmth and compassion she had shown all along in her dealings with Dylan. She had counted on that warmth to help Ian see the school's side. Dylan, beside her, swallowed with difficulty, his throat obviously dry from nerves. Helsi, her hands shaking, poured him a cup of water from the amber glass pitcher on the table. Ian, sitting at Dylan's other side, coughed and put his arm on his son's shoulder.

Brian Glover followed Hope with his comments. "Bringing a knife to school is a very serious thing." He looked at Dylan and waited for his eye contact. Seconds seemed like minutes in the deathly silent office. The entire building was quiet. Ian wondered how 500-plus students could be so quiet all at once. He squeezed Dylan's knee. Dylan looked sideways at him with head down. Ian nodded toward Mr. Glover. Dylan slowly lifted his eyes.

"Dylan, it's important that you understand why it is a serious matter to bring a knife to school. That's why I am here; that's why your parents are here. Dr. Fleming cares about you and wants to make sure you learn from this mistake." He asked Dylan several questions about whether he had shown the knife to other students, or opened the blades, or threatened to use it. Dylan answered in a low voice, full of fright.

Why can't they just tell Dylan his consequence and end this trial? Ian agonized. But he had to admit that they needed to make an impression on the boy.

Dr. Fleming laid the red-handled pocketknife on the table. Ian immediately recognized it as Sean's scout knife. "What were you doing with your brother's knife, Dylan? You know Sean doesn't want you using it."

"I know he's been whittling with it. I saw a carved piece of wood by his bed." Helsi recalled then the sense of uneasiness she had felt when she discovered the evidence.

"Whittling can be ok, Dylan. At home. With your parents' approval and supervision. Heck, I used to love to whittle. Even carried a pocket knife in my pants." Mr. Glover looked at Dylan with kind eyes.

The man's a human being, after all. Ian studied Brian's face.

"Dylan," Dr. Fleming looked warmly at the boy. He looked at her with intense eyes. "Please help us. We need to know that you understand what could have happened when you brought Sean's knife to school. Why it was a bad choice. You said you had the knife in your book bag. What could have happened if someone, without your knowing, had taken it out of your book bag? " Hope kept her voice calm and even, her warm eyes on Dylan.

"Could've hurt themselves." Dylan spoke softly but held eye contact with Hope.

"Or someone else. Right, Dylan?" Hope continued, "If a kindergartner had gotten his hands on that knife, he could have opened the blades and caused someone or himself to be injured. Whose responsibility would that be?"

"Mine," Dylan dropped his eyes.

"Why would you be responsible?"

"I brought it here."

"Exactly, Dylan. You would be responsible. You understand that. And you are certainly too nice a boy to want to see someone hurt because of you. You understand that you must never bring a knife to school again?" Dylan nodded yes.

Now they're going to tell us how this will be on Dylan's permanent record for the rest of his life. Aching to get on his feet, Ian shifted his weight in the chair. He barely listened to Brian and Hope explaining board policy recommending a ten-day suspension for bringing a *weapon* to school and how allowances may be made for the child's age, behavior record, and mental ability to understand the seriousness of the infraction.

He thought of his suspension meeting with Sister Domenica and his father when he was just a few years older than Dylan. He and two classmates had beaten up Cornelius, the class bully, and his cohorts, inflicting black eyes and ugly bruises. Sister's eyes said *"Thank-you, Cornelius had it coming."* But her voice said, "Fighting is absolutely not tolerated. Ian and his two accomplices will be suspended for three weeks."

"Yes, I agree." Helsi's voice startled Ian back to attention. "Three days of suspension is long enough to make an impression on Dylan and the other kids. And if Mrs. Cooper sends work home, we will see that he completes it; so he doesn't get any further behind."

Three days when she could've given him ten! Maybe there's hope for the doc after all. Ian joined his wife in thanking the officials for their time, stood, and shook hands with Brian, Hope, and Mrs. Cooper.

"I know you will see that the three days are not fun days off. They are to be restricted and structured around school work and other tasks." Hope looked directly at first Helsi, then Ian to make her point.

That's the doc I know. Ian took the scout knife from her outstretched hand and led Dylan and Helsi through the door. He glanced at the clock in the hall. *Forty-five minutes for that little kangaroo court? Doesn't that just beat all!* But in his heart he knew the school had to have the hearing, and it was right that Dylan be suspended.

CHAPTER TEN—HOPE

Hope was stunned by Ray's news. And surprised about his relationship to Millie. Neither of them had mentioned it to her. She wondered if the entire staff knew they were cousins, not that it mattered much; but some districts frowned on nepotism.

Hope shivered in her navy wool suit with the belted jacket. She had worn it for warmth because of the forecast of an approaching cold front and the fact that it took awhile for the school to warm up on Mondays. The building had the chill of November despite the rumbling of the two large boilers reverberating from the heating vents as if behemoths were caged inside. Hope tried the door of the storage room where cleaning chemicals were kept to make sure it was locked. Worried that an audacious student from an adjacent classroom might get into unsafe chemicals, she had spoken to Ray about finding the door unlocked several times. She was pleased to find it properly locked.

Hope continued through the second-grade wing, admiring colorful handprint turkeys on black construction paper, featured on the floor-to-ceiling bulletin board.

She tried to remember the extent of the cancer treatments her friend from college had had last year. Mia looked well now. Or at least, she had when they ran into each other last month. But she had gone through rough bouts during the chemotherapy, Hope found when she dropped in with homemade soup. She wondered if Millie would have the same sickness. She felt drained. *I pray that Millie will come through this all right.*

And her class. What about her class? Millie had several of the neediest third graders in the school because she handled them so well, gave them the emotional support they needed so they could be more receptive to learning. She typically volunteered to take more than her share of struggling students. She knew how to break down skills for them, too. Millie really understood how to individualize instruction, how to set children up for success. *What about those students? No one can keep them feeling secure and motivated as Millie does.*

Hope canvassed the third-grade wing where she was charmed by three-dimensional, tempera-painted turkeys displayed on a tabletop in the hallway. She wondered how frequently Millie would need a substitute. She couldn't bear to think of not having her to count on, even for a few weeks. She felt selfish. She was concerned on many levels: finding a suitable substitute for Millie, meeting the security needs of her students, helping parents deal with their despair, working with colleagues to give support to her and her family, and the awful possibility of losing Millie to the cancer.

Hope came to Millie's room and was surprised to see the light on at 7:15 in the morning. She could hear a chair scraping and walked into the room to see what Ray was doing. She felt the presence of life but saw no one at all. Her eyes scanned the room, taking in all the evidence of good teaching: children's written work featured, interactive bulletin boards, math manipulatives arranged around problem-solving questions, lists of sensory words and synonymous verbs, clay sculptures ready for the kiln, cheerful-looking computer center with appealing task list posted. Hope's heart sank.

"Oh, good morning, Hope." Millie's salt-and-pepper-hair peeked out from behind the red-and-gold puppet theatre. She stood up in a cloud of dust. She wore a red paisley smock over her hunter-green suit.

Relieved to see her looking so well, Hope smiled. "Good morning, Millie. You're here early." She reminded herself that Millie did not know she knew about the cancer. "What are you into back there?" Trying to act as natural as possible, she walked to the theatre where she saw papers sorted into neat stacks on the floor next to a large cardboard carton filled with more such papers.

"Just digging through archives. I'm looking for a social studies simulation project that I used two years ago. A town-planning unit. This class would do well with it. These kids may be slow, but they can be responsible. I can just see Jeremy as planning board chief. He'd relish that, telling everyone what to do." She looked at Hope but averted her eyes quickly.

"Sounds wonderful. Good for you for taking it on. Simulations are such a lot of work. Most teachers kind of give up on them once they've done one. May I see the overview?" Hope bent over the paper piles.

"I just had it." Millie rifled through one of the piles, locating it near the bottom. She handed it to Hope, moving next to her to point out key parts. "Every student takes a responsible role." Her finger moved down the list, guiding Hope's eyes. They discussed the organization of the project, the many learning objectives, and the length of time the class would spend on it. "It can run four to eight weeks, depending on how in-depth the children are able to go. The last class I did it with stayed interested for about—oh— six weeks, maybe. They begged to go on when we stopped, but I could tell they'd had enough."

Hope chuckled. "That's how children are, isn't it. Try to keep the fun going after it's run its course. Like trying to drag them away from an amusement park."

Unspoken words hovered in the air. Hope looked at Millie, who, again, held eye contact for only an instant. She began moving the papers to her desk, crossing each stack on top of the last one to keep them sorted. Hope helped by bringing several stacks herself, carefully keeping each stack separated. To break the silence, she asked, "How long do you expect this class to work on the town planning unit? You know them pretty well now."

Millie sighed and looked out the window. "If I do my blue-ribbon intro, I should get a good four weeks out of them. But—well—I have to—Oh, drat! I'd best tell you the whole story." Millie turned and looked squarely into Hope's eyes. "My cousin told me you know about my diagnosis. Thank you for letting me bring it up." Millie kept her voice steady. "Let's sit down. The whole thing's rather complicated."

Bella's voice came over the public-address system, calling for Hope; she looked at the clock and was surprised to see that it was 7:50 already. Millie and she had talked for over half an hour. Hope's head was swimming with all the dates and times in Millie's treatment schedule. She looked at what she had jotted on the post-it note and could barely read it. Millie promised to give her a legible copy. Hope stood to leave. Millie stood as well. They faced each other, both wanting to hug but neither initiating it. They smiled artificially at each other. Hope put her arms around Millie; and they hugged with intensity, both fighting back tears.

Hope hurried down to the office to see what Bella needed. Must be a new student, she thought when she saw an unfamiliar man with a child of about six in tow. The secretary introduced Hope to them and explained that Travis had been home schooled and was coming to public school for the first time. Hope led Travis and Mr. Baron into her office where they could talk privately.

After Travis was enrolled in Pam Thorpe's third-grade class, Hope looked at her in-box. The usual assortment of hand-written notes, typed memos, and envelopes bulged in a pile. She sat down at her desk to sort through the pieces. Carmen Ricci wanted her to preview a plan for the Christmas musical. There were notes from fourth-and fifth-grade and special-education chairpersons, objecting to copy-paper rationing and restricted days for laminating. There was a pink quarter-sheet phone-message in Bella's large, illegible scrawl: call Brain ASAP re: Ian Bradford. *Of course, she means Brian.* There were a thick, blue packet of third-grade-test practice skills and a less-thick packet of the revised district student code of conduct.

Hope placed the two packets in her to-read-with-lunch folder and left the notes near the phone. She dialed Brian's number and waited while his secretary located him "somewhere in the building." Ian Bradford must have called him about the suspension's staying on Dylan's record since he had voiced objection to it at the hearing. Hope had been surprised and pleased that Brian had not backed down but knew that Ian and he might well come to a good-ole-boys' agreement about that later.

An out-of-breath Brian finally came to the phone. Hope took careful notes while he described Ian Bradford's complaint that older boys had been bullying Robbie for two weeks and nothing had been done about it.

"To whom did Robbie report this bullying?" Hope probed her memory, desperately hoping it had not been reported to her on the run and slipped her mind.

"The playground supers," Brian kept his voice even. "Don't you have a couple who have been there too long, forty years or so?"

"I do. Thirty-eight years, that is. Lucille Maroney. But she's a good aide. Thorough and fair. If she got the report, I would know about it. I'll look into it, Brian. And ca—"

"Call Ian today, Hope. You have that—what's it called— fester-free policy, and he's already festering. No sense having him fester all weekend."

"Non-festering policy. But I like your term better. A fester-free school, fester-free families. I'll call him, Brian. Thank you." Hope replaced the receiver. She looked at her watch. There was just time to catch the playground supervisors before their shift began.

Hope spoke to the team of lunch aides and found that none of them recalled or had recorded a bullying report from Robbie Bradford. The aides were all local residents and knew the Bradford children since the large brood was highly visible in the neighborhood. Hope made a mental note to speak to Robbie during lunch recess.

She walked through the bustling cafeteria filled with seven- and eight-year-olds, beside themselves with Friday excitement. Fridays always brought excitable students and staff members, thrilled to be having a weekend off school. Hope was excited, too, about her luncheon date with George tomorrow. She wondered how he'd look. How he might have changed in four years.

"Dr. Fleming, will you sign my cast?" A sturdy looking seven-year-old girl with a mass of red curls swiveled away from her table as Hope walked past. She extended her left arm, encased in a thick blue cast from wrist to elbow.

Taking the yellow gel pen the girl offered with her right hand, Hope began writing her name on the hard plaster. "How did this happen, Francine?" The yellow ink was barely visible on the blue surface, so Hope traced over her signature again.

"I fell off my cousins' new playground set," Francine flashed a broad smile and shrugged her shoulders in *oops* fashion.

"Did your hands just slip, or were you hanging upside down on the bar?" Hope smiled back.

Francine lowered her chin. "Hanging upside down," she grinned, wide eyes sparkling.

"Francine, Francine, what are we going to do with you?" Hope shook her head adoringly at the child.

"My dad said I'm lucky I didn't break my collarbone. That's what happened to him when he was my age."

"You'll remember to sit on the bench during recess, won't you? I read your mother's note requesting that you do." Francine nodded her head emphatically.

Hope approached Robbie's class table and searched for his thick, dark hair. She spotted him and tapped his shoulder. "Robbie, please come to my office before you go outside. After you visit the lav and wash your hands." Robbie nodded faintly with unsure eyes. Wanting to avoid embarrassing him, Hope deliberately spoke in a loud voice that his classmates could hear. "I need your help, Robbie."

"Dr. Fleming, please come see Philip." Hope's eyes followed the voice to Flo Brady, one of the lunchtime supervisors. She was standing next to a small boy with bushy blonde hair, seated alone at his class table.

"Philip, have you done a good job eating today?" Hope asked as she inspected the remains of his lunch. "Did you bring a whole sandwich or a half, Philip? You've only one-quarter left."

Philip beamed proudly, "A whole sandwich! I ate almost all of it, see!" He waved the small piece of cheese sandwich at Hope.

"Good for you, Philip. And I see you've eaten most of your apple, too; and your milk is gone. It's only twelve minutes after 11:00; you still have most of your recess left. Your mother will be pleased. Your brain will be ready to work this afternoon. Mrs. Brady, are you ready to dismiss Philip."

Flo dismissed Philip and turned to Hope. "This is his fourth day eating a decent lunch. I think he gets it now. No eat = no recess. His mom knew what she was talking about after all."

"She appreciates our help. Thank you, Flo, for the extra time you've spent monitoring Philip. I've admired the way you've managed not to lose sight of the task in this busy lunchroom." Flo smiled and nodded then headed across the room where two children had raised hands.

Hope stopped to watch students at the tray-return rack. Children greeted her; some waved shyly. They replaced their sectioned trays correctly, each one nesting into the one below. "Good job placing your trays, Third Graders. What a help you all are to Mr. Sellers." Many pairs of eyes turned toward Ray, inserting new plastic bags into a large trash can nearby. He looked up and smiled at the children. Hope walked over to him. "You've trained them well, Ray." He shrugged his shoulders, but he was smiling shyly. Hope could see he appreciated her noticing.

Glancing at her watch, Hope hurried to the office. She saw an ill-at-ease Robbie standing quietly outside her door.

Robbie did not seem to know names of the bullies he had complained about to his father, nor could he identify them in the school yearbook. He was unable to describe them other than naming the colors of their shirts and calling them "bigger boys." In actuality the eldest children on the playground the same time as Robbie were other third graders. Hope found it significant that Robbie's description of their tactics was vague as well. "They were bugging me," he kept saying. When she tried to pinpoint the area of the playground in which the alleged bullying had taken place and how many times it had happened, Robbie contradicted himself several times, thoroughly confusing her. Hope knew that sometimes during these *hearings* one gets a clear sense of what probably happened. This was not one of those times.

"Robbie, I have nothing to go on, no clues to help me find these children. None of the playground supervisors took a report from you. You did say that you could not report the incidents because they always happened just as the bell was ringing when you had to line up." She looked into Robbie's deep blue eyes. He swallowed and broke eye contact. Measuring her words carefully, Hope asked,

"Your father is under the impression that you have been reporting these incidents, Robbie. Help me understand why he thinks that." Robbie did not raise his eyes. He said nothing. "Did you perhaps report the bullying to your teacher?" He shifted his weight to his other foot, nodding his head without meeting Hope's gaze.

"Yes? You did report it to your teacher?" Hope gently lifted his chin, and his eyes looked into hers. In a barely audible voice, Robbie said,

"She didn't hear me. The kids were being noisy." He pulled at the front of his sweatshirt. It seemed to Hope that, real or imagined, the so-called bullying had not happened to Robbie, maybe to someone else and was observed by him. She wondered if the report were an attention-getting device aimed at his father.

"How do you get to be one of those—convict—mangers?" Robbie asked, suddenly responsive.

"Conflict managers? The boys and girls who help kids work out their disagreements?"

"Yeah." Robbie's eye contact was improving.

"You have to be recommended by your teacher or principal, and your parents have to send written permission. Then you go through training. Would you like to become a conflict manager?"

"Kind of. Maybe."

"You do know that you must give up some of your recesses, don't you? The training takes place during lunch recess. And you're on duty during recess. Sometimes there are meetings, and they're during lunch recess as well." Hope searched Robbie's face for a sense of his true feelings about giving up recess. He looked squarely at her.

"Games aren't good at recess. Too many kids. They act cool. Can't get going. Conflict mang-ing would be more fun." Robbie had obviously thought through the matter.

"I'll speak to Mrs. Blackwell, Robbie, about your joining Poore Pond Conflict Managers Corps. We'll send a permission slip home for your parents to sign. I admire you for wanting to help and for having the courage to try." Hope guided his right hand into a handshake, emitting a shy but proud smile from the boy. "And remember, if someone bothers you right before—or even right after—the bell rings, you are still to report the incident to the playground supervisors. They are there to help you until your teacher takes your class back inside the building. Will you remember that?"

Robbie replied affirmatively and, Hope noted, with some confidence. She escorted him out of the office. "You still have twelve minutes of recess left, Robbie. Enjoy it."

After watching the last line of fifth graders file into class at the end of recess, Hope returned to her desk. She picked up the pink quarter-sheet message atop a small pile of incoming notes and papers. The names Jeremy Baker and Heather Baker stood out from Bella's uneven scrawl. After careful scrutiny, Hope deciphered the whole of the message. *Jermy Baker still absent. No he's not sick-Heather Baker keeping him home for what she calls persnal resons.* Hope buzzed Bella who confirmed the message as per her telephone conversation with Heather this morning. There had been no explanation from Heather Baker of the nature of the personal reasons.

Hope knew she would have to make a house call. Maybe she could get away early today since it was Friday and most of the staff left promptly, trucking their paperwork home with them for the weekend. Only a few stayed late on Fridays in order to avoid taking work home. Still fewer stayed late working and carried home papers or workbooks to grade as well.

Surprisingly, Friday afternoon passed uneventfully. The usual high number of weekend-minded parents picking up their children had queued their cars into a long line, slowing the arrival and departure of buses. But everyone seemed to be patient, so the process went smoothly, sparing Hope the need to pacify an angry parent or bus driver or an errant child. Hope was grateful for the unusually smooth-though-crowded Friday dismissal.

Sticking a post-it note containing Heather Baker's address to her dashboard, Hope noticed the car clock registered 3:30. It was even earlier than she thought. If she kept her visit to the Baker's short, she could be home before 5:00, in time to relax and plan the best approach to use with George tomorrow. She did not want to make a mistake, say the wrong thing or ask too many questions and drive him back into estrangement.

Hope's grey Volvo tooled along the parking lot fronting the two-level rows of garden-type apartments. Her eyes scanned the addresses for Heather's number, which she spotted on a sign with an arrow pointing to the second level.

She parked her car and walked to the stairway, noting how quiet the area seemed and how surprisingly well maintained the grounds were for a low-rent complex. It was encouraging to see that Jeremy was living in a clean environment. Steeling herself for a possibly awkward encounter, Hope sounded the doorknocker. She could see a tiny peephole inserted in the door and wondered if Heather were peering through it. She heard a barking puppy, a muffled voice, and footsteps. She waited for what seemed minutes before the door opened slowly. A pajama-clad Jeremy draped himself around the door edge and looked at her.

"Hi there, Jeremy Baker." Hope smiled.

Heather appeared behind him, her thick blonde hair disheveled and an oversized tee-shirt hiding her trim figure. She managed a weak smile and motioned Hope to come inside. Drawn drapes darkened the room and a small television set on low volume sounded in the background. Heather switched on a lamp. She looked at Hope with despair in her eyes and asked if she'd gotten her message.

"That's the reason I'm here, Mrs. Baker. It's unusual for Jeremy to miss school unless he's sick. I was concerned that you may need help." Hope kept her voice soft and warm.

"I know I shouldn't have kept Jeremy out of school. But I had no choice. He was hungry. His clothes weren't clean. And yesterday he ripped the sole of his shoe almost clear off. " Heather looked at the floor.

"So you need groceries and laundry detergent? And Jeremy needs shoes." Hope looked at Jeremy, wide-eyed and listening and wished that he would leave the room. "Jeremy, go watch tv in Mommy's room with Puddles. It's OK. While Dr. Fleming talks with me." Reluctantly, Jeremy walked down the short hallway. "Close the door, Jeremy, so Puddles can't get out."

Heather looked at Hope but did not speak. Hope could feel her discomfort. She searched for the right words to ask how she could help, words that would allow Heather to keep her dignity.

"We have money in the Thanksgiving basket fund that you would be entitled to for emergency groceries, Heather. Would that—"

"Yesterday I got laid off. Jeremy doesn't know. I can't believe it. I was the fastest worker on the line. I always beat my quota in pieces. Every day. Can they do that, just lay you off for no good reason? Don't I have rights?" Heather's eyes, brimming with tears, pleaded with Hope for answers.

As it turned out, Heather's final paycheck would not be issued until regular payday next Friday. And now it would be half a check. Her rent was overdue and she was down to her last ten dollars.

Hope knew she must help Heather and, especially Jeremy, with this dire emergency. But she wanted to make sure there was no chance for any money to be misdirected. Heather seemed sensible, but how had her affairs gotten so out of hand when she had a steady job? Could she be involved with drugs? Gambling? Or a free-loading boyfriend? Her mind raced while Heather was tending Jeremy in the bedroom. She looked around the sparsely furnished room. It was clean and orderly though Heather had not known Hope was coming. That said something about her.

Hope finally convinced Heather to borrow the rent money from her on the condition, Heather insisted, that she would repay it when she "got back on her feet." And Heather would accept the grocery money from the school outreach fund. They agreed on a plan. Heather would accompany Hope to the rental office where Hope would write a check for the rent. Hope would go to the superstore on the next street and purchase a gift certificate while Heather found a neighbor who would look after Jeremy while she shopped for groceries and Jeremy's shoes.

*

Hope arrived home full of gratitude for her education, her salary, her home, her car. She turned the key in the lock and savored the tasteful beauty of the large foyer. She placed her briefcase and purse on the cherry deacon's bench. She opened the louvered door and hung her trench coat in the empty closet. She knew she had saved the day for Jeremy and that he and his mother could enjoy a peaceful weekend. But she could not shake a sense of having missed the mark, of having failed a fellow human being. The mahogany schoolhouse clock chimed four notes, and Hope saw that it was 5:15. She had made good time. Unable to come to terms with the Baker family incident, she sat down on the bench. She could feel a small knot of anxiety growing in her stomach.

Heather had thanked her, but apparently she had sensed Hope's reluctance to give her cash, and stopped short of a genuine expression of warmth. Hope regretted this. She knew that a gesture of trust could have boosted Heather's confidence immeasurably. She remembered her own skyrocketing self-esteem when Mary Baldwin had given her, a mere nineteen-year-old, check-signing authority. Mary Baldwin's wisdom shone through the years.

Feelings of utter desolation washed over Hope. She did not want to remember Mary Baldwin now. Mary's kindness to her had compelled her to help Heather and Jeremy, she realized for the first time. It was Mary's legacy. Hope knew she should feel gratitude, but a sense of profound guilt overpowered all other feelings when she recalled Mary Baldwin. Mary had trusted her. The vote of trust had come at a time when Hope was feeling low, awaiting word of college scholarships, without which she could not continue as a college student, not at an exclusive four-year school. She would have to join the ranks of junior college students, those with low grades and no money, the bottom of the social hierarchy. She would never be able to join Mary Baldwin's world by going to junior college.

Hope could still feel the despair she had felt. But when Mary gave her responsibility for paying her accounts, Hope felt empowered, more motivated, determined to meet her goal of a degree from a prestigious university. She grew certain that the scholarship would come, and it did. She was awarded full scholarship to Vassar College for women. Mary's gift of trust had given her the mindset and drive to succeed. *I could have done that for Heather, on a smaller scale, of course; but the result would have been similar. Why didn't I?* Hope did not want to open the doors of dark thought in her mind.

Shivering, she walked through to the kitchen. She filled the kettle at the sink and put it on the stove to heat. She switched on the small white television mounted under the cupboard. She welcomed the drone of the news broadcast to get her mind off painful, unforgiving memories.

Hope took one bite of the microwave-baked potato topped with butter and cheese and realized how famished she was. The small green salad with grape tomatoes tasted heavenly with the potato. She ate every drop while staring at the television. She made herself a second cup of tea, then rummaged in her purse for half a chocolate bar left over from lunch. When the new young weatherman came on the screen, he reminded her of George and their luncheon date tomorrow. She decided that she would talk as little as possible and just listen to him. And if he hadn't much to say, she would talk casually, about safe subjects. She could tell him about Poore Pond. She would wait for him to express affection, when he was ready. She could be very patient when it counted.

*

After a night of fitful sleep Hope awoke later than usual. Her mind had kept filing images of faces, Mary Baldwin's face so proud when Hope thanked her for her trust; Heather's wounded face as she waved good-bye at the superstore; George's face smiling at her as she approached his table; George's accusing face as they argued angrily. She sat up in bed and rubbed her eyes. She was flooded with a feeling of disappointment. She had so wanted to be in top form today for her first contact with her son in four long years.

She rose and went into the adjoining bathroom, her eyes caught off guard by the sun drenching through the skylight. Well, at least it's a fine day, she thought as she splashed her face with cold water.

Downstairs in the kitchen Hope considered how much time she had before leaving the house by 11:45. It was now 8:48 and she needed an hour to shower and get dressed. She could afford a leisurely breakfast and some think time. She must plan what to wear, nothing stiff and business-like such as she wore to work. And yet, she did not want to dress so casually that George would read it as psychological decline. She wanted him to see that she was strong, living a satisfying single life, thriving in her new position. She munched on half-a-slice of whole-wheat toast, uncharacteristically slathered with peanut butter and raspberry jelly to boost her spirits. She decided on grey wool flannel pants, cut fashionably trim, and a coral cashmere cardigan over an ivory silk shirt. Classic weekend attire for a well-dressed professional.

The important what-to-wear decision out of the way, Hope focused on the best attitude for dealing with George today. In order to be forearmed, she tried to recall what had triggered his anger in their past disputes. She finished the glass of orange juice and poured a cup of tea from a small blue teapot. Stirring the milk and sugar, Hope then drank deeply from the big English breakfast cup to quell the anxiety in her stomach. Revisiting angry confrontations with George was too painful. She would not do that.

Hope finally came to terms with the question by deciding to simply treat George as her long-lost son whom she loved deeply. That was really all that mattered. She must not put him on the defensive for the past, nor allow him to put her on trial. She envisioned a loving reunion with pent-up warmth flowing between them. She wanted George to realize that her love was still unconditional and how very much she had missed him.

Hope lost her early edge when she had difficulty finding parking space outside the restaurant. The trendy sandwich house, surrounded by upscale specialty shops, was a popular Saturday spot for those who cared about an *avant-garde* image as well as those who just enjoyed good sandwich fare. She had counted on arriving first, so she could watch George enter the restaurant and study him a bit from a distance. Now it looked as if he would be the one studying her. Her eyes scanned the vast dining room with its many nooks and cubicles. She inquired of the hostess about a young man alone and was directed to the broad-shouldered back of a male figure in a secluded corner booth. Approaching close range, any doubt she had that it was actually George dissipated as she recognized the blue-grey muted glen plaid wool blazer she had bought George for his freshman year at university. That would have been nearly six years ago, and he was still wearing it. She had recklessly selected it on her own and surprised them both when it was to his liking.

"George?" she spoke to a thick, long shock of brown wavy hair bent over a newspaper.

"Oh. Mom. Hi." He stood to greet her as casually as if he'd seen her just yesterday. She was awed by how tall he was. They stood like that, smiling at one another. A hug seemed in order, but neither of them moved to initiate one. Hope took his hand and hugged his forearm to her chest. George giggled. "Sit down," he said, still smiling and motioned toward the seat opposite him.

Hope sat down and realized that George was not unshaven; he had an emerging beard, one level beyond designer stubble. Actually he wore it well, along with his collar-length hair which was darker and wavier than she had remembered. Both set off his strong chin and sculpted cheeks handsomely. She noticed a slight trace of receding hairline, following the genetic pattern seen early in her father and uncles.

A waitress arrived and George ordered cappuccino for both of them. Hope could not tear her eyes away from him to look at the waitress. She drank in every inch of him: his broad shoulders; the faded-red broadcloth shirt worn open-collared under the threadbare blazer; the faded blue jeans; and worn, natural-cowhide boots. He looked the epitome of success and self-assurance, secure enough to dress in uncontrived, comfortable clothes with no regard for a moneyed image. But she could not help wondering in what sort of workplace his facial hair would be tolerated.

"This place has changed. Bigger, isn't it?" George's eyes scanned the room.

"It's under new ownership. Recently renovated. Still always busy." Hope, though flooded with memories, was reluctant to mention the many times they had eaten there together, both as a family of three and then just the two of them. George always ordered the super-sized hot cheese steak sandwich on a toasted sesame bun.

"I remember coming here with Dad," George said with a nonchalance that caught Hope off guard. She felt herself stiffen at the mention of Michael.

"How is your father?" Hope asked, trying not to sound hostile.

"He's OK. Good. Wants me to come work for him." Hope immediately felt jealous that Michael might have regular contact with George. She was fiercely curious as to how frequently they were seeing each other now. *If he's having "business reverses," how can he afford to hire George? Oh, of course, free labor. So-o Michael.* She was on the verge of asking when queasiness in her stomach stopped her.

"Are you looking for a change?" she asked safely.

"I don't know." George looked off in the distance. "I try to stay always open to new opportunities." He turned, smiling, to look in her eyes. She returned the smile.

"It's wonderful to see you, George. I've missed you terribly." Breaking her own rule, she reached across the table for his hand. He allowed her to take it and returned the grasp briefly. The waitress arrived and George engaged her with humor and questions about the menu.

George ordered his old favorite and a large serving of French fries with vinegar. Hope ordered the house special, a cooked vegetable salad with steak.

"When did you start using vinegar on your fries?" Hope chuckled.

"I don't know. Just saw everybody else doing it. Now I can't eat fries without vinegar." Hope was impressed by his easy manner, his calm. Gone were the old tension and irritability, the need to lash out. His ability to make small talk was remarkable. He must be working in some sort of public relations, or sales, she thought, to have fine-tuned this skill to such a second-nature level. She took a large drink of water to busy herself.

"Here it comes. Wow!" George's face lit up at the food, much as it had when he was eleven or twelve. Hope enjoyed seeing his enthusiasm again.

"Anything else?" the waitress asked after emptying the tray.

"We'll want dessert, won't we, Mom? Later." George smiled boyishly at his mother and then at the waitress.

Hope asked, "How about a triple-threat sundae? That's what your eleven-year-old appetite always craved after a hot cheese steak sub. Remember?" George laughed heartily. Delighting in his good humor, Hope laughed, too. It was impossible not to notice how George wolfed down his food. His appetite was ravenous, as if he hadn't eaten for a week. He ordered a second batch of fries with more vinegar. Hope finished half her salad and toyed with the rest.

"Are you going to eat that?" George asked, aiming his gaze at her salad.

"No, would you like it?" Hope lifted the plate in his direction. George set the plate down near him and attacked it with his fork. While George was passionately involved in eating, Hope welcomed the break in conversation. She needed time to think of more safe subjects. She realized she had not talked about Poore Pond yet. That would be her next bit of small talk.

"How did you know where I worked?" she asked to open the subject.

"Didn't I tell you? I saw an announcement in the Gazette. I wanted to congratulate you, but it was an old issue of the Gazette. It had been months since you'd been appointed. So—well, you know—too little too late." He flashed her a dazzling smile. "So congratulations now. Sounds like your thing. In charge of a whole school." They both laughed. *What a handsome adult he has become. And so personable.*

"It is my thing. Very hard work, but I'm enjoying everything about it."

"If I recall correctly, hard work has always been your thing." George said with no trace of emotion in his voice. Hope searched his eyes. *Is he being sarcastic? Or just objective? Oh stop it! Don't try to analyze anything. Just enjoy the company of your long-lost son.* Hope smiled.

"You're right about that, George. Your mother always was a masochist. It must have been annoying." George laughed a little too heartily, and Hope joined him.

"Tell me, what do you like so much about working nonstop in a school?" George seemed genuinely interested. Hope went on to tell him about the lovely historical building, the charming children who so wanted to please, the large staff— the whole gamut of personality types, the diverse and involved parent population. George made her feel she had his full attention, that he was engrossed in the details of her life at Poore Pond. *He is so unlike his father in that respect.*

It was after 3:00 when they left the restaurant, having made a date to meet there again next week, same time. Driving home, Hope reviewed the entire afternoon. Funny how she had worried ahead of time about getting into a contest with George over who would pay the check. It was important to her to pay the check; she wanted George to see her as self reliant, and she needed to give him something to celebrate their reunion.

But when the black leather folder was placed on the table, George had seemed not to notice it. He had shown no discomfort, no sign of awareness of what she was doing as she calculated the tip and counted out bills. In fact, he had said goodbye and slipped out while she was waiting for change from the waitress, mentioning something about another appointment. *I had so wanted to see what kind of car he was driving.*

Stopped at a lengthy red light, Hope realized that she still had no telephone number or address for her son, no way to get in touch with him at all. She had to own the fact that she was still bristling from his refusal to give her that information on the phone; therefore, her pride would not let her ask again. Once she thought about it, she had drawn her own conclusions about his not wanting her to have his phone number. After seeing him today, how he'd become so nonchalant about life, she realized that she may have read malice into his innocent comments. The light went green and she accelerated more than necessary as her heart jumped with happiness. She noticed other drivers smiling at her and realized she was smiling broadly to herself. When she pulled into the driveway, her home, the entire world seemed perfect.

Preparing for bed, Hope indulged herself with plans to become involved in George's life. *I'll help him fix up his apartment. Or no, get him to move in with me, back to his old room. We'll redecorate it, make it more sophisticated. We can have meals together, long talks by the fire. Make up for all the time we never spent together.*

She thought of Michael and was instantly chilled. He was trying to sell this house out from under her. Her house. The ignominious way he informed her of the fact sickened her.

She crawled under thick covers and fled into the bedside novel she could always count on for escape.

CHAPTER ELEVEN—RAY

Ray awoke early to a soft snowfall and bolted out of bed. The snow meant he would have to clear the walks and possibly call the grounds crew.

When he reached Poore Pond, he could see little accumulation although a light snow continued to fall. He brought out the hand blower and blew the scant snow off the walkways, knowing it would have to be done again just before student-arrival time. But he wanted to show Hope he was way ahead of her with snow removal. He knew he'd have to hurry in order to get her office vacuumed before she arrived around 7:15.

Ray felt anxious to see Hope and tell her he could not speak at the teachers' meeting. The more he thought about it, the more frightening it became. Why, he would be leaving himself wide open. They could gang up on him and really criticize his work. He had to admit that he didn't always empty each pencil sharpener or clean every sink if he was running late, especially in classrooms of the neater teachers.

As nice as the teachers were to him one-on-one, their humor, especially the upper-grade teachers,' was always a little more biting when they were grouped together. He tried to avoid the teachers' lounge during peak times for that reason. He had never gotten over their sarcastic remarks about his "Mommy-Poo doing everything for him. "

It all started the time he had forgotten his lunch and Caroline caught a ride with a neighbor to bring it to him. It was a good lunch: beef stroganoff and fresh asparagus left over from the night before. Caroline used a lot of double cream in her beef stroganoff, so it didn't keep well. She insisted she would have to throw it away if it weren't eaten the next day. The teachers wouldn't understand.

Ray joked quite a bit with individual teachers, but neither he nor they ever resorted to sarcasm in those small exchanges. He could just imagine how they'd work him over if they were all there together with fifth-and sixth-grade teachers leading the pack. No, he would just post in every classroom, the signs he had hand lettered, listing the do's and don'ts for managing pets, refreshments, and a few other things. He was glad he had gone to Kopy Kwik yesterday. The signs really stood out on the green neon paper. He'd paid extra for the color; but it would be worth it, make them hard to miss.

Ray vacuumed Hope's office quickly, skipping the area under her desk. He took a stapler and the neon posters to every classroom, checking for stray dust or litter in each one. No sense giving them "rocks" to throw at him when they saw the lists. Posting the neon paper in Jeff Master's classroom, he stepped back and, for the first time, was troubled by the uneven lettering. He had tried to be so careful in shaping the letters. But now they seemed to him like a child's irregular scrawl. "Oh cripes," he said as he stared at the poster. "How's anyone going to take this list seriously? It looks like a kid did it."

Ray walked to the window. His eyes scanned the parking lot for Hope's grey Volvo. His van was the only vehicle in the lot. He looked back at the poster. It was still blaring its juvenile message. Anxiety rose in his stomach. He went quickly to the wall and removed the poster, digging the staples out of the corkboard with his nails. He tore the poster in half angrily. What a waste of time and money, he thought. He rushed back through all the classrooms where he'd left posters then down the hall to his boiler room. He dropped the stapler on the desk and tore at the stack of neon paper. It would not tear. "Oh that's just great!" he moaned as he took a few sheets and tore them easily. He ripped through the entire stack a few sheets at a time until they were all in shreds. He deposited them in a covered trashcan near the door. He heard Hope's heels tapping down the hall and slammed the lid.

"Good morning, Ray," Hope said from the doorway. "Did you have a good weekend?" She smiled.

"It was OK, just a weekend."

"What have you decided about the faculty meeting?"

Ray sighed and looked at the covered trashcan. He did not want Hope to know about the wasted posters. Silence filled the room. Hope waited, smiling all the while. With the failure of the posters he had no alternative to give her. Ray looked at the floor and rubbed his forehead. He felt trapped. He began to remove the soiled head from a large dust mop.

"Can you see your way clear to speaking to the teachers at Wednesday's meeting?" Hope's blue eyes searched his downcast face.

"I guess I'll do it." Ray was shocked to hear the words fall out of his mouth. "But I can't stay long, only about ten minutes." He could see the relief on Hope's face.

"Good for you," she smiled, patting his arm. "We'll put you first on the agenda. Have a good Monday. And by the way, the walks look great."

Ray watched her step lightly down the hall, his heart heavy. Now I really have to get to work, he thought. *I can't just blurt out those rules from the list. I'll have to use nice words and explain each point. Cripes.* He tried to form phrases in his mind as he laid out the flag for the student helpers. But he could think of no nice way to tell the teachers to do a better job cleaning pet cages. Or wiping spills. Or seeing that kids did not forget their homework.

He went to the closet for the hand blower then realized he had left it in the lobby. He pulled his sweatshirt hood over his head and put on his wool jacket, still thinking about words to use at the meeting. The more ways he tried to say things, the more trivial each point seemed. *How did I get myself into this?* He headed for the snow blower.

Ray was surprised at the amount of snow accumulation he found. It had been only about fifty-five minutes since he had blown the snow. Now it looked as if it had never been done. He cleared the main entrance then moved to the south entrance, then the east, then the north. The small blizzard the blower created invigorated him. A hard patch of ice had formed right by the doors, so he brought a bag of rock salt and sprinkled it heavily. He began to blow snow around the patch and blew much of the salt away, too. *Stupid me. I can't think straight.* He scattered more salt and walked back into the building. He avoided the teachers' lounge although he really needed a cup of hot coffee. *I'll wait until after the bell when the teachers are all in their classrooms. I'm in no mood for chit-chat.*

Back in his safe haven, Ray removed his jacket. He pulled the sweatshirt over his head. "Mr. Sellers to the office, please. Mr. Sellers to the office." Bella's smooth voice came over the boiler-room speaker. *What now?* His stomach was full of frustration.

"Dr. Fleming wants you to clean the clinic lav. There is dust in the corners by the toilet, " Bella announced. Ray turned on his heel and went back to get the small mop.

"This is going to be one of those days," he said to the corridor, now bustling with student helpers and parents bringing in children. The floors were wet with melting snow. *I don't think I'm ready for this weather. All those munchkin feet dragging in snow and ice.*

Ray finished dusting the corners of the clinic toilet. He gave the sink a quick swish with a wet paper towel.

As he passed Hope's office, he could hear a loud discussion between Carmen Ricci and Hope. He busied himself adjusting the floor mat at the entrance to the outer office.

"I've been using Christmas carols in our program for the past three years. Keith let me. We always got positive comments from parents about it." Ray could hear indignation in Carmen's voice.

"And I'm telling you that we are sitting ducks when we do that. There are people who attend these programs just to see if we are violating the Constitutional separation of church and state. They kick up a big fuss." Hope was holding the line, at which she was very good, Ray couldn't help thinking. He meticulously dusted the file cabinet drawer fronts along the wall next to Hope's office.

"Sometimes we just have to take a risk." Carmen's voice blared through the open door and into the outer office. Bella looked at Ray and rolled her eyes.

Hope closed her door noisily, and only muffled voices could be heard.

"What's that all about?" Ray asked her in a low voice.

"I guess Hope is worried about heat from the ACLU." Bella spoke so softly that Ray had to strain to hear. "She's still festering over the woman who called the Board president after Parents' Night. You know, about the lack of females on a bulletin board. Some kind of famous Americans display. Anonymous caller. Hope was furious."

"That's stupid. I can see why Hope was upset. The buck stops with her. Us peons don't have to worry about it." Bella giggled. Ray's chuckle was obscured by the sound of the second bell.

Ray mopped the wet snow at the entrance doors and adjusted the mats. He placed yellow caution-wet-floor signs at each one. The brilliant yellow signs reminded him of another reason he had to use them, which was, to protect the school from liability should anyone slip on the wet floor and become injured. He thought of Hope and Carmen's argument on which he had just eavesdropped. *I have to do certain things to cover us legally.* Hope wanted to prevent any legal action for violating the Constitution. Carmen wanted her to take a risk. *Carmen's right. She should stick to her guns, fight for her beliefs. Everyone knows today's kids need to learn the Bible. But I wouldn't want to be in Hope's shoes. No sir.* He whistled softly.

From the corridor Ray could faintly hear Hope's voice on the public address system, starting announcements. He entered the lounge where the speaker sounded more clearly. He poured himself coffee in a styrofoam cup, added two sugars and a spoonful of dry creamer. He thought Hope's voice sounded tense on the speaker. Her list of reminders for the week included the Wednesday faculty meeting. After the student-led Pledge of Allegiance Ray walked gingerly down the corridor with his hot coffee. The faculty meeting haunted him. He had to work on his words. Even a ten-minute speech had to be right. He had to know what he was talking about, sound like an authority if he wanted the teachers' respect.

Ray bundled trash bags from the morning Latchkey Program and carried them out to the dumpster in his shirtsleeves. He shivered all the way back to the building. He glued new backs on three kindergarten-sized chairs. He looked at the boxes of supplies that needed to be unpacked and checked off the purchase order. Ray looked at his watch. He had just forty-five minutes before he had to set up for lunch. He would work on his speech, finish it before it niggled him to death. He took a big gulp of cold coffee and sat down at his desk. He took out a yellow legal pad and tried to think of a friendly way to open his talk. To get his mind going, he pulled out a file of memos from Hope. She always called everyone *colleagues* in her memos, teachers, secretaries, cooks, custodians; they were all colleagues to her. They seemed to like that, sort of put everyone on an equal basis. He would do the same, call them *colleagues.*

Ray noticed that she mentioned the children a lot. Everything they did was for the children. Maybe he could do that. We're here for the kids, he heard himself say. That sort of made everyone feel guilty, as if they were trying to get out of a little work instead of going the extra mile to help the kids. "Hot dog!" he sang. He was on a roll. At the end of the day Ray found a copy of the meeting agenda in his mailbox. The agenda read: I. Welcome, II. Ray Sellers - Cleanliness and Safety. His name jumped out at him. He had to admit it looked pretty important. He smiled to himself. Hope had stuck a pink post-it note in the corner on which she had written *Thank you for your help, Ray. Good luck, even though you won't need it. Hope.* Ray felt proud. He almost looked forward to Wednesday. He folded the paper and tucked it into his pocket.

*

The note on the dashboard of his van grabbed Ray's attention as soon as he climbed into the driver's seat. Good thing since he had forgotten that he was to pick up Caroline at the church. She was working there all day, helping with the small food bank and store of clothing the church maintained for needy families. She never missed a Monday helping out there and always took a plate of home-baked cookies or strudel to share with fellow volunteers as well as a tightly wrapped box for the food bank. Sometimes she combed rummage sales for children's clothing to donate to the church program.

Ray pulled into the church parking lot and waited for his mother. She soon came out, walking slowly with heavy steps. Ray jumped out of the van and helped her into the high seat. He could hear her breathing heavily. "How'd it go, Ma?"

Caroline settled herself into the seat, buckled her seatbelt. "It was a banner day," she said with a smile. "Three women from Abbey Gardens subdivision came in with carloads of kids' clothes—good, expensive. Hardly worn. And toys and games, even a bike, like new." She paused to take a breath. "Everything like new. Clean and pressed. Games in original boxes, not a mark on them. Toys hardly used."

"Good deal!" Ray cheered. "St.Catherine's will be giving you a raise, with all that inventory to manage," he teased, pulling into the busy street.

Caroline laughed. "How did your posters work out?" Her serious eyes looked into Ray's face.

Ray coughed and kept his eyes on the road. "Not so good. Well—I changed my mind. I decided it would be better telling them in person. More fair, you know. So I'm going to speak at their meeting Wednesday." He coughed again.

"That's too bad. After all that money you spent on those Day-Glo copies. Are you sure you're up to giving a speech? The Sellers family isn't known for its oratorical talent, is it?" She chuckled.

"I've got it all ready, Ma. No problem." Ray's voice rang with pride.

"That's just great, Rayley." She sighed heavily. "Do you think we could stop at Pizza Bazaar?" She nodded toward the corner store. "I'm too tired to cook dinner tonight."

"Sure, Ma. I'll even treat." He slammed on his brakes to keep from passing the pizza shop and made a sharp right turn.

*

Tuesday was hectic at Poore Pond. Ray lost nearly an hour repairing a broken window in the servery before the cooks arrived to prepare lunch. The scuffed hardball lay conspicuously in the sink among shards of glass where it had landed when it came through the window. Although all the broken glass seemed to have fallen into the deep, wide sink, Hope insisted he vacuum the entire servery and adjoining corridor where the children's lunch line formed.

All the students in each lunch shift had finished eating and gone to recess. Ray rushed to clean the lunchroom so that Carmen could start rehearsals by 1:30. There was so much tension between Carmen and Hope about the Christmas music that Ray could feel it in the air. After the multi-purpose room was all set up for rehearsal, Ray tried to stay out of both their paths. At one point Carmen sent for him to help adjust the sound system. He was disappointed to find Hope positioned near Carmen, watching every move. Her solemn look did not change, nor did her body move. She looked like one of those living statues.

Ray heard later that Hope had agreed to observe the run-through today and then decide whether or not Carmen could keep the religious music in the program. Bella said Hope wanted to see the entire program and how dominant the religious theme seemed to her. Ray felt suffocated from the thickening tension in the room. I like Hope much better when she smiles, he thought, which she nearly always does; the realization surprised him. "I'm glad I'm just a peon," he muttered.

Just before the end of rehearsal when Ray would clear the room and set up for the after-school Latchkey Program, he was called out to the parking lot. There he found a rattle-trap car, overheated and smoking. The hood was raised; and he could see thin, shapely legs in tight jeans below a small waist and shoulders bent over the engine. His heart quickened.

"You could use a little help, I see." Ray forced his voice not to shrill. A mop of blonde hair and big blue eyes turned toward him. Ray swallowed. *What a pretty woman.* Under a white cotton shirt he could see the shape of her firm, pointy breasts through her open black simulated leather jacket. He felt his face redden and looked away. He pulled a shop cloth from his back pocket and used it to unscrew the hot radiator cap. "Step back," he said to her as burning steam surged out of the opening. He motioned her further back with a wave of his arm, brushing against her accidentally. "Excuse me," he said, the strength of his voice pleasing him.

They stood watching the steam erupt. "My neighbor told me this car's an oil guzzler," she said. "But I didn't know it could overheat like this. I just drove it a few blocks." She looked at Ray and smiled. He smiled back. "Oh—my name's Heather," she offered her hand. "Heather Baker. I'm here to pick up my son."

Ray shook her soft hand firmly. "I'm Ray. Ray Sellers."

"Ray Sellers. You must be Mr. Sellers." She giggled, "Jeremy talks about you all the time. Jeremy Baker. My son. Third grader."

"Jeremy. Oh sure. He's one of my helpers. Good one." Ray could not control his widening smile.

Ray told Heather the car needed time to cool down and offered to help her get it going afterward. But Heather, late for an appointment, made a telephone call from the office; and a tall man came to get Jeremy and her. School had been dismissed by then, and the parking lot was nearly empty. Heather's friend said he would return later for the ailing car. Ray watched the three of them head toward a silver sedan, relieved that he did not see any touching between them or any sign of a close bond. Maybe that was her brother, he surmised. But there had been no friendly chiding between them either. I could have gotten that car going for her, he thought as he watched them drive away. "Oh well," he said aloud. "It's been that kind of day."

Ray looked at his watch as he entered the building. It was 3:45. He was leaving fifteen minutes late without letting Caroline know. *I'll have to listen to Ma now. She'll go on about being worried and not knowing how she'd get along without me. That's just what I don't need after a day like today.*

"Ray!" He turned to see Hope waving toward him from the office door. She motioned for him to come.

Ray sauntered down the hall. *What now? I've had about all I can take from these females today. Except for one.* Visions of Heather Baker's engaging face and to-die-for figure filled his head. He felt his groin quiver.

"Do you have a moment, Ray? Let's go in my office." Hope led the way. "Have a seat." She gestured toward a chair at the table and sat down next to him. He could hear Bella's printer swooshing out pages.

"Are you all set for tomorrow's meeting? Do you have any questions, you know, about words to use?" Her tense mouth managed a tight smile. She folded her small, white hands in her lap. Ray noticed how tired she looked.

"No, I'm all ready." Ray leveled his eyes straight at Hope. "I've thought a lot about what to say. And how to say it, Hope." *Oh great, now she has doubts about me. What happened to her good-luck-although-I-know-you-won't-need-it mood? Oh no, she's not going to do a job on me.* He pushed his chair away from the table. Reddening slightly, in a too-strong voice, he said, "I wouldn't have agreed to do this if I couldn't handle it." He met Hope's gaze with cold eyes.

"You're way ahead of me, Ray," Hope said in an uncharacteristically flat voice. She smiled weakly and dropped her eyes. Then her face brightened when she told him how kind it was of him to help Heather Baker with her car. She explained Heather's dire straits and that she thought it was time she had a break. "She really does try hard to be a good mother and provide for Jeremy. I admire her fortitude. We need to watch her though. She isn't one to ask for help, even when she needs it badly."

"She sure is pretty," Ray heard himself say. He felt his face redden and smiled broadly.

"That she is." Hope looked at Ray with understanding. "I pray she has food in the house. She's too proud to let us know."

"Things are that bad, that she may be going hungry? Jeremy too? Good grief, Hope." Ray's voice rose. His eyes widened. "There are so many places to get help, food banks, churches. My mom's church runs a hunger program. Maybe I'll talk to her." His voice trailed off as he remembered Caroline's comments about the food bank.

"Thanks again, Ray. See you at the meeting tomorrow morning."

"Right. Will it be in the library or the computer lab?" Ray knew it would be in the library; but he was reluctant to leave this rare, more vulnerable Hope, talking like a friend instead of his superior.

Hope stood. "The library. I'll need the overhead projector and screen, too, Ray," her smooth, back-in-charge voice ended the conversation. Ray left.

*

As tired as he was, Ray picked up his notes to review right after he got home. He sat down in the cushy recliner in the living room. He could hear Caroline closing cupboards and pot lids as she prepared their meatloaf dinner. But he had difficulty concentrating on the speech; Heather Baker's intriguing face clouded his mind. He kept seeing Jeremy's innocent eyes and freckled nose. He could not bear to think of them as hungry. He went into the kitchen. "Ma, what does it take to get help from your food bank?" He straddled a chair backwards, resting his forearms on the top rail.

Caroline lifted a roasting pan from the oven. The aroma of hot buttered cabbage and meatloaf, covered with baked-on catsup, filled the small room. Ray wished he had somehow arranged to bring Heather and Jeremy home with him for dinner.

"St. Catherines?" she finally responded. Ray nodded. "Just go there. You give your name and get to sort of shop the shelves. Why?"

"No charge or proof you're poor?"

"Nothing like that. We do ask your name, if you've been there before. We try to keep records." She began slicing the meatloaf. "You know, see how many people need us over a long period of time. Otherwise, no questions asked. Why do you want to know this?" Caroline set the platter of sliced meatloaf on the table and riveted her eyes at Ray.

His voice cracked as he explained about the student helper and single mother who were struggling.

"Tell her to come over. Hours are from 9:30 in the morning to 4:00 P.M." Wielding a slotted spoon, Caroline scooped cabbage into half a divided bowl. She spooned mashed potatoes into the other half and placed it on the table. "Let's eat, Ray."

After dinner Ray showered and retired to his room early, telling Caroline he wanted to go over his speech.

"Oh, tomorrow's your big day." Caroline said without looking at him. She switched on the television remote. "You'll do fine, Son."

Ray sat on his bed and recited his speech. He remembered most of the points readily. He undressed and crawled into bed.

*

Ray grew nervous as the library began to fill with chattering, laughing, rested-looking teachers, some carrying their favorite drink mugs. Many of them helped themselves to juice and quarter cuts of bagels, already spread with various kinds of flavored cream cheese. Hope had laid the refreshments out on colored construction paper and paper doilies. Several teachers cornered her with small discussions. Others chatted among themselves about events from last evening or this morning. A sinking feeling invaded Ray's stomach as he watched their numbers grow. He busied himself pretending to adjust the projector, then the screen.

Remember to use the word <u>colleagues</u> *and to say, "for the kids" a lot.* He knew he had his points down pat. He hoped the words he planned to use were soft enough without making him look niggling and lame. He was fully aware of, and not bothered by, the fact that he was less educated than everyone else in the room. But he could not bear to be seen as weak and whiny.

Hope called the meeting to order promptly at 7:45. She smiled brightly while she thanked everyone for being on time. Speech teacher Maddy Marenko slipped sheepishly through the door and stood against the wall; kindergarten teacher Melanie Armstrong followed, lowering her chin and shrugging her shoulders. Some teachers smiled from their chairs at the latecomers. Hope appeared to take no notice and continued speaking.

"I know there has been some confusion over several issues that affect our custodial department. Some of you have come to me with constructive suggestions. So Poore Pond's Head Custodian has agreed to talk with us to help sort out these issues. I know you will give a warm welcome to our own Ray Sellers." Ray stepped forward to resounding applause and wide smiles. His own broad smile conveyed his pleasure.

Ray stood next to Hope in front of the first table. He cleared his throat. He was relieved when Hope moved to a vacant chair at the farthest table. He looked at the sea of friendly faces, all eyes on him. He could not help but smile back.

"Friends, Colleagues, and Bosses," Ray said, trying to keep his voice steady and loud enough for all to hear. The teachers roared with laughter. "I want to thank Dr. Fleming and you for giving me this opportunity to do what I can to," he cleared his throat. Vertical lines formed between his thick eyebrows. "help us understand each other better. Talk about what you're up against in the classroom and what I'm up against keeping the whole school clean for our kids." Again, the teachers applauded roundly. *What was I worried about? This is one respectful group.*

He moved to stand near the next table, carrying the 3 x 5 note cards covered by his palm. He felt so relaxed he thought he may not need to refer to them at all.

"Let's talk about floors. I know how much you like clean floors. Why, some of you even sweep your own rooms every day. Or have the kids sweep. And you wipe up spilled drinks with paper towels. I know because I get so many students hunting me down for fresh rolls of towels. Also, I see the piles of used ones in your trashcans. So I know you like clean floors as much as I do." He paused, amazed that he enjoyed being the center of attention. "But those sticky sweet drinks the kids bring in, those box juices and those Little Hugs in plastic bottles," he held his hands flat, palms facing, one about three inches above the other, "things like that. They stick to the floor unless they're washed up with soap and water, not just plain water. Then Marty and Rosie and I try to sweep, the dust mops keep getting hung up on sticky spots. The sticky spots—on the floor and on the mops now—attract ants. So there's another problem. I don't want our kids to have to be trying to learn with ants crawling around, up their chair legs, on their desks, in their book bags and lunch boxes. And I know you don't want that either."

Ray looked around at the faces of the teachers. A few began to talk softly to their neighbors. *I hope I'm not losing them.*

"Why can't we just reinstate our old rule against beverages? Nothing allowed except water?" Carmen Ricci called out.

"Some kids need the energy boost from juice. Water won't do it for every kid," a voice called out from the table by the windows.

"I need the energy boost," Boris Mathews exclaimed, laughing through his words. "Water won't do it for me either. A beer would." He looked at his colleagues for a sign of approval, which no one gave him.

"How about we all keep mop buckets, those wringer ones, in our rooms?" Trudy Cooper asked.

"I don't want to worry about mopping floors. Those mops are heavy, and the kids make a game of using the wringer." Lou Ann Newhouse punctuated her statement with a frown. "I don't mind once in awhile, after art or a party, or something. But not daily."

"Where would we keep a big bucket like that?" called a voice from the last table.

Ray looked at Hope. He could not read her blank face. Oh no, he thought. What have I done? How do I get out of this mess?

The teachers continued debating solutions among themselves, oblivious to either Hope or Ray. Ray saw Hope look at the wall clock. It was 8:07 and she had a long agenda to get through. Ray's eyes fell on a copy of the agenda on the table. He felt a surge of pride at seeing his name in print. *Mr. Ray Sellers.*

Finally Pamela Thorpe stood. "The third-grade teachers think we should all have a spray bottle of soapy water, not some chemical cleaner that may cause allergies or kick up someone's asthma, or anything like that. But fresh soap and water. Ray could make a pump dispenser available in each wing. We or the kids— the older ones— could mix fresh soap and water every day or so."

"That way we could clean the drink spills easily and properly," Pamela's fellow third-grade teacher, Lou Ann Newhouse, interjected. "Of course, our soap consumption will go up. Those kids don't know what *sparingly* means yet."

Ray noticed that his cousin Millie Blackwell, though conferring with her third-grade colleagues, did not volunteer an opinion. He was grateful for her good sense.

Ray jumped in while he could. "You told me our colleagues would have good suggestions," he called to Hope across the room. "You were right." He eased into the related subject of cleaning up after classroom pets, ready this time for active debate. *I hope they come up with a reasonable solution to this one.*

Since the keeping of classroom pets was limited to largely primary grades, those teachers debated while most of the intermediate-grade teachers socialized. It was 8:25 when Melanie Armstrong stood and projecting her voice over the din, asked, "Do we have a budget for more plastic garbage bags? Because if we do, we could just shake the whole cage bottom into a fresh garbage bag every time we clean it. No holding it over the trash can and missing it, ending up with half the mess on the floor—"

"And leave the kids out of it," Jan Wheaton interrupted.

"And leave the kids out of it," Melanie repeated. "Maybe the parents' group could buy extra bags for us, at the wholesale club?" She smiled and sat down again.

Teachers with pets agreed good naturedly to Melanie's suggestion, as did those without pets.

Ray decided not to get into the issue of parents coming back after school for forgotten homework. There wasn't time. The teachers were getting restless; and Hope walked toward him with a stack of handouts, ready to get on with the agenda. Ray wanted out of there.

"Ladies and Gentlemen," Hope projected her voice; and one by one, the teachers grew quiet and attended. "Thank you, Ray, for your time and interest in the welfare of Poore Pond students and staff." Applause broke out. Ray, grateful that he did not have to speak again, murmured, "Thanks," and walked into the hall. He could hear Hope's assured voice introducing the topic of practice tests as he closed the door. *My moment of fame is over,* he thought with utter relief.

Ray had always felt that student-arrival time was a time when he should be highly visible, working busily about the school; and he did so most mornings, tending to tasks in the lobby or corridors. Today he needed to review the meeting in his mind, so he tried to appear purposeful as he paced down the hall.

Overall, the meeting had gone quite well, Ray thought. He felt self-satisfied. No one had attacked him; they were actually very friendly. Though it had thrown him at first, he admired the way they could disagree freely and no one seemed offended.

Crossing the lobby, Ray spotted Heather Baker coming up the walk, carrying Jeremy's book bag while he dug in his pockets. She was wearing the black leather jacket again, with a white turtleneck and a red miniskirt. Black platform shoes emphasized her gorgeous legs. "Good morning, Mrs. Baker, Jeremy." Ray smiled and opened the door for them. "Did you get your wheels running?" He laughed.

"Barely," Heather said with fleeting eye contact. Jeremy nodded. "I left it running now, hope it doesn't die." She hurried down the hall.

"Let me know if it does; I'll help you," Ray called to her back.

"Thanks," he heard her reply without turning around. Wanting to stay near the door in case the car stalled, Ray looked around for a task. He pulled out his shop cloth and began polishing the glass covering on the fire extinguisher case. He put great energy and concentration into rubbing the glass. He saw Hope's reflection in the glass as she walked past to the office and was reminded again of the meeting.

Yes, it had gone pretty well. I used colleagues *and "for the kids" several times without feeling like a fake, and it worked. The teachers came up with reasonable solutions that wouldn't cause too much extra work. I'll just have to remember to order all those spray bottles and extra soap and large garbage bags. I'd better tell Rosie and Marty to stock their areas as well and keep them stocked.*

Still feeling relief that the meeting was over and proud of his performance, Ray wanted to talk about it to someone. He gave the glass one last swipe and walked into the office just as the first bell rang. He glanced into Hope's office, but she was on the telephone.

"Good job at the meeting, Ray," Dave Myers, physical education teacher, spoke from the photocopier. Ray walked over to him. "Your invasion-of-the-ants scenario was a blast."

"Thanks." Ray stood next to him at the copier. "Those colleagues of yours sure do have opinions, don't they?" Ray laughed. *Is he telling me I went over the top with the part about the ants?*

"Oh, yeah. Forty people with forty different opinions. This morning wasn't so bad. Sometimes they get really heated. They mean well, but it takes up so much meeting time. I try to miss the meetings when I can. Most issues don't apply to me anyway. Hope likes me to be there, says I need to know what's going on. She's right, I guess." He removed the collated paper stacks from the copier trays and placed them, crossed, on the worktable. Ray could see sharply drawn diagrams of game positions on the sheets.

"Well, at least you had another guy there this morning," Ray chuckled.

"What do you mean?" Dave began stapling each stack and did not look up.

"Me. I was there. Or were you sleeping?" Ray flashed a teasing smile.

"Oh, right. One more male. That made five, didn't it? That's right. Maybe you should come to our meetings more often, give us more token males." They both laughed. Ray wanted Dave to say more about his speech, but he started talking about last night's NFL game and the lousy outcome.

The second bell rang and Dave hurried out. Ray noticed Hope at her door, frowning at Dave's last-minute departure to sentry duty in the hallway. *Sometimes she is so easy to read.*

"I saw you holding the door for the stunning Mrs. Baker, Mr. White Knight." Bella, her desk window finally free of parents and children, chided Ray.

"I always hold the door when I'm there," Ray felt his neck redden. "My mom taught me well."

"I'll look forward to that the next time I come in when you're there," she said with a straight face. Then she laughed. "Maybe I'll get myself a miniskirt and platform shoes."

Hope stepped out of her office and began conferring with Bella about misspelled names on the Christmas concert program draft. Ray left the office. *I suppose Heather Baker's car kept running.* He was disappointed that he had missed her when she returned to the parking lot.

Ray passed the children's lavatories and heard loud laughter and talk from both the boys' and the girls' lavs. He stepped inside the boys' lav and saw intermediate-grade students sprawled on the floor, finger painting on large, glossy white paper. Patches of green, blue, and red paint were smeared on the floor and some on the wall. Two of the sinks were covered with paint.

"What are you kids doing?" Ray demanded.

"We're making place mats for our parent breakfast," a small, wiry ten-year-old with closely cropped, red-blonde hair, shrouded in a varsity jersey three sizes too large, explained. "Aren't they cool?"

"Does your teacher know you're in here?"

"He sent us. Mr. Mathews said finger painting is too messy for the classroom." All the children stopped working and stared at Ray. "We came to school early. Supposed to finish before the bell." The boy's eyes pleaded with Ray to understand.

"All right, then," Ray's steady voice did not reveal the anger he felt. He headed straight for Hope's office.

Ray waited a long five minutes until a parent came out of Hope's closed door. He waited longer while she took a telephone call. To counter his impatience, he adjusted the levelers on Bella's lateral file until she nodded toward the phone-line board showing that Hope had ended her call. He collided with Annie Klements at the door. Annie motioned for Ray to go ahead of her. Breaking his own rule on deferring to teachers, he rushed inside. Hope rose abruptly from her chair.

"What is it, Ray?"

"You've got to do something. He's done it again."

"Who? What has he done?"

"Boris Mathews. Let the kids take over." Ray fairly spat the words at her. "His whole class is smearing paint all over the boys' lav and the girls' lav. It's only 9:25 in the morning. The sinks were still clean, hardly used yet."

Hope brushed past him and sprinted down the hall. Ray was torn between wanting to witness Hope's handling of the matter and not wanting to face the children after reporting them to the principal. It wasn't their fault the teacher didn't know better. He headed to the servery to check the coolers.

*

A heavy snow began to fall early in the afternoon. Weather forecasters predicted falling temperatures and six-to-eight inches by rush hour. Superintendent Amiston instructed Hope to have students ready for dismissal fifteen minutes early, so buses could be boarded quickly. Visitors tracked snow into the building, and Ray kept busy mopping up slush and placing caution signs in wet areas.

Through the large arched windows in the lobby, Ray watched the snow accumulate quickly. He knew he would have to stay a little later today and help direct traffic. Parents of children who walked to school would come in droves to collect them, depriving them of the opportunity to romp in the delicious white fluff. He never understood why so many people went into a panic state with the first heavy snowfall. *This is the northeastern United States. Snow falls here. Heavy snow. Every winter.*

But at the first big snowfall parents of bus-riding children would sign them out for early release. This would cause conscientious bus drivers to take time verifying where their missing charges were; thus, losing the time edge intended by the early boarding. The line of cars would back up for blocks. Some harried parents always managed to park in the buses-only lane, infuriating the drivers who would fuss until they knew the principal was outside intervening.

Although this was Ray's first year with Hope, he knew she would need the same help he had always given Keith when a snowstorm hit. It was important to Ray to maintain his own personal standard in that regard. So he telephoned Caroline and told her he'd be he-didn't-know-how late. Her voice held the same note of worry that the voices of those here at school held.

When snow fell rapidly like this, teachers, even those who typically worked hours after dismissal, would rush out of the building, looking worried and talking excitedly of a possible snow-day furlough the next day.

About forty-five minutes before time for early bus boarding Ray put on the thick anorak he kept on a hook in the boiler room. He was happy to find his wool-lined suede gloves in the pockets. He went outside with the small snow shovel and a broom to clear walks and try to head off potential traffic bottlenecks. He found the cold air and the swirling snowflakes invigorating and smiled at his vision of the soon-to-come show of human nature at its most illogical. He had never admitted to anyone how much he enjoyed watching the drama of Poore Pond dismissal on a snowy day. He felt guilty. It wasn't that he took serious matters too lightly; he just found all the scurrying and worrying entertaining.

Finally, all students and parents were safely on their way home except for two children whose parents had called to say they were stuck in traffic across town. Hope had registered them in the after-school Latchkey Program. The parking lot was empty of teachers' cars except for Millie Blackwell's vintage white station wagon.

Bella swooped into the office carrying a tray holding styrofoam cups of steaming hot chocolate for everyone. She had ferreted the cups and chocolate and a dusty box of stale goldfish crackers from the parent-group storage cupboard.

"Bella, just what we need," Hope smiled at the secretary. "Come on, Ray. Sit down." She gestured toward the worktable. Ray sat down. Hope took the chair across from him. Bella ran to answer the persistent telephone.

"Goldfish. Goody." Ray laughed. "I love those things." He passed the box to Hope who took a handful.

"These must be left over from the August picnic," Hope joked as she chewed the stale crackers.

"Reminds me of that old saying, how's it go?" Ray glanced sideways, thinking. "Something about fish and houseguests get stale after four days. I guess it's true." Hope laughed. Bella walked over and stood by the table, drinking her hot chocolate. An awkward silence fell as Hope and Ray drank.

"I've been meaning to ask you, Hope." Ray looked at her. She smiled. "How did you get the boys' lav back in order so fast? I went in there about 10:00 and everything looked clean."

"Let's just say that Boris Mathews learned something this morning about school sanitation regulations and about child labor. It's okay to use it, but you have to supervise. I stayed with his class while he oversaw the cleanup."

"I hope it sticks," Ray chuckled. "All those projects he's always doing, it'll come up again. Bound to." Ray's face grew serious as he examined his styrofoam cup.

"It was thoughtful of you to stay after and help with dismissal, Ray." Hope's eyes sought his. "Things would have been chaotic without your help. You direct traffic like an expert. With authority. People listen to you."

"Oh, I don't know. They just—. Thanks, Hope." Ray's face reddened. He wished he had not given her such a hard time when she first came to Poore Pond last August. *Who would have thought she'd turn out to be a nice person?* He felt guilty.

CHAPTER TWELVE—IAN AND HELSI

Enjoying the quiet kitchen, Ian Bradford poured himself a second cup of coffee. *It's great to have a day off.* His muscles ached and his eyes burned. He had worked half the night, assisting at a passenger-train derailment in Coshocton, forty miles away. He had tried to sleep late, but that was never possible with five kids and a business-as-usual wife in the house. They were all at school now, and Helsi was chaperoning a field trip with Rachel's preschool. Ian felt a twinge of guilt to be enjoying the solitude so much. It was a rare thing. He couldn't remember when he'd last had the house to himself.

Ian looked around at the kitchen, light flooding in through the large, curtainless window, the yellow laminate countertops bare, just the way Helsi liked them. The wide arched, 50's vintage doorway into the living room seemed charming to him this morning. He admired the two candleholders Helsi had asked him to mount on either side of the doorway, skonses, she called them. They were her quick substitute for the electrical sconces she really wanted. They gave a sort of dining-room feel to the kitchen eating area, especially on holidays and birthdays when she would put a fancy cloth on the big, round table and lighted candles in the sconces. *I'm lucky to have a wife like Helsi. She puts her all into making a home for the family.*

Ian carried his cup into the small living room. He set the cup on the table and stretched his tall body expansively, then sat on the sofa with its stiff cotton slipcover. He looked at the vases of pussy willows Helsi had scattered on tables, a large one on the floor by the door. *What she could have done with a doctor's income.* Melancholy overtook him. *I could have bought her a mansion, or at least a new house like those in Abbey Gardens. She would have been in her glory.*

Why didn't I stick to my plan? I could have. Just let Mom go on welfare after Dad died. I could have done more for her later with a big income. I wanted nothing but to be a doctor, a physician. It was all I ever wanted. How did I lose sight of that? What am I now? A piddling paramedic. And where's Mom? She's gone. Lived only long enough after Dad died to see me get off track. Then I met Helsi; we got married and that was it. We were powerlessly lovesick; the kids came so fast. And they kept coming.

Ian lifted the remote and switched on the television. Last night's train accident came to life on the screen. He could see his white emergency van off to the side, his partner's back at the door. Ian had to admit it had felt great being able to help all those injured people, knowing what to do on the spot, calming them, looking after them. Just like a doctor, really. But he didn't feel great helping them into the hospital. *Those emergency-room docs are pompous asses, think they're so much better than us paramedics. Could see it in their faces when we briefed them on patients. Only difference between them and us is their big break at college and their big incomes now. Shoot.* He changed the channel.

*

Ian felt more awake after a hot shower and clean clothes. Helsi had left a note on the shower curtain: *Don't forget Robbie's reading class play at school. 10:30. He's expecting you. Bring a canned good for the food bank. Take a can of spaghetti.* Good thing she left the note. He had put it out of his mind. Didn't want to think about going to that tight-arsed school with the dragon principal.

Ian remembered the last time he was at Poore Pond. It was for the so-called hearing about Dylan bringing Robbie's scout knife to school. The principal made a big deal of it, even had her uptown boss there. It had not been pretty. Ian had left the hearing feeling more like an outsider than ever. *Well, today I won't go near the office,* go *straight to Robbie's classroom. I know where it is; the number's on the invitation.* He rummaged through a pile of papers by the phone and found the folded blue paper. *Room F-2.*

But Ian wanted to see Dr. Fleming about her having questioned Robbie on the bullying incident. Robbie had told him that he didn't think the principal believed him and that nothing was done. Ian had bristled at Robbie's account and would have contacted the school right then, but it was the weekend. Then the workweek started off in a rush and the entire matter lost its importance. He did recall a telephone message from Dr. Fleming stating that *she was sorry. She had investigated all sources, but she had too little information to identify the perpetrator.*

Ian left the house early, wondering what he could bring to Robbie's class to make an impression on the teacher, the other parents. For Robbie's sake. He had seen his wife do that. She'd taken cupcakes or even small plastic bags of raisins and dry cereal to the children's classes. Not for special holidays or functions, but just because she happened to be stopping at the school for business with the office or the teacher.

The invitation said there would be refreshments. Should he bring more food? Donuts? Bagels? He stopped at the small bakery down the street from school. He knew Bud and Selma, the owners, from his CPR classes. They attended every year for a refresher course. Bud always talked about the pastry orders they got from the school, bagels for teachers' meetings, donuts for kids' birthday parties, special cakes.

"Good morning, Ian," Selma smiled. "Did you work the train wreck last night?" Her face turned grave.

"Yeah, it was pretty bad. And now I'm off to Poore Pond for Robbie's class play." He didn't want to get into last night. "Thought I'd bring the kids a treat. Maybe donuts." He walked to the end of the glass display case. There were so many varieties of donuts, he didn't know where to start.

"Actually, Mrs. Newhouse bought four dozen doughnuts this morning. For the after-play party." Selma showed Ian other pastries: thickly frosted cupcakes; chocolate chip muffins; small, white-glazed danish. They finally settled on cookies, alphabet cookies with colored frosting. She suggested four-and-a-half dozen, two of every letter of the alphabet and a few of the meatier ones like A's, B's, M's, W's. Layering them with waxed paper, she lined them carefully into a big, white box.

"You're going to make Robbie proud of his dad, Ian." Selma smiled again. "Being so nice to his classmates. And alphabet cookies for reading class, that's very clever of you."

"It was you suggested it, Selma. You're the clever one."

Ian pulled into the parking lot, complimenting himself for thinking of bringing the cookies. Somehow, it made going to the school a little easier.

When he walked in the front door of Poore Pond, Ian, relieved, saw no one he recognized, nor did he encounter anyone in the hallways. On the stairway up to F-wing he passed a small boy who muttered, "Hi, Mr. Brafford," in a soft voice. He said Hi back without knowing who the child was. He found himself checking his posture, standing straighter. He hardly knew this reading teacher of Robbie's.

His son beamed at him when he entered the classroom, squeezing into a line of fathers wearing visitors' badges and looking as ill at ease as he felt. Mrs. Newhouse, wearing a wide, fixed smile, nodded at him and sent a child to get him a visitor's badge from the office. She instructed the fathers to sit on the children's chairs while the children were standing against the chalkboard, positioned in three rows. Ian gingerly wove his large frame around the crowd to give her the box of cookies and can of spaghetti.

He saw the red and white paper tablecloth laden with plates of donuts and jugs of juice, sending him instantly into doubt about the cookies. There were also goldfish crackers and a large electric coffee urn. Mrs. Newhouse accepted the box with an oh-no-not-more-food expression in her eyes. She lifted the lid and squealed with delight.

"Mr. Bradford, alphabet cookies for a celebration of reading? Just too perfect! Thank you so much." Ian's eyes met Robbie's proud eyes and smiling face. He felt as if, for once, he'd gotten it right at Poore Pond. He worked his way through the crammed cluster of fathers and sat down as unobtrusively as he could on a child-sized chair.

The children began reciting, two at a time. The pairs read first in unison, then as speakers in dialogue. Each pair carried large drawings that depicted scenes from the story in their reading books. At first Ian thought they had memorized the passages verbatim and marveled at their memory, secretly fearing that Robbie, who could not remember the days of the week, would forget his part. Then a red-faced child dropped her poster, and the fathers could see the neatly printed text on the other side of the drawings. When it was Robbie's turn, he was smiling so much he could barely speak, let alone read. But the audience found him delightful, and he managed to finish his turn respectably.

Once his son had performed, Ian relaxed somewhat and almost forgot where he was. The fathers roared with laughter when a freckled boy in black-rimmed glasses stepped forward without a partner and began changing his voice to portray two different speakers. He finished the part masterfully and received long and hearty applause. Mrs. Newhouse explained that Frederick's partner was absent and he wanted to cover both voices himself. The fathers applauded her words robustly.

After the performance the children served refreshments to their fathers, moving like mice in a maze through the crowded room. The fathers agreed that they would serve themselves coffee to prevent unsafe mishaps. The children then helped themselves to treats and sat on the floor near their fathers to eat. Ian was happy to see that nearly all the children opted for alphabet cookies, most trying to get their own first or last initials. Robbie noticed it, too, smiling up at his dad again and again.

When it was time to say goodbye, Mrs. Newhouse informed Ian that he needed to stop in the office and sign the permission slip for Robbie to be a conflict manager. She thanked him again for the cookies and for coming. "Just see Dr. Fleming. She'll take care of you." Robbie, his eyes reluctant, said good-bye to his father at the classroom door.

In truth, Ian wanted to avoid the office and Dr. Fleming. For the first time he had had a lovely morning at Poore Pond and did not want to spoil it. But he diligently headed that way. The closer he came to the office, the tenser he became.

Bella said the principal was in a classroom and was due back in ten minutes. Would Mr. Bradford have a seat in the lobby to wait? Ian sat down on the smooth oak bench near the front door and stretched his legs. A thin, pale man with a receding hairline came in the entrance doors. He looked around nervously, checked in at Bella's window, then returned to the lobby.

"How are you doing?" Ian greeted him.

"Fine, thanks. How are you?" The man sat down at the other end of the bench.

"Are you waiting to see the principal, too?" Ian asked, wanting to put him at ease.

"Sort of." He stood to remove his rumpled suit coat and sat back down. "Do you know her? What kind of person is she?"

"Okay, I guess. But a real stickler for rules and procedures."

"Sounded kind of harsh on the phone. Told me to pick up my kid. Emergency removal. All he did was have a little scuffle in the boys' bathroom." He glanced furtively toward the office.

"Yeah, she likes to do those emergency removals. She did that to my son a few weeks ago. The kid wasn't listening to her or the teacher and he punched another kid. You know how boys are." Ian made a boxing motion with his fists. "So he gets out of line, and she gives him a day off from school. 'Some punishment,' I told my wife."

"Well, that's what I said. Didn't make much sense to me. What happened to staying in for recess? Or after school? These schools today. I'll tell you." He rose and began to pace.

Bella came to tell Ian Dr. Fleming would see him now. "She'll be with you in a few minutes, Mr. Swanson," she said, looking at him. He nodded. Ian followed her into the office.

Hope waited at her door. "Hello, Mr. Bradford. It's nice to see you. Did you enjoy Robbie's program?" Ian told her it was great.

"Sit down, David. You're not to touch the copier. Your father is waiting to see Dr. Fleming. You don't want to get in more trouble than you already are." Bella's stern voice carried through the outer office.

Ian winced. Hope sighed. She closed the door and invited Ian to sit down. "You're here to sign Robbie's conflict-management permission form?" She took a green folder from her desk and sat down next to Ian.

"We need to talk about that, but first I want to know what's been done with the bully," he heard himself say. Hope explained the process she had taken Robbie through and the lack of any information to help her locate the perpetrator.

"So you see, Mr. Bradford, I had nothing to go on. I could not take the process any further. I did counsel Robbie to please report such incidents immed—"

"Robbie said you think he's lying. He was upset." Ian did not want a confrontation, but he was unable to stop himself. Hope looked at him with warm eyes.

"I explained specifically, the lack of information, point by point, to Robbie." Her brow furrowed. "But I never suggested that he wasn't telling the truth." She stiffened slightly. "I am sorry if that was his perception. He seemed to understand everything I told him. In fact, it was he who mentioned conflict managers. At that very meeting. Said he wanted to be one." She sat still as a statue, her eyes riveted to Ian's.

Ian wanted to think that Hope had changed the subject to divert him from the truth about the bully. But no information is no information. He squirmed in his chair. Will she ever stop staring at me? He coughed and she averted her eyes. She removed a paper from the green file and laid it in front of Ian, placing a pen on top. She handed him a paper with the heading: *Conflict Management Parental Fact Sheet.*

"Please take a few moments to read this, Mr. Bradford. If you have questions, I will be happy to answer them for you." She rose and went to her desk where she began sorting through her inbox.

Ian began to read the question-and-answer format. *1. What is conflict management? A program that trains selected students to assist peers in solving disputes at school.* Ian found it difficult to concentrate with Hope just a few feet away. His eyes skimmed down the page and stopped abruptly at question *8: What are the difficulties the conflict managers face?* Good question, he thought, reading further. *They must not lose sight of their role. Their job is to simply guide the children in conflict toward their own resolution, using the above-stated simple steps.. They do not make suggestions for specific resolutions, nor do they evaluate solutions the conflictees identify.* Ian, a sinking feeling in his stomach, stopped there. How can kids do that? Heck, grownups can't even get people to do that. No, Robbie is not going to be put in that position, not my son. He looked toward Hope who now sat at her desk, apparently deep in thought. She sensed his eyes on her and looked at him. She rose and joined him at the table.

"Do you have a question, Mr. Bradford?" She smiled.

"No—this is not for Robbie. I can't see him doing it. Or any other kid, for that matter. Sounds more like a program for grownups. Who dreamed up this one?"

"Kids do it every day in thousands of schools across the country and parts of Europe." Her eyes met his.

There she goes, laying that high-intensity eye contact on me again.

He glanced out the window above her desk. "Little kids? Robbie's age?" He did not look at her.

"Yes, elementary-school students, usually from age seven. With good results."

"How do we know it works?" He looked fleetingly at her face.

"Actual programs have been well researched. Schools with a strong program in place experience fewer disciplinary problems, detentions, and the like. The training is good and children tend to take ownership in the program. I think Robbie would do that. Why not let him go through the training and try it? It will be good experience. If either you or he feels it's not for him, you could withdraw him. But—"

"I know already it's not for him—"

"Please let me finish." Hope looked at him with determined eyes. "It's important that we not lose sight of what's best for Robbie."

"Exactly!" Ian interjected.

"If you or I do not respect his desire to be a conflict manager, what are we saying to him?" Hope's eyes challenged him to respond, but Ian's brain had shut down as it often did in tense situations. Not during paramedic duties, but outside his field of expertise, like now. The silence tugged at him.

"We'll be saying that he can't think for himself, his own goals are not valid, won't we?" Hope's entire body language compelled him to respond.

"I know my kid. Other kids don't listen to him. No. No. It would be a disaster. Look, I've got to go. I'll talk to Robbie." Ian stood abruptly and left the office hurriedly.

*

Ian waited on the sofa while Robbie finished his after-school snack. He sat on the floor with Dylan and Rachel in front of the television, watching *Wishbone*. Ian could see why they loved that show. They didn't know they were learning history. They loved the antics of the winning little dog who looked ridiculous in period costumes. The children sat mesmerized as they munched on peanut-buttered crackers, deftly lifting small glasses of juice with sticky fingers while their eyes never left the screen.

When the show was over and the snacks consumed, Dylan and Rachel went off to play. "What did you want to talk to me about, Dad?" Robbie asked, ducking inside Ian's sinewy arm and making up-close eye contact.

"About Conflict Managers." Ian breathed deeply.

"Did you sign my permission slip? There's training tomorrow." Robbie's face was full of hope.

"Do you know what you're getting yourself into, Robbie? You need to think about that." Ian's face turned grave.

"I know." Robbie dropped his chin. Neither spoke for a moment.

"Robbie, it's a hard job. Big responsibility. Kids will be getting mad at you for trying to get them to be sensible. Besides, you—"

"But I want to be one," Robbie howled, surprising Ian with his intensity. "I want to be trained and use those words. I want to wear a green pinny. I want my picture in the yearbook." He slumped down dejectedly on the sofa next to his father.

Why is this so hard, Ian thought. He was not prepared for such resistance. Robbie usually just took Ian's advice at face value and that was that. "Well, it doesn't have to be this year, does it? Why not wait until next year? You'll be in fourth grade. You'll be bigger. You could practice—"

"I want to be a third-grade conflict manager, Dad. I want to be already used to it when I get to fourth grade. That's when everybody turns tough, in fourth grade. That's when all the fights start. Fourth graders start all the fights. Every recess." His eyes appealed to Ian, driving straight through his heart.

"But, Son." Ian pulled him onto his lap. He could feel tension all through his thin little body as he held him tightly. "You don't have to fight just because you're in fourth grade, do you?" He remembered what it was like to be nine-years-old and frightened. Afraid to fight, yet hating your cowardly thoughts.

"They'll make me! They make everybody! They have a chicken test. You have to fight or you're a chicken. When you get to fourth grade. Ask Sean." The despair in Robbie's voice made Ian's chest hurt. He felt tired again. He didn't know how to help his son. Robbie sank into his lap and he sat holding him. He remembered Hope's words, *Why not let him go through the training and try it? It will be good experience...*

Ian heard himself tell Robbie he could try it. He would stop at school tomorrow morning and sign the permission form, so he could attend the training meeting during lunch recess.

Robbie's face shone with happiness. Looking like a new boy, he went off to play. Ian felt relief and defeat. He didn't relish going into Hope with his tail between his legs, admitting to her that she was right. But he would do it for his son.

Hope was not in her office when Ian stopped there, but Bella said she had left the form in case he came in to sign it. A vague sense of resentment set in as he quickly signed the form. "Will you see that whoever's in charge of conflict managers gets this? Before lunch? So my son can go to the meeting?"

"Of course, Mr. Bradley," Bella flashed him a flippant smile. "Oh, here's Dr.Fleming now."

"Good morning, Mr. Bradford," Hope smiled brightly. She saw the signed paper on the counter. "I see you've changed your mind about Robbie's becoming a conflict manager. Good for you for reconsidering. I admire your open-mindedness." She reached to shake Ian's hand. This time he did not rebuff her. He shook her hand firmly and made good eye contact. "I'm sure Robbie will fill you in on how the training goes for him. Have a good day." She smiled again. Ian smiled back, surprising himself.

Am I mistaken or is the doc getting nicer? He no longer felt resentful that Hope had anticipated his returning to sign the permission form. "She sure had me pegged," he chuckled.

*

Robbie arrived home from school, full of excitement, carrying a folded piece of neon green fabric. Helsi stopped peeling potatoes at the sink and sat down on a kitchen chair. Rachel and Lucy ran into the kitchen to join the excitement.

Robbie unfolded the green pinny and slipped it over his head. He fastened the metal rings at each side of his waist, sliding the ties through easily as if he'd been practicing. He looked at his family with shining eyes.

"You look so official." Helsi smiled.

"What's that say?" Rachel pointed to the round logo on the upper right of the pinny's front.

Robbie lowered his chin as much as he could and looked down at the logo. He fingered the heavy embroidery. "CM, for conflict manager," he said, tracing the letters with his finger. He ran his fingers over the small writing that circled the CM. "Poore Pond School Conflict Resolution," he read with surprising accuracy and precise diction. Lucy and Rachel looked at their brother with awe-filled faces.

"I want to be a confit manger," Rachel said, looking at Helsi.

"We didn't have conflict managers when I was at Poore Pond," Lucy moaned. "You're lucky, Robbie."

Robbie beamed. He walked to the floor length mirror in the hall and admired himself. "When's Dad getting home?" he called to Helsi.

"Right about now," she laughed as Ian opened the side door. She stood at the sink and watched her husband and son.

"Hey! What have we here? A law enforcement officer?" Robbie ran to his father and hugged him. "Let me look at you." He held him at arm's length. Lucy and Rachel, now bored with all the attention their brother was getting, went back to their play.

Ian was amazed at how proud he felt.

"Dad, Dad, I know the ground rules now. We have to set down ground rules first. *No interrupting. No arguing. Wait your turn to speak.*"

'That's great, son." Ian sat down and hoisted Robbie onto his lap. Helsi returned to her potatoes.

"Dr. Fleming said you made a special trip to sign my permission form. She said I was lucky to have a father like you. She said it in front of the whole lunch line." Robbie put his forehead against Ian's chin. Ian swallowed.

"She did? Well, isn't that nice. You weren't embarrassed, were you?" Ian turned Robbie's small shoulders so he could face his father.

"No. I felt glad." Robbie put his lips to Ian's ear. He whispered, "I don't like it when you get mad at the principal. Dylan doesn't either. It makes us feel—you know— funny."

"OK, Son. Don't you think you should take off that uniform now, so you don't spoil it?" Ian said, aware of how unnatural his voice sounded. He lifted the boy off his lap and stood. Robbie went to his bedroom, unfastening the ties as he walked.

Helsi, adjusting the gas flame under the pot of peeled potatoes, looked warmly at Ian. She could see the discomfort in her husband's face. He walked over to her and they embraced. "You did a good thing for Robbie, Ian. Letting him join that program. I know it wasn't easy, worrying about him and all. I'm proud of you."

"What time's supper," he asked in a gruff voice.

"Thirty minutes," Helsi smiled.

"I'm going to the garage." He walked out, closing the door firmly behind him.

CHAPTER THIRTEEN—HOPE

Hope had stayed up late, baking date-nut bread. She wanted the teachers to feel appreciated and pampered at the meeting. She brought along cream cheese and several choices of juice. She laid out red poinsettia cloth napkins and placed the treats on matching place mats instead of the usual colored construction paper. Teachers praised Hope for the lovely spread as they eagerly helped themselves to refreshments before taking a copy of the agenda from the pile and sitting down at the table.

The December meeting of Poore Pond's grade-level chairpersons was called to order promptly at 7:45 A.M. in the library. The agenda was crowded with updates and reminders as well as decisions to make about Christmas sing-alongs and January conference schedules, keeping supplies purchasing within budget, and implementing the next phase of practice tests.

But the category called *OTHER* was likely to fill most of their time this morning. Hope had heard from the grapevine that staff members were divided over the mechanics of the academic-improvement plan. First-grade teacher, Trudy Cooper, leader of the opposition, was sure to bring it up.

Hope had learned to place category *OTHER* at the beginning of the agenda because it often ended on a negative note. It was important to her that closing discussions be kept positive, especially at morning meetings when teachers would carry their attitudes back to their classrooms. She wanted them to have issue-free minds to help them give their students an upbeat start to the school day.

Trudy was the first to comment after Hope opened the meeting. The faces of the other chairpersons showed tension the moment she began. Trudy, speaking for "first-grade teachers and a lot of other-grade teachers as well," contended that weekly progress checklists and class analyses should not have to be submitted to Hope; the teachers should be trusted to maintain them without supervision. Secondly, it was next to impossible to assess every child every week in reading progress, so how could they be expected to begin the same assessment schedule in math starting January 5th? Especially with conferences looming when the semester ended January 18th?

Tense discussion followed with second-grade chair, Katrina Davis, sharing Trudy's view on submitting weekly progress checks. Katrina spoke in an even voice, "That's not treating us as the professionals we are." Hope tried to make eye contact with Katrina whom she respected as an outstanding teacher and possibly the most consistently professional member of Poore Pond's faculty. Katrina did not look at her during or after her comment. On a more supportive note, she further explained that she understood the need to begin weekly math assessments on an individual basis and suggested the use of parent volunteers to help with that. She believed that math weaknesses were easier to diagnose, involving more concrete skills than reading, so it was not as necessary for teachers to conduct their own math assessments as it was for reading.

Good point, Hope thought, this time making successful eye contact with Katrina. Her eyes shifted to fourth-grade chairperson, Brad Kushner. She had been warned that he was in agreement with Trudy and planned to issue an ultimatum at the meeting. Brad was active in the teachers' association, serving as district elementary representative and as regional representative at state level. Brad returned her gaze, his face blank. Hope looked at her watch, which read 7:55.

Kindergarten teacher, Melanie Armstrong, looked at Hope with warm eyes. She spoke about the need to regularly assess reading and math skills in kindergarten because parents at that level were so anxious about their children's progress. "And we'd better know what we're talking about and in very specific terms." She spoke with the authority she had well earned as an outstanding teacher of reading and math readiness skills to five-year-olds.

"We know Dr. Fleming wants to follow how every child is doing—academically—." She interrupted herself with her hearty trademark laugh. "How often does she just happen to come in your classroom when you're doing large-group reading or math opening activities, to watch kids recite?" Several teachers chuckled. Trudy and Brad remained poker faced. "I'm sure reviewing our weekly checklists helps her stay current with individual students." She and Hope exchanged kindred looks.

Third-grade teacher, Pamela Thorpe, and fifth-grade teacher, Annie Klements, spoke about the importance of the assessments in this "age of accountability." Pamela, in pleasant voice, stated that assessing groups of three similar-level children at the same time was do-able with practice. Annie, in neutral tone, said her high-ability students needed regular assessment in the basics just as much as average students because some of them had poor retention of basic skills although capable of higher-level thinking. She felt students took the assessments more seriously, knowing that Dr. Fleming would be reading them.

Music teacher Carmen Ricci gave her view of reading and math skills going hand-in-hand with music theory skills, that each class complemented the other in developing those skills. Her vast experience in facing an audience showed as she unabashedly reminded her colleagues of extensive research proving that children exposed to regular music education, both theory and application, showed higher academic achievement across the board. "We know, we know, Carmen," her colleagues chided her for getting on her soapbox yet again.

Dave Myers, physical education teacher, emphasized the way his classes provided practical reinforcement of math skills through game playing and score keeping. The take-charge, no-nonsense manner he used with his students crept naturally into his voice.

Maddy Marenko, speaking softly, described the language reinforcement she provided in speech classes, also math reinforcement through board games as occasional rewards for good effort. Her expertise came through despite her reddening face and quiet voice.

Hope saw that Trudy and Brad were the sole dissenting members of the team although Katrina, in her own inimitable way, supported parts of both sides. She looked at her watch and wondered when Brad would drop his bomb?

"Before I forget, Hope," Carmen's clear voice chimed. "Mrs. Luther and Mrs. Franks—you know they're helping with costumes— said they and all the moms they talk to like the Christmas music. They think we should have traditional carols in our program, even if they are religious. Thought you'd want to know that." She smiled her winning smile, turning to flash it at her colleagues as well. Hope noticed that Trudy and Brad did not return the smile though others did.

"Well, getting back to weekly assessment. I just can't go along with all this busywork." Brad blurted the words as if they'd only just occurred to him. Hope noted that it was 8:35, leaving twenty-five minutes maximum for the rest of the agenda. She hoped he would not provoke a long debate. "I know what my kids are doing, in reading and in math and in every other subject. Why do I have to analyze progress reports for some dusty file at the Board office?"

"That's right," Trudy affirmed. "Nobody ever reads all those records we have to keep. Those analyses are ridiculous, like graduate-course assignments." She and Brad looked unsmilingly at one another. Hope felt creeping tension in the room. She took a deep breath.

Hope was about to tell Brad that Brian required only the quarterly progress checklists and analyses submitted to his office when Brad continued.

"I'm already spending five hours a week on individual reading assessment. Where am I going to get another five hours to do math assessments?" His voice rose as he finished his remarks.

"The checklists for fourth grade are longer, too. In reading and in math. More skills to cover. And the analyses take longer. First grade ones are short; I will say that." Trudy looked at Brad. Hope could feel the tension mounting further. "Why can't we just do the quarterly assessments as we've always done? Whose idea was it, anyway, to do weekly checks? And those silly analyses?" She looked at Hope with adolescent eyes blinking.

"They're written into our district continuous improvement plan," Katrina responded, taking Hope's words right out of her mouth. Katrina served on the district continuous improvement committee as Poore Pond's representative.

"Well, I think we maybe need to file a grievance to get this nonsense stopped," Brad dropped the militancy bomb Hope expected.

"You can't grieve adopted board policy, Brad," Carmen said. "Once it's adopted, it's official policy and procedure." Hope could have hugged her, the well-taken point was much more effective coming from another teacher than from the principal. As a standing member of the negotiating team, Carmen was knowledgeable in all areas of the teachers' contract.

"But——" Katrina paused for effect. "You can time-slip the extra hours you spend on record-keeping—that would be the analysis part—over and above your planning periods. That provision is built into the plan as well. So submit a time slip, Brad."

"Getting paid doesn't help me find the extra time I need to do the work," he said weakly. It was obvious to Hope that he had not known about the payment provision.

"Don't forget about volunteers," Katrina piped, directing her comment at Brad with warm eyes. He gave her a half-smile.

"Do you have those lists of parents willing to volunteer, Hope? You know, the ones we put out at Parents' Night?" Trudy surprised Hope with her on-board attitude change.

"Yes, I do have them, Trudy. I will ask Bella to publish a master list and get it out to each of you." Hope smiled, wanting to move forward.

"We don't necessarily have to use our own kids' parents as volunteers. They could be parents of kids in other classes." Annie smiled at everyone, reminding Hope of how congenial she always seemed.

"It would be better if the volunteers did not have a child in your class," Hope spoke clearly. "No risk of comparing her or his child with everybody else in the class. And, of course, you all know that we should hand-pick the volunteers." Teachers uttered agreement. "Most of our regular volunteers are quite savvy about confidentiality in the classroom. They respect the children's privacy. But we do have a few busybody types who can't resist spreading inside information in the gossip mill."

"Mrs. Weaver. Brittany Weaver." Several teachers chimed. Hope did not know that side of Mrs. Weaver, John and Monica's mother. She had impressed Hope as a very knowing person with high integrity.

Hope, thinking of Mrs. Billings, met Annie's gaze. She felt certain that Annie shared her recall of an angry Victoria Billings demanding the transfer of her daughter, Alana, from Annie's class to Marsha Klements' class the first month of school. Alana had complained of several classmates who were deliberately making her feel left out and unpopular. Mrs. Billings blamed the teacher for not taking steps to unify the class. A bewildered Alana, not expecting her mother to take such a drastic step, went quietly to her new teacher. A lovely child with high ability and low self-esteem, Alana had been recommended by fourth-grade teachers for Annie's class. Annie had a strong track record of successfully raising students' self-esteem.

"Are we getting back our test profiles to go over at conferences?" Pamela Thorpe asked, marking the end of the assessment debate as she referred to the next item on the agenda. Hope sighed with relief. She glanced at Trudy and Brad who looked down at their agenda copies as if ready to move on to the next topic.

The committee moved fairly smoothly through the agenda, stopping just before the practice-test item. The wall clock showed 8:58, and the teachers had to report to their classrooms. Hope promised to cover practice tests in a forthcoming memorandum and adjourned the meeting.

Carmen kept Hope with several questions about risers for the chorus and bell-choir performers.

The first bell rang as Hope reached her office. She stood by her door, still carrying the armload of leftover meeting folders and handouts, watching students file into the building. The outer office was busy with parents, teachers, students, and ringing telephones. Bella and Marie were handling everyone efficiently, the former glib and detached, the latter warm and nurturing.

"Andrew Billings—He's going on the field trip with Mrs. Klements' class—just say he's sick," Hope overheard a parent say to Marie Harris, the attendance secretary. Hope knew that Mrs. Billings was chaperoning her daughter's fifth-grade field trip to the health museum, which filled her with dread since the class would be experiencing human-reproduction lessons and exhibits. Less troublesome parents than Mrs. Billings occasionally disagreed with the way museum staff presented the sensitive subject matter.

Was she really keeping Andrew out of class to accompany her? And worse still, expecting the secretary to lie on the attendance record? She asked Marie if she had overheard correctly. Indeed she had, Marie assured her, her face full of disappointment and disbelief. Filled with dismay, Hope could feel her blood rushing. *I cannot let this go by.*

Hope walked outside where she saw a group of parents, waiting to board the field-trip bus. Mrs. Billings, a classically stunning blonde, was easy to spot. Hope approached her. "Please, Mrs. Billings, may I have a quick word with you? In my office?" Victoria Billings walked alongside her.

"It's nice of you to volunteer to help with the field trip, Mrs. Billings. I know how busy you are with your new job and moving into your new home."

"That's all right. I enjoy being with the kids," Mrs. Billings said assertively without smiling. Hope could not help noticing that she felt more uneasy than Mrs. Billings seemed. She recalled their previous confrontation with trepidation. The two women entered Hope's office; Hope closed the door slowly, summoning courage.

"Mrs. Billings," Hope began, speaking calmly and managing to hide the emotion she felt. "I can understand your wanting Andrew to accompany his sister on the field trip." Hope paused, breathing deeply as inconspicuously as she could. "But I know you as a caring parent. I know you do not want to send the wrong message to Andrew and Alana."

"What are you talking about?" Mrs. Billings asked in an edgy voice.

"Keeping Andrew out of class to go on Alana's field trip with you is not showing respect for Andrew's education or for the school. I know you do not want to do that."

"It is my prerogative to choose when my children are together for special activities. If I want Andrew with his sister, Andrew will be with his sister." She stared at Hope with cold eyes. "And it's not your place to tell me how to raise my children." She opened the door and strode out.

Completely wilted, Hope sat down in her desk chair. Looking into the outer office, she saw Bella's concerned face. She sank back into the soft cushion and stared out the window at the courtyard. She watched Shelton, the elusive turtle, sunning himself on a pond-side rock and was conscious of her good fortune in seeing him. Shelton's rare appearances were a popular topic around Poore Pond School. Shelton flexed his tiny limbs, stepped backward, then forward, plunging into the water as if rendering Hope's interest unwelcome.

Hope's thoughts returned to Mrs. Billings. I should have known better than to advise a woman like her, she chastised herself. Knowing how audacious she could be with school officials, it was foolish of me to try to appeal to her sense of rightness. I was criticizing her, and that was obviously all she heard. Of course, she had to save face. I know she has gone through a bitter divorce and "that can certainly spoil anyone's disposition," Hope spoke aloud.

And the subject matter, Hope lamented, realizing she'd had no opportunity to remind Mrs. Billings that human reproduction was not an appropriate topic for six-year-old Andrew.

"Dr. Fleming, we're here to read our stories to you," a pair of charming second graders suddenly bloomed in her office. A sturdy little red-haired boy in camping shorts and black running shoes handed her a note while a tall, pretty girl in pigtails and navy velour sweater and pants pulled a chair alongside Hope's.

"Alex and Jenna! You're just what I need right now; your timing is perfect," Hope chirped, resisting the urge to hug them. She looked up to see Bella at her door with a knowing look on her face.

"Thank you, Mrs. Kurowski, for sending them in." The secretary nodded.

Hope enjoyed hearing the children read their original stories, Alex's about a race-car driver and Jenna's, a child rock star. She welcomed the insight into their developing language skills. Both children waited patiently while she wrote brief comments on their papers and added fuzzy animal stickers.

As the children left, Hope noticed Mia Drake waiting near her door. She smiled and motioned her into the office. Mia had reservations about the upcoming field trip to city hall. They both sat down at the small table.

"I'm not sure the children have enough background for the field trip," she said. "We have not finished the city planning simulation, not even to the point where they understand the different jobs in city government." She looked at Hope, her palms raised to emphasize the dilemma. Hope looked at Mia's trustworthy face, reminding her yet again how fortunate Poore Pond was to have found such a capable substitute for Millie Blackwell. A veteran teacher, Mia had resigned from teaching to raise a later-in-life baby. Wanting to keep her hand in the profession, she had agreed to take the class the three half-days a week Millie needed off for treatment.

"What does Millie say?" Hope felt she knew the answer.

"Millie thinks the trip will be meaningful at any point in the simulation. I'm not sure—." Mia opened the folder she carried with her. She took out a hand-drawn diagram. "I made this diagram and color coded it." She pushed the paper toward Hope. Hope saw that the words *mayor, police chief*, and *fire chief* were written in red. There were other labels on the diagram written in pencil. Mia explained that the children had learned well, the work roles of those in red while those in pencil had been only touched upon in class by either Millie or her.

After some discussion, they agreed that Mia should focus on the building inspector's role before the field trip. That would help the children see one connection between city government and both homes and businesses, broadening their understanding of the concept of city.

"Millie is amazing," Mia said as she stood to leave. "She is so thorough with lesson plans, even has all the materials laid out for me each time I come. And small anecdotal information about individual children."

"Brian's on the phone, Hope," Bella called from her desk. "Says it's urgent."

"She knows those children well, doesn't she?" Hope stood. "She has been an inspiration to us all, the way she takes her treatments, then right back to work without missing a beat."

"It's good for the children, too. They don't seem so worried about her. Time to go. Thanks, Hope." Mia dashed off to pick up the children from music class.

"Good morning, Brian," Hope spoke into the receiver, picking up a pile of free-and-reduced lunch program applications to categorize while she listened to Brian.

"I don't want to alarm you, Hope, but there's been a terrible incident at a high school in Grove City, just down the road." Brian's somber tone gave her chills. She laid the applications on her desk, listening as intently as she could. "Are you there, Hope?"

"Yes. Yes."

"There's been a shooting. An assistant principal and a custodian. Man walked in off the street with a sawed-off shotgun. Assistant principal's dead; custodian's in serious condition." Brian's voice, though clear and even, echoed unmistakable pain.

"Thank God no children were hurt. Were they?" Hope felt desperate.

"Well, yes. Not badly. Two kids waiting outside the clinic were grazed by gunshots. They're not seriously injured. But traumatized, no doubt."

Hope moaned softly. She felt angry. She wanted to cry.

"It's still on tv." Brian said.

"Is the guy—the perpetrator, in custody?"

"Yes. A student on hall duty called 911 from his cell phone. Police came right away."

Hope felt sick. She wanted to vomit. She barely managed to hear Brian's instructions. She was to go personally to each teacher with a written message asking them not to leave the building unless absolutely necessary, during lunch or planning period until the end of the day. "Parents will be calling and coming in droves," he said. "We need all staff on site to help make everybody, parents and students, feel safe. There will be a security meeting right after school, as soon as you can get to the board office."

Hope replaced the receiver and sat, staring at it. She replayed in her mind, the entire conversation she had had with Brian. What if something like that were to happen here? At Poore Pond? She felt numb. She reached for a folded paisley shawl and tied it over the shoulders of her grey flannel suit. She stood and glided, trance-like, out of the office, meaning to check every classroom, every corner of the building.

Oh, the message to the teachers, she remembered, standing still in the rear lobby. She went back to her office and typed a succinct message on the word processor. She waited for it to print out, then gave it to Bella. "Fifty copies, please, Bella. Quarter-sheet strips. Colored paper. I need it ASAP." She could hear the phone ringing repeatedly. Bella nodded as she lifted the receiver.

"She's right here, George. It is George, isn't it?" Hope pointed to her office, walked to it, and closed the door.

"Hi, George Dear. It's good to hear your voice." She tried to muster cheer.

"Hi, Mom. I just wanted to see how you're doing.' I heard about the school shooting at Grove City. Isn't that just down the road from you?"

"Yes. Yes, it is. I only just heard. It's very unnerving.

"I can imagine. You're strong, Mom. You'll need to be for your people. They'll be frightened. All those little kids. How—"

"I know. I know. It all falls on me. But I'm frightened, too." Hope felt her eyes tear. She was grateful that George had phoned, but hearing his voice just now triggered in her ear, the voices of all 600 Poore Pond students, looking to her, pleading for reassurance. She could hear all the phone lines ringing at once in the outer office.

"It'll be OK, Mom." Hope was shocked to hear the emotion in George's voice. He really was worried about her.

"You have no idea how much it means to hear from you at this moment, George. Thank you, Son. See you Saturday? Same time same place?"

"Yeah, sure. I've got to go. Bye, Mom." Hope heard the dial tone. She stood and stared through the window at the courtyard, her subconscious noting the recurrent background traffic noises whenever George called.

"Here they are. Hot off the press." Bella handed Hope a neat stack of lavender strips of paper. She had typed the message in fourteen-point font, not exactly what Hope had in mind. It was too easy for young eyes to read if a teacher inadvertently left it in a child's line of vision. But there was no time to republish. *I should have specified.*

Hope grabbed her clipboard with the staff roster attached and set out to deliver the important word. She looked at the wall clock: 10:38. If she hurried, she could catch every teacher before lunch. Backing into her office, she stepped out of her black kid, French-heeled pumps and into the cordovan leather loafers under her desk, the better to speed down terrazzo floors. She headed to the kindergarten/ first-grade wing since those classrooms started first-lunch shift in about fifteen minutes.

A few teachers took the message subtly with expressionless faces, not missing a beat in their instructing. But most took time to read the message in front of Hope and the children. She watched each one as their faces grew ashen and they struggled to keep calm expressions for their students.

"Principals have a meeting on security right after school today," she whispered to each teacher, attempting to reassure them. "Please destroy this message before it's seen by students." Her lips formed a weak smile, but her eyes shone with fear. In each classroom she could feel the children's faces on her back, turned deliberately toward them for privacy.

Hope had seen every teacher except Lou Ann Newhouse whose empty room had caused Hope to ponder only a moment about leaving the message on her desk for her to find. Having thought better of it, she now circled back again to Lou Ann's room where she found her quietly grading papers at her desk while her students were in physical education class. Hope sat down at a child's desk near her and waited while Lou Ann read the message. It was a relief to have the children out of the room.

"Oh my heavens." Lou Ann closed her eyes and shook her head. "This is getting too close now. Those other incidents out west seemed so far away." Hope could see tears forming at her lower eyelids.

"Administrators do have a security meeting right after school today. I'm sure Brian and Ed are working on guidelines right now." Hope looked at Lou Ann and tried desperately to conceal her own naked fear.

"I hope the cafeteria staff can feed all of us," Lou Ann said, obviously trying to focus on a less-terrifying issue. "As you know, Hope, half the staff goes out for lunch most days.

"You're right, Lou Ann. I'll go see food service now. We might have to send out for pizza or something." She stood to leave. "Thank you for the reminder. Don't forget to destroy the message before your students return." The air was heavy with empathy each felt for the other. And for the children.

Holly Hapwell, PTA president, came through the main entrance just as Hope crossed the lobby. Her face looked drained. "Do you know about the shooting, Dr. Fleming?" Her voice echoed as she rushed up to Hope. Hope's eyes scanned the area for children who may be within earshot. "I'm sorry, I'm sorry," Mrs. Hapwell squeaked. "Is there a plan for situations like these? To, you know, keep the kids calm?" She whispered into Hope's face.

Hope reminded Mrs. Hapwell that the children would have no way of knowing about the shooting unless parents came into school and told them. But she secretly worried that the children would be sensitive to tension in the air and would surely notice the absence of the usual lunchtime comings and goings of staff members.

She also knew that visiting adults were likely to make comments about the shooting incident within earshot of students.

"Well, I'm sure more parents will be concerned and show up here," she aptly pointed out to Hope. "What can we do to help? Patrol the halls? Be visible?"

"Mrs. Hapwell, will you stay in the lobby and greet those parents who do come in; that is, those who come out of concern, with no other school business to handle? If you could keep them collected around this table here, so it looks as if you're just having another committee meeting. You would be on hand in case we need assistance, without behaving differently and alarming the children. Isn't there a PTA issue that needs discussing?" Hope was determined not to let the parents' concern cause disruption, but she appreciated Mrs. Hapwell's desire to help. She knew that the presence of extra, familiar adults in the building could be reassuring and that she or the teachers may need assistance.

"We're still deciding what to do about the Father/Daughter Dance, whether or not to have it. Charge for it. Limit it. We could meet about that." Hope looked at the PTA president with grateful eyes and smiled weakly. *Holly Hapwell is a godsend.*

Hope went straight to the servery. Spaghetti and tossed salad were the lunch menu. The kitchen manager thought there would probably be enough extra food for teachers. "I can add tomato, cucumber, carrots, ham maybe, to the menu salad for those who want a chef's salad," she said. "And we have a ton of bread sticks."

"That would be great," Hope said. "I'll ask Marie to make a quick menu sign for here. And I'll announce it —no, better not announce it for the children to ponder. We'll put quick signs in the teachers' lounges. Thank you, Helen. I'll try to get back here to help cut veggies." Hope dashed off to find Marie.

"I just want dismissal time to come," Hope thought as she stood in her office, trying to collect herself before supervising the lunch line. Get the children safely out of here and see what the administrators say at the meeting. *What a morning this has been.* She sighed and rubbed her temples. She could hear commotion in the primary wing and knew it was time for first lunch. She took a deep breath and walked to the rear corridor. Her empty stomach growled, but she knew she could not face food nor take time to eat.

The children, sweet tempered as usual, chatted with Hope as she supervised the lunch line. She savored the distraction, not allowing herself to think of them in terms of the tragedy at the back of her mind.

Taylor Pruett greeted her teacher, walking past with a lunch tray. "Mrs. Cantrell, you're eating lunch at school! You never do that."

Ali Cantrell's eyes met Hope's. "Well, sometimes I do, Taylor." Ali's natural smile shone at Taylor.

"May I help you in the room during recess, then?" Taylor's body wriggled with eagerness.

"Not today, Sweetie. I have a meeting with other teachers." Noting Taylor's exaggerated expression of disappointment, Ali said, "We'll do it another day. When we change bulletin boards. You're so good at that." She patted the child's shoulder and continued down the hall. Undaunted, Taylor ran to catch up with the moving line.

"Will you be in your office in about twenty minutes, Dr. Fleming?" Carmen Ricci, using the formal title in the presence of students, asked as she passed with tray in hand. "I need to tell you what my friend who teaches in another state had to say about the subject in your note." Carmen's eyes looked toward the second-and-third-grade students approaching the back of the lunch line.

"I'll be around. Either here or in the cafeteria, or my office. Just come find me." Hope found herself smiling easily at her charming colleague. *Carmen always takes a global view.* She felt grateful for her interest and input in total-school matters.

"Why aren't you wearing your high heels, Dr. Fleming?" Francine Hapwell's sweet voice rose above the din of the emerging second-lunch line.

Hope looked at her loafers, smiled at Francine. "To keep my feet from getting tired, Francine. I've done a lot of scurrying around the school today."

"I know. I saw you come to our room. With that purple message. What did it say?" Francine looked at her with innocent eyes.

"Just a matter for your teacher, Francine." She sighed. "Your cast is gone!" Hope exclaimed, successfully diverting her. Francine launched into a detailed description of the actual removal of the cast, undaunted by the frequent interruptions of other students in the line.

Third-lunch students, fourth-and-fifth graders, seemed quieter as they queued up near where Hope stood. *Or is it my imagination?* She noticed Alana Billings' guarded look when she asked how the field trip had gone. *Some parents have no idea how their lack of school support affects their children's emotional security needs.* She smiled widely at Alana. She kept smiling until Alana smiled back weakly, averting her eyes and following the line forward.

"Thank you for remembering the no-jacket rule in the lunchroom, Tommy," Hope said to tall, brown-haired Tommy Grant. "Are you and Anthony still being nice to each other?" Hope gave him her I-mean-business look. Tommy nodded yes, not dropping his eyes although she could see he wanted to. "Good for you and Anthony. If Poore Pond fourth graders don't stand by each other, who'll stand by them?" She smiled broadly at Tommy.

"Well, I'm in a different class now." He returned the smile slowly, shaking his thick, shaggy hair out of his eyes.

"Why is it indoor recess?" Tommy asked giving Hope only fleeting eye contact.

"Weather forecast. Possible storm." Hope looked toward the large window wall in the rear lobby, feeling a bit guilty. The sky was clear and the playground was dry. It was cold though, with borderline wind chill; so the judgment call could go either way in schools across the district. The storm forecast was for later in the day. She nodded to Tommy as he followed the line forward.

Perhaps, I'm wrong to have indoor recess. The children do need to get out and run. But I cannot bear to have them outdoors and vulnerable. Not today. Not after what happened in Grove City. She wanted to put them all in one room and keep them there with her until dismissal. But, of course, she could not do that. She could not wait to attend the security meeting. Her heart ached for answers.

*

A light snow fell on icy streets as Hope drove home in the early darkness. The meeting had been long. A feeling of utter despair had permeated it although she had found it comforting to commiserate with colleagues. As superintendent, Ed Amiston, knew that parents would need a forum in which to give input; he had spent the day fielding phone calls from anxious parents wanting to know what steps the district would be taking to prevent a Grove City happening in Salem Schools. He announced a schedule for parent meetings to be held next week at the three middle schools, each meeting including parents from elementary schools that feed into the respective middle schools. Ed required principals to definitely attend the meeting for their own buildings and encouraged them to attend every meeting 'to get a good sense of parents' issues and suggestions.'

"Make no mistake about it," Ed had said in a dire voice. "School security against this type of assault is going to change the way we operate on a daily basis. It will take more of my time and your time. Time none of us has to spend. But we must spend the time. Whatever it takes to make our students and their families feel that school is a safe place to be."

"And our staff members," Hope heard herself call out, remembering the distraught faces of her teachers when they first heard of the shooting.

"And, of course, our staff members," Ed echoed, looking at Hope.

Brian announced that elementary principals and parent-group representatives would be meeting with the local police department tomorrow morning, before school, so as not to leave buildings without administrators at this critical time.

Walking out of the meeting with fellow principal Belva Carmichael, Hope had expressed fear that they were venturing into unknown territory, that this defensive thinking would be leading them who knows where.

"I'm sure Ed has had feedback from school administrators in those western states where the other shootings happened. When he emphasized the time cost of all this extra security management and p.r. —you know a lot of it is public relations— he knew what he was talking about. "I don't think I've ever seen Ed so vehement." Belva said, meaning it.

"So much of our work is p.r.," Hope responded. "But this issue is such an emotional one, for us all. We can't afford to make mistakes, or panic will set in quickly." They agreed to meet for breakfast at 6:00 A.M. and said good-bye.

Hope noticed how lovely the snow-covered streets and lawns looked in the lamplight. She drove past Mill Pond Middle School, where Poore Pond students go, its white-blanketed campus the epitome of American suburbia, orderly and peaceful. The irony made her want to cry.

Trying to relax by the fireplace, gas logs burning invitingly, Hope sipped hot tea with lemon and pulled her red fleece robe close to her legs. She wanted so to let go of the trials of the day, but they kept intruding on her pleasurable thoughts, thoughts of George's phone call, his voice full of concern. She was touched.

Hope remembered that she had not followed through with Trudy Cooper's request for her to counsel Dylan Bradford on his attitude. She had promised Trudy she would come see Dylan in the classroom and observe his behavior during math and language. But she had lost sight of her promise. It was as if she had been glued to the phone; Brian rang three or four times with new information and instructions on what to say or not say to parents, staff, or students. A number of mothers and two fathers rang to voice their concerns and ask questions regarding how to talk to their children about the school shooting incidents, every phone conversation heavy with emotional undertones.

Draining her teacup, Hope made a mental note to observe Dylan in class first thing tomorrow morning. Thank God it would be Friday. A weekend is just what we all need, she thought.

*

Friday dawned brightly, sun shining on slight traces of new snow accumulation. Snowflakes shimmered in the sunlight, transforming bushes and picnic tables in the courtyard into fairy castles Hope enjoyed from her office window. She glanced at the headlines of the newspaper Ray had considerately left on her desk. She began reading reports of the Grove City shooting, complete with photographs of the victims, but soon turned away. She did not want to dwell on the tragedy; it was too debilitating. She needed to think of today as a normal day at Poore Pond.

Hope waited a few moments to give Mrs. Cooper time to get the class settled in before going down to observe Dylan. The buzz of the intercom intruded on her thoughts.

"Mrs. Bradford's on the phone, calling Dylan in absent, wants to talk to you about it." Bella's transmitted voice was matter-of-fact.

"Good morning, Mrs. Bradford. How may I help you?"

"Good morning, Dr. Fleming." Helsi said in a strained voice. "I need to talk to you about Dylan. He refuses to go to school today. Told me some disturbing things about yesterday."

"Yes, please go on, Mrs. Bradford. By the way, is Dylan listening?"

"He's downstairs watching cartoons," she said, letting Hope know they could speak freely. "Says he's sick. Says he spent almost the whole day in time-out yesterday. Even during afternoon free time." Helsi's voice grew shrill. "Do you know what's going on with Mrs. Cooper?"

"Did you get a note from her?"

"Not a word."

"Did you ask Dylan if his teacher gave him a note? He may have left it in his book bag. Children will do that. Their avoidance strategy. Do you want to check and ring me back?"

"Yes. Just give me a few minutes." Hope heard a dial tone.

When Helsi Bradford rang back, she told Hope she did find a note from Mrs. Cooper in Dylan's book bag. "Claimed he had forgotten to give it to me. The note said that Dylan had a bad day: poor choices, insubordinate. Showed unusual attitude. Asked me to contact her ASAP to arrange a conference."

"I must apologize to you, Mrs. Bradford, as I have to Mrs. Cooper. She asked me to come observe Dylan's behavior in class yesterday and talk to him. I never got there. The Grove City thing kept me chained to the phone."

"Why didn't she just send him to your office? Instead of humiliating him all day in front of the other kids?" Anger crept into Helsi's voice.

"I presume she was waiting for me to follow through but was considerate enough to be patient. She knew the turmoil we were in after the Grove City shock."

It's dubious that Helsi would understand the direct effect of that incident on our school; how could she? Hope immediately wanted to rephrase her comment in softer terms.

"Well, she wasn't very patient with Dylan, was she?" Helsi's escalating anger was apparent. Then abruptly, her voice warmed. "That was such a terrible thing. Grove City. Those poor children. And teachers. The principal. Custodian. Everybody."

"Yes, we are all feeling despair over it. We've never experienced anything remotely like it. There is a letter from the superintendent coming home today. He's holding parent meetings. Discussion forums." Hope dropped her voice, wanting to die rather than discuss Grove City another second.

"Maybe that's the real reason Dylan won't go to school. He's afraid," Helsi pondered. Seconds of silence indicated to Hope that she was awaiting validation of this possibility.

"Are you prepared now to set some tentative times you might meet with Mrs. Cooper and me?" Hope asked, reaching for the master schedule of teachers' planning periods. They agreed on three possible dates and times and closed when Hope promised to get back to Mrs. Bradford with confirmation. Hope, feeling reprieved, replaced the receiver.

Recalling Ed's caution about keeping all but the main entrance doors locked and television reporters trying to catch schools out in this respect, Hope set off anxiously to check all eight sets of outside doors. Her smiles and cheerful words were met in kind by individual staff members, students, and parent volunteers she encountered on her rounds. She was heartened to see that despair from the Grove City tragedy had not dampened the feeling of exhilaration that typically permeated the building on Fridays. *Ah, the strength of the human spirit.* She looked forward to lunch-time supervision with the children, always the bravest of little soldiers.

Trudy Cooper caught up with Hope in the afternoon, waving Hope's quarter-sheet goldenrod note. They agreed on a date and time to conference with the Bradfords.

"Something has to be done for Dylan," Trudy said, her troubled eyes underscoring the simple statement. "He simply cannot do first-grade work. His reading readiness skills are not there. He needs more tutoring than I can give him. His self-esteem is going down fast. I know that's why he's acting out. He sees the other kids completing work. Knows he can't do what they are doing. It's a no-win situation for him." She stopped to take a breath.

"Hopefully, the Bradfords will be open to our feedback. Do you think Dylan's ability may be lower than our tests indicated? Or does he just require more teaching time to master concepts?"

"He definitely needs more reteaching and more drill and practice. The few basic skills—all the consonant letter/sounds he's mastered—are ones that I personally have drilled him on repeatedly. And when I'm not working with him, I have him using every approach I can fit in: flash cards, manipulatives—you know, those Fun-to-Learn kits we made at the workshop, computer programs, audio-tapes, see-and-say bingo, peer partners, volunteer moms." Out of breath again, Trudy threw up her hands. Hope could feel her frustration.

"You've sent devices—games and kits, flashcards—home as well?" Hope asked, knowing the answer.

"Of course I have. But who knows how far they took them." She sighed and shifted her weight in the chair. Trudy took a deep breath. "Is there any chance we could put him back in kindergarten and," she paused for emphasis, "and get him one-to-one with Debbie in reading lab three or four times a week?"

"Well, having placed him in first grade is clearly not working. If we do a good job explaining that, in terms of very specific skill deficiencies, and the same with his escalating behaviors, maybe the Bradfords will draw their own conclusions. Suggest it themselves. We just have to be careful not to be seen as exaggerating the behavioral incidents. " Hope looked deeply into Trudy's eyes, wanting her to understand the fine lines to be tread, especially with Ian Bradford. Trudy did not drop her eyes.

Thinking aloud, Hope continued, "Perhaps we will want to present our observations, then bring Dylan in and try to elicit his view on how he's doing. Before we invite the parents to comment. Children often reveal profound judgments during such conferences, particularly with parents who have been in denial as has Mr. Bradford. But then, some children are more in touch with themselves than others are."

"I'm glad you're going to be there," Trudy said. "It will be a difficult conference. And Mr. Bradford scares me, the way he seethes."

"No educator ever died from exposure to seething parents, Trudy. You know that." They both laughed heartily, probably more heartily than the joke warranted.

Hope stood; Trudy followed suit. "Dylan didn't really spend all day in time out yesterday, did he?" Hope asked softly, her eyes warm.

"As a matter of fact, he did. Practically," Trudy remarked, undaunted. "Why? Did his mother tell you that?"

"She was quoting Dylan."

"That's why I wanted you to observe him. He had such attitude yesterday." Trudy laid her hand on Hope's arm. "Like nothing I've seen before from Dylan Bradford. At one point, when I reprimanded him for visiting other students during seatwork—for the twentieth time—he said, 'I'll just go to time out and stay there.' And he did. Took his books and papers and sat in the time-out corner the rest of the day. Of course, he was still up and down. But he kept going back to time out." She inched toward the door.

"What did the other children do?" Hope asked, remembering Helsi's complaint about humiliation.

"They didn't quite know what to make of it. Stared at him for awhile. Then just ignored the whole thing. They're probably still trying to figure it out." Trudy snickered and backed out of Hope's office with a small wave of her hand.

*

Hope and George sat in silence, not looking at each other. The bright white of the snow-covered landscape filled the large windows, lighting up the restaurant cheerily. All around them lunchers laughed and talked amid pungent aromas of spicy tomato sauce and freshly baked bread.

George, coarse woolen muffler still around his strong neck, toyed with his apple cobbler. Hope sipped hot coffee daintily, wanting to avoid further spills on her cream cashmere sweater. George scrutinized the list of specials clipped to a small, metal, tabletop stand. Hope looked out the window. *How can I break this tension?* She stole a look at her son's face, still indignantly set. She looked at his squarish hand on the table, so like Michael's. She remembered being strangely attracted to Michael's hands when she first met him. Honest, strong hands. Hands that took care of life's challenges.

"I've got to go, Mom. See you." George threw a crumpled ten-dollar bill on the table and rushed out, slipping his worn, grey duffel coat on as he walked. Hope, speechless, watched him go through suddenly tear-filled eyes.

Stubborn tears continued to flow for minutes—long minutes. Hope was unable to stop them. She dug in her black leather handbag for sunglasses and put them on, grateful that the tears were silent ones.

Bearing the pain, she tried to recall her entire conversation with George. Their meeting had begun with characteristic warm greetings and small talk, each just enjoying the other's company and eye contact.

It was during dessert when George was talking openly about how much he had learned of life, obviously proud of his personal growth. Hope was admiring how in touch he was with himself, his emotional strength and maturity.

That was when he dropped the bomb. No lead-in, no preparation, 'Mom, I have to tell you this and it's not pretty,' or some such warning. No. When she asked him if he thought living alone may have helped him discover himself, he simply said in an even voice, "I don't actually live alone, Mom. There are people all around me. I live on the streets. One of those homeless persons you read about." His eyes met hers fleetingly before scanning the other restaurant patrons in a show of nonchalance.

Hope remembered feeling paralyzed with shock. When George finally looked at her, his eyes reflected the horror he saw in her face. She had always been easy to read. "What did you say?" she shouted. "You live where?" She could feel the stares all around her. George looked uncomfortable. He pulled off his muffler.

"Homeless? How can you be?" she raged.

"Mother. Let's discuss this calmly."

George's use of the formal term was not lost on Hope. She grew more enraged. "Calmly? My only son—my only child—says he dwells in the street, with derelicts, druggies, and criminals; and I should be calm?" She was powerless to stop the flow of venom. "You were not raised that way, George Michael Fleming. You were raised with high standards, and you know it!" She felt the staring continue but did not lower her voice. The waiter came to ask if they needed assistance. He looked at George for direction. George gave the briefest of nods and waved him away.

"Mother, we are not going to have a big debate in this public forum. You know it's not your style, and it's not mine either. So stop." His voice low but knife sharp, he looked at her with the starkly serious face of his boyhood days. She felt like a chastised child. Too exhausted to challenge him, she accepted his parental approach and fell silent. She reached with trembling hand for the coffee cup, spilling the brown liquid down the front of her sweater.

Shaking as if to erase the memory, Hope took out her wallet and picked up the black leather folder containing the check. Her eyes rested on George's crumpled ten-dollar bill. She pulled out a ten and three one's to pay the $22.72 check. *Why did George leave that money? He's never done that before, all these weeks of our luncheon meetings.* She felt consumed with sadness. She stared at the crumpled bill, thinking it should be smoothed out. But she could not bring herself to pick it up. She pulled a twenty from her wallet and inserted it inside the folder with the three one's. She put on her camel-hair walking coat and left the restaurant.

Hope welcomed the soft, wet snowflakes on her cheek as she walked to the car. She steered the grey Volvo cautiously down the snowy streets, feeling suddenly chilled. She turned the heater switch to full power. She felt tense with anger and yet, overwhelmingly sad. Familiar feelings, they made her think of Mary Baldwin.

I've given everything to providing a proper upbringing for George: culture, intellect, elegance, she told herself. *At great risk. I could have gone to prison. If anyone ever audited Mary Baldwin's estate, I could have been found out. I needed that money. A scholarship was only the beginning. One cannot be a Vassar girl without the right clothes, the image. I wanted to give my child the best, the advantages the well-born enjoy, not the barely adequate upbringing I had.*

Suddenly, stopped cars materialized ahead of her. Hope slammed on the brakes, skidding sideways in the snow. She narrowly missed hitting the slick town car beside her in the turning lane, the driver shaking his head disgustedly at her. The red light seemed to jump at her from its post, demanding attention. Her entire body tense, she stared at it until it went green, thankful for anti-lock brakes. She heard the town car surge forward but did not look its way.

"Pompous ass!" she said aloud to the vacuum of the car's interior, resenting the way the driver made her feel. "Men," she spat the word. *Are they all out to demoralize me?* She tried to think of one man in her life who had not let her down. *Dad? Hah! He made such a miserable living with his pathetic little watch-and-jewelry-repair service. 'I have to be my own boss,' he always said when Mother would urge him to seek a better income.*

Michael? Hope continued the torturous analysis. *Turned out to be cold and insecure, resentful of my hopes and dreams, jealous of my achievements. And now George.* The tears started again. Still, she kept thinking dismal thoughts. *George? George is punishing me. For what, I don't know. Divorcing his father? Having fine expectations for him?* She tried to visualize his living on the street. She just could not reconcile the vision of her healthy, clean, intelligent son, with the street people she had seen, if only through her peripheral vision in the cowardly way most people sneaked looks at them. Unkempt, raggedly dressed, cloudy-eyed misfits she preferred be kept invisible.

Brilliant mid-day sun reflecting off snow-covered lawns blinded Hope's vision as she drove home, sobbing uncontrollably the entire way.

CHAPTER FOURTEEN—RAY

Ray sat at his dilapidated but freshly painted wooden desk. It was after ten o'clock when he finally found time for a break. He stared at the printed form in his hand, not knowing what to think. He had dreaded the performance review with Hope early this morning, but it had gone surprisingly well. Friendly and warm, she asked for his comments on every point on which she had rated him. She had marked him *Above Average* in nearly every area. Except two. He looked again at the *Outstanding* rating Hope had marked for the item: *Identifies with the school as an organization and works to improve total building conditions for the benefit of students, staff, and parents.* She explained that she appreciates the way he obviously feels a part of the school and tends to see the big picture. For example, his helping parents with stalled cars which "really saves the day for them and is good public relations for us." She particularly appreciates, she told him with earnest eyes, the way he employs some of the more-disruptive students as his maintenance helpers; thus, keeping them from the playground with all its potential for inciting them.

"The children are smart enough to know what we're doing, but they also know they are better off avoiding that entire recess scene. And they're happier for it, don't you think?" Hope smiled and looked at him as if he were the world's expert on unruly kids.

"We're all happier for it," Ray laughed. "I have those kids begging to help me, day after day, the same ones."

Ray enjoyed thinking about this part of his meeting with Hope. She had made him feel important and appreciated. He wanted to keep that feeling alive as long as he could.

His eyes moved to the item rated *Needs Improvement.* Hope had marked him down on this one: *Seeks opportunity for skill advancement,* because he does not attend workshops and seminars that she suggests, she explained. He had persuaded Rosie to attend the workshop, "Clean More Classrooms in Less Time." He had sent Marty to "Preventing Boiler Breakdowns," Hope reminded him.

He couldn't deny it. She was right. He just hated those seminars. They always gave him a been-there-done-that feeling. Or they taught some so-called scientific way to manage the ventilation system or whatever, nothing but textbook rigmarole dreamed up by college-educated maintenance "engineers" barely old enough to shave. He'd rather stay at school and do his work.

But at the same time, Ray did not like the look of the words, *Needs Improvement*. They stuck out like a red flag and spoiled the whole evaluation form.

Ray's eyes moved down to the *Additional Comments* section of the form. Hope had written: *Ray is working to build a memorial to a deceased Poore Pond student. I commend him for being a caring role model for the students, staff, and parents as well as a courageous example of spirituality.* He smiled to himself. This was another one of the good parts. He and Hope had made a shortlist of ideas for remembering Bucky Ames. And she had offered to find funding for the project. Ray grew excited just imagining the outcome.

A small knock sounded on the boiler-room door. He noted that today was Monday when Mr. Mathews' class presented their current issues, pretending to be newscasters. *It's about time for them to borrow the small lectern.*

Ray opened the door and saw a red-faced Heather Baker. She stood so close he could smell her gardenia perfume. "Ohh—Jeremy's moth—Mrs. Bak— Heather," he stuttered, stepping back. He felt himself grinning uncontrollably.

"Hi, Mr. Sellers," she said in a breathless voice as she shivered in a grey sweatshirt over a black turtleneck and grey sweatpants tucked inside short, black boots. "I just wanted to thank you for the stuff from St. Catherine's, the groceries and toys. Jeremy loved them, and I found these neat black boots." She looked down at her feet, her hair falling forward. Ray noticed black fur earmuffs underneath her thick, blonde hair and wondered why she wore no coat. She handed him a small package. "It's homemade pumpkin loaf," she said, smiling shyly. Jeremy and I love it. I wanted to thank you." She turned to leave.

"Oh, that's nice," Ray giggled, unwrapping the package nervously. The silly grin persisted. The russet loaf was still warm. "I'll have that for lunch," he chuckled, "with my coffee. Thanks, H—." He shook his head. "I never know what to call you. Mrs. Baker sounds too old for such a pret—young woman." Her eyes met his briefly before she dropped them.

"You can call me Heather," she said smiling toward the hallway.

"OK, Heather. Do you need another delivery? From St. Catherine's? Call me if you do." He wanted to keep her there.

"Not now. But I might later. Thanks. Should I call you here at school?" She began to relax.

"Sure. Or at home." He moved to his desk and jotted his number on the back of an envelope. "Here's my home number." He handed her the envelope. "Let me know if there's anything—"

"There is one thing," she looked him directly in the eye. "My sister's letting me have her old dryer if I can haul it myself. She got a new one. Mine died. Do you think you could haul it for me? She just lives over by the reservoir." Her blue eyes glistened.

"Sure," he laughed, delighted to be asked. "When?" He looked at the clock and saw that he was five minutes late starting lunch setup.

"I shouldn't bother you here. You're busy," she said, backing down the hall.

"Send me a note with your sister's address and what day you want to go." He followed her as she backed down the hall. She waved and turned to walk forward. Ray watched her walk, her trim derriere charmingly round under clingy sweatpants.

Ray enjoyed the quiet lunchroom, typical for a Monday when students seemed tired from the weekend. Jeremy Baker ate his lunch and rushed to help Mr. Sellers manage garbage cans. He loved pushing the cart that hauled the thirty-gallon cans to the boiler-room door. Jeremy dropped his eyes sheepishly when Ray mentioned his mother's pumpkin bread and how delicious it looked. "That sure was nice of your mom to give me that pumpkin bread," he said. Jeremy, unable to look at Ray, busied himself with out-of-kilter lunch trays. *I wonder if he can see how much I like her.* He took several wire twists from his pocket and asked Jeremy to tie the filled plastic garbage bags. Jeremy ran eagerly to the boiler room.

Ray passed the courtyard as he rolled the cumbersome mop bucket down the hall. He stopped and looked at snow-covered rocks around the small corner pond. Bucky helped dig that pond, he recalled suddenly. That's where his memorial should be! This pond has Bucky's name written all over it. He helped pull up the thick ivy. He dug for three days, never getting tired. He watched the nurserymen install the liner, barely containing himself until time to lay the large, flat, limestone rocks around the edge. He was way ahead of the other students and teachers who worked to turn the entire courtyard into a land lab. Every photograph of the work in progress had Bucky in it somewhere.

Ray grew excited again. He wanted to sit down and write a list of ideas for a memorial in the land lab. But he had to get back to the lunchroom and get it cleaned as soon as possible. Carmen would be trooping in with her recorders and microphones to set up for rehearsal. He would have to roll in the piano and whatever else she needed.

"Beautiful, isn't it?" Hope's voice from nearby startled him. He turned to see her standing there and immediately looked at her feet to see why he hadn't heard the tap of her low stiletto heels. She wore rubber-soled loafers.

"Uh-yeah. It's beautiful all right." He felt his face redden. "I was just thinking this courtyard would be a good place for Bucky's memorial," he explained, wishing he had a stronger case for being caught off task. But there was the mop bucket.

"Because of its beauty, its serenity?" Hope asked, looking at the mop bucket.

"That and the fact that Bucky did more work building this pond than anyone else." Ray explained Bucky's part in the project.

"We're not changing the land lab, are we?" Marsha Klements joined them. "My fifth graders do a science unit out there. Every fall we have water day. We like it just the way it is. Unless you were going to add a butterfly garden. We'd like that for our cocoon study in the spring.

"No, I was just thinking it would be the right place to put some sort of remembrance of Bucky Ames. Remember him? Fourth grader. Died of Batten Disease." Ray looked at Marsha.

"How long ago?" she asked with a frown.

"Three years ago, winter of 96/97." Ray swallowed and dropped his eyes.

Surprised by his exact recall, Marsha said softly, "I came to Poore Pond spring of 97, Ray. I didn't know Bucky." Her warm eyes met his. "But it's a great idea. A memorial in this beautiful little oasis." She turned and walked toward the lobby.

"We can get everybody's input, Ray. It'll be a school-wide effort, just like you described the land-lab project." Hope smiled. "Are we all set for Carmen?" He nodded and gestured toward the cafeteria. She nodded and left.

*

Ray carried the small ladder to the landing, opened it, and climbed up, light-bulb cartons bulging from his waist apron. He pulled out a screwdriver and unscrewed the glass ceiling-light cover. He heard the children's chorus singing sweetly from the lunchroom. He put in the new bulb, screwed shut the cover, and climbed down, closing the ladder and moving to another darkened light fixture. Melanie Armstrong came toward him, looking like a schoolgirl in navy cropped pants and a short red jacket. Ray noticed she wore navy leather platform shoes, nearly as high as Heather Baker wore.

"Do you have a minute, Ray?" Melanie asked, her voice uncharacteristically serious. Ray snapped the ladder securely open and turned to face her. Through tense lips, she said softly, "I heard you were planning a memorial to Bucky Ames, who died three years ago." Her eyes searched his. He looked at her, brow furrowed. "Well, I lost Colin French the year before that. To leukemia. And we never did a memorial for him. I don't think it's fair. Even if he was just in kindergarten," she said, meaning it.

"Oh, well—we were just talking about a memorial. Nothing's definite. I just told Hope it would be nice..." Ray's voice faded.

"I guess it's really not your problem. I'll talk to Hope about it." She turned to walk away.

"Yeah, talk to Hope about it. We'll work something out." Ray called to her back, stepping onto the ladder. *Good grief. How did word get out already? Marsha must've gone right around broadcasting it.* He began to remove another light cover. The screwdriver kept skating out of the screw from Ray's too-tense hand pressure. *Dadgummit. Politics again. Who would've thought that something as innocent as a memorial would stir up the troops.*

*

"Hot dog!" Ray said aloud as he pulled in the driveway and saw Aunt Patsy's red compact car. He hadn't seen her since his mother's birthday bash when she had, to his great relief, said nothing further about his bad attitude.

"Well, look who's here!" Aunt Patsy smiled as he came in the door. They hugged soundly. Ray removed his wool jacket and joined her at the table. He smelled seasoned roast beef cooking in the oven and realized how hungry he felt.

"Hi, Mom," Ray said as Caroline came up from the basement, carrying a bowl of raw potatoes. Her face was deep red, and she was out of breath. She sat down at the table.

"Why didn't you ask one of us to get those, Ma?" Ray looked at her, his eyes full of concern.

"Oh, it's nothing," she said not looking at him.

"Caroline's got that Weyand stubborn independence, Ray. You know it runs in the family." Aunt Patsy laughed. Caroline laughed, too; and they began one of their giggling spells. It always cheered Ray to see his mother and her little sister having fun together.

Aunt Patsy offered to peel potatoes, but Caroline insisted on doing them herself, placing a saucepan on the table and sitting down to peel. Ray's eyes met Aunt Patsy's; neither of them had ever seen her peel potatoes anywhere other than the sink.

"Ray and I will keep you company, then." Aunt Patsy smiled at Ray. "So what's going on at that school on the pond?" she asked, poking Ray's elbow. Ray told them how busy he was with music rehearsals, snow removal, and all. He brought up Bucky Ames and the memorial. He told them about his idea to memorialize Bucky in the land lab, that he was trying to think of ways to do it.

"You could plant a nice tree in his honor," Caroline offered, "with his name engraved on a brass plate."

"How about a statue of a child, a boy? You know, those cast ones you find at garden stores?" Aunt Patsy added.

"It needs to be something that can withstand all kinds of weather," Ray said. "I was thinking a flower garden, maybe, with bulbs and perennials, something like that." The three of them talked at length about possible memorials. Caroline asked Ray to explain to Aunt Patsy about Bucky, how he died. Both women listened intently as Ray went into great detail about Bucky's antics and how hard it was to watch him get sicker and sicker.

"Rayley always did have a tender heart," Caroline looked at him with adoring eyes. Ray's face reddened; he shifted his weight on the hard wooden chair. He told them about the kindergarten teacher's resenting the memorial for Bucky. Both mother and aunt told him not to worry; it would all work out.

During roast beef and mashed potatoes, the conversation returned to memorials. The three of them agreed that any memorial should honor both Bucky and the kindergartner and include provision for, God forbid, future memorials. A park bench was suggested, as was a sturdy wind chime.

Aunt Patsy insisted on washing countertops and stovetop while Caroline loaded the dishwasher. Ray, feeling peaceful and content, swept the front walk in the sharp winter air, fretting about his mother's unusually loud breathing and obvious fatigue.

Tuesday morning Jeremy Baker came to Ray's boiler room and handed him a folded paper. It was a note from Heather asking him to meet her between 4:30 and 6:00 at her sister's house at the corner of Lake and Grove Roads. She would be watching for him.

Ray, from the moment he read the note, looked forward to going to Lake and Grove Roads. Every time he thought about seeing Heather, his heart raced. He dialed his house to tell Caroline he would be late getting home. The phone rang and rang.

While shoveling snow, he saw Heather's sweet face. Then his mind heard the ringing of the unanswered phone, echoing through his house. His thoughts kept returning to those two visions as he finished lunchroom setup.

When Jeremy and a classmate reported to him to help, he forced himself to focus on directing them. Not feeling up to chit-chatting with them as he usually did, he gave the boys spray bottles and cloths and assigned them the job of cleaning finger marks off lunchroom windows.

After trying several times to reach his mother, Ray asked Bella to keep trying and give her the message once she reached her.

By mid-afternoon Ray began to worry about his mother. He thought about calling his sister but did not want to hear her complaints. Imagining the worst, he ruled out calling one of the neighbors. If Caroline were in real trouble, he knew she would want a family member with her. He had visions of her falling down the basement stairs. Finally, he called Aunt Patsy at work; and she agreed to go check on her sister. Needing to move about to deal with his apprehension, Ray made rounds to refill paper-towel dispensers.

"Ray Sellers, to the office, please," Bella's smooth voice came over the speaker, interrupting Carmen's rehearsal. Ray walked briskly to the office with pounding heart.

*

Caroline lay still as stone under the white sheet, oxygen mask covering her ashen face. Claire kept fussing with linens on the narrow hospital bed. Ray paced the floor. Aunt Patsy sat in a chair at the head of the bed, holding Caroline's limp hand. Everyone was silent.

"It's 6:30, Ray. Isn't that when Mom takes her heart medication?" Claire's voice broke the silence, startling him. He looked at his sister, his face blank.

"Honey, the doctors here are medicating her, probably different medication," Aunt Patsy said, looking at Claire with warm eyes. Claire burst into tears.

"Stupid me. I know that." Claire shook her head. "I'm just not thinking straight."

"None of us are, Honey," Aunt Patsy said in her soothing voice. "We're all so worried about Caroline."

Ray had not seen his sister cry since she was twelve; he felt he should go to her and hug her or something. But his feet remained planted to the floor. "Six thirty?" he thought, suddenly remembering his appointment with Heather between

4:30 and 6:00. For a moment he felt torn between rushing over to Lake Road at Grove and staying with his mother.

"Anybody want a cup of coffee?" He announced, desperate to busy himself. To his delight, both women said yes. Ray headed toward the elevator. He brought back four styrofoam cups of steaming coffee, "One for Mom, in case she wakes up," he explained. Claire looked at him with wild eyes. Aunt Patsy smiled.

*

Ray pushed the clumsy vacuum cleaner down the dark corridor to Hope's office. He felt himself moving stiffly this morning. Slowly and deliberately, he began vacuuming the tiny office. He moved chairs and vacuumed carefully under them. He vacuumed as far as he could reach under Hope's heavy wooden desk, knocking a folded newspaper off a pile near the corner. He stooped down to pick it up, glancing at the blue-shaded logo. He read the large-print heading: *THE HOMELESS GRAPEVINE*, his eyes shifting below to a blurred photograph of a weathered face with intense eyes, wearing a thick knitted cap. Faintly curious about Hope's interest in a street publication, he replaced it on the pile atop the desk. "She is kind of a bleeding heart," he thought, recalling her genuine concern for Heather Baker's plight several weeks back. "Her eyes got a little misty, too, when I told her about Bucky," he said to himself, dragging the vacuum cleaner through the door.

"Good morning, Ray. We missed you yesterday. How's your mother doing?" Hope approached him from the outer office.

"She's doing OK, I guess. As well as could be expected." He shrugged his shoulders. "Thanks for asking though. You're here bright and early." He smiled slightly.

"As are you," she said with a wide smile. "Of course, neither of us has any reason to have trouble sleeping, do we?" Ray's eyes widened and he dropped his chin, agreeing. "Is your mother still in the hospital?" Hope looked concerned.

"She'll be there probably the rest of the week, doctor said. Makes her mad as sin, too. She wants to go home. Giving those nurses a hard time about it. Doesn't want them all waiting on her." He chuckled.

"What is her prognosis, Ray?"

"Well, as I understand it, her heart just slowed down. Doctor said it's early stages of congestive heart failure. She has to rest and eat right. Then gradually build up to an exercise routine, walking—nothing strenuous though." He took steps forward.

"Well, she's a strong woman, from what you've said. I'm sure she has the right attitude to get better. Let me know if I can help in any way, Ray." Hope looked at him with earnest eyes. He walked away.

"Oh," he said, backtracking, vacuum cleaner trailing behind. "Did Mrs. Baker—Heather—come in here yesterday looking for me? I was supposed to haul a dryer for her Tuesday night." Ray tried to keep his voice even.

"No. No, she didn't. And Jeremy was absent yesterday. Bella tried all day to reach them for absence verification. I'm anxious to see if he comes today. Sure hope nothing is wrong." Again, concern clouded her eyes.

"I feel bad, you know. I stood her up. Just didn't get there, what with Mom going to the hospital and all. I could help her today if she wants me to." He felt an uncontrollable urge to grin, stifled when the thought struck him: how could he manage to help Heather and visit Caroline as well.

"Do you want us to give her that message if we hear from her?"

"That would be a help. Thanks." He started off again.

Back in the boiler room, Ray stood staring into space. He could not think what his next task should be. Normally, he had a mental list of priority tasks for the morning and another list for the afternoon. He pushed the vacuum into the storage room and looked around. He picked up a red resin chair back on his workbench and examined it, remembering that it had come loose from its metal frame. He looked around for the frame, practically stumbling over it on the floor under the bench. He lifted the child-sized piece to the work surface, took a cloth and dusted the still-attached seat. He pulled four large-headed screws from a jar and began to reattach the chair back. He noticed how slowly and deliberately he moved but seemed unable to change to his customary faster, smoother pace.

"Hello, Handsome," Bella's clear voice echoed through the cavernous boiler room as she entered. "Have a message for you." She smiled and handed him a note written on pink message-pad paper. Ray returned the smile and read the note: *Hether Baker spoke to Hope. Evicted from her apt. Won't need dryer. Thanks anyway.*

He looked at Bella. "She finally called Jeremy in absent," she said. "What were you doing? Free hauling for her? Wouldn't have anything to do with how hot she looks in those mini-skirts and platforms, would it?" She laughed heartily. Ray felt his neck redden and turned away.

"It might," he said weakly, unable to think of a snappier comeback.

"That's what I like: an honest man." Bella walked away, giggling.

Ray, wanting to be alone with his thoughts, was relieved to see her go. Heather. He wanted to think about Heather. He had missed an opportunity to be with her, help her. *Evicted? She's been evicted? Where will she go? What about Jeremy?* He found these thoughts unbearable.

Back at the workbench he resumed work on the chair. He thought of Claire's old bedroom at home, unused except for storing the ironing board. He thought of Caroline's bedroom, now empty for who knows how long.

He wished the doctor would call him about Caroline's progress. He had left two messages with the receptionist this morning. He could still see her in the hospital bed, looking smaller than usual in gaping hospital gown, wires and I.V. coils attached to her body. Her usually resonant voice sounded weak when she spoke.

I'll take her a copy of the Enquirer when I visit the hospital today. She loves to read tabloids.

"Mr. Sellers," two students stood at his open door, knocking softly on the frame. They carried stacks of folded art paper. "Our class made cards for your mother," a dark-eyed, ten-year-old girl with heavy bangs almost to her eyes said. "Mr. Mathews told us she's in the hospital." She smiled and held out the bundle of cards. Ray was touched.

"Well, thank-you," he said, returning her smile. A tall boy, same age, with closely cropped hair, medium brown except for a bowl-shaped, bleached patch on top, handed him a second bundle.

"Our class made cards, too," he explained. "Miss Klements teaches art to both our classes." He smiled a crooked smile.

"Trevor? Is that you with that funky hair?" Ray laughed, recognizing the boy as one of his frequent helpers a year or two ago.

"Yes," Trevor responded, laughing with him.

"I can't believe you wear your hair like that. You were old stick-in-the-mud when you worked with me. Always doing everything by the book. Remember? " Trevor grinned widely. "Yeah. I used to worry a lot. About getting in trouble and everything."

"You're older and wiser now." Ray said. Trevor nodded. "Well, I sure do appreciate you kids thinking of my mom. She'll be tickled to get these cards. Thanks, again." The two students left happily.

Ray glanced at the clock and saw it was nearly time to set up for lunch. But first he wanted to ask Hope if she had more information about Heather and Jeremy. He walked to her office and saw the door closed. He sauntered past the corridor window that looked into her office; she was seated at the table with a man in a business suit. He headed back to the boiler room and rolled out the four-wheeler holding three large garbage cans. He went into the lunchroom and began folding down tables from storage frames on the wall. *I'll try to track Heather down later.*

Ray looked again at the clock and wondered if his mother were eating lunch right now. He hoped he heard from the doctor before he went to the hospital. He did not want Claire to know more about their mother's condition than he did. She would throw it up to him.

After the lunchroom was vacated and cleaned, Carmen's rehearsal gear set up, and Ray's own lunch finished, he tried again to catch Hope. She was seated at her desk, office door open, reading a thick pack of stapled paper.

Hope explained that Heather had said she was staying with her sister for awhile and would try to get Jeremy back in school by Monday. She had told her there was just too much to do, and Jeremy had to help.

Ray spent the afternoon inventorying on-hand supplies before completing a purchase order. He listened to the student rehearsal, sweet, clear voices spilling into the corridors. The holiday music made him think of Heather and Jeremy. "What kind of Christmas are they going to have?" he thought. In between inventory tasks, he fretted about how to get in touch with her.

Ray walked past the cafeteria enjoying the rising volume of children's singing as he came closer. He remembered he had promised Marla Sutton he would put the artificial trees in front and rear lobbies for the mitten drive. He would do that after he finished the inventory. Knowing Marla, he was sure she had already lined up students to announce this afternoon the start of the mitten-tree collection.

The clinic was empty except for Elaine Sunfield, the school nurse, who was at her desk writing entries in green folders. Her salt-and-pepper pageboy hair fell over her care-worn face. "How many refills of disinfectant do you have, Uh-laine," Ray asked, catching her by surprise.

"Oh! Well, let's see." She chewed on her pencil and looked around the room. "Where did I put them?" Ray's eyes scanned the room along with hers. He noticed the black binders, grade-levels printed neatly on the spines, shelved above the phone. The pink forms. He knew they contained personal data on every Poore Pond student. "Oh, I know. I put them in the storage cupboard back of the office. When I reorganized this clinic. After you moved it all around to strip the floors. I'll just go count them." She rose from her chair. "Be right back." She hurried out the door.

Ray went immediately to the third-grade binder and searched nervously for Baker. He found Jeremy's page and noted the names of other people to contact if parents were out of reach. *Hannah Walsh, aunt.* There it was. That must be Heather's sister. He quickly jotted down the phone number on a square of scrap paper, stacked neatly next to the phone. He replaced the binder on the shelf just as Elaine returned.

"Two-and-a-half bottles," she announced from the door. "Next time, could you get the scented kind, pine or something? This unscented stuff smells so strong. The children always comment and hold their noses after I sanitize the cots and things."

"I'll try," Ray said, feeling uncomfortable about his secretiveness. "Thanks for your help, Uh-laine." He left the clinic, nearly bumping into a tiny, blonde boy, holding his bleeding thumb stiffly and crying wildly. "Excuse me, Sport," he said as he deftly dodged the sturdy little figure.

Back at his desk Ray dialed the number scrawled on the scrap of paper. He recognized Heather's little-girl voice when she answered the phone and felt his heart race.

"Mrs. Bak—Heather? This is Ray. Ray Sellers." He spoke loudly to be heard above blaring television intruding from the background.

"Oh, Mr. Sellers. From school. H-hi." Silence. "How are you?"

"Fine. Hop—Dr. Fleming told me you're having a few problems. You moved?" Silence.

"I was just wondering if you needed any help or anything," He began to regret making the call.

"N-no, not that I can think of right now. Don't you—isn't your—is your mother still in the hospital?" Her voice faded.

"Yeah. She'll be in for awhile."

"I'm sorry to hear that, Ray," she said, more responsively.

"Can you and Jeremy come to my house for dinner. Tonight?" he asked, shocked by his own words.

"Tonight? Your house?" she asked incredulously.

Ray explained that he would pick them up and drop them off; and after covering the receiver while conferring with her sister, Heather accepted the invitation.

"OK, then. I'll pick you up at 5:30. Bye now." He hung up the telephone with pounding heart. He sat at his desk, staring. *Where on earth did that invitation come from?* He had given no conscious forethought to such a preposterous idea. *Obviously, I can't trust myself where she's concerned.* Helpless to stop thinking of her, he reviewed every encounter he had had with her: her curvy figure in tight jeans, those remarkable legs in a miniskirt. Even sweatpants did not disguise her charms. He could smell her flowery scent, hear her sweetly innocent voice.

He looked at the clock. Scarcely half an hour until dismissal time. Where had the time gone? His heart felt so full he could hardly breathe. Needing air, he put on his wool anorak and gloves and went outside early to head off impending traffic problems in the parking lot.

He felt a cold blast of air when he opened the door. It was just what he needed. He took a deep breath to keep excitement from getting the best of him. The parking lot was fairly empty, only three cars, all with parents behind the wheel, waiting for the bell to ring. Two yellow buses had taken their places in the curbside bus lane; the two drivers congregating in the front bus while idling diesel engines sputtered clouds of fumes in the frosty air.

"What'll I serve for dinner?" he asked himself. "Take-out? Ma's leftovers? What's in the freezer?" His mind flitted. He tried to remember the last time he had attempted to prepare a meal. It had been twelve years ago, after Caroline's knee surgery. He'd made macaroni and cheese from a box and hot dogs. She had fussed about it as if it were fine cuisine. But Ray knew it was substandard. He knew box macaroni and hot dogs were out of the question tonight.

He decided to stop at the superstore deli and buy something already cooked. Something nice like lasagna or roast chicken. He would have a short visit at the hospital, then stop at the deli and go set up at home, just in time to pick up his guests by 5:30. He would have to hurry.

*

Ray could hear Claire's strident voice as he neared his mother's room. *Drat! That doctor never got back to me.* He carried two women's magazines under his arm, but not the tabloid he had wanted to bring since he forgot all about it until he arrived at the hospital. The gift shop had no tabloids. He felt tension take over his body as he walked into the room, the slick magazines sliding to the floor.

"Hi, Ma, how are you feeling?" He bent down and gave a hugging motion to her shoulders. "Glad to be rid of that oxygen tube?"

"Hi, Rayley," she beamed up at him with watery eyes. "Sit down." She gestured toward the armchair.

Ray stooped to pick up the magazines. "I wanted to get you an *Enquirer*," he apologized, handing them to her. "But I didn't have time to stop." He could feel Claire's eyes burning his back and swallowed, not looking at her.

"Thanks, Son. That's all—"

"Didn't have time?" Claire, interrupted, looking at him incredulously. "Where're you going? Got a hot date?" Her voice dripped with sarcasm.

"As a matter of fact, I have," Ray kept his voice strong and looked her in the eye.

"Who with, may I ask?"

"A new girl I met. At school."

"Not a twelve-year-old, I hope." She smirked and looked at Caroline.

"I'll just pretend you didn't say that, Claire." Ray wanted her to feel ashamed. Distress clouded Caroline's eyes. She lifted her white hand in protest. "Please, stop. Don't fight. I can't...," her voice trailed off.

Claire rushed to her mother. "I'm sorry, Ma," She dropped her eyes. "Ray." Her shoulders drooped. To Ray, she looked defeated. He didn't like seeing his overbearing sister lose her fight. He wasn't used to it. She looked pitiful.

He just wanted to go get ready for Heather and Jeremy. But he forced himself to go to Claire and hug her. She looked away but hugged him back, hard. It felt good, Ray thought. He looked at Caroline's face, lit with joy.

He broke out of the hug, "We better quit this; we're really scaring Ma now." He laughed. Claire laughed with him. Caroline smiled.

"You two go get a bite to eat," Caroline said, her voice faint. "You must be starved."

"Good idea," Claire said quickly and looked at her brother. "How about a little fast food? I'll treat."

Ray looked at the clock. It was already 3:55, and he had to stop at the deli and get set up before leaving at 5:15 to get Heather and Jeremy. He looked at his sister, her face full of anticipation. "OK," he said. "But I've only got about twenty minutes. It has to be really fast, fast food." They walked out laughing.

                                                    *

Ray took a last look at the table before leaving. It was all set with Caroline's company dishes, white ironstone, laid on her pale blue plastic mats. He had folded white paper napkins, the thick ones he had seen his mother use for guests. He smelled the deli lasagna warming in the oven and hoped he had it at the right temperature. He had taken the rose-colored glass votive candleholder Caroline kept on the mantel and placed it in the center of the table. *Looks pretty good, if I do say so myself.*

Ray looked at the clock: 5:25. He pulled the scrap of paper from his pocket and dialed Hannah's number. When she answered, he asked her to tell Heather and Jeremy he would be a few minutes late. He ran across the porch, down the steps, and into the van.

*

Ray rinsed the last dish and placed it in the musty-smelling dishwasher. He wondered why Caroline never liked to use it. He dumped leftover apple juice from tall water glasses and placed them in the dishwasher. He rooted around under the sink for dishwasher soap and found a green box of powder. Shaking the box to loosen the lumpy granules, he filled the small cup in the open door of the dishwasher, locked the latch, and turned the dial to ON. He heard the motor lurch, then the sound of water rushing.

He went to the refrigerator and removed the half-piece of chocolate eclair that Jeremy was not allowed to have. Heather had insisted Ray give him only half a piece because of all the sugar and fat. She, however, had eaten a whole one, as had Ray. He poured himself a glass of cold milk and took a fork from the cutlery drawer. He sat down at the table, and savored the rich pastry. He had hardly tasted the eclair he'd eaten earlier with his guests, his stomach was churning so. The rich cream filling caressed his stomach, adding to the warm glow he felt from being with Heather. It had been a lovely evening. The lasagna, though somewhat dry, was tasty. The deli Caesar salad, pathetically limp, tasted all right. The dinner rolls were just perfect, crusty on the outside, soft on the inside. Jeremy had eaten four. Both Heather and Jeremy had eaten heartily, causing Ray to wonder how many meals they had missed.

I'm glad I had them here tonight. I don't know if Ma or Claire, for that matter, would want me to. But I'm glad I did. It was nice. Maybe I'll do it again sometime soon. What they don't know won't hurt them.

CHAPTER FIFTEEN—IAN AND HELSI

Early for his appointment with Hope, Ian waited on the oak bench. He looked at the smallish artificial Christmas tree nearby, covered with colorful mittens, gloves, hats, and scarves. He recognized the pairs of mittens and gloves that his children had chosen when he took them to SaveMart. *That's a good thing to do for needy kids.* He felt grateful that his own children were donors, not recipients, of the warm clothing. *I can certainly afford to buy my family what they need to keep warm.*

"Dr. Fleming will see you now, Mr. Bradford," Bella materialized in front of him. She led him into the principal's office. Hope greeted him warmly and offered her hand. Ian shook it firmly and sat in the chair she offered.

"It's good to see you, Mr. Bradford. Thank you for coming in so we could discuss your concerns. I know how busy you are, but face-to-face discussion is so much better than on the telephone. We do have our meeting about Dylan set for next week, but today you want to talk about Robbie."

Ian, leaning forward, looked at her. "Like I said on the phone, Doc, Robbie's having a great time being a conflict manager; and he's good at it, as far as I can see. But he's getting behind in his work, and that comes first." He sat back in his chair.

"You're right; Robbie is one of our best conflict managers, reliable and calm. But you think he's not finishing class work during in-class study time? What does he give you as a reason?"

"Well, he must be talking about work done in class. We always see that he gets his homework done. Says the teacher calls quitting time before he's barely even started. And they go on to science or social studies or something." Ian looked at Hope with worried eyes. "You know, schoolwork has never come easy for Robbie. He's always trying to catch up. He can't go on being a conflict manager if his work's not getting done."

Hope glanced at the group photograph of smiling, proud conflict managers on her desk. "I understand, Mr. Bradford." She looked into his eyes in that unflinching way she had. He turned away. "So please let me clarify your point. You think

time spent on conflict management: meetings, duty, et cetera, infringes on Robbie's
study time? Time he would normally use to catch up on his work?"

Ian shifted his weight in the chair. "Exactly," he said, trying hard to suppress
the old belligerence he once relied on to control school situations.

"We really need the teacher's input here, Mr. Bradford. How's your time?"
She glanced at the wall clock.

"It's all right. I want to get this resolved."

"Excuse me a moment, please." She stepped out of the office.

Ian tried to remember precisely what he and Helsi had discussed. *Was it a
case of Robbie's wasting time in class or not getting a chance to make up work
during recess?* He could not remember the details. He remembered only that
Robbie was not getting his work done. *What's keeping her?* He scrubbed his
hands, rapidly losing patience.

Hope returned with a warm-faced youngish woman in a soft, long, flowered
skirt and dark blazer, introducing her as Mrs. Drake, Mrs. Blackwell's substitute.
"You know that Mrs. Blackwell is undergoing medical treatments, so she needs to
be away from time to time?"

Ian nodded. "Yes. I was sorry to hear. She's really something, the way she
gives the kids those great rewards—incentives she calls them, I believe. Robbie
was so excited about going to the circus with her and her husband, all he wanted to
do was practice reading that book." He looked at Hope and Mia, laughing with
pleasure. "Is it true that she rewards every child in the class like that? And it
works; they all get a great treat like Robbie did?"

"Yes, it's true. And every one of them masters reading of Book I by the end of
term. Of course, the incentives are really special. And she pays for them out of
her own pocket. With a little help from the parent group this year, for the first
time." Hope turned up her palm. "It only goes to show what children can do when
they buy into the stakes."

Ian nodded. "How is she doing?"

"As well as could be expected, I believe," quickly adding, "We are fortunate
to have Mrs. Drake. And she is working closely with Mrs. Blackwell." She looked
at Mia Drake.

"Yes, that's right, Mr. Bradford. Millie—Mrs. Blackwell— keeps me in touch
with individual needs of students. She knows Robbie very well and told me I must find
creative ways to give him one-on-one help as well as extra time to complete work."
She smiled at Ian. He smiled back. "That's what I'm trying to do." She laughed.

Hope sat back as Mia and Ian analyzed Robbie's particular problem. Ian
noticed that she smiled proudly when Mia described Robbie's genuine effort in
class. But when Mrs. Drake said that conflict management was possibly too much
responsibility for a struggling student like Robbie, Ian saw Hope flinch ever so
slightly. It was then that she resumed control of the meeting.

"You may not have had an opportunity to discuss adjusting assignments
with Mrs. Blackwell, Mrs. Drake." Ian could see the respect Hope had for the
interim teacher. "But we need to look at adjusting Robbie's workload to make

it more manageable for him." She looked at Ian. "Robbie is benefiting a great deal from his position as conflict manager, and we don't want to take that away from him. His self image, his motivation, his leadership skills; they're all developing well."

She guided the discussion along the lines of adjusting the length of certain assignments to fit Robbie's skill needs. Since Mrs. Drake felt that a lack of time in the school day was Robbie's biggest problem given his tendency to be a slow worker, they looked for ways to extend his day. Ian agreed to Robbie's staying after school a half- hour several days a week to make up work.

"His mother and I will follow up at home, you know, when he needs someone to sit on him." Mrs. Drake agreed to stay with him and offer assistance when needed. She would design a schedule. Hope agreed to send home an extra set of textbooks, so Robbie would not have to haul them all home each day. She went off to gather the textbooks while Ian waited.

"Robbie is lucky to have you for a father, Mr. Bradford," Mrs. Drake said with a level of poise earned only from experience. "Caring enough to come in and work these things out for your son."

"Oh, I don't know." He felt his neck reddening. "It's no more than any other father would do." He frowned at her. She looked mature yet too youthful to be of his generation. "I'm trying to do a better job. Work with you people. I used to be pretty obnoxious about it." He grinned at her. "Gave Dr. Fleming a hard time about everything."

Mrs. Drake nodded understanding. Her serene manner encouraged him to continue confiding. "But my son told me," he looked out at the courtyard at sparrows on the bird feeder. "My son told me he doesn't like it when I fight with his school. Said his brother doesn't like it either." He shook his head. "I don't know what I was thinking. It was really hard for Robbie to tell me. Had to whisper it in my ear." He gave her a false grin, unable to mask the utter remorse he felt.

Hope returned with a stack of colorful, glossy-covered books. She released Mia Drake and handed Ian the books, thanking him for his time and interest.

"Thank—you—too," he stammered, wanting it to sound natural when, in truth, he rarely used the words. "The extra books will be a big help." He offered his hand to a surprised Hope, who shook it warmly.

"Come in anytime you have a concern," she said, meaning it. "Oh, but we'll see you next week—Mrs. Cooper and I—about Dylan, won't we?"

"That's right." He hung near the door looking thoughtful. "I don't know. My wife and I try to do everything right for our kids." He cocked his head and scratched it. "They still have problems. You see these people, straight-A kids." He gazed out the window. "You have a Ph.D. You tell me: how do they do it?" He studied her face.

"It's not easy being a parent, Mr. Bradford. I used to think if your kids turned out well, it was ninety-percent parenting and ten-percent luck." He laughed, and she smiled at him. "My own son is a college dropout." Ian noticed she did not lower her eyes although her voice grew a little thin. "Now I think good parenting is ten-percent skill and ninety-percent luck." They both laughed heartily.

Ian waved and walked out the door, smiling. He had a sense of really connecting with Hope this time. *I can't believe she has a son who's a college dropout. And I really can't believe she would tell me about it, being such a by-the-book person.* He climbed into his mid-sized car, heaving the stack of books onto the front passenger seat. His mind still on their conversation, he waited too long at the stop sign before pulling slowly out of the parking lot.

He noticed the school sign, it's bright red-and-white logo: Poore Pond School, Rich in Opportunity. Is that a new sign? He could not remember ever seeing it before. He read the messages on the sign announcing the upcoming music program, mitten trees, and holiday parties.

Still warmhearted from his exchange with Hope, he felt a twinge of pride in being part of this school. He could see Robbie, grinning from ear to ear in his neon-green conflict manager's pinny. He could see Lucy as a sixth grader, stroking her red honor-roll ribbon the last day of school. "This is their world," he said to himself, recalling how he had withheld support for the school—their school. His stomach felt sick with guilt. He thought of Dylan, struggling every day in first grade, not wanting to go to school just because his stubborn dad overrode the professional judgment of Hope and the teachers.

He wanted to go home and be with his children. But they were all in school; even Rachel was at preschool. He wanted to make up for letting them down with his lack of loyalty to their school. *That would have been the best thing, wouldn't it? Show them by example. Where else were they going to learn loyalty?*

He had to go back to the fire station. At that moment he understood, for the first time, the unequivocal loyalty he had for his colleagues and the work they did together. *How could I have been so blind?* He could not stop chastising himself. *Robbie and Dylan feel the same way about their school. And the people in it. It's their workplace.*

Dad was right. He parked in the lot behind the station and turned off the ignition. *I never forgave him for not seeing that Sister Maribeth stopped the other kids' taunting me. He told me to handle it.* He took his duffel bag from the rear door and slammed it shut. *Too sorry for myself to see how wise he was.*

CHAPTER SIXTEEN—HOPE

Hope sat with funereal reverence, waiting and hoping for George to arrive at the restaurant. Today was the day and time of their standing luncheon date. It also marked exactly one week since he had given her the frightful news: he was homeless, living in the streets.

She looked at her watch and ordered coffee. She felt anxious, her emotional circuits overloaded from this tension with George and disquieting issues at Poore Pond. She still had not come to terms with the idea of her own son living so primitively, exposed to who-knows-what unsavory and dangerous elements. She had managed to tuck it away in the back of her mind all week, only to be ambushed by the reality of it when the weekend began.

Overcome with fear that she may never see her son again, she had tossed and turned all night. In the morning she had moved robot-like through the ritual of getting dressed, preparing for the standing luncheon date they had kept religiously for weeks although she was unsure that he would meet her today. Nevertheless, she had to be there in case he did come. And even if he did not appear, she had to keep the ritual for her own sake. She remembered nothing of the drive to the restaurant under an ever-darkening, cold December sky.

Hope watched as families and extended families entered the dining room, laughing happily and enjoying one another. Sadness enveloped her. The four years she had been out of touch with George had begun painfully. But as time wore on, she had managed to insulate herself against the pain until the fact of her having a son receded, for the most part, into the background.

Once they were reunited; however, sweet contentment replaced the cold, aching knot suppressed deep in her heart. And then this breach had spoiled it all. She was caught off guard with no insulation.

Now, in the light of a new day, she could see how wrongly she had responded to George's news. It must have been difficult for him to disclose to his mother, the extreme way he lived. And she had done nothing to make it easier for him, nothing to indicate she cared more about how homelessness may be affecting him than for what learning of it did to her. She found her lack of compassion chilling. What would she have done if George were one of her students, or a Poore Pond parent? She would have thought first of him, how he was faring, and been eager to help. Had the emotional bond between mother and son, in some twisted way, altered to the point that her own needs superseded his? Was that the case with Mary Baldwin as well? Had Hope's own needs come before Mary's? Hope knew only too well the answer. Abruptly, she turned her thoughts to this day, to George. Would he keep their date?

She motioned to the waiter and ordered a cup of potato soup with a crusty roll. She took pad and pencil from her purse and, to collect her emotions, began off-handedly jotting down appropriate words to use in the upcoming Dylan Bradford conference. She had noted only poor self-image and giving his all when the steaming soup arrived. She smiled weakly at the waiter. She spooned the hot, creamy stock into her mouth and felt instantly comforted. Repressing all thoughts of countless pots of soup she had never made for her family, she broke a piece of crusty bread and buttered it sparingly.

"Mother." She heard the cherished voice beside her and looked around. George stood at the table, his eyes searching her face compellingly. He wore a scuffed, soiled sheepskin jacket two sizes too large for him and a discolored cream, fine-wool muffler. His normally clear eyes were red rimmed, his face puffy from the bitter cold.

Hope leaped to her feet and hugged him with all her strength. She could feel the wetness of both their cheeks. Other diners broke their conversations and stared at them, but they continued hugging.

"You're here! You're here!" Hope said, pressing her head into his broad shoulder. "I am so sorry, My Son," she said, undaunted by the raw emotion in her words.

"Me too," George said with husky voice. He broke away and sat down opposite her place. "Sit down, Mom."

"Can you ever forgive me, Son?" Hope asked, reaching into her purse for a tissue. "It's just that—well, it was such a shock—I had no idea." She looked at him with tender eyes.

"I know, Mom. It was my fault. I should have prepared you a little." He stood to remove his heavy jacket, then sat down.

"I think you did try to prepare me. I was just too blind to pick up on it," Hope said flatly, uttering what she had only just discerned. "You balked at giving me an address or phone number." She smiled warmly though her subconscious mocked her cloddish initial angry response. She should have been concerned enough to analyze George's position, to consider the possibility that he may be unable to afford a permanent residence.

"I confess I was having a little fun with that one," George laughed. "I programmed myself to wiggle out of that question each time you asked it."

Hope's smile belied her self-disgust. "Then when you ate ravenously at our meetings here, practically eating the furniture, I gave it only momentary thought."

George raised his hand in protest. "Now, Mom, don't beat yourself up—"

"And did I take notice when you ignored the check, never offering to pay?" She looked at him with eyes full of self-condemnation. "You, who insisted on paying what you called 'your share' of the electricity bill during the energy crisis? You were fourteen years old, for heaven's sake; your only income was five dollars a week for fetching Mr. Sykes' paper and feeding his cat!" She banged her palm against her forehead. George reached across the table and gently lowered her hand to stop her.

"That's enough, Mom. It's counterproductive," he said, delighting Hope by echoing one of her favorite expressions. He looked around for a waiter, waving at one near the kitchen door. He broke a piece of bread and popped it into his mouth.

The waiter came and took orders for George's pasta and salad, Hope's eggplant sandwich.

"You've got to realize, Mom," George leaned toward Hope. "I am not suffering. I'm working and learning. I have learned so much about people, about social systems, about myself." His hand thumped his chest. "I've met some of the wisest people in the world. Street people—the ones I've met—are very knowledgeable about things that matter. They are not stoned or spaced-out or deranged castoffs, most of them. They know what's going on." His blue eyes shone with the intensity he felt. He devoured another bit of bread and butter.

"But no shower, no clean bed, no place of your own, George? Those are basic physiological and psychological needs," Hope countered, scooping into her mouth the last bit of soup, which had now gone cold. She sat back in the booth, relaxed and pleased that they could be having this objective conversation.

"I shower every day; West Haven Shelter has showers, or Oscar lets us use the shower at his car wash on Bellaire Avenue. I sleep in warm shelters or abandoned buildings with my friends. Have a down-filled sleeping bag I inherited from Willie, my streetmate. I used to push his wheelchair across the high-level bridge for him every morning. He's the one who really taught me how to survive—no, not just survive, to live—on the street. Unfortunately, he died last February of complications from emphysema and left me his most prized possession, the down sleeping bag." His eyes misted with sadness and pride.

"But what about your degree? Do you plan—?"

"Did you know, Mom, that this country has the widest gap in the world between the haves and have-nots? Year after year the gap grows." He took a large drink of water. "There's been a major shift of personal wealth in this country, from the bottom eighty percent of the population to the top twenty percent! American CEO's are paid more than thirty times what the typical factory worker earns." He stopped abruptly and sat back in the booth as if waiting for his facts to sink into Hope's consciousness.

Hope looked at him and saw not a misfit son, but an informed young man, embracing a passionate cause. He was obviously using the good mind he'd been blessed with, albeit without generating a livelihood.

"But what will you do with all this information, George? Where will it take you?"

The waiter arrived and set hot plates of food before them. Hope placed the top of the bun on her crispy, breaded eggplant sandwich, which she cut neatly in half. George covered his hearty serving of pasta with grated cheese and plunged a huge forkful into his mouth, following it with an even larger bite of oil-drenched salad.

Holding her sandwich mid-air, Hope watched George eat with the gusto of a refugee near starvation, the way he had done every week, of course, and to which she had been all but oblivious.

"The United States is the only one of the world's advanced industrial countries that just accepts the poor as an inevitable permanent social class, an unavoidable Act of God," George managed to say between chews.

"I get your message, George. You obviously know what you're talking about. And I agree with you; it is shameful. But where do you plan to go with it?" Hope put the last bite of her half sandwich into her mouth without taking her eyes off him.

"I want to get the media to give it more coverage, foster public outrage. So far, I've been unsuccessful. I try to dress so they can't tell I'm homeless myself, but no one listens. It's just not a matter of concern to anyone but the homeless, and we're powerless. We need advocates." He pointed to the other half of Hope's sandwich. "Want that?" Before she finished nodding no, he transferred it to his plate and attacked it.

Welcoming the change of subject, Hope responded to George's question about how things were going at Poore Pond, limiting her account to positive events and anecdotes about amusing children. She did, however, describe the plight of Heather and Jeremy Baker, knowing that he would relate to it. Overall, he seemed genuinely interested in her school life, but did not take up the matter of the Baker family's bad luck.

Sensing the fact that their conversation had run its course, they bundled themselves against the frigid temperatures and walked out together. An icy wind blew across their faces, frightening Hope with the thought of George's spending the night out in the bone-chilling, dangerous cold.

"Why not come home with me, George? Stay warm by the fire for awhile." Afraid to crowd him, she added, "Just for awhile. Build up your body heat reserves before braving the cold again." She forced a chuckle to make him think the offer was a casual one.

In the end George agreed to go, just for awhile, to see the old homestead, watch a little television. Maybe even play a video game. He carefully kept the situation casual as well.

*

The unusual brightness in the bedroom woke Hope early. She left her bed, pulling a white fleece robe around her as she hurried to the windows. Deep snow blanketed the backyard, the trees, the garage, the driveway, the walks. Warm feelings rushed her as she passed George's room and saw through the half-opened door, his thick mop of hair on the chambray-covered pillow. It felt wonderful to have him in the house again. She hurried downstairs and looked into the street from the living room.

"There must be two feet of snow on the ground," she gasped. The clock said 5:05, just ten minutes earlier than her usual getting-up time. Knowing that Ray would be awake, she went to the small Rolodex near the kitchen phone. A sharp ring startled her. She lifted the receiver and heard Brian's jovial voice.

"I have bad news, Hope," he drawled. Hope felt tension run through her body. "No school today. Snow Day." They both laughed. "Do you mind calling all your people? Bella will help, won't she?"

"I call grade-level chairs who, in turn, will call their grade-level colleagues. Ray and Bella call the classified staff. That's the plan. We have a dynamite steering committee, remember?"

'That's right. You do. Well, get the wheels rolling. Thanks, Hope. Enjoy your break. Good-bye."

Hope put the kettle of water on and immediately began her list of calls, starting with Ray in order to catch him before he left for school.

Ray answered right away but gave clipped responses in a hushed voice. Hope concluded that his mother must have come home from the hospital, and he did not want to disturb her. He told her that the boilers should be in good order, but he would go in to check them later. She told him to phone her before 3:00 o'clock in the afternoon.

Hope checked the hall thermostat and turned on gas logs in the fireplace. She poured boiling water over an Earl Grey teabag in a red-patterned stoneware teacup and sat down by the fire. She switched on the television to hear a forecast; four-to-six more inches were expected by nightfall with temperatures below zero. "Dear God," she prayed with closed eyes. "Thank you for keeping George here with me, warm and safe from this dangerous weather." She shook her head forcefully to keep her eyes from filling. She stood and walked to the window. Looking out at the tundra her lawn had become, she tried to think of a way to persuade George to come back home to live. If she could convince him to stay at least until the storm subsided, she would have time to devise an enticing reason for him to live at home again.

Hope heard water running and doors closing upstairs. She went to the kitchen and filled the coffee maker for George.

"Good morning, Mom," George coughed behind her. He wore grey sweatpants with heavy fold creases and a faded, shapeless, navy blue university sweatshirt. It was obvious that he had dug into drawers of his old clothing, which Hope had never been able to deal with discarding. "That coffee smells good."

"Good morning, Dear. Did it seem strange, sleeping in your old bed?" She smiled at him.

"Just sleeping in a bed seemed strange to me," he laughed. Sensing what she needed to hear, George added, "Actually, it felt good to be back in my own bed, in my old room, in this house." His eyes swept the kitchen.

"What will you have for breakfast, George? Blueberry pancakes? I have frozen blueberries."

"Don't go to any trouble, Mom. You have to be at school."

"No. No, we're having a snow day today. It's a very rare thing, you know. So we can have a nice breakfast together." She searched her mind for words to use to keep him there after breakfast was over. "And after breakfast, if you don't mind, maybe you could hoist a few boxes into the attic for me, books and old mementos I'm not ready to part with yet." She pulled pancake flour from the pantry and eggs and bacon from the refrigerator. She took a square plastic container of blueberries from the freezer.

"I could have toast and cereal. But blueberry pancakes would be great. I'm famished. Maybe I'll go jump in the shower while you're cooking. Unless you want me to help," he asked, delighting her with his manners.

"No, you go ahead. I need a little time to finish our breakfast feast." Hope watched his broad back as he headed for the stairs. Midway, he turned around and called to her.

"Do you have a snow shovel, Mom?" His voice echoed through the uncarpeted hallway. "I'll shovel the drive."

Hope walked toward him. "The wind chill is minus six, George. Shoveling can wait awhile. But thank you; that's nice of you." She heard the bacon sizzling in the pan and went back to the kitchen to turn it.

They basked in warmth and contentment after the hearty breakfast, enjoying the comforting fire. "When did you learn to make breakfast like this, Mom?" George chided. Hope surprised herself by laughing heartily. In the end, he agreed to stay until the winter storm was over if she would let him earn his keep.

He hoisted boxes into the attic, shoveled walks despite thick snow that fell nearly as fast as he shoveled. He repaired a broken frame and climbed a ladder to clean ceiling-fan blades. He filled all the bird feeders and swept the steps. He asked if he might use the computer in her study to go on the Internet.

"Of course," Hope said, knowing she would have agreed to anything that would keep him occupied here. She walked to the window and looked out at the glistening expanse of the front lawn. The round, brass thermometer registered three degrees above zero. She shivered and looked toward her study off the dining room.

George had left the door open, and she could hear the rapid sounds of a computer program booting. She went to the front foyer and lifted her briefcase, which she took into the kitchen. She pulled a neon pink file folder out and spread its contents on the kitchen table. She took the cordless phone from the counter and carried it to the table. She scanned her to-do list of phone calls, intending to complete as many as possible from home since she had been given this bonus day. She started down last year's list of volunteers who helped with the traveling science program, hoping to recruit many of them again this year. Looking for a familiar name, she moved down the list and stopped at Sue Pruett, Taylor's bright and supportive mother who always had a positive attitude about life.

Before she could place the call, she heard the doorbell ring through the house and went to answer it.

Peering through the side glass, she saw a short, balding man in a pinstriped suit bulging through an open wool overcoat, carrying a briefcase. His back to her, he pressed the bell again just as she opened the door.

"Yes?" Hope held the door partially open, chain still fastened.

"Mrs. Fleming?" He flashed a business card in her face. She read, *Century Real Estate Appraisers.* She looked blankly at him. "I'm Hank Hanlon. Your husband sent me to appraise the property." He grabbed the door as if to open it further.

"Excuse me," Hope said, giving him a direct look. "I have no knowledge of such arrangements. Who sent you?"

"Your husband, well, I guess maybe—your ex-husband?" Hank's face reddened slightly. "Mike. Mike Fleming."

"He is my ex-husband; you're right, Mr. Hanlon. But, unfortunately, he did not inform me of this possibility. So I am sorry; I cannot accommodate you. At this time." She closed the door and watched through the sidelight window. He pulled out a cellular phone and began to use it. Apparently failing to make his connection, he thrust the phone back into his overcoat pocket and dashed off the steps. Hope watched him climb into a red thunderbird and drive away.

Still not grasping the meaning of Hank's visit, Hope sat down on the foyer bench. *What was that all about? Century Real Estate Appraisers,* the card said. Then it dawned on her. Michael must be serious about selling the house. Their house. Her house. She was shocked. Never mind that ludicrous business reverses clause he tried to use. She was given the house as part of the divorce settlement. To reside in for ten years, after which they would renegotiate the agreement, one buying the other out or selling the property and splitting the profits. *He can't— what year is this?* She knew it was December, 2001, and distinctly remembered the date of their agreement was January, 1992.

She would never forget; it had been a day much like today with record-breaking cold and snow. She had picked up George at school, signing him out for early release because she could not bear to go home alone. *Not now. Now that the marriage, however miserable, was officially dissolved.*

Michael's getting a jump on the situation; I know he is. Wants to know ahead of time the current market price of the house, so he can build his case. That's just how he operates. The telephone rang loudly, and Hope picked up the receiver on the hall table.

"Good morning," Hope answered cheerily, forgetting she was not at school.

"Hello, Hope," Michael's strident voice jolted her psyche, instantly arousing long-buried exasperations.

"Hello, Michael." She could not keep her voice from sounding tired.

"I know I didn't notify you ahead of time. But the ten-year period is up, and it's time to renegotiate our agreement. You have a calendar, don't you?"

His patronizing manner cut right through her stomach. Old feelings flooded her.

"Hope?" His voice carried years of impatience in that one word.

Hope rubbed her face with both hands, cradling the phone on her hunched shoulder. She took a deep breath and responded in a calm, neutral voice. "We have more than a month, actually a month and a half, before the agreement expires, Michael. This is not a good time for me to deal with that."

"Still putting everything off until the last minute, Hope? When are you going to grow up and learn to be proactive?" Hope was reminded of how much she loathed everything about Michael's speech: the husky voice, those clipped inflections, the arrogant tone. She'd rather have major surgery than continue this conversation another moment.

"Mommmm," George called from the study.

"I'm on the phone, George. In the kitchen."

"George is there? Our George?" Michael sounded indignant.

"Yes, he is."

"Let me speak to him."

Hope walked toward the study, cordless phone in hand. "It's your father," she said to him in a low voice. He punched *enter* on the keyboard and took the phone.

"Hey Dad," he chirped, his voice full of love. "How's it going?"

Not wanting to intrude on his privacy, she left the room although she tried to eavesdrop from the kitchen doorway. She heard George laugh several times and say, "Yeah, yeah, that's right," more than once. Finally, "I'll think about it, Dad. I'll get back to you. Yes, by next week. You too. Yeah. Bye now."

George, still smiling, came into the kitchen. "I didn't know you and Dad ever talked."

"We don't. But today he was after something."

"Well, he sure sounds great. His business is going well. Said the smartest thing he's done was to diversify into polymers. He wants me to—." George's voice faded as he saw the stricken look on his mother's face.

It took everything Hope had for her to say, "It's good that you and your father have a close relationship. It's the way it should be." She did not look at him.

"Yeah, my days of wanting to punish both of you for splitting up are over. I get it now. It just wasn't working." He smiled broadly.

"You've grown up a great deal, George." She walked over and hugged him firmly. "Probably more than either of your parents have."

George started toward the study. "Do you need your study, Mom? I can get off the net if you do."

"No, Son. I need to get dressed now anyway. Stay on as long as you like." He went back to the computer, and Hope went upstairs.

*

It took only until next morning for Hope to devise a carrot to keep George home. She awoke before 5:00 with the idea. Her sorority sister worked for a newspaper, fairly large in circulation in Des Moines. Not the well-known *Des Moines Times Register,* but its competitor, *The Chronicle.* Ellie had worked her way up and was now editorial assistant, next in line to succeed the editor. She could contact her about George's doing a feature story on the homeless. Maybe she'd even come for a visit. It would be great to see her, to have a reunion.

Hope, adrenaline rushing, ran to the windows to check the weather. Freezing in her thin cotton nightgown, she noted that streets and walkways were clear; there was no new snow accumulation. She was sure there would be school.

She decided to deviate from her regular routine and shower and dress before going down to breakfast. Perhaps George would be up by then and she could tell him about Ellie.

*

"That's wonderful news, Millie. Thank you for telling me so promptly." Hope walked down the hall with her. "I know how relieved you and your family are about your clean bill of health." They smiled at each other. "Tell me, Millie, was Mia able to move the class along as much as you had hoped?"

"Oh yes. I've never seen such follow through with a sub. She was just what we needed."

"Just the person I want to see," Carmen rushed up to Hope. "Since we lost yesterday, I need double rehearsals today, both A.M. and P.M. in the gym. Thursday will be here before we know it."

"I'll catch both PE teachers now about holding classroom gym periods and notify teachers and students during morning announcements."

Hope hurried to the office to call their rooms on the intercom. Both teachers were pleasantly agreeable to the change, making her feel grateful for their flexibility.

Right after announcements Hope slipped quickly out of the office before anyone could detain her. She had not had a single minute without a teacher, student, Ray, or Bella wanting her attention since she arrived at 6:45 this morning. The snow day had interfered with everyone's plans, and adjustments had to be made quickly. Actually, the entire re-entry process delighted Hope; it underscored the concern for the children's education that Poore Pond faculty and staff shared. She appreciated their ability to carry on with alternative approaches. And most of them did so cheerfully. She felt a great need to tour the entire building and all the classrooms to makes sure everyone's needs were met in light of changed schedules. She knew too well that there would be a few individuals who did not handle last-minute changes as well as most, and she wanted to prevent any festering resentment. She had learned years ago that personal attention was the only effective way to do that. *The best fertilizer is the farmer's foot,* her British literature professor had termed it.

She entered Annie Klements' fifth-grade classroom where pairs of students were completing Civil War posters. They chatted noisily as they worked on large lettering and charming, hand-drawn symbols. Bits of rubber eraser spilled over white poster board like fairy grass clippings as they feverishly erased lettering deemed unacceptable by their critical young eyes. Jars of tempera paints were everywhere, amazingly upright and unspilled. Elaborate plastic stencils were passed back and forth.

Hope's eyes scanned the room searching for Annie. She found her fitted comfortably into a child-sized desk, working on lettering with a student who, she explained, had preferred not to have a peer partner. She smiled at Hope and stood. "Good morning, Dr. Fleming." She waited for the children to echo the greeting in unison, smiling at them with pleasure after they promptly did so.

Hope smiled at the class. She moved closer to the teacher and asked in a low voice, "Have you managed to regroup after losing a school day yesterday, Miss Klements?" Annie had followed her directive to use titles and surnames in front of the children, and she was careful to follow suit.

"We're fine. We're spending a little longer today with our posters to make up for yesterday. The students were to present them today, but now they'll do that Wednesday. They asked to review for the language test on their own; we usually do a class review. Use that time for their posters." She bent to point at a misspelled word on the child's poster. "Aren't they doing awesome work here?" She proudly led Hope to work of other children, pointing out unique slogans, well-drawn symbols, or striking color combinations.

"These slogans are very relevant. And they show such good sense of design." Hope admired several, asking the artists specific questions about their intended message. She gazed at Annie. "You must have worked with them on design principles first."

"Actually, Mrs. Billings came in and taught several art lessons on design." Annie's face reddened. "I put a note about it in your box ahead of time." She frowned.

"That's right, you did. It's just that I did not know what concept she would be covering." Hope smiled widely at Annie. "She has some sort of artistic background?"

"Yes, she has a master's degree in graphic arts. And owns her own graphic arts business. She taught them sooo much." Annie turned to address a child waiting patiently beside her.

"Is there anything you need, any way I can help you?" Hope asked after the child, question answered, returned to his desk.

"Not that I can think of. But thank you. Oh, there is one thing. Do you mind if we invite the other fifth grades and the fourth grades to see our posters? Thought we'd set them up in the small gym. In the afternoon when it's vacant." Her eyes turned from the students to Hope.

"Let the children explain their work to the visitors? The relationship to the Civil War? Is that what you were thinking?" Annie nodded. "Of course. Just remember to sign up for the space with Bella so you won't be preempted." Hope waved herself out the door.

She continued her rounds feeling, as always when getting a school-wide view, how very like the perfect school Poore Pond seemed. Hands-on teachers providing good-natured, one-on-one assistance to students as needed, not teaching from their desks; students actively involved in learning through all their senses; a relaxed, purposeful atmosphere. *This is the way a school should function.*

She found herself in the primary wing. Here teachers were running intense reading instruction using small-group oral reading; pairs of students reading or flashing word cards to one another; individual children, business like in headsets plugged into tape players while they followed print in oversized books. Some children were completing skill sheets and skill games at their seats or at a table with volunteers guiding. In Jan Wheaton's class a small, curly-haired boy with freckled nose read to a large, shabby teddy bear.

Trudy Cooper's first graders were sharing their original stories, taking turns reading their writing from a chair placed center stage. Trudy tiptoed over to Hope and whispered, "Oh, Hope, I missed my planning period yesterday because of the snow day. I had planned to bind the children's books then. Parents are coming tomorrow for our holiday tea; they're supposed to get the books—they're gifts from the children—at the tea." She looked at two children seated at their desks, hands waving in the air.

"Excuse me," she told Hope and went quietly to each, explaining that they would have a turn to share their stories.

Applause broke out as the child "on stage" ended his story. "That was a warm story, Joshua. You really love your dog, don't you? Who's next?" Trudy asked.

A classic-faced girl with dark brunette braids raised her hand tentatively. "Right, Maria's next." Trudy smiled at Maria. "Thank you, Joshua. "

Maria carried her small book to the designated chair. The teacher listened as she began reading her story about a Shetland pony. Hope, impressed with Maria's complex sentences, forgot about the time and listened eagerly. She applauded with the class when Maria finished.

"Maria, do you really have a Shetland pony?" she asked the reserved child.

"No, but I want one more than anything," she said with shining brown eyes. "Mrs. Cooper said we could write about our real pets or about one we wish we had. The only pet I'm allowed to have is a fish. He doesn't do anything worth writing a story about."

Hope smiled and nodded. "Thank you, Maria." Trudy commented on Maria's interesting plot, then directed Cameron to read, before returning to the principal.

"As I was saying," Trudy whispered, "those books must be bound by tomorrow. They've made wrapping paper and everything. I don't know when I can get to them. I'm meeting with Mary Kate's parents right after school, and I have a dentist appointment at 4:30." She looked at Hope with pleading eyes. "Help," she said comfortably.

Hope noticed that Cameron's voice was so low it was barely audible.

"Cameron, do you want to use the microphone?" Trudy, obviously sharing the observation, asked in a neutral voice. "It's right next to you on the table. Pick it up."

Cameron, tousled brown hair full of cowlicks that framed his elfin face comically, looked pleased and took the microphone, checking the ON switch. He began reading again, clearly delighting in the sound of his amplified voice. The other children watched with envious eyes.

"How much time do you need?" Hope whispered, feeling rude for talking during the boy's presentation. She motioned Trudy toward the door. They stepped into the hall to speak, and Trudy stood in the doorway, her body angled toward the children. "How much time do you need?" Hope repeated.

"About thirty or forty minutes if the binding machine cooperates." Trudy watched as Cameron, big brown eyes shining, interrupted his reading and audaciously began fielding questions about his story, from classmates. "I have to go," Trudy blurted, poised to take command of the room.

"I'll take your class while you bind. Between 1:00 and 1:30 this afternoon? Send me a note confirming or suggesting another time." She walked away while Trudy rejoined the children. She heard her voice over the microphone calling for attention. *Trudy kept close track of each child's writing progress; she had such specific comments. She understands so well how writing is an important strand of teaching reading. We need more of that sort of in-depth teaching.*

Hope glanced at the hall clock and saw that she had just a few minutes to visit the kindergarten classes. But she found both groups in the throes of preparing to go to lunch so opted to see them in the afternoon. She would try to get down there before she relieved Trudy or, barring that, afterward. She wished for an uneventful afternoon so she could meet her commitments.

She gazed out the lobby windows to a fresh coating of light snow on the walks and playgrounds. It looked so peaceful and quiet, yet frozen and bitter. *How fortunate I am to be in this warm, full-of-life school on such a cold, lonely day.* She felt energized by stimulating teachers and motivated children whose classes she had visited.

I wonder if George went into the city as intended, to take blankets and all those sweaters and fleece sweatshirts he was dredging up this morning. He had told her of his concern for homeless friends who may not have found space in shelters, which are always full in weather like this. And their favorite niches in abandoned buildings may be blocked by drifted snow. *I hope he doesn't decide to stay with them.*

Hope returned to her office to see a grim-faced parent waiting beside Bella's desk.

"This is Mrs. Egan, Dr. Fleming." Bella widened her eyes to signal the problematic nature of this visit. "She needs to see you as soon as possible." Hope smiled at Mrs. Egan. "And Brian wants you to call him. Before 12:30."

Hope, feeling the tension Mrs. Egan exuded, led her into the office where she sat in a chair Hope motioned her toward and waited for the principal to speak first.

"I hope you weren't waiting long, Mrs. Egan." She smiled warmly as she took the chair opposite and, leaning across the table, looked into the woman's troubled eyes. "How is school going for Francis?"

"That's why I'm here." Ashen faced and unsmiling, she looked at Hope. "I have a problem with Mr. Myers, the way he runs his gym class." She gazed out the window, swallowing discreetly.

"Would you like a drink of water?" Hope asked, rising to reach one of the unopened, eight-ounce bottles of water she kept on her shelf for just such occasions. She placed the bottle in front of Mrs. Egan, who unscrewed the cap and took a sizeable drink.

"Thank you," she said, her voice still tense. She looked directly at Hope. "As I was saying, Mr. Myers is doing some questionable things in gym class. Francis tells me he is required to run backwards into the wall." Her voice rose with indignation. "Now that's dangerous."

Hope looked tenderly into Mrs. Egan's troubled eyes. "Have you spoken to Mr. Myers about this, Mrs. Egan?"

"No. No, I haven't. I was so upset I came straight to you." She fluttered her hand. "I know you like parents to go first to the teacher; but I was too upset, didn't want to say things I'd regret. You know, and have him take it out on Francis."

Hope cringed inside. She had never understood how teachers could be vindictive toward students whose parents criticized them, although she knew there were a few of those who resorted to that sort of petty response. She had been careful to emphasize to the faculty—the entire staff—that it was in everybody's best interest to win over critical parents and their children.

She had reinforced that expectation with individual teachers when situations arose, noticing that the more professional of the experienced ones agreed instinctively. The less-experienced ones seemed to be of two groups: those who understood the logic of her direction, committing to it; and those with low emotional IQ's who refused to see the logic and became defensive, often escalating the situation. She felt confident that Dave Myers epitomized the experienced professional.

"I will see if I can bring Mr. Myers down now, so you can talk this through." Hope offered. "How's your time, Mrs. Egan?"

Mrs. Egan looked at the chrome watch she wore facing the inside of her wrist. "O—kay," she said with some reticence, eyes still fixed on the watch.

Hope stepped out of the office, returning several minutes later. "Mr. Myers will be right down," she smiled into Mrs. Egan's unresponsive eyes. She moved her chair to the side, making room to pull out a chair for Dave Myers.

"Francis seems to enjoy being a Library Club Reader, doesn't he? And he's good with the kindergarten children, patient and calm. Has he told you about reading to them?"

"Yes, he told me he had to do it. That's about all." She looked at Hope with flat eyes.

"Will your family be going away for the holidays?" Hope tried again.

"No, just to my sister's on the other side of town." Mrs. Egan folded her arms and lowered her chin.

Finally, Dave Myers bounced through the door on cushy running shoes. Though not a tall man, his manner and crisp black-and-white athletic suit exuded the authority of a winning coach. "I'm Dave Myers," he said confidently to Mrs. Egan and offered his hand, meeting hers for a quick shake.

"You're Francis' mom?" Without waiting for her answer, "You raise cockatiels? Francis told me all about it. He knows so much. And can really articulate what he knows. He's an interesting kid."

Hope gestured toward the chair, and Dave moved lithely into it. She noticed Mrs. Egan's face softening, watched her pat her hair and open her mouth to speak.

"Francis tells me he wants to be more athletic," Dave spoke before she could begin. "I've given him little strategies to use. He tries hard." Dave took a breath and flashed a dazzling smile at Mrs. Egan.

"Is that why you're having him run backwards, Mr. Myers?" Mrs. Egan asserted in a strong voice. Hope, surprised by the accusing tone, stood as if to deflect a resurgence of anger.

Dave Myers patiently explained that running backwards was a standard skill in the fitness curriculum, that the children are taught to keep checking their proximity to the wall to avoid colliding with it. That it develops the hand-eye coordination and body control needed for physical dexterity and all-around fitness. "Francis balks at doing it, but he knows he needs it; and I watch him closely. The kids that fear it need it the worst; and I watch them closely, so they don't get hurt." Dave's voice rang with sincerity. His eyes were tender as he looked at Mrs. Egan. Hope saw the tension around her mouth ease again.

"You mean there are other kids who don't want to run backwards?" She asked, her voice ringing with discovery.

"Oh yes. Every year a few. They all get past their fear. And then they're proud of themselves. Francis is determined. He'll do it." He stood, poised to leave. "May I help you with anything else, Mrs. Egan?"

"No. No. I guess I understand the reason you're doing it now. Thank you for your help." She stood. "It's just that Francis complains—he told me nothing of how you're helping him become more athletic," she suddenly blurted, interrupting herself.

"Kids have a way of doing that. They act okay in class, then go home and complain. It's just their way sometimes. But you don't have to worry about your son. He has a good mind, and he knows his limitations. He's trying to improve. And he will. He's a great kid." He offered his hand; they shook hands, warmly this time. "Keep those cockatiels coming," he laughed.

"Thank you, Mr. Myers," Hope said as Dave left. She turned to Mrs. Egan. "I'm glad you came in today, Mrs. Egan, instead of festering away at home. Are you satisfied with the outcome?" She stood at the doorway.

"Yes." Her eyes toward the floor, she paused a moment, staring. "Yes," she said, looking at Hope. "I understand." Her eyes narrowed. "Do you think I should mention it to Francis?"

"Mention what?"

"All those things he hasn't told me. You know, the deal he has with Mr. Myers to get more athletic. Complaining at home then going along in class."

"Sometimes the less said, the better. Children have to be free to vent when they come home from school. Just as adults go home and complain about their jobs. Francis seems to be doing fine with Mr. Myers. And he has a good record here at Poore Pond." Hope shook her head. "I would not dredge it up if I were you. Save the attention for a more crucial issue that may come up in the future."

They shook hands and said their good-byes. Mrs. Egan departed, leaving Hope to ponder the outcome. It seemed to her that Dave had won her over in sincere fashion, and the matter was closed.

But there had been other occasions with other parents when Hope had seen situations end on a seemingly positive note, only to hear from Brian or Ed that the parents had brought their dissatisfactions to them. She could not be sure the matter of Dave Myers' requiring Francis Egan to run backwards in gym class was closed. She wished she knew Mrs. Egan better. But she had to admit she had known those other dissatisfied parents quite well; and they still managed to surprise her when they went over her head.

She dialed Brian's number and left a message on his voice mail.

Late for lunchtime supervision, Hope slipped the strap of her portable microphone case over her shoulder and hurried to the cafeteria. From the hallway she could hear a rising tide of young voices chatting animatedly. She stopped at the assigned table for Pamela Thorpe's class and realized that second-lunch shift was more than half over. She smiled at the children and asked them if they were ready for the music program tomorrow night. A chorus of happy voices shouted, "Yes," while one student, a sturdy little girl with bushy, short brown hair said she wouldn't be there.

"My mom just had a baby," she said proudly. "So I can't come." Her face registered appropriate disappointment.

"You have the best excuse of all for missing the program, Shannon." They exchanged smiles. Holding the microphone in the child's face, Hope asked, "Do you want to announce your new—." She whispered, "Sister or brother?"

"Brother," Shannon said faintly and away from the microphone.

Eyes wide, she shook her head no vehemently. Noon aide Lucille Maroney rescued her when she came to dismiss the table for recess. Hope walked to the servery to supervise the third-shift lunch line. Nine-and-ten-year-olds chattered and squirmed in the line, some facing the child behind them. Guilty-faced children turned to face the front when they saw the principal.

"Thank you for remembering to face forward in line, Morgan, Tommy, and Hugh," her voice blared through the microphone. Some children flinched dramatically at the sudden sound. Morgan, a slender, lovely fifth grader who towered above her classmates, smiled sheepishly at Hope. Tommy, a husky boy with gleaming white teeth and closely cropped dark hair, met Hope's gaze with innocently blinking eyes. Hugh, a thin boy, looking smart in fitted red sweater vest over a plaid shirt, a surly look on his small face, glared at the principal. Hope stepped over to him and put a hand on his shoulder. He turned his face away. "How was your morning, Hugh?" Hope's voice was tender. "Is everything all right?" He turned to look at her and shook his head yes, swallowed, and dropped his eyes. "You certainly look smart in that vest." She said, patting his shoulder. Still unsmiling, his brown eyes warmed. *Poor Hugh. I see what Brad meant. He takes everything as a personal affront. Perhaps some sort of leadership role would help him be more positive. I'll talk to Brad.*

Hope watched as the line moved past the food table, students balancing sectioned plastic trays of mashed potatoes and turkey gravy, dark dollops of cranberry sauce, carrot slices, and buttered rolls. She could smell the hot turkey bits and gravy as they passed her en route to their tables. She realized she was hungry but not for the yogurt and granola she'd brought from home.

"Would you like a bit of lunch, Dr. Fleming?" Helen, the kitchen manager, asked with a warm smile on her pretty face. Hope noticed a new short, haircut with attractive blonde highlights that made Helen look much younger than her fifty-some years.

"You look smashing in that new hairdo, Helen."

"Oh thank you," she shrugged with shy eyes.

"Yes, I will take a turkey lunch, thank you. The whole schpiel. But please, don't give me full portions, just child-sized portions. It looks so good, and I have no will power today. Don't want to eat my way out of a business frame of mind for the afternoon."

Hope took the tray into the lunchroom and looked for the best place to sit. She noticed noise and commotion coming from Brad Kushner's fourth-grade table and went immediately there.

The table was filled, so she sat at the overflow table directly opposite, carefully slipping the microphone off her shoulder without tilting the tray. She sat down as gracefully as she could on the end of a bench that was too close to the table, and looked over at the students. A few girls smiled at her; Mark Pryor, Poore Pond Student Council President, asked her how she was; others worked their food and conversed nonchalantly, pretending not to notice the principal's close proximity.

Stretching the coiled cord, Hope placed the microphone on the table, at the ready, in case she needed to redirect a student at any of the eighteen tables in the large room. No further unnecessary commotion arose from Mr. Kushner's table, and conversation continued in a normal tone.

Hope knew that the blasé attitude of the intermediate students was typical behavior. Primary students, on the other hand, would have called out to her and chattered away, thrilled to have THE PRINCIPAL join their table. Most days Hope enjoyed the interaction. But today, at this moment, she welcomed a small respite to savor the hot comfort food.

*

Driving home on icy streets, Hope felt agitated. The overcast winter sky and biting air cast gloom. The heater in the Volvo seemed slow to produce. She worried that George would not be home when she got there. And she was fighting feelings of resentment toward the two teachers' association representatives who had come to her right after dismissal to complain about student discipline. Desiree—Rae she preferred—Osmond and Chuck Taylor had come in with grave faces to say, "Something must be done about the lack of student discipline at Poore Pond." They noticed that "it had deteriorated of late;" and "many" of their colleagues had "complained" to them, they contended.

Hope did not want to think about this now. She would think about it later. All she wanted was to get into her snug house and find George waiting for her, comfortable and cozy by the fire. She wanted a cup of hot tea. She wanted to change into her fleece shirt and woolly slippers.

The stately white house had that vacant look that houses have when no one is home. No lights burned, despite the growing darkness. Still curtains framed lifeless windows, staring like hollow eyes in a mammoth beast.

Hope reached over the visor to press the garage-door opener and drove into the uncluttered garage. She pulled her purse and briefcase from the seat and pressed the button to close the heavy overhead door.

The house felt warm and inviting as she removed her coat and hung it in the foyer closet. She set her things in her study and went into the kitchen, switching on lamps and wall sconces as she passed. She filled the stainless-steel kettle with water and put it on the stove, turning the burner to high. She went upstairs to change clothes.

Hope descended the stairs on soft-soled slippers and heard the kettle whistling in the kitchen. She brewed her tea and sat at the table, leafing through mail. It suddenly occurred to her that someone had placed the mail there. *Who would have removed it from the outside box? Would Michael have brought that appraiser here and gone through the house? It would be just like him to look through my mail for something about which to criticize me.*

Uneasiness overtook her; she rose and walked through the familiar, lovely rooms, looking for what, she did not know. Thoughts of identity theft and derelict companions of George's moved rapidly through her mind. She covered the first floor and climbed the stairs, looking first in the guestroom, then the spare room where she kept the ironing board standing. Nothing seemed out of order although the window was still open a crack; she had obviously forgotten to close it when she finished ironing in there Saturday.

She came to George's room where the door was closed and hesitated before entering. Sure that she had left the door open—she loathed closed doors—this morning, she felt apprehensive. Her dry throat burned. She could hear her heart pounding. She turned the knob slowly, opened the door slightly, and peered in.

To her great relief, she saw her son sprawled on the bed, covered in a thick, flannel duvet, sleeping like a bear in hibernation. There was no sign of another person. She laughed to herself and said a quick prayer of thanks. Plastic bags stuffed with clothing and blanket rolls littered the floor as well as a tangle of blackened aluminum saucepans and skillets tied to a dingy rope. A large, dirty canvas bag crammed with magazines and papers leaned against the dresser. *Does this jumble represent all George's worldly goods? It certainly seems so.*

She tiptoed out, closed the door gently, and went downstairs exhilarated. *George looks so at home here. Michael is not selling this house. George will live here with me for as long as he wants.*

CHAPTER SEVENTEEN—RAY

Ray pulled into the black asphalt sea that was the Riverview High School parking lot, regretting that he had agreed to work overtime to set up for the music program tonight. He would much rather be helping Heather and Jeremy sort through their possessions in Hannah's garage. Marty or Rosie usually helped with the music programs on their shift, but Marty had called in sick. There were no substitute custodians available, and Rosie had to oversee Poore Pond.

Ray climbed out of his van and walked into the sprawling, yellow-brick building. The odor of well-trampled plastic floor mats mingled with adolescent perspiration offended his olfactory senses as he passed the weight room. Two muscle-bound teens in long, limp jersey shorts stood near the door, gulping cans of cola. He continued down the low-ceilinged corridor, the slick-surfaced, concrete-block walls reminding him of the old high-school gym where Centerville Peewee Wrestling League once held its matches. "I should have stayed with wrestling," Ray said to himself. "I was good. Could have had a college scholarship, probably, if I had stayed with it through high school." In his head he could hear his kid brother, Rory, cheering him on, his shrill voice ringing above the crowds of proud parents. The way Rory looked up to him at those matches made Ray feel like a hero. No one since Rory had ever made him feel so tall.

Ray did not mind working the music programs occasionally. He'd been asked to do so only a handful of times since they had been moved several years ago to the high school. Poore Pond's parking lot and gymnasium were too small to accommodate the growing crowd, which now often included stepparents and grandparents along with biological ones. It was not uncommon for one child to have a party of six or eight family members in the audience.

But now that he found himself pressed for time to help both his ailing mother and the unfortunate Heather, Ray preferred not to have the extra work, though the money would surely come in handy on both counts. He seemed to be going through cash quickly of late, buying take-out meals for home and extra gasoline for driving Heather around to apply for government aid and look for apartments. It was easier to just drive her himself than to keep that rattletrap car of hers going. He actually enjoyed driving around with her in the seat next to him, so pretty and fresh smelling. And he liked having Jeremy in the back seat, chattering away and laughing. He loved to treat them to ice cream sundaes or French fries or pizza; they enjoyed it so.

He hung his jacket on Darryl's hook in the boiler room and headed toward the sound of metal folding chairs banging and scraping. At least, he would get a glimpse of Heather and Jeremy tonight. She had told him Hannah was bringing them to the program to see Jeremy perform with his class. Ray had taken them to Deal-Mart to buy the required white shirt for Jeremy to wear. He wanted to treat, but Heather insisted on paying for it herself. He had cringed, watching her unroll eight dollars from a skimpy roll of bills she took out of her purse. He wondered if that roll were her last bit of money in the world. He'd earn enough money tonight to buy six of those white shirts for Jeremy. But Heather always took care of her own expenses. She would let him do favors for Jeremy and her, drive them places, haul things, take them to dinner; but she never let him pay for items she bought. He liked that about her. In fact, that was one part of her personality that he knew Caroline would like. She always liked self-reliance in women. He wanted his mother to approve of Heather.

"Hey, Ray," Darryl called from the other end of the gym. Ray waved into the bright mercury lights and began unfolding chairs, adding them to the rows in front of the band shells in the center of the plastic-covered floor. He wished he could reserve front-row seats for Heather and Hannah. He could tell that Hannah was getting a bit edgy from having Heather and Jeremy living with her all those days. Choice seating would probably cheer her up a little. But he could not think of an inconspicuous way to save the seats.

Parents and children began to trickle in although the program's starting time was fifty minutes away. Performing students were not required to arrive until twenty minutes from now, but he knew that parents came early for the best parking places and the best seats. Their little kids climbed all over the bleachers, sending thumps from the engineered synthetic soles of their cushy athletic shoes reverberating throughout the cavernous space. Like ants in a child's ant farm, performing students ran to and fro, in and out of the gym, feeling important in regulation white shirts and black pants or skirts. Ray had forgotten what a big night this was for the kids.

Carmen Ricci came in, laden with canvas bags, costumes draped over her arm, and a suitcase-sized black handbag bulging with sheet music. She minced across the floor on those open-backed, nothing-little shoes with thin, shaped heels that Ray had seen so many women wearing lately.

"Hi, Ray," she smiled. "Would you get the portable mike and extension cord from my car?" She tossed him her keys, which he caught easily. "It's parked by the band-room door."

"Hi, Mr. Sellers," Ray heard a familiar voice behind him as he shifted the heavy sound-system case to open the door. He turned around to see a smiling Heather and Jeremy, his hair all wetted down and combed to the side.

"Well, hi there," Ray smiled back. "You're looking spiffy, Sport, in that dress shirt and mousse on your hair." He stood aside to let them pass, catching up to Heather afterward. Jeremy walked briskly ahead of them, following the stream of people. Ray walked as closely as he could to her, inhaling her flowered scent. His arm brushed hers, sending tiny electrical shocks through his midsection. She turned to look at him, her face framed by a crisp white collar under her black faux leather jacket. Her lush lips shone with pearly pink lipstick; and she wore her thick blonde hair clipped atop her head, long, silken strands escaping down her cheeks. His heart raced to look at her. "She looks like a movie star," he thought, struggling to take a complete breath. The very air around her seemed charged with electricity.

Jeremy waited by the bleachers for them to catch up with him then hugged his mother before joining his class behind the band shells.

"Maybe you can find an empty seat on the floor, Heather." He motioned toward the folding-chair section. "I'll be right back." She nodded. Ray carried the sound system over to Carmen, standing dead center before the band shells. The din of hundreds of excited voices filled the air.

"Oh thank you, Ray," Carmen said with feeling. "You know where the closest outlet is?" She raised her voice above the hubbub. "Over by the side box," she pointed with her palm. "Remember?" Ray opened the case and plugged the speaker into the extension cord. Then he trailed the cord over to the outlet, dodging parents and kids, warning them to step over the black cable. He walked back to the case and turned on both microphone switches, red indicator lights affirming the power connection. Carmen gave him a thumbs-up and smiled.

He looked for a yellow caution sign and quickly found a folded one resting against the wall. He stood it over the cord where it crossed the aisle.

"Anything else?" Ray asked, anxious to have another word with Heather.

"Can you find a few more chairs? The floor section is nearly full already. See, a few more spaces on each end?" She motioned toward the chairs, now occupied by eager parents and grandparents waiting to see their students shine.

"That will work," he said, happy to have spotted Heather in the middle of the second row. "She found a good seat after all," he said to himself. He carried chairs, four at a time, from the four-wheeler in the back hallway. Two adolescent boys asked to help, and the chairs were placed quickly. A young mother in a denim jumper and a grey-haired woman, an older version of her, waited to sit on two of the chairs, their faces registering delight with the good seats and determination to be first to get them.

He looked across the rows at Carmen. Seeing that she was about to open the program, he felt confident that she needed nothing else. He turned to make sure Heather was still there and left to find Darryl.

The house lights went down, and Carmen signaled the chorus to begin. Young voices filled the vast gymnasium as the children sang their hearts out, beaming smiles. The enthralled audience gave rousing applause to every number, some whistling and hooting, Ray knew to Hope's dismay. *I wonder if she's giving her headmistress stare to the audience wherever she's sitting.*

He helped Darryl sanitize the workout room, listening for Jeremy's class to start the angels number. He heard the introduction and stepped into the gym, laughing at Jeremy's little face, concentrating as he sang the words with heart and soul. His chest filled with emotion, and he blinked tears from his eyes. He chuckled along with others in the audience as the children waved paper angels in the air with unexpected grace. He applauded soundly and went back to his work as a troupe of dancing girls pranced to center stage.

Everyone cheered and applauded at the close of the concert. Hearing the applause, Ray stationed himself near the door to catch Heather. Family after family streamed out; but there was no sign of Heather, or Jeremy, for that matter. Disappointed, Ray hurried over with the four-wheeler to fold and load chairs. It occurred to him that Hannah had not come. He wondered if Heather had driven her wreck of a car and knew if she had, she would need help getting it started. He continued folding and loading the chairs in flat piles of ten, then twenty, trying to watch with his peripheral vision for Heather. All the chairs were folded, plus the band shells. Everything had been trucked to the storage room. Ray, along with Darryl and his colleague, Sam, had swept the plastic floor cover. Ray had loaded Carmen's gear into his van. He checked out with Darryl.

"Guess we're all done, Darryl," Ray drawled.

"Right, Ray. Thanks for helping. You haven't been over here in awhile. Nice to see you." They shook hands "You going back to school?"

"No, I was put on just to help over here. I'm done for the night."

"OK, Buddy. Too bad that sweet thing by the door's not waiting for you." Darryl laughed, his face turned toward Heather.

Ray looked over and saw Heather, standing quietly by the door trying not to look ill at ease. Jeremy swirled large paper angels around in the air.

"I bet she's got car trouble," Ray called to Darryl from his brisk walk away.

"You hope." Darryl smiled and shook his head.

"I've got to get my own place," Heather said softly as Ray's van traveled down Main Street. He looked over and saw the strain in her fair face.

"Did Hannah say that?" Ray asked, lowering his voice when Heather turned nervously to look at Jeremy, chattering to himself as his finger traced lines in the steamed windows.

"She didn't have to say it. I can feel it. She's always in a bad mood, and that's not like her."

"What about that duplex over on Cross Street?" Ray turned onto Reservoir Road, the pitch darkness abruptly causing him to let up on the accelerator. "You said it was nice. And the rent was cheap." "It was OK." Heather did not look at him. "That family in the other half though." With a sidelong glance behind her, she lowered her voice. "Did you see how trashy their place looked? Toys all over the yard, torn screen door, ragged-looking dog chained to a tree." She looked at

Ray with despair in her eyes. "I can't let my son live like that." She gazed toward Jeremy, now silent. "I can't live like that." She licked her dry lips.

"Mom, I liked that house. That dog's nice. And there's a playground across the street. Remember?" Jeremy piped from the rear seat. Heather raised her eyebrows toward Ray.

"See, Mom, Jeremy knows what's important, don't you, Jeremy?" Ray turned toward the boy and laughed, hoping to cheer Heather. But she sat stiffly forward, her forlorn face cutting right into Ray's heart.

"What I should do is stick it out with Hannah and save enough money for a bigger deposit, get a better place. Frank said he'll probably put me back on full-time after the first of the year. And who knows, maybe Jeremy's dad will sell his front loader. He's supposed to give me half of that; I helped pay for it. I think I'll call him. See how close he is to selling it." She sighed and sat back in the seat just as the van pulled into Hannah's neat, hosta-lined driveway. Hannah appeared at the window, waving weakly.

Heather gathered her purse and the bag with Jeremy's bow tie in it, then turned to look at Ray. "Thanks for driving us home, Ray. You've been good to us. I owe you."

Ray, his heart overflowing, looked at her with serious eyes. "I would do anything for you and Jeremy, Heather. You know that." His eyes searched hers, and for a brief moment their gazes locked. Ray felt electrical shock again and leaned toward her. He wanted to kiss her; but she was out of the van in a flash, gathering Jeremy and his paper angels from the back seat. She closed the doors and stood beside Jeremy waving, looking toward Ray, avoiding his eyes.

He watched them go inside and waved again at Hannah as she held open the door. Hannah gave him a slight wave back and closed the door.

Ray pulled onto the dark, two-lane road. He switched on the radio, and soft rock music filled the van. His thoughts turned to the loveliness of Heather, the joy of being in her company. She seemed so vulnerable. And yet there was staunchness to her, a determination. She obviously had a certain standard, in regard to mothering Jeremy, that she struggled to maintain.

Ray decreased his speed to round a sharp curve on Reservoir Road. He could see the silvery surface of the water ahead of him. He passed Love's Point where several cars were parked under the trees, separated, yet each strategically facing the lake. He wondered how it would feel to be there with Heather. But that was silly. She was a grown woman, a mother; and he was no longer a hormone-driven teenager. Still, his imagination lingered on the illusion.

He saw lights ahead and knew that he was approaching the highway. Waiting at the junction in the glare of streetlights and other headlights, his mind turned to more practical thoughts of Heather, her housing dilemma.

He didn't like to think of Jeremy and her having to depend on a weary Hannah for their shelter. He remembered, as a boy, having to stay at Aunt Swoosie's when Rory was born. His delivery had been a difficult one; he was a breech birth, and Caroline stayed in hospital for two weeks. It had taken its toll on Rory, too.

Underweight, exhausted, and refusing to eat, he had remained in the hospital for another week after Caroline was released.

Ray was completely cowed by Aunt Swoosie, the harsh-speaking, former-prison-guard sister of his father. Aunt Swoosie had openly resented what she saw as an imposition, having responsibility for her nephew thrust upon her with no way out of it. He could remember, as if it were yesterday, how unsettling it was to be trapped with a cold aunt who clearly did not want him. He could neither eat nor sleep, and the anxiety-ridden days stretched long and dark. How tickled he was when his doting Aunt Patsy collected him and took him to her sunny little house.

Ray wished he could bring Heather and Jeremy home to his house to stay. He wanted to be their *Aunt Patsy*.

*

The familiar grey bungalow stood starkly silent against a bright evening sky. Ray could almost see the biting chill in the air as he walked across the driveway, his heart racing. There was no flickering television screen reflected in the windows although it was barely nine o'clock. He hoped his mother was all right.

Ray dropped his keys, trying to unlock the side door quickly. He managed to unlock it and stepped inside, the utter quiet bearing down on him as he rushed down the short hall to his mother's room. Her door was ajar, and he could see her resting comfortably under the blue-flowered duvet Claire had given her. He walked up to her to make sure she was breathing.

"That you, Rayley?" she said in a dry voice.

"Yeah, Ma. It's me. I'm home. You doing all right?" He touched her arm and helped her sip water from a bedside carafe and glass he had bought for her.

"I'm fine, Son. Just tired," her voice faded, then revived. "Would you put out the rubbish, please, Ray? Remember, we didn't get it out last week; and the cans are overflowing." She did not look at him, but, lying flat on her back, faced the ceiling.

"I know, Ma. I'm sorry about that. I'll take it out now. Don't worry about it. Get your rest." Ray went to the pantry garbage can and stepped on the pedal to raise the lid. He pulled out the plastic bag, heavy with food scraps, and tied it closed. He took a fresh bag from the pantry shelf and inserted it neatly into the empty can. Opening the back door as quietly as he could, he carried the bag to the garage where he placed it in a large plastic bin. He snapped the lid to lock it and hauled it out to the curb, his feet noiseless on the snow-covered ground. He was glad Caroline had not tried to do this herself the way she used to when he didn't beat her to it.

Ray stood a moment on the back stoop, enjoying the brisk air. Up and down the street post lamps and porch lights cast a warm glow on the snow and filled his heart with peace. He thought about his mother. She had not snapped back as quickly this time as she had the previous times she'd been hospitalized. She did not complain, but he could see it. She moved slowly about the house, bent over and weak. She insisted on trying to keep up her normal work, but it was clearly too much. She had taken to going to bed earlier and arising later. Ray worried that she might need help running the house, more help than he could give her.

Claire insisted on coming over on Friday nights to help with laundry and see that there were proper groceries in the house. In her inimitable way, she made Ray feel as if he weren't capable of running a house, despite the fact that he earned his living looking after a forty-thousand-square-foot building.

Ray would keep out of her way by dusting and vacuuming the rooms where she wasn't working. He was always tired on Friday nights and preferred to relax and watch a movie with Caroline the way they used to, but he forced himself to keep working while Claire was there. Caroline, as uncomfortable with her daughter's obsessive fussing as Ray was, would invite Claire to sit down with them in front of a movie; but Claire would have none of that and martyred on with work.

So their mother usually ended up just stopping the movie early and going to bed once her bedroom had been cleaned. Friday nights used to be a special night at their house. Now they had become a weekly endurance test. Neither Ray nor his mother ever talked about this unpleasant disruption, and they did not try to redirect Claire.

Feeling the cold now, Ray opened the door softly and went inside, relishing the heated rooms. He looked in on his mother then sat down in the living room with a glass of tomato juice. He needed to unwind and clear his head.

Tomorrow was Friday and Claire would be storming through again. Ray dreaded it already. Perhaps he should start buying groceries on Thursdays, so he could tell Claire not to come. She didn't shop right anyway, kept buying the same fresh meat and vegetables Caroline used to buy when she was able to cook them. Now she was asking for more prepared foods, frozen dishes and deli concoctions. Ray knew that Caroline willed herself to cook the food Claire bought to keep from hurting Claire. But she couldn't do it every day, and the freezer was backing up with roasts and chops while Caroline sent Ray for take-out dishes three or four days a week.

Unbeknownst to Claire, Ray had thrown out fresh vegetables like peppers, beans, and spinach that had gone uncooked. He remembered now the yellow squash mouldering in the refrigerator. He retrieved it, dropped it, soggy and dripping, into a recycled plastic bag. He hurried, jacket-less and shivering, out to the curb to add it to the bin.

Finishing his tomato juice, Ray removed his shoes and stretched back in the recliner, the coarsely woven upholstery massaging his tired back and aching legs. He wanted to think about the possibility of bringing Heather in to help Caroline with meals and housework. He wanted to devise a plan that would help Caroline and him and, at the same time, give Heather and Jeremy a temporary home. But he dared not think along those lines. Convincing Caroline and dealing with Claire were more than he could manage. His subconscious would not allow him to develop the idea.

*

Ray was in the throes of replacing ballasts on light fixtures in the rear hallway when Jeremy brought him a folded paper. Ray climbed down the ladder and took the note.

"What are you doing here so early, Sport?" He smiled at Jeremy.

"Came to Latchkey," he said proudly. "My mom had to go to work early, so she let me come. I never get to be in Latchkey." Ray noticed how thrilled he was, unlike those children who attend every week, to be in the before-and after-school program.

"That's a good thing?" he asked. Jeremy nodded vehemently as Ray unfolded the note. *Ray, I have something for your mom, a homemade pumpkin loaf. I want to take it to her to wish her a quick recovry. Would tomorrow after school be all right? Jeremy wants to come with me? Sincerely, Heather Baker.* Ray noticed that she had dotted the I in *sincerely* with a line drawing of a tiny heart and wondered whether it was meant for him or if she always closed her letters that way. He was deep in thought when Jeremy coughed and cleared his throat.

"Tell your mom that tomorrow would be fine, Jeremy." He looked into Jeremy's expectant face. "Tell her I'll pick her—and you—up at 4:15. We can stop for pizza and eat it at the house." He could see that Jeremy was pleased. He watched him skip away and mentally calculated how much time they would have Friday before Claire arrived around seven. He could order the pizza ahead and pick it up at 4:30 at Pizza Shack on the way home. That would give them nearly two hours with Caroline. He would get the stuffed-crust pizza he knew Jeremy liked. He would also get large coca-colas and those little fried cherry pies Caroline loved. He could hardly wait for Friday to come.

After their conversation, every time Ray encountered Jeremy around school, they would flash smiles and chant, "Friday," their thumbs pointing upward. When Ray and Hope were standing near the entrance door discussing its deterioration, Jeremy walked by and flashed teeth and thumbs. Hope, her eyes puzzled, laughed and watched the boy amble across the lobby to the boys' bathroom.

"He's certainly looking happier these days, isn't he?" She looked at Ray. "His mother must have worked through their problems."

"Yeah. She's still living with her sister, looking for her own place. I've been trying to help her when I can. Feel sorry for her." Ray dropped his eyes and fiddled with the loose panic bar.

"I saw you talking to her after the Christmas concert and wondered if she had car trouble aga—Walk please!" Hope interrupted herself to call out to fourth grader Sharon Richter as she flew past in a full run, obviously not seeing her principal at the door.

Sharon, looking sheepishly at Hope, stopped abruptly on her thick-soled, black leather Mary Janes and in a barely audible voice said, "I'm sorry, Dr. Fleming," before continuing on her way.

"Actually, I gave her a ride home. Her and Jeremy." Ray swallowed. "Her sister was supposed to come to see Jeremy perform but ended up just dropping them off. Ray opened the door, letting in a blast of cold air, and adjusted the panic-bar connecting rod. "I get the feeling things are wearing a little thin at Hannah's house with Heather and Jeremy staying there so long." He continued fiddling with the door and did not look at Hope.

"Those arrangements always turn sour. People nowadays need their privacy. I can understand that. My little rituals at home are very important to me."

"I'm thinking of taking them in at my house for awhile." Ray blurted, surprising himself. "Heather could help with cooking and that. Until my mother is getting around better." He closed and opened the door several times, watching the mechanism. He felt a slight tension as Hope's eyes bore into his back.

"How is your mother, Ray? Still not fully functioning yet?" Now that they were on a little safer subject, Ray turned to look at Hope. "No, she's not. Still tired and weak. That's not like my mom." "So you're thinking she could use some help, and Heather might be able to give that?"

"Yeah, kind of a good arrangement for everyone. Heather could help Mom run the house, and she'd have a place to stay till she gets her own. And Jeremy would certainly liven things up for all of us." Ray smiled broadly and chuckled.

"That he would. That he would." Hope tried the panic bar and it worked as it should. "Well, what does your mother think about all this?" Her eyes searched Ray's face.

"I'm going to talk to her about it tonight if she's up and around. See what she says. Course I'll have to deal with my sister, Claire. She always has opinions, usually negative ones." Ray looked off across the lobby.

"I know how that is. Once the big sister, always the big sister," Hope said, smiling at Ray. "Let me know if I can do anything for your mother, Ray. Or you," she added, meaning it. She hurried off toward the sound of young voices shouting in the fifth-grade wing, leaving Ray to work on the adjacent door.

Ray opened the door for two mothers in anoraks, jeans, and athletic shoes. He recognized them as volunteers for Santa Shop and had been told by Hope that they would need to set up in the library after school today.

"Hello, Mr. Sellers," they chimed, smiling at him. "We're here to set up for Santa Shop."

"I know. Dr. Fleming told me you'd be coming. The library is open." Ray gestured toward the room across the lobby. "You probably need help moving tables around. The night crew will be here soon, so just tell them what you need." The two women walked toward the library.

When Hope walked past Ray, he told her that the Santa Shop volunteers had arrived. She reminded him that they would need a key to keep the library locked once their merchandise was arranged. Ray followed her to the office to get a file key.

*

Ray looked around the kitchen table. Jeremy took big bites of the stuffed crust pizza and, heeding Heather's warning look, tried not to lick his fingers. Ray handed him a fresh paper napkin.

"I'll trade you this clean one for that crumpled one in your lap, Sport." Jeremy retrieved the ball of tomato-stained paper and handed it to Ray. He took the clean one and spread it carefully in his lap. "A guy needs industrial-sized napkins to handle this pizza. It's loaded with sauce," Ray said with a knowing look. They exchanged smiles.

Heather and Caroline, deep in conversation, glanced warmly at Jeremy then resumed their discussion.

"Hannah sure sounds like a good sister to you, Heather," Caroline said, searching Heather's face. Heather chewed a bite of pizza and nodded yes. She took a larger drink of cola.

"She's always been there for me," Heather said solemnly. "And for Jeremy, hasn't she, Jeremy? Aunt Hannah?" She looked proudly at her son. The child, with squirrel-like cheeks full of pizza, nodded in agreement.

The two women continued their ardent discussion. They covered the importance of families sticking together, how difficult living with relatives could be, and how expensive apartment rentals were. Neither was at a loss for words; and, to Ray's delight, they seemed to be relating quite well. Ray sat across the table observing, trying to decide when and how to ask his mother about taking in the small family. He knew he would have a better chance of getting her to agree if Heather made a good impression.

Ray removed the pies from a grease-stained white paper bag onto a clean plate and heard Heather ask Caroline if she should make coffee. Heather got up from the table and followed Caroline's directions in locating the filters and coffee. He watched Heather carefully measure the scoops of coffee according to his mother's preference for a not-too-strong brew. His eyes followed the movement of her hips in figure-hugging black stretch pants and her tiny waist accented by a cropped white sweater as she brushed the few spilled coffee grounds from the countertop into her hand. He noticed that Caroline was watching, too.

"She sure is pretty, Ray," she said to her son as if Heather weren't there. Heather turned and smiled at her.

Ray laughed and said, "You're telling me?"

"And that son of yours, Honey." Caroline beamed at Jeremy who was sitting quietly, savoring every drop of soda pop and obviously full of pizza. "He's a winner, he is." Jeremy smiled broadly.

Everyone but Heather ate two fried cherry pies, carrying on an entire conversation about how greasy good they were and about other favorite desserts, such as, chocolate- chip cookies from the sub shop, sundae parfaits from the frozen custard stand, and funnel cakes at the annual Community Days Festival. Then Heather took Jeremy into the bathroom to wash his hands and face. Ray and Caroline heard her say, "Don't touch anything," as she closed the door.

"I can see why you like her, Ray. She sure is pretty." Caroline said in a low voice.

"I know, Mom. And she's a good mother, too, don't you think?" Ray kept his voice just above a whisper.

"It's a shame she has to stay at her sister's and be uncomfortable." Caroline said, giving Ray hope. She slowly eased herself out of the chair, her weak state still in evidence. "But you can't blame Hannah. Almost a month she's had them. No wonder she's at the end of her rope." She looked at the clock on the range before taking small, slow steps toward the living room. Ray's heart sank. He stared into space, absorbing the full meaning of her remarks as they pertained to his plan for Heather and Jeremy.

"What time are you taking them home, Ray?" Caroline asked in a tired voice. "Claire will be here in half an hour."

"I guess I'd better take them now, then. Before Claire comes." Ray said, sounding defeated.

He bundled them both into his van, complete with two pieces of leftover pizza and the last fried pie wrapped in plastic wrap. Caroline called, "Thanks again for the pumpkin loaf, Heather. Bye, Jeremy, from the back door.

"Close the door, Ma. You'll catch your death," Ray called.

*

He watched Hannah repeat her weak wave when he dropped them off at the neat white house on Reservoir Road. How he wanted to rescue them from that tense situation, for Hannah's sake as well as Jeremy and Heather's. He waved again and backed out of the drive.

The road was a little icy, and Ray had to concentrate on keeping the van straight. He wanted to think about a new plan for Heather. An oncoming car forced him to concentrate on getting over and holding the van on the road at the same time.

The two cars passed successfully, and he thought again of the evening with his mom. He could not believe how closed minded she had seemed about taking people in, Hannah's taking in Heather and Jeremy, her sympathy more for Hannah than for Heather. It wasn't like her. She usually sided with the underdog.

*

The sight of Hope's Volvo in the parking lot surprised Ray when he arrived at school at 6:25 on Monday morning. He tried to recall a parent function that might be scheduled for today and could not think of one to explain her early arrival. It annoyed him to have to deal with his supervisor before he'd had a chance to look things over and settle in for the day, especially on a Monday. He prided himself on his thorough checks for weekend vandalism, weather-caused mishaps, and the like. He did not want to hear about conditions of his building from others, especially Hope.

So as not to frighten her, Ray began whistling when he approached her office. He could see her desk lamp lighting up a patch of the hallway.

"Good morning, Ray," she called through the open office doors as he walked by.

"Good morning, Hope," Ray called back, entering her office to find her poring through a stack of garden catalogs.

"Look at these, Ray." She waved her hand toward several open catalogs spread on the table. "I don't think I told you the survey that the steering committee completed showed an overwhelming majority of students and staff members, parents, too, favored some sort of garden-type memorial. One that could be added to for future needs, God forbid." She handed him a catalog, its pages marked with post-it notes. "I liked your idea of a bench with a commemorative plate on it. There are nice teak ones in here. And this one," she handed him another catalog, "has lovely cast-concrete angel figures like you had suggested."

Ray did not want to think about bench or angel memorials. He had his rounds to do. "I'll look these over," he said. "OK if I get back to you?" He rolled the two catalogs together.

"I'm meeting with the parent-group board this afternoon; and I promised to bring ideas for the memorial, so they can order soon. Remember, they allocated several hundred dollars for this project." She shot him one of her intense looks.

"What time is your meeting?"

"One thirty."

"I'll look them over when I eat lunch and get back to you early." Ray backed toward the door.

Hope thrust another catalog at him. "This one has all sorts of small trees and bushes. Take it along, too. Just let me know what your preferences are. I want the decision to be ours."

After the board meeting, Hope stopped at Ray's desk in the boiler room where he was busy writing a purchase order from a hand-scrawled list of cleaning supplies. She saw paper towels written on the list.

"We're out of paper towels already?" she asked, giving him an incredulous look.

"Well, yeah, we are. I guess your big hand-washing campaign has worked," Ray laughed. "Soap, too. We keep running out of soap."

"Let's see if the spread of colds and flu has decreased along with it," Hope said. "If it has, the cost will be well worth it."

Hope went on to inform Ray that the board had liked his preference for the small, cast-concrete angels. "They had no difficulty visualizing your memorial garden of angels, each wearing a brass plate with the name of a deceased child on it. I told them you would help students plant a border of flowers to define the area. The cost is affordable, too."

"Good. That takes care of Bucky and the kindergartner, then. So Melanie should be OK with it. When do we start?"

"They're going to order the angels right away. And Mrs. Fraser knows the owner of Smalley's Trophy Shop, thinks she may get a discount on the engraved nameplates. We should be ready for a ribbon cutting by spring. Thank you for the input." Hope smiled at Ray.

"That's great,"

"What can you tell me about the Bakers?" Her eyes searched Ray's face. He looked blankly at her. "Is your mother up to taking them in for awhile?"

"Nooo, I guess she's not well enough yet to have extra people living with us." Ray stood. He took a cloth from his back pocket and began wiping the dusty black telephone.

"I can understand that," she said, picking up Ray's list and, taking a pencil from his desktop, adding *waterless soap* to it.

"How critical is the situation at Heather's sister's, would you say?"

"Pretty critical," Ray looked directly at her.

"I'll think about it and see if I can come up with any ideas. Jeremy really needs a stable environment." She took steps toward the door. "I'll get back to you."

"Okay, Hope."

She took another step, then stopped, her finger on her lips. "How independent— self reliant—. Would you say Heather has enough pride not to take advantage of people wanting to help her?" She looked inquisitively at Ray. He had never before seen her struggle to find the proper words for what she wanted to say.

"You mean keep leaning on them, take the easy way out?" Hope nodded.

"Naw, not a chance," he said with feeling. He immediately worried that he had spoken too soon; he didn't really know her that well. He wanted to take back the words. He could feel his neck reddening. "At least from what I can see," he added, dropping his chin to hide his swallowing.

"I know you've been a big help to them, Ray. It's very kind of you. Heather seems to really try." The piercing sound of the first dismissal bell startled them. Hope turned to the bell sounder attached high on the wall just outside the boiler-room door. "That thing is loud."

"As I was saying, there's something about Heather that draws one to her, isn't there?"

"Yeah, there is," Ray said, his face quickly reddening. He swallowed. "I don't know what it is; she seems sort of helpless somehow." He straightened the papers on his desk.

"She has a vulnerability about her, I noticed. And a sincerity. You really like her, don't you?" Hope asked, her directness throwing him off guard.

"I do," Ray said. "She's beautiful. I like her very much." He surprised himself with such candor.

"She certainly is," Hope agreed. "And she seems to know what's important for Jeremy."

"That's right." Ray appreciated Hope's comments. It was as if her words validated his high opinion of Heather.

"Well, I hope we can help solve her housing problem." She looked at her watch and dashed off just as the final dismissal bell sounded sharply behind her.

Ray hurried into his jacket and outside to help direct traffic. Cold hung in the afternoon air, and the overcast sky echoed the chill. Ray welcomed it. He needed to cool down after his heated thoughts of Heather. She had that effect on him, and talking with Hope about her only intensified his body heat.

Cars were backed up at the flagpole, the designated pick-up point. The line was already ten cars deep. Ray went over to direct drivers exiting the flow-through lanes, hoping to prevent angry words from impatient parents on tight schedules. He smiled at a distressed-looking Mrs. Hapwell whose car was angled half in and half out of the lot, blocking other anxious drivers who had already collected their children. Francine smiled and waved from the back seat as he guided her mother smoothly out of the lot. The cars behind her swished past him, their drivers waving appreciatively at Ray. Exhaust fumes filled his nostrils. He saw Hope, bundled in her full-length fur coat, portable microphone strapped over her shoulder. She was calling to students whose bus had not yet arrived, instructing them to line up at the edge of the walkway. As accustomed as they were to their principal's voice over the microphone, they were always caught off guard by it when they hadn't seen her wearing it. They complied in short order.

CHAPTER EIGHTEEN—IAN AND HELSI

Helsi moved about the house quickly, making beds, gathering dirty laundry, placing stray books and toys on shelves. She kept hearing Dylan's words from last night's homework session.

"I'm the dumbest kid in my class. Probably the dumbest in the whole first grade." He had said it so matter of factly, and that was what bothered her the most.

Robbie was trying to help him, flashing word cards to him, giving clues to words Dylan did not recognize, which was most of them. Robbie would add those to the back of the pile and flash them again and again until Dylan called them correctly. After repeated attempts with the same simple words, Robbie grew frustrated when Dylan did not apply his clues and made wild guesses.

"Don't be such a dumb kid!" Robbie had shouted.

That was when Dylan responded in cavalier fashion. "I'm the dumbest kid in my class." It disturbed Helsi that he hadn't defended himself, that he seemed resigned to the low rating.

She recalled Hope's words the day she had placed him on emergency removal for acting out. When Helsi had gone to school to collect him, the principal had appealed to her by saying, "Dylan needs our help. His self-esteem is suffering."

There is still more than half the school year left. He needs to spend it back in kindergarten. Should she ring Ian and ask him to agree? Or should she simply book the appointment at school and take care of it herself? Save Ian the stress and time of dealing with it again. But that wouldn't be fair. They had always made joint decisions about the children's education in the past. Helsi aimed to preserve that unity in their relationship.

She dialed Ian's number at the fire station. Sally, the dispatcher, told her Ian was in a new-equipment briefing and unable to come to the phone.

Helsi wanted to schedule an appointment with Dr. Fleming and get it over with immediately. If she didn't hear from Ian by lunchtime, she would do that.

Wouldn't it be a wonderful Christmas present for Dylan to go back to kindergarten. She hoped he would take it in just that way. *Then in September he could go on to first grade but this time with proper skills.* At the evaluation team meeting the point had been made that Dylan's IQ was below average. Though Helsi was mindful of this, she refused to think about it. *No. He would repeat more than a semester of kindergarten and then be ready for first grade. Being half a year older, he would have a better chance of succeeding. Even the teachers on the team had said that just a few months of maturity can make a difference in learning.*

·   *But what about the other kids? If they already say he's dumb, what will they say when he's put back?* She could feel her heart breaking at the thought of their child-like remarks. *"Dylan has to go back to kindergarten because he's too dumb for first grade," from the crueler ones. And from the kinder children, "Dylan's the same age as I am, so why does he have to be in kindergarten again?"*

But it can't be any worse than what the kids are thinking and saying now if Dylan, himself, says "he's the dumbest kid in his class, probably the dumbest in the whole first grade." No, that is far worse. If Dylan believes it now, he will believe it the rest of his life unless we intervene. We've got to.

*

Dr. Fleming, looking festive in a dark red suit and red-and-green-houndstooth silk shirt, greeted the Bradfords in the lobby with warm handshakes for both. They could feel excitement in the air fueled by the Christmas tree, its branches laden with brightly colored mittens and hats; the showcase full of clay menorahs and bright blue dreidls alongside soft green fir trees and red and yellow Kwanzaa banners. From the door of the multipurpose room flowed the sweet, high voices of Poore Pond School Choir leading students and teachers in a sing-along. Everyone they encountered was dressed in holiday colors, smiling ecstatically, and calling "Happy Holidays!"

They turned toward the office just as a classic-faced brunette in a red sweater woven with a green Christmas-tree pattern and tiny silver bells, approached Hope.

"Excuse me," she said, looking right at Ian and Helsi. "I just want to tell Dr. Fleming how beautiful the holiday concert was." She smiled warmly at Hope. "Those kids were outstanding."

Hope shook her hand. "It's good of you to tell me that, Mrs. Carren. Mrs. Ricci certainly knows how to get the best from the children, doesn't she?"

"She does. The way she features so many of them with small solo parts is wonderful." She widened her eyes at the Bradfords. "Even some of those rowdy boys you wouldn't expect to see behaving so well." Everyone laughed.

"These are the Bradfords, Mrs. Carren, Helsi and Ian," Hope touched Helsi's arm lightly. "This is Sarah Carren. She has two children at Poore Pond." They exchanged handshakes and greetings.

"It was great though," Mrs. Carren resumed. "I especially appreciate the way she uses traditional Christmas carols." Lowering her voice to a whisper, "I know she stretches that separation-of-church-and-state thing a bit, but the parents I spoke to were all for it."

Ian saw Hope's jaw tense slightly. "Not really," she said, giving direct looks first to Mrs. Carren then to Ian and Helsi. "Mrs. Ricci teaches the carols in her music classes as part of an emphasis on the history of music. She relates various styles of music to their origins." Ian could see she was defensive.

"Sure she does," Sarah Carren said, still smiling widely. "My mother drove all the way over from Fairfield to see the concert. She wanted me to tell you how much she enjoyed it as well."

"I believe I met your mother at Grandparents' Day last fall, is that right?" Ian admired the way Hope quickly regained her relaxed charm. "She was wonderful, I remember, said very kind things about Poore Pond."

"Oh yes, she comes every year. Looks forward to it. Buys a new outfit." Mrs. Carren looked laughingly at Helsi and Ian who laughed with her.

"Please tell her how much we appreciate her support. And thank you for your support, too, Mrs. Carren." Hope shook her hand again.

Ian and Helsi chorused "Glad to meet you" and marveled at Hope's unfailing charm.

*

Helsi was pleasantly surprised by the calm nature of the meeting. Ian made nothing but kind remarks about the school. Hope, her shoulders and mouth relaxed, listened attentively and let them take the lead. She withheld comment when Helsi described Dylan's self-deprecating words during the homework session. She did not react when Ian said that Dylan may have had a better chance in first grade with a male teacher. She did not respond when Helsi got off the subject of Dylan and commended the Conflict Management Program and how it had benefited Robbie. She waited for the Bradfords to state their own conclusions regarding the best way to help Dylan succeed.

This is how a meeting between parents and principal should go. Helsi credited her husband's improved attitude and Hope's nondirective approach for the comfort level of the meeting.

In the end, after Helsi had planted a small seed of the idea that Dylan should return to kindergarten class, Ian put forth, as if original with him, the benefit of repeating kindergarten. To Helsi's delight, he endorsed it as the best possible solution for their youngest son. No mention was made of the fact that his decision echoed the original recommendation of the intervention team.

Plans were laid for Dylan to come early the morning of the first school day after break and be installed in the kindergarten room with Mrs. Armstrong instead of his former teacher, Miss Fox. Hope's only directive comment was that returning to Miss Fox's class might trigger in Dylan old feelings of failure. A second chance in kindergarten with a new teacher whose style was different would truly be a fresh start. The Bradfords agreed.

"I will explain our rationale to Miss Fox so she understands that in no way are you criticizing her teaching," Hope said, her eyes imploring them to feel her sincerity.

"Of course," Helsi agreed while Ian nodded yes.

Hope waited for Ian to conclude the meeting. Standing, he offered his hand, which Hope grasped readily. "We can't thank you enough for working with us—your patience—letting us see for ourselves. We get it now," Ian said, meaning it. They shook hands warmly then broke for Helsi and Hope to follow suit.

"We apologize for giving you such a hard time," Helsi said with honest eyes and a warm grasp.

"Not at all," Hope said serenely. "Good luck in your talk with Dylan. I like your idea of getting a sitter, so you and Mr. Bradford can take him for a special lunch to discuss the matter. He'll feel quite grownup, I expect."

During the drive home Helsi sat back in the seat and sighed with relief. She looked out at the peace of snow-covered streets and lawns, the joy of cheerful holiday decorations on homes and shops. Street light poles decorated with pine roping and red-striped candy canes bobbed past. She looked lingeringly at the life-sized nativity in front of Trinity Church and felt hopeful for Dylan.

She looked at her husband and they exchanged smiles. He reached for her hand and their fingers entwined. "One more day of school for our rugrats," he laughed. "Then they're all ours for ten days. Are you ready for that, Hon?"

"Do I have a choice?" she chided.

Since there were forty-five free minutes before Rachel had to be collected from preschool, they decided to stop at the donut shop for the rare treat of actually eating a donut on the premises with a relaxing cup of Christmas coffee.

*

Ian and Helsi were not prepared for the family fallout after they had had their special Saturday luncheon date with Dylan. The initial discussion went rather smoothly. Dylan asked a few questions: *What should he tell his friends in Mrs. Cooper's class? What if Miss Fox thinks he hates her? What if Mrs. Armstrong doesn't want an extra kid in the middle of the year?*

In each case Helsi or Ian counseled their son in positive terms. "You need more practice with letters and sounds," they explained should be the stock answer to the why questions.

"Dr. Fleming promised to speak to Miss Fox and make sure she knows that we think she's a good teacher; you just need a fresh start all around," they told their son.

"How could Mrs. Armstrong not like you? She loves all children," they said with conviction in an attempt to reassure the boy.

But the real shock came from Lucy and Sean.

"I can't believe a brother of mine is so lame," Sean quipped. "How'll I face my friends? A five-year-old with the brain of a five-month old. Who would have guessed Dylan's oversized head held such a pea brain?" Sean lapsed into his usual early teen response to serious issues, biting sarcasm. He swaggered into the living room and switched on the television, turning the volume a little too loud.

"How could you do that to Dylan?" Lucy moaned. "He'll be remembered forever as the kid who got sent back to kindergarten. It's worse than just staying in kindergarten another year." Her eyes filled and her face turned bright red. "At least when you repeat a grade, everyone knows you weren't ready to go on." She stood resolutely, hands on hips to make her point. "But when you pass to the next grade and can't cut it, you let everybody down, teachers, your mom and dad, your brothers and sisters. They had high hopes for you, gave you a chance, and you let them down." She spooled her emotions into such a feverish pitch that Dylan and Robbie raced inside from their tin-can hockey in the driveway.

"Oh Dylan," Lucy wailed. "You poor thing." She ran to him and scooped him into her arms.

Dylan looked confused and afraid. "What? What, Lucy?" He untangled himself from his sister's arms.

"That's enough, Lucy. Go to your room now," Ian said in raised voice.

"Let's go," Robbie said to Dylan and they went out the back door, opening the door too widely and sending a rush of wintry air into the kitchen.

Lucy huffed out of the room and up the stairs.

Helsi's gaze met Ian's. "You don't suppose Lucy's right, do you, Ian?" she said through tense lips.

Ian plucked a grape from the small bowl on the sink and popped it into his mouth. He looked into his wife's eyes. "She might well be," he said, plucking another grape and studying it. "But she's a kid. She's giving us a kid's point of view. That's all." He looked at Helsi's strained face.

"But it's a kid who has to deal with this, isn't it? Our kid." Helsi shrugged her shoulders. "We should have talked to Lucy and Sean first, gotten all this out in the open; so Dylan wouldn't have to hear it."

She peered out the window at her two younger sons, intensely involved in the whereabouts of a battered soft-drink can they scrambled to hit with long sticks. She raised her eyes toward the upstairs and thought of Lucy, simmering with disappointment. She glanced toward the adjacent living room where Sean escaped into a mindless television sitcom. Helsi was struck by the different ways the children dealt with the issue.

From outdoors came the sound of small voices shouting and sticks splatting against a metal can. "You're right, Ian. Look at Dylan. He's more interested in his game with Robbie than school." She gestured toward the window.

Ian went to the window and looked out, smiling at a memory of himself as a boy delighting in the game of kick the can. "Look at that," he laughed. "Lucy will get over it, too." He looked toward the next room. "So will Sean. Everything's embarrassing when you're thirteen or fourteen. We did the right thing for Dylan. That's what matters." He hugged Helsi briefly. "Where are your keys? I'm going to get the van washed."

Helsi went into the next room and sat down with Sean. She asked him to turn down the volume on the television. "You know, Sean, you could be a big help to Dylan in this move."

"How's that?" Sean muttered, his eyes riveted to the television.

"Well, you could let him know you understand what he's going through, that he'll have to adjust." She knelt down next to Sean's chair, her face close to his. He flinched exaggeratedly.

"How is that done, Ma?"

"Just look for an opportunity. When the two of you are alone in the kitchen, or outside." Sean shot her an I-don't-get-it look. "You know, tell him it won't be easy, but it's the best thing for him."

"And why is it the best thing for him, being humiliated like that?" Sean could not let go of his teen-age attitude.

"It's the best thing for him to have more time to learn his basic kindergarten skills." She spoke loudly and deliberately, her eyes fixed firmly on his. "So he can go on to learn to read properly. You know as well as I do, Sean, how important that is. Will you help? Help Dylan and help Dad and me?"

"Sure thing, Ma," Sean spoke weakly, not looking at his mother. But Helsi knew Sean would take her suggestion to heart. He knew that Dylan idolized him, and he would want to do a good job encouraging his small brother. Helsi, on several occasions, had seen Sean show affection for Dylan. But she knew he wanted to keep his warm feelings secret.

The Christmas holidays were hectic and flew by. There was no more family talk about Dylan's class change or about school at all. A few days before the end of break Dylan received in the mail a small, neatly addressed off-white envelope bearing a large snowman sticker. Opening it excitedly, he found a handwritten note from Mrs. Armstrong and carried it to his mother to read to him.

Dear Dylan,

I am looking forward to having you join our class in Room 12. We call ourselves The Room Twelve Try-Hards *because everyone always tries their best to do good work. I know that you will fit right in because I have been told that you try hard to learn.*

When we learn something new, we practice it 12 ways and earn a sticker each time. The stickers are placed in a row next to your name in a class chart book and earn you special treats like stories and extra computer time.

I have made a nametag for your desk, so you can find it easily the first day.

Your teacher,

Mrs. Armstrong

Dylan proudly showed the note to everyone in the family and kept it at his bedside at night. Helsi felt re-encouraged each time she saw the small envelope.

*

School resumed and the Bradford family settled back into a daily routine with Dylan happy to have only half days of class. Seeing how the morning kindergarten schedule suited him so well, Helsi felt convinced that their decision had been right. Dylan spent his afternoons playing outside or in his room with a new super-sized set of building logs. Helsi interrupted his play for a mid-afternoon snack followed by a short practice session on letter identification and sounds. The short list of those he knew grew gradually longer. Just when Helsi and Ian began to feel he'd made solid progress, he stumbled, unable to recall several of those he seemed to have mastered.

Then the notes and telephone calls from Mrs. Armstrong started. She gave suggestions for specific strategies they could use at home with Dylan and sent materials in his book bag, flashcards and small manipulatives matching sounds and pictures to letters. Dylan seemed to enjoy using the practice materials and spoke often about centers the children worked in at school.

But his sporadic recall loomed over his positive attitude. Helsi tried to conceal her concern from him but discussed it at length with Ian.

"Maybe you should visit Dylan's class and see what those *centers* are all about. Get more ideas to use at home. Dylan likes them so much, maybe that's the key. Everybody knows we learn what we like."

So Helsi, to Dylan's great delight, arranged to be one of Mrs. Armstrong's classroom volunteers on learning-center days. He would smile and look sheepishly at his teacher when his mother arrived and wanted to linger at the particular center she was running.

Though Helsi picked up useful ideas, such as letting Dylan configure letters in a tray of sand with his finger, she gleaned far more. She saw how quickly most of the five-year-olds grasped new skills. But she could not miss the reality of how difficult learning seemed for Dylan, who had already turned six. While he approached each task with enthusiasm and a façade of confidence, it was clear that he could not retain mastery from one session to the next, often not within the same session. One turn he recognized letters m and n as well as their correct sounds; the next, he confused the two or made wild guesses. Picture cards did not help. He could face an illustration of a monkey, recite monkey, then match it with a letter d or g beginning-sound card.

One particular day Helsi found it all frustrating. Her face grew red with emotion and embarrassment. Tears of concern filled her eyes. She tried to will away the tears so neither Dylan nor the other children would see. Mrs. Armstrong, sensing her dilemma, stepped in to give her a lavatory break.

In the faculty women's restroom Helsi found herself face to face with Marie Harris, the attendance secretary.

"What's wrong, Mrs. Bradford," she asked softly, her eyes warm.

Helsi, taken aback that Marie knew her name, managed only to nod her head.

"You're not well?" Marie said and hugged her as one would hug a distressed child. "Do you want coffee? I'll get you coffee. You sit here; I'll be right back."

She gestured toward the small plastic-covered settee barely fitting against the wall in the cramped restroom. "Do you take milk and sugar?"

Helsi, her eyes moist, nodded yes. Marie left quickly and Helsi dabbed at her eyes with a wet paper towel. "Get hold of yourself," she said aloud. "It won't help matters if you fall apart." She was torn between loathing Mrs. Harris and feeling grateful for her kindness. She sat back down and fished a folded tissue from her sweater pocket.

Marie soon returned with a styrofoam cup of hot coffee. She handed it to Helsi and sat down next to her. "That should make you feel better," she murmured in a voice full of kindness. "You must be volunteering in Mrs. Armstrong's class today. Your son Dylan is in that class, isn't he?" She looked into Helsi's eyes.

"Yes, you know Dylan?" Helsi asked, turning toward Marie.

"Oh yes," Marie smiled. "He always chats with me when he comes to see about his lunch card. He and I are buddies. He is such a nice boy, so pleasant."

"That's Dylan. All charm and personality." Helsi said, steeling her voice not to crack. *And not much substance.* She immediately felt disloyal.

"Unfortunately though, he's really struggling in school," Helsi, shocked, heard herself say. She hardly knew Marie Harris, had spoken to her occasionally in the office and on the phone; but that was the extent of their relationship.

"I know about his class change," Marie said softly. "That must have been a hard decision for you." She looked at Helsi with tender eyes. "I thought about you when the changes on his class rosters came across my desk. Trying to make the right decision for your child's education is heart wrenching, isn't it?"

Helsi nodded, mopping with tissue the tears that suddenly spilled down her cheeks. "The hard part is trying to hide my disappointment from him. I feel so guilty." Her voice rose with emotion. Marie, embarrassed for her, glanced away.

"I went through the same thing with my daughter and her little son. He wasn't learning to read like the other kids were. My daughter and son-in-law helped him every day at home, but he had to repeat first grade." Marie fidgeted with the folds in her skirt. Helsi knew she avoided looking at her and appreciated the gesture of respect.

"Did he do better the second time in first grade?"

"Not much better. He ended up in a special tutoring program. That's when things got better. Now he's in fourth grade and doing OK. But he'll never be a straight-A student." She looked again at Helsi. "His mother was a straight-A student all through school. It's hard." She stood, poised to leave. "But he's the dearest boy, smart as a whip in other areas. Charms everybody."

Marie extended her hand to Helsi, and they shook warmly. "You're not to worry, Mrs. Bradford. Everything will work out for the best. You have a good day now." She left the room.

Helsi sat, savoring the hot coffee, the warmth she felt as it ran down her throat. *What a caring woman Marie Harris is, taking the time to comfort me like that.'* Helsi was grateful that it had not been Hope Fleming she encountered in this emotional state.

Helsi looked at her watch and realized her volunteer duty would finish in fifteen minutes. She drank the last of the coffee in one long drink, blotted her mouth on the napkin Marie had brought with the coffee, and checked herself in the mirror.

She returned to the room in time to help the other volunteers clean center areas while the children, congregated on the carpet and listened to their teacher read a story. Dylan turned to make eye contact with his mother, his face full of concern. She smiled weakly at him; and he, apparently reassured, directed his attention back to the teacher.

Helsi waved quietly at Mrs. Armstrong and closed the classroom door softly behind her. She checked out in the office with Mrs. Kurowski and Mrs. Harris, smiling warmly to hide her heavy heart. *Why had she volunteered to help with centers?* She was at a loss as to what the next step for Dylan should be. What were his real limitations? Was he *brain damaged? Retarded? Dyslexic?* The entire subject chilled her to the bone.

She shivered violently in the cold car as she waited for the heater to work before pulling out of the parking lot. Staring across the snow-covered grounds of Poore Pond, Helsi noted the beauty of the stately building, enhanced by the snowy setting. The structure bespoke a sense of security and stability that Helsi, at that moment, did not feel. She suddenly feared she might give up on Dylan. Frightened, she pressed too hard on the accelerator and shot into the street.

She dreaded seeing Ian and had no idea what she would she say to him.

CHAPTER NINETEEN—HOPE

"Do you know why Jeremy Baker is absent today, Ray?" Hope asked as he came to her office in answer to her intercom call. She backed into the tiny inner office and motioned for him to sit down.

Ray shook his head. "I have to get right back. Dumpster pickup is in 15 minutes." He gave her a let's-get-on-with-it look and began, "Well, I guess Hannah issued her an ultimatum yesterday, either get out by the end of the month or pay her $600 a month until she finds a place."

"But if Heather could pay her sister $600, she could afford to get a place. What is she thinking?" Hope's brow furrowed.

"Exactly," Ray laughed.

"Telephone, Ray. Line one," Bella called from her desk.

Hope moved away from her desk to make room for Ray near the phone. She stood poised to leave the room if the conversation became personal.

"Well, hi there, Heather," she heard Ray say, his voice full of pleasure. Hope waited to glean the nature of the call, busying herself by looking through a pile of mail. She could tell from Ray's sympathetic comments that Heather was upset. When his responses became more emotional, Hope stepped out of the office, quietly closing the door behind her.

Bella rolled her eyes at Hope. "Trouble in paradise?" she asked. Hope shrugged her shoulders.

Ray opened the door, his face troubled. Hope stepped into the office and closed the door against Bella's curious ears.

"Is Heather in crisis?" Hope asked softly.

"Yeah, it's a crisis all right. She and Hannah had it out. Now she's all packed to leave." Ray paced back and forth, as far as he could in a ten-by-ten office. "Wants to stay at my house temporarily. Store her stuff in our garage." He looked helplessly at Hope. "I'm going to call Mom. See what she says." He opened the door. "I'll keep you posted.

"Did she say where Jeremy was?" Hope asked, thinking how frightened he must be to have seen his world crashing in amidst so much emotional tension. "Playing outside in the snow with his cousin, she said. Poor little guy." Ray's eyes grew more desolate. "He should be in school," Ray said as if reading Hope's mind.

Hope glanced at her watch; she had half an hour before the lunch lines would start. She sat down at her desk and resumed her check of the mail. She dropped envelope after envelope of advertising in the trash can and nearly discarded an ivory letter-sized one when the heavy bond paper and the return address jumped out at her. McElson- Bourney and Associates, L.P.A.

Her heart froze. It had been years since she had seen that name. Mary Baldwin's attorneys. With trembling fingers, Hope turned the envelope over in her hand. It was full and tightly sealed. The word confidential, stamped carefully to the right of the school address, blinded her. Her heart raced. Her chest burned. Needing a large drink, she reached for her water bottle. But her throat was so constricted she could take only a sip.

Hope stumbled to the door, bumping her knee on the desk. She peered into the outer office where Marie and Bella were both working intently on computers, and closed the door tightly.

She thought for a moment that she should leave the building and take the letter home to open it. "That's silly," she said aloud. "Get hold of yourself, Hope." She sat back down and picked up the dire envelope. It had been twenty-six years since she had worked for Mary Baldwin.

*

The two of them had related well from the beginning. The dowager's spirit, and no less her wealth, immediately enchanted Hope. Mary had admired Hope's intelligence, ambition, and most of all, her mature character. She'd often said, "You've got a strong sense of right and wrong, Hope Minster." Her steely blue eyes locked into Hope's. "You'll go far if you keep it." She said that to an eighteen-year-old Hope only one month after hiring her. She said it again to Hope at age twenty-two when she completed her final summer of working for Mary. She had just graduated summa cum laude, thus fulfilling her dream of an honors degree from a prominent women's college. Mary was as proud of Hope's accomplishments as Hope was herself.

"Can you work a few more hours a week? I want you to start managing my accounts," Mary had said after employing Hope for one year. She thrilled the nineteen-year-old Hope, who felt deeply honored. She could use the extra salary; indeed, she was desperate to increase her income. She was already struggling to maintain a distinctive upper-class appearance, sometimes living on popcorn when she used her food allowance to buy such necessities as a cashmere sweater or snakeskin pumps.

"Wherever did a girl like you from a working-class family acquire such a mark of the aristocrat?" Mary would comment bluntly. Hope had proudly explained her father's heritage: his mother, Laura Thomas, was the great granddaughter of an earl, the Earl of Stratford. The heir apparent had emigrated in 1848 from southern England to Charleston, South Carolina, where he'd become a wealthy landowner and tobacco farmer. When his family summoned him back to England to claim his rightful title, he declined, not wanting to give up his opulent plantation life in America.

Unfortunately, the earl's heirs squandered their tobacco inheritance generation by generation. Hope's father, though well educated, was not fired with ambition and did not have the ancestral love-of-lavish-living blood in his veins. He was a solitary soul who earned a modest living as a watchmaker, housing his submissive wife and two daughters in a small brick row house.

As a young girl, Hope was drawn to upper middle class peers and managed, on the strength of her classic beauty and regal bearing, to be included in their exclusive circle. Her scholarship to Vassar set her on the road to living her dream. When her path crossed Mary Baldwin's, she experienced genteel life in Mary's twenty-eight-room family mansion, ultimately sealing her determination to live the life of an aristocrat.

Mary paid well for her work as companion, which actually entailed far more than the word connoted. Hope ran errands; coordinated social engagements, medical and business appointments; indeed, oversaw Mary's entire calendar as well as performing all duties of a corresponding secretary.

Eventually, Mary became dependent on Hope to drive her to appointments and on outings, seldom using Mock, her full-time chauffeur-gardener. She felt comfortable with Hope and seemed to find pleasure in grooming her for the aristocratic life. When Hope would drive her to the hairdressers, she would insist that she, too, have full-service treatments: hairstyle, manicure, pedicure. Hope accepted graciously and learned to anticipate these benefits, scheduling them—since she managed Mary's master calendar—for times that suited her own needs. She liked to look her best for important campus functions.

After managing Mary's accounts with precision for fourteen months, Hope readily understood the pattern. Monthly amounts for each account remained somewhat static. Deposits in the checking account magically appeared from the investment firm on the first of each month, always the same six-figure amount. Household expenses, clothing and personal care, travel and entertainment, and gifts and donations varied little in amount from month to month.

On the first day of the month—always the first day—albeit the weekend or a holiday, Hope was expected to sit down at the handsome mahogany desk in Mary's library and methodically pay the accounts. She wrote the checks by hand, using a carefully mastered calligraphic stroke she had taught herself after admiring Mary's bold, artistic handwriting.

Hope would deduct the checks from Mary's balance in the check record of the business-sized, eight-and-one-half-by-eleven, leather check ledger. Although the payable amounts seemed exorbitant to Hope, total deductions for the checks she wrote never exceeded the monthly deposits. Therefore, Mary's balance in the checking account kept growing. This seemed strange to Hope whose college minor was finance, so she had learned that one of the basics of money management was to keep one's money working.

When she broached the subject with Mary, Mary complimented her on her financial prowess before flatly stating, "I have my reasons for growing that balance. Your job is to write the checks and balance the account." This was in keeping with Mary's independent spirit and sense of privacy. She opened certain doors widely to Hope. Others remained securely closed. "Just pay the accounts on my list, Hope, and balance the figures. Put them in stamped, addressed envelopes, and see that they are posted on the first day of the month. That's all you have to do. That's all you have to know." She punctuated each directive with a strong tap of her silver-handled cane on the polished cherry wood floor, her pale eyes flaming, her face set.

In her junior year Hope was desperate for a large sum of money to pay for winter term abroad, which the scholarship did not include. Every one of the sorority sisters she was close to was going, and Hope had optimistically scraped together the $200-deposit to reserve her place. The balance, $5200, had to be paid by November 10, and Hope had no prospects of finding the money.

She sat at Mary's elegant desk in the hickory-paneled library on 1 November, invoices, bills, and check ledger spread on the glass-topped surface. She transferred from the deposit slip, the new six-digit figure and added it to the still-sizeable account balance. For the first time, the amount of money in Mary's account struck a chord in her mind. "She would never miss a paltry $5200 from this enormous balance," she thought. Frightening herself, she looked away, out the nine-foot tall French windows spanning the north side of the room. The day was gray and cold, the sky overcast with muddy clouds. Drops of water from intermittent rain stuck to the windows.

Hope looked again at the large balance. She wondered how she might go about extracting from Mary's account, the tiny bit of money she needed. How could she issue herself a check, beyond the bi-monthly paychecks she was responsible for drafting. Twice a month she issued herself, according to Mary's direction, a check for $600. Only one more digit. That's all she needed to solve her problem. She gazed toward the door.

Would Mary notice the small discrepancy during her sporadic inspections? Would bank officials notice? Occasionally agents from McElson-Bourney reviewed the accounts, she knew. They would call and speak to Mary, after which she would direct Hope to deliver pages of the check record to them. How closely would they scrutinize it, she wondered. Her heart raced. She took deep breaths.

No, she could not do it. That was stealing. She was not a criminal.

She picked up the list of accounts and began writing in her careful script the corresponding checks, clipping them to the bills and laying them atop envelopes.

She wrote checks to: *Wholefoods Market, Municipal Power, Willowscape Gardens, and Hope Ministries. Hope Ministries,* she stared at the payee and noticed as she had numerous times before how very like her name this televangelist group's name looked. And sounded. Mary had specified on her November list, as she did each month, a $6000-donation to the group.

Six thousand dollars would pay for winter term abroad and leave Hope $800 for other expenses. A few strokes of the pen would solve her problem instantly. Just a few strokes. Hope stared into space. She heard faint strains of Verdi's *Rigoletto* from Mary's sitting room above the library. She faced the leather-framed desk calendar and saw November 10 looming very near. She looked again at the fat balance.

It was too much to resist. She took the broad-tipped pen and painstakingly blended the first is in Ministries into a wide s. She wrote over the ri and the es, changing them to er.

She took a deep breath, checked Hope Ministries off the payables list, exhaled, and inserted the check into a blank envelope which she tucked into the pocket of her Ralph Lauren corduroys.

Partaking of tea with Mary was part of the bill-paying ritual. Edna, the stalwart cook, brought it on an immense silver tray: silver teapot of steaming Earl Grey tea, silver pitcher of heated milk, miniature scones with Devon cream and biscuits or fruit tarts, precise little lemon wedges. Hope calmly sipped and nibbled as she conversed at length with Mary, answering questions about her classes and instructors, her goals. All the while she was conscious of the stiff envelope folded in her pocket.

*

The first-lunch bell sounded, startling Hope. Still, she had not opened the ivory envelope. She stood. She looked down at the envelope. She picked it up and reached for the letter opener, her heart racing.

Hope sighed heavily. She laid the letter again on the desk, the opener next to it, and slipped the strap of the portable microphone over her shoulder. She headed resolutely toward the cafeteria, nearly colliding with a child.

"Well hello, Sophia," she said to a serene-faced third grader.

"Dr. Fleming, my mom wants to know if you could take me home to get my valentines." Hope chuckled before realizing that the child was dead serious.

"You forgot to bring your valentines for the party today, Sophia?" The child nodded, her eyes wide and her bluntly cut, glistening brown hair bobbing.

Hope glanced at the clock, considering for a moment the girl's proposal, then said, "You may bring them tomorrow. Mrs. Thorpe will let you give them out then." She smiled.

"I need to call my mom and ask her if that's OK."

"We won't bother her at her office, Sophia. You'll tell her when you get home from school today. Let's go back to class now." Sophia's mouth was poised to speak, but Hope guided her out of the office and started her down the hall. The bustle of students coming to the lunch line filled the hallway near the servery.

"There's my class now," she blurted, hurrying to join the girls' lavatory line. Pamela Thorpe stood at the head of the line and smiled knowingly at Hope.

"Did you get Sophia's problem sorted out, Dr. Fleming?"

"Yes, we did." She stepped close to the teacher and lowered her voice. "She's going to bring her valentines tomorrow and give them out then."

"Have you ever had a child ask you to take her home for that reason?" Pamela asked with a chuckle, keeping her voice low. "And she said her mother suggested it." The teacher laughed heartily, her dark eyes dancing.

"No, I can't say I have. And I can't believe I actually considered it for a moment. Before I realized what a precedent I would be setting." They both laughed, attracting the attention of all the boys and girls in the two lines. Feeling the tension of so many pairs of curious eyes, Hope quickly remarked, "Mrs. Thorpe thinks we should have two days of valentine parties, Children. Isn't she funny?" The children laughed and several high voices called, "Yeah! Two parties!" as Hope walked away.

Finding it difficult to engage in friendly banter with students and practice their names as she often did, Hope moved rapidly up and down the lunch lines. First-lunch children seemed to be squirmier and noisier than usual. She found herself reprimanding too many of them, startling those who did not hear her natural voice, by repeating their names on the microphone. The line of five-and-six-year-olds grew quiet and still. They looked at Hope with confused, sullen eyes. Their faces made her feel guilty, and she loathed herself for depriving them of their customary personal exchanges with an interested principal.

When second-lunch classes began to file through the cafeteria line, Hope vowed to be more herself with the eager second-and-third-graders. But her resolve faded when she had to remove Frank Branchello and Joey Masterson for scuffling in the line and being disrespectful to Helen when she chastised them. Hope asked Helen to send the boys' lunch trays to the office with a student helper, then she escorted the two to her office where they would eat lunch while watching behavior-modification videotapes dramatizing the importance of respect.

Frank, stout and strong, and Joey, tall for his age, followed her with surly and embarrassed faces. She cleared spaces at her worktable and instructed them to sit down facing the television set. Fourth grader Mark Pryor, looking poised and responsible, entered the office balancing a lunch tray in each hand. The smell of overcooked potato nuggets filled the small office.

"Thank you, Mark. Just set those trays on the table." Mark did so and left quickly. Hope pulled a video from the shelf and inserted it into the videocassette player.

"Frank and Joey, you are to watch this video while you eat lunch. There will be no talking." She gave them her intensive eye contact. Frank swallowed and examined his food. Joey looked at her with defiant eyes. "Afterward, you will write about your behavior and some of the points on the tape. I will give you instructions then."

Frank raised his hand and looked at her with face of pure innocence.

"Yes, Frank."

"Will we get to go to recess after we write?"

"That will depend on what you learn from this episode." Hope broke their eye contact to switch on the tape player.

Hope stepped out and asked Marie, who sat at Bella's desk, to please monitor the boys for talking.

The fourth-and-fifth-grade lunch line seemed to be flowing nicely although the children seemed unusually noisy and active as had been the previous groups. *It's too bad we've had so many indoor recesses. The children really need to get outside and work off excess energy.*

"Dr. Fleming, Dr. Fleming, Katie's crying," a shrill voice called. Hope moved toward the voice.

"Yes, Alana."

Alana spoke for Katie who stood next to her, head down, hands over her eyes. "She's sick, Dr. Fleming. Feels rotten." Alana cast sympathetic eyes toward her friend.

Hope put her arms around Katie's shoulders and said, "Come with me, Dear." She steered the child, heat emanating from her entire body, into the clinic.

"Mrs. Sunfield, Katie Flanders feels ill and has not yet had lunch. I will have her lunch sent in in case she feels like eating." Elaine Sunfield helped the child to a cot and gently placed a digital thermometer in her mouth. She picked up the telephone.

Hope returned to her office where Frank and Joey were watching the tape, their empty lunch trays pushed aside. Hope followed the tape, knowing the end was near.

"May I see you a moment, Dr. Fleming?" Marie's warm voice asked. She stood at the doorway. Hope joined her and they stepped into the outer office. "Elaine has to leave; her mother's been rushed to the hospital." Marie spoke in hushed tones. "I've called for a clinic sub, but they couldn't tell me—personnel will get back to us. Oh," she lowered her voice to a whisper. "The boys were very quiet." Marie always puts a positive spin on the situation.

"Thank you, Marie." Hope dismissed Frank and Joey with instructions to write a paragraph about their behavior in the lunch line, what rules they had broken, and what better choices they could have made, as discussed on the tape.

"Bring me your papers before lunch time tomorrow if you expect to be considered for recess. Take your trays to the servery, thank you." The boys left with their trays and relief on their faces.

Hope went into the clinic. Elaine, slipping into her coat, explained, "Katie Flanders has a temperature of 102 degrees. Her mother, Mrs. Sawyer, said she would be here as soon as she is free to leave work. Katie is resting comfortably." Elaine looked at Hope with worried eyes.

"You go on, Mrs. Sunfield. We'll manage. I hope things are under control with your mother."

"Katie's temperature should be taken again in about fifteen minutes," Elaine called over her shoulder as she left hurriedly. "And Thad needs his taken now."

Hope moved to a chair near the sink where Thad waited patiently and inserted a thermometer into his mouth without comment. She checked to make sure Katie was comfortable. She went to the desk and looked at the stack of clinic slips, placing Katie's and Thad's on the side.

"May I help? I live next door to Sawyers." A small woman in a red Poore Pond School sweatshirt and pressed chino pants stood just inside the clinic door. Katie sat up slowly and waved weakly at the woman.

"Of course," Hope said. "Come in."

The woman went over to Katie and patted her hair.

Katie lay down again. "What's the matter? Not feeling so good?" she asked warmly. Katie nodded.

"I didn't realize you lived next door to Katie
Flanders, Mrs.—is it Mayfield?" Hope asked.

"Mayhew," the woman smiled. "We're good friends. Alana Billings—she lives on our street, too—saw me in the hallway unpacking new playground materials. I could see she was worried. She told me Katie was in the clinic." She stroked Katie's small hand as she talked. "Our families are close."

A faint beep sounded and Hope retrieved the thermometer from Thad's mouth. "Ninety-eight, point two," she read. "You do not have a fever, Thad. That's good." The husky-faced boy looked at her with disappointed eyes. "Let's have you rest on the cot for awhile, and maybe you'll feel better." Hope knew Thad as a chronic clinic patient who often needed a little TLC. Her natural tenderness emerged.

Careful to maintain his sad face, the boy shuffled to the cot as if he may not make it. "My head hurts," he muttered.

Hope looked at Mrs. Mayhew and smiled. Mrs. Mayhew smiled back knowingly.

"Have you reached Katie's mother?" Mrs. Mayhew asked. "I could take her home. I'm leaving soon." She looked tenderly at the child who lay relaxed on the cot, eyes closed.

"That's very kind of you, Mrs. Mayhew. Mrs. Sawyer said she'd be here as soon as she could get away." Hope ran water over a coarse paper towel, wrung it, and folded it into a neat rectangle. She applied it to Thad's forehead.

"This cold compress will help your headache, Thad."

"I hate to see her having to wait it out here when she doesn't feel well," Mrs. Mayhew said. "I'll be done in fifteen-to-twenty minutes."

"Why don't you check back before you leave; and if her mother hasn't arrived, I'll try to reach her and get permission for you to take Katie home." Hope took blankets from a drawer and covered both Katie and Thad.

"That's good. Did the nurse get sick? Is that why you're taking care of the clinic?"

An energetic nine-year-old danced into the room, and Hope went to the locked cupboard where students' prescription medications were kept. "Hello, Steven," she said.

To Hope's great relief, the substitute nurse arrived for the last hour of the school day. Anxiety over the letter had kept Hope's mind fragmented to the point that focusing on clinic duties and young patients was more stressful than it should have been. She walked resolutely to her office, prepared to face the words of *McElsen-Bourney* and get it over with at last.

Closing the door behind her, Hope felt it resist. She turned and saw Ray wearing his fur-lined anorak. He entered the office and gave her a perfunctory greeting followed by a series of questions. "Does PTA have an emergency fund Heather could use today? Do you know the cost of a room at the Junction Motel on Forbes Street? Do you have today's paper, the classified section?" He pounded his fist into his palm repeatedly.

Hope could answer yes to only the last question. "Yes, Ray, the paper is in the trash can under my desk." She fished it out, dusting off pencil-sharpener shavings.

"I only need the classified section," Ray repeated. He took the page from her and began to scour down the columns. "Thought maybe there's a room for rent in here somewhere. Temporarily, you know. So they have a place to stay tonight. Buy some time."

"I take it the Bakers will not be staying at your house?"

"Naw, Mom's not up to it. Well, that's not exactly right. She said she's not up to fighting with Claire over it." He folded the paper and placed it back in the trash can. "Nothing there," He said.

"I don't know what to do for them," he said, his face frantic. "Any ideas, Hope?" He was clearly sacrificing his pride.

"Has Heather contacted Family Services?" Hope grasped for ideas. She felt a confusing twinge of guilt.

"Not yet. She still thinks she's going home with me." Ray looked at the clock. Thirty-five minutes until dismissal. He paced the floor. "I don't know how I can tell her. Let her down like that." Emotion crept into his voice.

Hope could see that he wanted to be Heather's White Knight. She both admired and abhorred him for it. Michael, in the beginning, had wanted to rescue her as well.

She simply did not want to deal with the Baker's plight. She needed to open the foreboding letter and face whatever terror it held. But she had to have privacy and a clear mind in order to do that.

She was torn between wanting to opt herself out of Heather and Jeremy's lives and just taking them home with her to be done with it. *Where did that come from? Well, I could take them home with me; I have that spare room, not to mention the pull-out sofa and private bath in the basement.* Eyes staring upward, she stroked her chin.

Ray was busy looking through the yellow pages under motels.

At that moment Hope understood the earlier twinge of guilt she had felt. She had the means to help this family. But sadly she did not have the generosity of spirit to do so.

"Ninety-three dollars? For one night? You've got to be kidding!" Ray fumed into the receiver. "Thanks." He hung up and looked at Hope, shaking his head.

Hope had the terrifying feeling she was going to ask Ray to bring the Bakers to her house. She thought of the letter from *McElsen-Bourney* and of all the help she'd had from their late client, her employer, her friend, Mary Baldwin. What was that movie she and George had watched on cable? Pay it Ahead? Repay Ahead? No. No. Pay it Forward. That was it. Pay it Forward. The concept intrigued her. George had said the world would be a better place if everyone would pay it forward. She agreed.

This was her opportunity to do a noble deed. She needed to do something noble. There was no way for Hope to repay Mary backward, but she could certainly pay the kindness forward.

Ray was dialing the phone, muttering about high prices.

"Ray, put down the phone." She met his gaze. "Heather and Jeremy may stay with me a few days. I have the room." Shocked at herself, she sat down. Apprehension flooded over her.

"Are you sure, Hope?" Ray asked, his face incredulous.

"Yes. Yes." She looked at Ray with serious eyes. "It's the right thing to do," she said flatly, meaning it. She felt it as well.

*

George called to his mother from her study when she walked into the house. "I'm on the net, Mom. Do you need your computer?"

"No, George. I'm going to make a cup of tea; would you like one?" she asked, her voice weary.

"No thanks, Mom. I'm in the middle of an orange juice. You carry on."

Hope removed her charcoal grey wool blazer, filled the kettle with water, and put it on the cooktop. She switched the burner to high and took a red-patterned stoneware cup and saucer from the cupboard along with a box of Earl Grey teabags and a small sugar bowl. Using a child-sized English coffee spoon, she placed a single brown-sugar cube in the cup and opened a teabag, placing it atop the cube.

She went to her briefcase near the door and removed the ivory envelope. The kettle whistled, and Hope brewed her cup of tea. She carried both the tea and the envelope upstairs to the writing table in her bedroom. She pulled the chain on the antique Tiffany desk lamp and sat down to open the envelope. Unfolding the rich bond paper, feeling its weight, she read first the engraved letterhead, then the letter itself:

Dear Hope Minster Fleming:
A matter concerning the estate of Mary Margarethe Baldwin and
you has been brought to our attention.
Please contact this office at your earliest convenience.

Best regards,

Maxwell A. Bourney
Attorney at Law

Hope gulped the scalding tea and burned her constricting throat. She dropped the letter, running to the bathroom where she cooled her mouth with handfuls of water from the faucet. The face in the mirror frightened her: drawn features, unnatural pallor, wild eyes.

"...a matter concerning the estate of Mary Margarethe Baldwin and you," What does that mean? *"...brought to our attention."* Who would have done that? Mary had no descendants except a nephew on the other side of the world, New Zealand or somewhere.

Hope splashed cold water on her face and blotted it with a thick towel. She inhaled deeply, exhaled, and went back to the writing table. The tea was now just the right temperature and she drank it lustily. She could have used a second cup but did not want to go downstairs just yet to get it. "I should have an electric kettle and tea fixings on a tray up here," she told herself. "Like my British friends have." She remembered winter term in Britain her junior year. She had fallen in love with the country estates the families owned and the elegant manor houses she visited. All that carved wood and faded chintz. And red brocade dining rooms. All the manor houses had red brocade dining rooms. The elegant china: Aynsley, Wedgewood, Spode, Royal Daulton.

Oh how I wanted to be part of the gentry. I never got there, did I? She tipped the teacup to her mouth and emitted a last drop of cool tea. *I got as far as the image and the education. That's as far as I got. Should have found an Englishman to marry. An aristocrat. Instead of Michael whom I had to support. He was always between get-rich deals."*

She sighed heavily and looked around the spacious master bedroom, noting that the look she had carefully created was much like those manor-house bedrooms, just as elegant, just as Old World.

I'll not let Mr. Bourney and his cohorts take this away from me. Not without a fight. But she knew in her heart how vulnerable she was, how defenseless. If her withdrawals from decades ago were discovered, she would be subject to criminal prosecution. But how could they have uncovered them? There would need to be collaboration with the televangelists' group, wouldn't there? Mary's donations had still gone to them, but once every other month instead of once a month.

The receipts they sent Mary for tax purposes would have revealed the discrepancies. Hope had been tempted to alter them before sending them on to the bookkeepers. But knowing Mary never reviewed them, she saved herself the impossible challenge of making undetectable alterations to the receipts and sent them on to the bookkeepers, risking everything. But nothing ever came of it. Until now.

The ringing phone shattered the stillness. Hope lifted the receiver and managed a husky hello.

"Hello, Hope," Ray said loudly, his voice unusually cheerful. Hope took that to mean he was in the company of Heather. "There's someone here wants to talk to you," he laughed. Hope heard whispering and shuffling.

"Hi—Dr. Fleming. I—want to—thank you for—." The line went silent. Hope recognized Heather's voice. She understood that Heather was too embarrassed to voice any reference to moving in with Hope, but she could not bring herself to say the words for her and confirm the invitation. "—everything you've done for Jeremy and me. We really appreciate it. Here, Ray."

"Hope?"

"Yes, Ray."

"Is it still all systems go? With Heather and Jeremy?" Ray's voice exuded confidence.

"Yes," Hope murmured. "When is this move to take place?"

"How about now? We already have the van loaded. We're at Pizza Shack now, just had dinner, so you won't have to feed them." He and Heather laughed simultaneously.

Hope could hear Jeremy whining in the background, "When are we going to the principal's house? I want to see my room."

Ashamed of her reticence, Hope summoned enthusiasm. "Now is fine, Ray. Jeremy needs to get settled in so he's ready for school tomorrow." She managed to keep from asking how many boxes of belongings they would bring with them.

*

Hope sat at the desk in her study reading progress reports. It was important to her to read every report card before it went home. She could not tolerate incorrect spelling, grammar, or inappropriate remarks sent to parents; and so she made time to read them every nine-week grading period. Because she sometimes found careless errors, the time cost was well worth it. She could appreciate the teachers' thoughtful comments as well.

She could hear Heather and George at the kitchen table, chatting like old friends. They were drinking colas and munching peanuts. It seemed strange to have so much young life in the house. She realized with surprise that she enjoyed it.

Hope had been relieved to see how little baggage Heather had brought: one suitcase apiece for Jeremy and her and two tightly bound, large cardboard cartons. They had settled nicely into the basement quarters where Jeremy now slept on the pulled-out sofa. George had moved plastic garment bags of summer clothes and boxes of linens from the large closet to the storage room. Heather had arranged all their belongings neatly and out of sight in the vacated closet.

She gave George little advance notice that the Bakers were coming, but he could not have been more accepting of them when they arrived. He immediately related well to Heather with no hint of sexual tension, just openness and natural warmth. Likewise, he treated Jeremy appropriately, so much so that Jeremy hung next to George at every opportunity until bedtime.

George carried the boy down the stairs on his shoulders, both laughing wildly. Hope was fascinated watching her son in a situation in which she'd never seen him before. She was proud of his ability to connect with these needy strangers and make them at once feel comfortable.

It had been a hectic but pleasant evening, full of surprises. After Jeremy's bath the four of them sat around the fire in the living room on Hope's white-linen-slipcovered chair and sofa. Hope in the broad chair next to Jeremy was reading aloud Henry the Uncatchable Mouse, George's favorite book as a boy. She had taken notice when George, answering Heather's where-do-you-work question, had replied, "I'm going to work in my father's business. Selling polymer products." He did not look at Hope.

"What are those?" Heather had asked, not at all self-conscious.

Hope listened intently with one ear while continuing to read aloud.

"Polymers are plastics, engineering thermoplastics. They're called engineering polymers because they have the combined physical properties of plastics, metals, and ceramics," George warmed to the subject. He raked his hair off his forehead with his fingers and continued. "My dad's company is a leader in using polymers to build engines, energy-efficient, low-noise, lightweight motors that are low cost." George sat back and took a breath. Only then did he look at his mother.

Hope smiled at him, wondering when he had acquired such knowledge of Michael's work and even more astounding, when Michael had become successful. She lost a beat in her reading and Jeremy looked up from the page. His eyes scanned the room.

"That's interesting," Heather said. "I know a little about polymers, I guess then. Resins? Are they a type of polymer?" She looked at George and without waiting for a response, continued in her child-like voice, "I work for a company that makes fasteners and small parts for electrical systems, and we just started using resin for some parts. They told us about its qualities, the same ones you just said: plastic, metal, and ceramic. And I've seen so many things, statues and things I thought were ceramic that turned out to be resin."

"Is that right?" George asked, somewhat surprised by her informed remarks.

Heather nodded. "Well, I'm –I've been laid off. Just getting called back now, for part-time only." She swallowed. "I worked there for two years before I got laid off," she said with pride in her eyes. "Got a raise every six months because I kept beating my quota."

"That was a blow to you, I'll bet," George said with tender eyes. "What do you do there?"

"Inspection. Just line inspection. Surface flaws, that's all. I know nothing about the parts, you know, how they're supposed to be built. It gets tiresome sometimes. But I have a pretty good eye." She sat back and sighed, having given her all to the conversation.

Hope was anxious to get more information from George about his affiliation with his father and about his specific plans. But she knew she would have to tread lightly to keep George from misjudging her motive. She resumed reading to Jeremy.

Now she heard movement in the kitchen. George and Heather were saying their good-nights and going off to bed. As Heather came to collect Jeremy, Hope looked at the stack of unread report cards, only slightly smaller than the stack of those she'd read. She removed her glasses and rubbed her eyes, yawning tightly.

George appeared at the door. "Good-night, Mom," he said with warm eyes. "You did a good thing today, helping Heather and Jeremy. I admire you." He smiled.

She smiled back, sending kisses with her eyes. "Some of you is rubbing off on me, I suppose. All your bleeding-heart talk about the homeless. What was I to do?"

"I think the real bleeding-heart is you. That has to be where I get it. We both know Dad doesn't have time for any of that, if it's not profit based." They both laughed. He turned toward the stairs.

Hope, not really up to paperwork but too full of anxiety to relax, picked up another report card.

*

Ray, having finished vacuuming Hope's office, coiled the cord in his signature figure eight. He wondered how Heather and Jeremy were getting along at Hope's house. He chuckled as he imagined them in what he thought would be Hope's hospital-clean home, scattering belongings through the impeccable rooms, throwing the entire kitchen into disarray with a simple cereal breakfast. He had been surprised at the way Caroline's kitchen had looked after serving them a quick supper of take-out pizza and fried pies. It looked as if a platoon had been fed there: soiled paper plates and napkins everywhere, pizza crusts and bits of sauce spilled on the table, greasy finger marks from the fried pies on drinking glasses. But Heather had diligently tidied it all up before he took her home, gathering trash and garbage and stuffing it into the waste can.

He heard Hope's footsteps down the dark hall and pushed the vacuum cleaner out to meet her.

"Good morning, Ray. Thank you for vacuuming early. You must have sensed I would arrive earlier than usual." She smiled at him, tired lines around her eyes, her mouth a little tense. She bent to set several plastic grocery bags on the floor.

"How did things go with your guests?" Ray's voice sounded too casual.

"Oh fine." Hope looked away. "They tried to be as obscure as they could, pretty impossible for an eight-year-old boy."

"Where is Jeremy? I thought you might bring him in with you."

"No. No. I dropped him off at his daycare after we took Heather to her factory. He'll get the bus to school."

"Some days he comes to Latchkey," Ray said, sounding disappointed.

"Will you please take these bags to the library for me, Ray. We have our steering-committee meeting this morning. Also, I need an overhead projector and the screen. Did I leave you a note yesterday about that?" Hope frowned.

"Yeah, you did. It's already set up. I'll take these bags down. Anything else?"

"No thank you. That'll be all for now, Ray." Hope was anxious to collate the pages she'd had Bella copy for the meeting.

Statistics on numbers of disciplinary measures taken this school year: telephone calls to parents, detentions, emergency removals. The statistics were part of her strategy for dealing with the discipline issue that Rae Osmond and Chuck Taylor raised. She had managed to piece together crude numbers from last year under Keith Broski, spending hours digging through scraps of handwritten notes in an envelope and copies of forms for parent notification of disciplinary action. She had no idea whether the set of forms was complete; she'd found them inside a crude log with alphabetized entries. Bella had printed from the computer a list of such consequences imposed on specific children in April and May, when Keith had begun recording them electronically.

Hope gathered copies of teacher-handbook pages spelling out disciplinary procedures she expected teachers to use as well as supervisory expectations that would, if followed consistently, help prevent opportunities for students to misbehave. It was important that teachers be reminded of the connection.

She laid the envelope from real estate appraiser Hank Hanlon on the desk to remind her to call him, and Michael, later.

Hope was a few minutes late getting to the library and was relieved that the teachers were helping themselves to juice and anise toast sticks while meeting their social needs. All of them except Rae Osmond and Chuck Taylor were chatting and laughing amiably. Rae and Chuck sat apart from the others, speaking in low voices, their faces serious.

Hope began the meeting and opened the floor for input under agenda item OTHER.

Pamela Thorpe commented on how well her volunteers were handling the math assessments for her. "They are the same parents who tutor my students twice a week in math skills, and the information they gain from doing the assessments helps them to better understand the kids' weak areas." Pamela made eye contact with every one of her colleagues at the table. "Sort of like—well—seeing the whole picture."

Hope admired her poise and professionalism and appreciated her putting a positive spin on the math assessments some colleagues had staunchly resisted.

Maddy Marenko complained that on indoor-recess days students, especially second-lunch, were being dismissed from the lunchroom and getting back to classrooms before the lunch supervisors. Blushing richly, she explained that she had no first-hand knowledge, but was quoting her special-education colleagues.

Brad Kushner responded that if the chronic ones happened to be Sam Richter and Francis Grey, he knew they were asking to go to the lavatory, loitering in there, and then heading back to class without returning to their lunch tables. He had caught them red-handed several times.

"Just a couple weeks ago I worked with Flo Bracco on it. She caught them skipping from the lav to the stairway and reprimanded them. I overheard and we both interrogated them." Brad's voice was serious. "Under pressure they finally admitted they would always ask a different supervisor for permission to go to the lav, so they wouldn't catch on. Those clever little stinkers had a real system, remember, Hope?" He laughed heartily and others, including Maddy, joined him. "They've been enjoying KP duty all week."

There was a knock at the door and Hope, sure that she had put the Meeting in Progress sign on the door, went to get it. She told the two students trying to return library books to come back later.

Trudy Cooper wanted to know why the new library books had not been shelved yet. "What is the problem?" She sniffed the air. "I'll help with the accessioning just to get it done."

"Carla's husband is still in the hospital," Melanie Armstrong explained before Hope, returning to the table, could interject. "Haven't you noticed the sub librarian we've had the past two weeks?" She looked at Trudy with mischievous eyes.

"Oh, that's who that perky woman in the library is! I thought she was a new, regular volunteer. She's a sub." Trudy widened her eyes and shrugged. "Well, what about Felice? Why can't she accession the new library books? Isn't that her job?"

"The truth is: now that our library collection is computerized, the processing comes on a CD. It's all done, accessions book and everything, on the computer. Felice does not know how to do it yet; she's still training." Hope explained.

Trudy groaned. "When will Carla be back?" Several people ventured guesses.

"She's hoping to return next Monday." Hope said. "I'll see if we can borrow a librarian from another school and get those new books processed before Carla returns. She'll have enough other catching up to do."

The next agenda item was DISCIPLINE. Hope asked Rae and Chuck to state their concerns, which they did, using the terms: permissive and lassez faire, building to negligent, chaotic, wild, and dangerous. The teachers responded in kind to their serious faces. The close of their comments was punctuated by total silence.

Hope, trying to derive meaning from the group's passive response to Rae and Chuck's strong remarks, distributed her statistics on disciplinary action last year and this year. They clearly reflected similar levels of action except Hope had used more emergency removals; in fact, she found no record of Keith having used the strategy at all.

After briefly discussing the statistics, Hope passed around the reminder pages on teacher supervision from the teachers' handbook. She led a review of the expectations: *greeting their own class lines at the entrance doors both in the mornings and at close of recess, escorting their own classes to specials, assemblies, lunch, group lav breaks, and the like as well as covering with consistency their assigned sentry posts at dismissal.*

This stimulated much animated discussion, which became heated at times. Pamela Thorpe and Brad Kushner boldly pointed fingers at unnamed teachers who were either chronically late to pick up their students or asked colleagues to escort their children back to class from music or PE when they dropped off their own class.

Dave Myers made one of his rare comments. "The best-behaved classes coming to gym have their teacher right there, setting limits." His eyes did not pan the room but looked straight at Hope. "Same thing leaving gym. If the teacher's on time, waiting for the kids to be released and directing and coaching, there's not much opportunity to act out." He turned to look at those colleagues who nodded in agreement.

"Coaching is a good word," Melissa said with a smile. "Especially for my kids."

Annie Klements made the point that setting high behavioral expectations for the class was a necessary correlate to close supervision during transitions. "You reinforce it hour after hour, day after day," she said, meaning it. "Not by in-their-face nagging, but quickly and clearly when you're giving directions and reviewing the schedule.

Hope let the discussion take its own course, observing with great interest. She was reminded of how aware teachers are of their colleagues' competency and effort. She was grateful for those with high standards—the majority actually—and the courage to speak out against any shirking of duties, for they assisted Hope immensely with this sensitive issue.

She looked into the faces of Rae and Chuck and saw detachment. She wondered when and how they would make their next point.

"So if everybody would just follow handbook procedures and take responsibility for supervising their own classes, a lot of these discipline problems would be prevented," Pamela summarized.

"And take it a step further," Brad advised. "Take the initiative, Folks. Intervene with kids you see breaking rules around school, in the hallways, the lavs, lunch lines, outside, even if they're not in your class." He smiled at everyone. "It's a team effort."

Rae and Chuck had no further comment.

The air became filled with escalating sounds of students shuffling in class lines, adults opening and closing doors, buses stopping and starting. Cold drafts of wind could be felt through internal doors, though closed. A sense of urgency took over the meeting.

Hope thanked the group for their work on the practice proficiency tests and distributed analyses charts of the results, giving them sets with enough copies to pass on to grade-level colleagues. She rushed them through key points reflected in the results in time to adjourn just before the first bell.

The teachers left quickly, some refilling juice cups and grabbing toast pieces before hurrying back to their rooms.

"I'll clean this up; my first class is not for another twenty minutes," Dave Myers offered. "Shall I take it all to the lounge?"

"That's nice of you, Dave," Hope said. "No, to the office, please. I like the secretaries to have a treat. Look at all that leftover toast." Hope gathered folders. "And thank you for your comment, Dave. It helped to quell the *coup d' 'etat.*" They laughed.

The ear-splitting first bell from the round metal wall unit above their heads interrupted their conversation. They waited for it to end.

"They just don't realize how obvious it is to us special teachers, how much they care or don't care about their kids' behavior," Dave said, loading his arms for a one-trip transport of leftover refreshments. "I always thought every teacher should trade places with us for one week. Even one day. Then they'd realize." He sailed out of the room in his athletic shoes.

Hope crossed the front lobby and saw the daycare bus unloading. She watched for Jeremy to disembark and soon spotted him trudging through the sparse snow, his boots in his arms. She greeted him and he returned the greeting, dropping his chin. She understood that his embarrassment stemmed from not knowing how to treat her in their new relationship. *It's a little awkward for me, too.* She stifled doubts about whether taking in the Bakers was the proper thing to do. *Oh well, it's only for a few days.* She hurried to prepare for morning announcements.

"There's our pledge leader," Hope said with a smile to Katie Flanders. "Feeling better?" she asked.

"Yes, thank you," she said, walking purposefully into the office.

After announcements Hope began to make her rounds, greeting classes in their rooms and checking for unlocked exterior doors. She relished making rounds first thing in the morning; students and teachers were rested and full of good cheer, excited about the day's planned activities.

Crossing the rear lobby, Hope felt the warmth of winter sun streaming through the tall, arched windows. She waved to Mrs. Brammond who sat at the round table on the other side of the lobby. She could see first grader Polly Chambers, brown pigtails bouncing as she walked toward her volunteer tutor. Hope knew there would be a good measure of phonics work going on there. Mrs. Brammond came every Tuesday at 9:30, and you could set your watch by her arrival. As grandmother of Poore Pond student John Brammond, she had really become a part of the school, volunteering as a tutor in not only John's class, but also in other classes.

What would we do without these volunteers? All the extra social activities would not happen, all the one-on-one help for children who do not qualify for formal tutoring programs. Hope, filled with admiration for Mrs. Brammond, walked up to her.

"How are you, Mrs. Brammond?" Hope smiled. "Good morning, Polly."

"I'm fine, thank you, Dr. Fleming. Just enjoying this sunny lobby." She smiled back at Hope and looked at Polly. "Of course, it's always sunny here, when Polly comes." The child laughed, trying to hide her embarrassment by shuffling work papers on the table.

"Are you staying for lunch today, Mrs. Brammond? We're having chicken with mashed potatoes. I can never resist that meal."

"Yes, I am. I gave my order to Marie already."

"You're way ahead of me," Hope said as she stepped away. "You and Polly." *A complimentary lunch is the least we can give for all her dedication.*

*

Lunch recess was over. Marie and Bella were back at their desks. The building was quiet. Hope seized the moment to think about Michael's plans to sell her house. She thought she would let him go ahead with the appraisal; she needed to know how much it would cost to buy Michael's share. She had no intention of selling the house.

Hank Hanlon agreed to come out week after next. Hope wanted to make sure the Bakers were gone.

She knew she should call Michael but dreaded the thought; his voice grated on her nerves so. She decided not to call him at all. Hank Hanlon would surely let him know she had followed through with the appointment.

Feeling stiff and out of shape, Hope stretched in her chair. She looked forward to meeting her friend and colleague Belva Carmichael, principal at Shake Rag School, at her health club. She invited Hope as her guest tonight as she had done twice before. Hope had felt invigorated from the treadmill and relaxed from the jacuzzi.

She also needed to get out of the house so she wouldn't foster Heather and Jeremy's dependence on her. There was that crock pot of chili waiting for them. Hope had decided to leave the chili, leftover from a batch she'd made for George and her when they were snowbound. After much deliberation, she had removed it from the freezer and explained to Heather where crackers and cheddar cheese were kept, urging her to enjoy a chili supper with Jeremy.

Hope was still getting used to the idea of outsiders living in her home. George had fitted nicely back into his former bedroom and had been so helpful with household chores. The sheer joy of seeing him every day, but without their old tensions, made her realize what she had been missing.

But now this new element, one of her students and his parent, actually living under her roof, seemed most awkward. They had spent only one night with her, but she knew clearly that it was a mistake. Taking in a family with no place to go is one thing. Taking in a student and parent from one's own school is quite another. *I should never have done it. I'm not up to it. An alternative must be found at once. Whatever was I thinking? I wanted to be more of a giver, give back, atone for my sins. Leave it to me to go too far the other way and lose my sanity.*

Do I want to be a formidable administrator or mother of the world? She laughed at her indecisiveness. *Could Michael have been right about my being weak?*

CHAPTER TWENTY—RAY

Ray drove along the curved street watching for Hope's address. He knew she lived on this fancy street with its English gardens and stately homes, but he'd never located her house. The addresses were stenciled on the curb, some obscured by traces of leftover icy snow; so Ray drove slowly.

"Why are you going so slowly?" Jeremy complained from the rear seat.

"Watch for 869, Jeremy. These numbers are hard to see." Ray inched along. He checked the rearview mirror and saw a white florist-shop van hovering behind him. He thought briefly of sending flowers to Heather, wondering if anyone had ever done that for her. Sensing impatience in the driver, he motioned for him to go around him. He stared down the driver as she passed.

"There it is!" Jeremy shouted.

"Where?"

"Over there. The other side of the street." He pointed with his open hand.

Ray pulled into the driveway and stopped. "Whewww, will you look at that?" He gaped at the white stucco, French Normandy, two-and-a-half story house. Brick trim, tall windows everywhere, and a massive wooden arched front door added to the imposing nature of the house. The driveway ran under a portion of the second floor, which bridged to the triple garage. "Which door do we use, Jeremy?"

"Drive under the *port cochiere*. There's a door right there." Jeremy was out of his seatbelt. "George is home; I saw him look out. Yes!" Ray could see how excited the boy was. He pulled the van forward, wondering how Jeremy could say *port cochiere*.

"Who is George?"

"The principal's boy. He's nice!" Jeremy could not contain himself.

"Boy? How old is he?" Ray asked, confused.

"He's twenty-six; he told me," Jeremy said proudly. "Just two years younger than my mom."

Ray felt an uneasiness creep over him. "Does he live here?"

"Now he does," Jeremy said with an I-know-the-whole-story ring in his voice. "He didn't used to. But he just moved back. He's back in his old bedroom."

"Hey there, Jeremy!" George called, holding open the wide glass door.

Jeremy climbed eagerly out of the van. Ray lowered the window and looked at George. *He's a handsome devil.* He noticed the broad shoulders, bushy hair, and piercing eyes above a cropped beard. *Looks like a college professor. That photo in Hope's office must be pretty old.*

George descended the steps and thrust his hand through the open window. "I'm George Fleming. You must be Ray. My mother—Hope—said you'd be dropping off Jeremy. Good to meet you." He smiled into Ray's face, and they shook hands. Jeremy hung on his leg.

"You too," Ray murmured, wondering what George's story was. *What does he do? Where has he been?* Hope had said very little about him at school. She had told Bella she had no way of contacting him. That was months ago when he was calling school a lot. Bella had told him about it every time George called Poore Pond looking for Hope. *Why is Jeremy hanging on him like that?* Ray felt resentful.

"Want to come inside?" George asked, his face friendly. "My mom's not home, gone to the health club." He lifted Jeremy up the steps. "She's left supper for us. Homemade chili. Would you like to join us?"

"Naw. I've got to get home. They're waiting dinner for me. Thanks, though." He shifted gears to pull out. "Can I circle around the garage?" George and Jeremy nodded. Ray pulled forward, "Bye, Jeremy," he waved. *Chili sounds good; I'm so hungry I could eat this steering wheel.*

Ray circled around the three-door garage and back to the main driveway. He glanced back but George and Jeremy were not there. Ray felt uncomfortable. He knew Hope would live in a nice house. But he wasn't expecting a mansion like that. *Well, maybe not a mansion, but it's twice the size of our bungalow.*

Ray pulled up to the stop light at Canterbury and Main. Bothered by an image of Heather and Jeremy having supper with George, he turned left toward Heather's factory. At the next stoplight doubt set in. "Oh heck," he said aloud. *I don't own her. Why, we aren't even going together or anything. I just help her.* He angled his van toward the right lane and waved at an approaching car. The driver, waiting, waved him into the lane. He circled the block and headed home. *She'll find her own ride home from work.* But he was still bothered by thoughts of Heather and George living under the same roof. He had to help her find a way to get her own place.

Ray stopped at the next convenience store to pick up milk for Caroline and a couple sticks of beef jerky for himself. He grabbed one of those free apartment listings from the rack near the door. He peeled the wrapper off a beef jerky and devoured it quickly, his hunger barely staved.

When he pulled in the drive, Claire's car blocked the garage. "Oh good grief," he muttered. "Just what I need."

"Where have you been, Ray? I thought you got off at 4:00," Claire, rinsing dishes at the sink, started the minute he entered the kitchen.

"Hi, Rayley," Caroline called from the living room. She sat behind a folding tray table eating soup and crackers.

"Hi, Mom. How are you doing?" Ray patted her shoulder.

"Sit down, Son. Claire's made potato soup. It's really good. Bacon in it. Claire, get your brother some soup." She turned her shoulders with some difficulty toward the kitchen.

The chilling expression on Claire's face ignited Ray. "I'll get my own damn— my own soup," he said, meaning it. He glared at his sister; she glared back at him.

"Why are we eating so early, Claire? Mom always eats at 5:00."

"Well it's nearly five. I got here at 4:30 and she was famished, munching potato chips, the worst possible snack for her, greasy chips. I expected to find you here already starting dinner. You work only fifteen minutes away, for gosh sakes."

Ray remembered the milk and went to get it from the car. Already agitated from the situation at Hope's house and seething with anger toward Claire, he reminded himself to calm down. *What was she doing? Checking up on him?* He felt edgy from hunger. It would not do for him to have it out with Claire again; it was too upsetting for Caroline. He set the milk jug on the step and pulled the other beef jerky from his pocket. A scrap of paper fluttered to the ground. Ray picked it up and saw the phone number Rosie had written for him. He opened the jerky and took a large bite, savoring it. She had told him about her mother-in-law's two-room apartment for rent over on Forbes Street. It was a nice area, but she didn't think her mother-in-law would rent it to anyone with a child. Said it had a big living-room/kitchen combination and a large bedroom with a tiny private bath. Rent was only $350. But she'd given him the number just the same, asking him not to say he worked with her. She didn't want her mother-in-law to give her a hard time if Ray tried to talk her into renting to a mother and child.

Ray heard the storm door open behind him. "Come on in, Ray. Mom's upset, thinks we're fighting again. We shouldn't upset her." She lowered her voice and said weakly, "I'm sorry."

Ray picked up the milk and followed Claire inside.

"Your tray's all ready, Ray," Claire said, not looking at him, keeping her voice neutral. "I gave you soup and a roast beef sandwich. You want grapes or chips?"

"I'll have a little of both, please." He poured himself a glass of milk, rinsing the empty jug at the sink. He stepped on it and put the flattened piece in the recycling bin in the pantry. Moving slowly he put the new jug of milk in the refrigerator, placing it carefully in its slot on the door. He dreaded seeing a dejected face on Caroline.

"Go eat, Ray, before your soup gets cold," Claire urged.

Caroline spooned vanilla ice cream into her mouth and looked at Ray with sad eyes behind her smile.

"You're on dessert already, Mom? I'd better get going." He sat on the sofa and drew the tray table over to him.

"Wasn't that nice of your sister to set out your dinner like that?"

"Yeah. Yeah, it was, Mom. Nice of Claire." Trying to keep things light, he added, "Think we ought to keep her?" They both laughed.

Ray expected Claire to join them with a tray table. When she didn't, he looked into the kitchen and saw her eating alone at the table. He pushed his tray table away, rose, and took another tray from the rack near the wall.

"We need your sparkling company in here, Claire," he said, stepping into the kitchen. He motioned toward the empty tray table. Claire picked up her tray and brought it into the living room. "Here we are, twenty-first-century family eating on trays in front of the TV." He laughed. "Anyone want to watch the news?"

"Let's wait for world news at 6:00," Caroline said forcefully. "Local news is all robberies and murders, child abuse, dog abuse, depressing stuff. Spoils my appetite."

"Yeah," Ray agreed. "I'd much rather watch world news; that's mostly just people abuse. By their governments." He chuckled and tucked into the hot soup.

"Ain't that the truth," Claire interjected. "All those hungry people in Bangladesh and the Congo." She shook her head and worked her mouth. "It's a proven fact that we produce enough food to feed the entire world population. Only governments don't figure out how to distribute it. Or they're so corrupt, they use it for their own schemes."

"They say that some of those children's campaigns on TV, less than twenty percent of donations actually goes for food. The rest goes to administrative costs. They don't care about those poor, starving kids." He swallowed, thinking of Jeremy going hungry.

"I can't watch those skinny little ones, their stomachs all distended like that from hunger. Makes me sick." Caroline said, her face aghast. She laid down her spoon.

They discussed other current world issues as they ate. Ray could not help thinking that this civilized conversation they were enjoying was a rare event in the Sellers' household. He actually enjoyed hearing Caroline and Claire's opinions and was impressed with how well up on the news they were. He knew his mother watched the news regularly but never felt she listened to much of it. And Claire, why she was so uptight about her little life: her job, her ex-husband's owing her, Caroline's health, and catching him out for not doing right by her. How could she concentrate on world issues?

They exhausted all the current issues, and conversation lulled. Ray stretched. Caroline shifted in her chair. Claire stacked dishes on her tray. "Know any cheap, nice apartments?" he asked his sister, wanting to prolong the easy exchange.

"Who wants to know?" she asked, voice bordering on her usual sharp tone.

"A friend of mine," Ray said, ignoring Claire's edginess. "You know that little kid that helps me in the lunchroom and his mother. Single mother."

"Oh, the one you're smitten with?" Claire said and laughed.

Ray blushed. "That's the one," he said clearly, refusing to be intimidated.

"She sure is a pretty little thing," Caroline said to Claire. "And that Jeremy is a fine boy." She furrowed her brow and looked at Ray. "I thought you said she moved in with your principal, that Hope."

"Well, she did. But it's just temporary. And now her son's come back home to live." Ray hoped his jealousy did not show. "Heather needs a place of her own." "Can Heather afford a place, Ray?" Caroline asked

"Well, yes. Not much of one, but a cheap place."

Claire knew of a one-bedroom in her building that rented for $600. The two-bedrooms were $725. "Lots of people make do with one bedroom," she said. "It was a single mother with two kids just moved out. Two boys." Claire stood and began gathering dishes off the trays. "She gave them the bedroom and she slept on the pull-out sofa. Lived that way for two years." She called from the kitchen, "You do what you have to do. There's a big difference between $600 and $725." She turned on the water and rinsed the plates.

Ray, seeing his mother's attempts to rise from her chair, put his hands under her shoulders and lifted her from behind. She made her way down the short hall to the small bathroom, breathing heavily as she went.

Ray joined Claire and began running hot water into the sink, squeezing liquid detergent under the flow. "I'll wash. You dry." He rolled up his shirtsleeves.

They chatted as they worked. Ray, watching Claire stack soup bowls on the wrong shelf, did not utter a word although it was tempting, just the type of infraction she loved to find him committing.

After the dishes were done, Claire managed to keep from complaining and left on a positive note. Ray even thanked her for coming two consecutive nights to help out although he secretly resented it. *If she could hold her sharp tongue the way she did tonight, she'd be good to have around. Like the old days.*

Ray sat in the living room poring through apartment listings he'd brought home. He circled those that rented for $600 or less. One in particular intrigued him. It was just a street away, above a garage. He knew the place, had watched the three-car garage go up two years ago and noticed that it towered over the small ranch house on the property. The vehicle-proud owner had a jeep, a boat and trailer, and a mid-sized car. The attached one-and-a-half-car garage would not house his prized fleet; so he had built the new one and, with an eye toward rental income, had included a three-room apartment above it.

There were a covered stairway along one side of the garage and large windows on every side of the apartment. Ray had followed construction progress and admired the finished structure. He had thought he might like to rent it for himself if Caroline were in better health. Now it was vacant again.

It was listed for $625 a month, but he could perhaps negotiate it down for Heather to $575. If he mowed the fellow's lawn or did some kind of maintenance around the place, he might come down on the rent. He would be happy to help Heather and Jeremy in that way.

Ray wanted to telephone Heather on Saturday and tell her about the garage apartment. But he could not bring himself to do it. Was he reluctant to have Hope know he was initiating contact with Heather? Or did he fear she might talk about George?

The sunny, cold day invited outings; and he busied himself taking his van to the car wash, picking up a few groceries and submarine sandwiches for his and Caroline's lunch. After lunch he swept out the garage, moving the garbage cans and gas grill to sweep thoroughly. He braved a chilly north wind to sweep the driveway and continued down to the street. Savoring the cold, he swept the sidewalk in front of the house and the front walk as well, all the while thinking about Heather and Jeremy in the garage apartment. All day he struggled with the temptation to call her.

Ray came into the warm house and poured hot coffee from the pot Caroline had brewed for him. He sat on the sofa and leafed through the apartment listings again, going over each one he had circled. He came to the garage one and stared at the photograph once more. There was neat tan siding on the building; and there were green shutters, too, matching the house. The outside stairway enclosure was sided, blending it nicely into the structure and avoiding any tacky, added-on appearance. The address, 245½, was visible above the solid green door. A separate strip of asphalt formed a driveway alongside the stairway and down to the street. *There's probably a storage area for the tenants under that stairway.* Ray scrutinized the photograph.

For dinner Ray reheated Claire's potato soup and made grilled-cheese sandwiches. Needing occupation and hungry for sweets, he mixed a microwave cake he found in the pantry. He merely had to add water and an egg to the dry mix and stir it right in the square paper pan. It baked quickly in the microwave and came out looking like real devil's food cake. He imagined Jeremy licking his lips for a slice of it and started thinking about the Bakers and the garage apartment all over again.

Caroline and Ray were just finishing their cake with large dollops of nondairy whipped topping when the telephone rang. He looked at the domed clock on the television. It was 5:23. If Claire was calling to check up on Ray and his dinner duties, she would not have a case. He picked up the kitchen cordless phone on the fourth ring.

"Hel-lo," he said with forced enthusiasm and cheer in case Claire was in a dark mood.

"Hi, Ray. How are you? Ray felt twittering in his groin as Heather's high voice came through the receiver.

"Oh, Heather. Fine. I'm fine; how are you?" He could feel a smile breaking across his face. "How's Jeremy?"

"He's okay. We're okay. We're good actually. Jeremy just left with his dad. Went to buy him a bike."

Ray was puzzled. This was the first he had heard of Jeremy's having any contact with his father. He thought the man lived 175 miles away in Clarkston. "His dad?" Ray cleared his throat. "I thought his dad lived in Clarkston." He could not keep resentment out of his voice.

"He does. Hardly ever comes to see Jeremy. But it was good he came today. He sold his front loader and gave me half the money. At least he told me it was half. You never know with Davey." Ray could picture her familiar expression: eyes growing wide, silent smirk on her lips.

"Well that's great, Heather. Now maybe you can get your own place. I've never met Davey, but his timing sure is good." He chuckled. "And he's buying Jeremy a new bike? That'll be one happy boy!"

"He is. He was so excited he couldn't stop talking. I could hear him all the way out to the car. Probably driving his dad crazy. Davey never did have much patience with him anyway." Anger rose in Ray's chest.

"I was wondering, Ray. Are you busy tomorrow?" She sighed audibly. "I mean for a couple hours in the afternoon or something. I need to look at some places," she dropped her voice significantly. "I need to get out of here."

"Sure, Heather. There's a—." He stopped short of telling her about the garage apartment. Better to see what she has in mind and bring it up tomorrow after he sees whether it fits her price range. There was also Rosie's mother-in-law's place.

They agreed to go at two o'clock, after he'd taken Caroline to church and stayed a few minutes for coffee hour. That would give him time to give her a proper lunch at home. Claire usually stopped over on a Sunday afternoon, too, so she would have some company.

Caroline told Ray that was a good time for him to be gone. Claire was coming over to shampoo her hair and blow it dry, which always took over an hour. She would be fine.

Ray carried the trays into the kitchen. He caught himself humming as he washed the dishes and wiped counters and stove. He even wiped the tray tables the way he'd seen Claire do, folded them and returned them to the stand.

He felt cheerful the entire evening, reading the daily paper, watching television news and a game show with Caroline. They both turned in at 9:45.

When Ray arrived at Hope's house to pick up Heather and Jeremy, they were already outside in their jackets. They waved as he pulled under the *port cochiere*. Then he noticed George coming out of the garage with two large, red frisbees in his gloved hands. He wore a thick Alpine sweater with a turtleneck that accented his strong jaw.

Ray climbed out of the van and shook George's extended hand.

"Good to see you, Ray."

"Nice to see you, George."

"Were going to the park, Mr. Sellers," Jeremy piped. "Taking George's frisbees."

"Are you riding your new bike?" Ray asked, feeling suddenly old. He glanced at Heather who was smiling widely.

"No. We're going to jog there. That's what George does. Says it's good for guys." He beamed up at George.

"I want him to practice on his bike before he takes it out of the yard," Heather said. "Right, Jere, you need to practice, don't you?"

"You ready to go?" Ray asked, almost looking at her.

"I'll just be a minute. Have to get my purse." She dashed up the steps.

Ray watched Jeremy follow George in and out of the garage.

"Does it look like frisbee weather to you, Ray?" George said, trying to fit a tall steel thermos into the pocket of a small backpack. Ray's eyes scanned the skies.

"It sure does. Perfect frisbee weather," Ray said, patting Jeremy's head. "You better watch yourself, George. This boy's arm muscles are awesome. Got them from lifting heavy garbage cans and pushing steel trolleys."

"He's told me how he helps you at school. Says he wants your job when he grows up."

"He's my main man at Poore Pond. In the lunchroom and on the grounds."

Jeremy twirled his small body until he fell on the pavement.

"Jeremy, are you all right?" Heather, shoulder bag careening, headed straight for her son. She helped him up and brushed off his jeans. Ray moved to the van and opened the passenger door for her.

"How long do you think you'll be, George? I mean, when do I need to be back for Jeremy?" Heather frowned seriously.

"Oh, we don't know. Not having a curfew is half the fun," George walked over to Heather. He looked directly into her eyes. "Take your time, Heather. We can manage if you're gone a long time. I'll feed him popcorn or something if he gets hungry."

"Well, I'll try not to be too long, George. I appreciate your helping me out like this." Ray noticed she looked easily at George's eyes. He also noticed how careful she was being with her speech, speaking clearly and not dropping g's. He felt strangely apprehensive.

Heather waved to Jeremy and George and climbed into the van. Ray closed the door gently.

"Have great frisbeeing, Guys," Ray called to them as they set off through adjoining property at the back of Hope's house. For an instant, Ray wished it were he going to the park with Jeremy.

He climbed into the driver's seat and looked over at Heather. They exchanged smiles, instantly warming him. He noticed she wore his favorite outfit: black miniskirt and black tights to show off her sensational legs, chunky white sweater that accented her fresh face, and her black imitation leather jacket. He buckled his seatbelt and turned the key in the ignition.

"That your list?" he asked, seeing the small pad she had in her lap. He had visions of helping her move in, setting up her new place, maybe buying her curtain rods, mops, brooms. A basketball for Jeremy.

*

In the end, Heather rented the garage apartment. She fell in love with it at once. Four spacious, light rooms and bath, everything in new condition. Jeremy could have his own room.

Ray was prepared to negotiate a lower rent for Heather, but the owner, Tommy Draco quoted $575 to her at first mention.

Heather looked over at Ray with puzzled eyes. He put his finger to his lips and she, without missing a beat, asked, "Is that due on the first of the month?"

"It's due whenever you want it to be," Tommy replied. He looked her up and down. "The first of the month, fifteenth, or last. Whatever works for you, Dear."

Ray saw tension in her face and felt it in his stomach. He could see Tommy's pink scalp through sparse strands of unnaturally red-brown hair.

"What about Mrs. Draco," Heather asked, to Ray's great relief. "I'd like to meet her since we're going to be neighbors."

"You will. Right now she's spending a week with her sister in Hoda." He smiled first at Heather, then at Ray. "Just make sure you pay the rent to me. That's firm. Joyce doesn't like to deal with business." He winked at Ray.

Heather looked around the apartment and pulled her checkbook from her purse.

"Didn't you want to look at those other places, Heather?" Ray asked quickly. "Mr. Draco, will you hold the apartment for twenty-four hours? We could get back to you tomorrow to finalize."

"Call me Tommy. Sure thing. You look at your other properties and call me." He looked at his watch. "By 5:15 tomorrow evening. I'll hold it till then." He shook hands with Ray, then Heather, enclosing her small hands with both of his.

"There's something about that guy, Tommy," Ray said as they pulled out of the driveway. Ray pressed the mileage button under the speedometer.

"He gives me the creeps." Heather's eyes were wide. "That eerie hair."

"Do you suppose you can trust him?"

"No, but if I see him coming, I can handle him." She looked at Ray and laughed.

"Just keep your door locked at all times. Limit his opportunity." He looked over at her. "Let's drive to your work and clock the miles." Heather smiled and nodded. "Then we'll stop at Baker's Oven for a bite to eat. Okay?"

Heather looked at her watch. "We should pick up Jeremy first though. I don't want to leave him too long with George. And Dr. Fleming's probably home from the concert already. I can't let Jeremy get on her nerves. She likes everything just so in her house, same as at school from what Jeremy tells me."

Disappointed that they would not be having their first meal alone, Ray turned right toward Canterbury. Darkness was setting in, and the air felt colder. Ray switched the heater to high and pressed the power button to the radio. Soft rock music filled the van; Heather took a deep breath and sat back in her seat. Ray stole a look at her stunning profile and wished again that they did not have to pick up Jeremy. At the same time, he loved her for not wanting to dump her son on someone else for as long as she could get away with it. George had certainly left the door open for her to do that.

Maybe I won't help her too much, just haul her stuff and let her set up on her own. Don't want to be a total schmuck.

CHAPTER TWENTY-ONE — IAN AND HELSI

Ian was surprised to see how few parents had come to the meeting. There were only ten or so scattered among different tables in the library; most of them sat tensely and silently and made no eye contact. He had his choice of several empty seats and chose one near the reading-lab teacher, Miss Maher, who smiled openly, obviously the only relaxed person in the room. He remembered how she had put everyone at ease in a similar meeting a few years ago when Robbie had started the remedial program. He recalled feeling intimidated by the idea of a public meeting for parents of kids who were too dull to learn to read. He wished he could say something that would alleviate the other parents' pain, their humiliation. He tried in vain to make eye contact.

"Hi, Miss Maher," he smiled at her. "How's the reading doctor?"

"Just fine, Mr. Bradford." She smiled back, looking bright and cheery in a spring-like pink-and-orange, diagonally striped short skirt and crisp pink shirt with straight hem skimming her small waist and ending just above her narrow hips. She was a breath of fresh air in a room full of somber-faced parents. Ian noted that the casual humor was entirely lost on them.

"Our Robbie," she smiled on. "He is a first-rate conflict manager, you know." Ian could see she wanted his help to combat the prevailing mood.

"So I hear. He's loving it, too. Wants to wear that neon pinny every day; he feels so important in it." They laughed together. Ian looked around for someone with whom to make eye contact and share the laughter. Again, no one met his gaze.

A young, confident-looking couple came in and smiled at Ian and Debbie Maher. She greeted the Petersons by name and introduced them to Ian. They shook hands and, with low voices, exchanged pleasantries. Ian was relieved that he wasn't the only parent who was not intimidated by this meeting.

Debbie Maher glanced at the clock and moved a few steps to the center of the room. She thanked everyone for coming although her eyes, scanning the empty chairs, betrayed her disappointment in the smallness of the crowd. Motioning toward the coffee and cookies arranged attractively on the counter, she said, "Maybe some of you would like coffee now, before we get started." She smiled at everyone and managed to provoke eye contact from a few of the somber faces.

Wanting to help her break the glacier-thick ice, Ian helped himself to refreshments. "Did you bake these cookies yourself, Miss Maher?" he smiled, his large hand daintily holding a cookie on a shamrock-covered paper napkin. He stood and waited for her response.

"As a matter of fact, I did," she said, her young voice full of exaggerated cheer. "But they're safe. I guarantee it. My fiance ate seven of them last night, and he's still OK." Ian and the Petersons laughed heartily, drowning the weak laughter erupting from a few of the others.

Miss Maher soldiered on, explaining the federally funded remedial reading program requirements for eligibility, how lab instruction compliments classroom reading instruction, and assessment. Ian had heard it all before and had to work to keep his mind from wandering. The tension in the room helped. He was so annoyed with the serious attitudes surrounding him, he thought of saying outrageous things to force them out of themselves. He waited for an opportunity to make a positive comment.

Miss Maher explained the pre-and post-testing she was required to conduct and the goal that every child show measurable growth of one month's achievement for every two months spent in the program. There must be for every child not meeting the standard, a detailed profile in place documenting possible reasons why growth may not have been attained as well as an individualized intervention plan of diverse strategies. She tried valiantly to engage everyone with her ongoing warm eye contact. But Ian and the Petersons alone rewarded her with their direct attention.

Emphasizing the accountability attached to the program, the percentage formula the Feds used to calculate acceptable growth of students not meeting the prescribed 1:2 growth ratio, she said, "Continued funding of the program is directly related to these growth rates." She looked brightly at each face, undaunted by the down-turned ones, and announced, "I am proud to tell you that Poore Pond's funding has remained stable; and because we take seriously the built-in accountability, ours is a strong program. Students are being helped. And you will be happy to hear that we are benefiting from your federal tax dollars coming back to our local school to help your children learn to read." She beamed with pride.

"That's the real point isn't it?" an angry voice called out. All eyes turned to a cloudy-eyed man in a rumpled business suit sitting alone at a far table. His slumped shoulders and haggard face revealed his weariness.

"Excuse me," Miss Maher replied in a soft voice.

"I said that's just the point. YOU are benefiting from this program. This trumped-up program!" His voice grew louder. Bodies shifted nervously. Tension thickened. Ian could feel heat rising in his chest. He looked at Miss Maher whose face remained fixed on the insurgent.

"You exaggerate the reading problems of kids—just enough kids to set up your lab classes—and label them deficient. Just so you can get the federal dollars and create more teaching jobs." Ian looked with contempt at the man. His face was now dark red and emphasized the thinness of his graying hair. "These kids don't need this program. They just need better classroom reading teachers, isn't that right, Miss?

"Mr. Sanderson, why don't you come with me. You raise some important issues. I will be happy to discuss them privately so the other parents can proceed with their agenda." Hope's calm, authoritative voice rose from the edge of the room. Ian had not seen her slip into the meeting.

Mr. Sanderson, unready to give up his audience, ignored Hope. "These other parents here should know the truth. You can see by their faces they're not happy with this program either."

"Just a minute, here," Ian heard himself shout. He looked at Mr. Sanderson. "No one speaks for me. And you have no right," his index finger punched the air, "to speak for anyone else in this room."

"I'm the only one here who'll stand up to the doc. The principal and the teachers are in cahoots to get those tax dollars. You know it as well as I do." His eyes dared Ian to respond.

"I have two kids who were helped by this program," Ian shot back. "I fully support Dr. Fleming," he glanced toward her, standing now next to the teacher, "and Miss Maher. They give their all to helping our children learn."

Applause broke out and Ian was flooded with gratitude. He looked around and saw not a somber face. Everyone smiled and clapped.

Mr. Sanderson slid toward the door and Hope hurried after him.

Miss Maher walked slowly to the door and closed it, obviously collecting her thoughts. She stood in front of the group and smiled broadly. She took a deep breath and exhaled. Parents looked at her with sympathetic eyes.

"May I just say, Miss Maher," Joe Peterson called, "you certainly kept a cool head during that crude attack." Others chorused agreement.

"Thank you, Mr. Peterson. But I don't consider that an attack. Mr. Sanderson's family has had more than its share of misfortunes lately. He's just, well, he's frustrated."

Ian could see tears glistening at the rims of her eyes.

The meeting resumed with all the parents clearly feeling more relaxed and open. Ian, Joe and Betsy Peterson shared personal anecdotes about their children's reading difficulties with winning humor and candor. Other parents read handouts carefully and asked pertinent questions. The discussion remained positive until adjournment.

As the group disassembled, Ian made it a point to introduce himself to a few parents and make small talk. He learned that Joe Peterson had once been a paramedic and was now a small-business owner with his wife, selling emergency medical equipment and supplies. They made plans to get together socially as couples.

The library emptied and Ian walked out with Miss Maher. "Thank you for your help tonight," she said turning toward him with a closed smile.

"You didn't need any help; you handled yourself well." He smiled back at her.

"Thank you. I can usually handle anything if I have a few supportive souls in the group. Without you and the Petersons I probably would have caved in," she laughed.

"I doubt that," Ian said, looking toward the office as they approached. "Dr. Fleming's still here; I'll pop in. Thank you, Miss Maher. Good night." She nodded and walked away.

Hope, hearing their voices, came to the door of her office. The outer office door was propped open and Ian strode through. "Have a minute, Doc?"

"Of course, come in." She motioned toward a chair. Ian sat down and she took the chair opposite him.

"How are you doing?" Ian asked in a sincere voice. "I mean, that crude guy, Sanderson. Did he come back to the office with you?"

Hope explained that he had refused to come to her office, and they had ended up having a pointed discussion near the exit doors. "That wasn't the real Dave Sanderson you saw tonight," she said. "His family has been kind of under siege by fate these days, and he is rather at the end of his rope. Needed to vent."

"Well, it's too bad he had to vent on Miss Maher. She didn't deserve that." He swallowed and continued without looking at her. "Kind of reminded me of myself, you know? In the days when I gave you such a hard time." He raised his eyes and met her gaze head on.

"Don't be too hard on yourself, Mr. Bradford. We all have our moments of utter frustration, moments we're not proud of." She looked away. "I certainly have my share of those."

"I don't know how I could have been so thick." He shook his head in wonder. "It's all clear to me now. You know, how much better it is for kids when the parents and the school are on the same side, the kid's side."

Hope said nothing, listening with all her senses, letting him talk.

"Such a simple concept. Yet we miss it. The Ian Bradfords, the Dave Sandersons of the world. We miss it." He looked out the window into the dark night. He could see moonlight reflected on the tiny courtyard pond.

"Ego. It's ego. We're so afraid of looking bad. We just. I don't know. Lose touch, I guess." He massaged his large hands. He knew Hope must want to call it a day, go home. But he couldn't help himself. He continued.

"I'm a paramedic. A paramedic. My big dream was to be a physician. But I wasn't determined enough, I guess." He began a biographical account, beginning with his early decision to earn a medical degree; to the death of his father and his mother's need for financial support; to his hopeless love for Helsi, their premature marriage and swift creation of family; ending with his regret that he'd settled for a career as paramedic.

He looked appreciatively at Hope who had not, at any point throughout his testimony, diverted her eyes or yawned or fidgeted. She had not once looked at her watch or the clock on the wall.

"Thank you for listening, Dr. Fleming. You are a patient woman."

"Not at all, Ian." She smiled and Ian wondered if she saw his surprise at her use of his first name. She leaned toward him. "You're still a young man, you know. It's not too late to further your dream."

"Aw, I'm too old for medical school; they'd never take me. And anyway, I couldn't do full time." He smirked and shook his head. "I have to accept the fact that I'm never going to be a doctor." He stretched his shoulders.

"What about a physician's assistant? You're practicing a form of medicine now as a paramedic. Becoming a physician's assistant would take you to another level of medicine." She paused as if checking his attentiveness. "City College has a fine physician's assistant program, one of the earliest ones offered. You could go there part time." She rose without breaking eye contact.

Ian rose, too, and knew it was time to leave. "Maybe I'll look into it," he murmured, knowing he wouldn't. "Good night, Dr. Flem—oh, I almost forgot. I wanted to talk to you about Dylan. My wife is worried to death about him. Well, another time."

"We are worried about him too. We just have to look harder for ways to help him. We'll schedule a meeting at your convenience and put our heads together." She folded her arms. "He's certainly enjoying school more now that he's on the kindergarten schedule. His face looks happier when I see him around the building." She walked him through the outer office; they shook hands and bid goodnight.

It was nine thirty and the meeting had adjourned at 8:25. Ian would get home too late to help even the older kids with homework. And he had promised to help Sean with a report on CPR for health class. *I hope it's not due tomorrow.* He drove home, enjoying the soft lamplight warming the darkness.

The streets and lawns had that March look: dry pavement washed clean from all the snow, rain, and wind; pale green sod bordered with small shoots of crocus and daffodil. He always felt energized this time of year, encouraged by a new spring suggesting fresh opportunity. He glanced into uncovered windows of warmly lit living rooms in houses he passed and longed to be home with Helsi and his sleeping children.

She met him at the door in her grey fleece robe. "That was a long meeting; want a cup of tea?"

Filled with unspeakable love for her, Ian hugged her hard and long. "Yes," he said finally.

*

Helsi stood at the sink grating eggs for egg salad and listening for Ian's car in the drive. She wanted to have lunch ready when he arrived, so he would not be late for his first time volunteering at Poore Pond. She chopped a quartered onion in fine pieces and scooped it with her hands into the grated egg. She spooned several large globs of reduced-fat mayonnaise into the bowl and mixed it well. She added a teaspoon of sweet pickle relish and generous shakes of salt and pepper, stirring robustly. She put whole wheat bread into the toaster oven and laid out two luncheon-sized plates. She forked green olives from a tall jar, arranging five on each plate. She scooped handfuls of low-fat ruffled potato chips onto each plate, giving Ian twice as many as herself. Taking the toast from the oven, she spread a thin film of mayonnaise on each slice and covered two slices with thick layers of egg salad. She took large pieces of damp romaine lettuce from a sheet of paper towel and placed them neatly atop the egg salad, following it with toasted bread. She cut both sandwiches in half, arranging the chips in between halves.

Helsi heard Ian's car in the drive as she filled tall glasses of ice with cold tea from a discolored white plastic pitcher.

Ian opened the door bringing a chilly draft in with him.

"How's it going, Hon?" He smiled at his wife.

"Lunch is all ready, Ian. Let's sit down." She smiled back and they hugged briefly.

"I'm starved," he said, taking a huge bite of the sandwich and catching the oozing egg salad with his tongue. He crunched a mouthful of potato chips.

Helsi took a bite of her sandwich and dabbed her mouth daintily with a paper napkin. "Are you ready for this?" she asked.

Ian took a few moments to finish chewing. "I think so. Talking about my job to a roomful of six-year-olds should be a piece of cake. I just wish I would've done it for Robbie's class. Remember how he begged me to come for Career Day, and I was too stubborn to go?" He looked at Helsi with sad eyes. She patted his arm.

"Well, you had other things on your mind. There was talk of layoffs, and you were worried about your job, remember? Robbie got over it."

"You don't think he's totally traumatized from it?" She furrowed her brow and shook her head. "Do you think he buries his anger in those endless tin-can hockey games?" He laughed as he said this.

"And that's why he can't wait to get out there with Dylan and whack the daylights out of that can every chance he gets? Because he really wants to whack his father for not speaking at Career Day when he was five years old?" She laughed heartily. "He probably beats that can senseless because he's angry with me for making him clean his room every Saturday morning. You know how we fight about that."

"I guess. What's for dessert? Any of those peanut-butter bars left?" Helsi went to the cupboard and brought out a square plastic container. Ian took a clean glass to the refrigerator and poured milk into it. "Want milk, Helsi?"

"No, thanks. I'll finish my tea with this." She placed the container on the table and they sat back down. "It would be nice if you had something to give the children." She swallowed a bite of peanut-butter bar and looked at Ian.

"I do have. We have stickers to give them. And brand new coloring pages showing when to call 9-1-1. The kids will love them."

"What time are you due? Is it one-thirty?" She looked at the clock on the range.

"Yes, one-thirty. I'll leave here about one-ten, so I have time to check in at the office." He took another bar from the square container. "These are great. Better with walnuts like this."

Ian managed to get out the door on time, leaving Helsi to wait for Rachel to be dropped off by her friend, Sophia's mother. She had been invited to lunch and play at Sophia's after preschool class. Anxious to make the most of the quiet house, Helsi settled on the sofa with a book she found at the public library just this week. The title, *When Children Can't Learn,* intrigued her and promised help in understanding Dylan's learning problems. She skimmed down the list of chapter headings in the table of contents and selected *Over-Age for the Class and Still not Succeeding.* Outside, the neighborhood was quiet. No sounds could be heard except birds chirping in the distance.

She read with fascination until Rachel burst in the door at three-fifteen. She dropped her armload of paper rolls on Helsi's lap and ripped off her jacket. Unrolling one of the large, white sheets, she pointed with her petite index finger to items in the drawing. She had drawn their house and placed each family member in a particular room.

"Did Mrs. Baldridge give you the idea to draw the inside of our house?" she asked, knowing that her friend, who had taught kindergarten before starting her family, could not resist engaging the kids who came to play with Sophia.

Rachel nodded yes. "She calls us her soo-doe class; Rachel Soo-Doe she says." She giggled then looked at her mother with serious eyes. "What is soo-doe again?"

"Well, I'm not sure, Rachel. Didn't she explain it to you?"

"Yeah, but I can't remember. Oh, I know—pretend. We're her pretend class," Rachel proudly recalled.

"Oh, pseudo. I get it." She smiled at her daughter. "You always have such a good time at Sophia's, don't you?" She hugged her soundly, nearly crushing the drawings.

"Watch my pictures, Mommy." She smoothed the papers and pointed to a small stick figure between two larger stick figures in a downstairs room, probably the living room. "Know who that is?" She looked into Helsi's eyes.

"That must be you with your father and me? Is that right?"

"No, that's me up here in the bedroom." She swept her hand to a small figure in a tiny room on the second floor.

"That's not Sean, is it, trying to make a deal with us to get new CD's?"

"No. Guess again." Rachel was thoroughly enjoying the game.

"It's Robbie, begging us to go to the movies." Helsi put her hands on Rachel's tiny waist as the child nodded no. "I give up. Tell me who it is."

"It's Dylan." She chirped. "Can't you see the flash cards in Dad's hands? Here's you," she pointed to the stick figure with full, dark hair, two lines curving up as a flipped hairdo. "See the book in your hand? That's Dylan's take-home book. You know, the one he couldn't read in first grade. Before they sent him back to kindergarten."

"I see. What are these other drawings?" Helsi watched and listened as Rachel explained a drawing of Sophia and her playing hopscotch in the backyard, as well as drawings of Easter baskets, colored eggs, and bunnies. Her mind wandered back to the first drawing as Rachel droned on, accounting the difficulty she had had deciding which colors to use for specific items. She was struck with how aware of Dylan's situation little preschooler Rachel was. She and Ian were always careful to discuss Dylan's problems privately. She knew that Dylan got on well with his little sister, often playing quietly with her in their bedrooms. Perhaps he had confided in her at times.

"Mommy, Mommy," Rachel pulled Helsi's sleeve. "You weren't listening. Look at this purple egg. Mrs. Baldridge let us use sparkle from her craft cupboard." She ran her fingers over the silvery glitter. "Don't you love it? Could we get some sparkles to color our eggs with?"

"Yes, yes, good idea, Rachel. Let's get you a snack now." She re-rolled the set of drawings and stood. They walked into the kitchen together.

Helsi spread peanut butter on saltine crackers and thought about how aware and ready to learn Rachel was. When Dylan was in preschool, he never gave detailed explanations of his drawings. He never included details in his drawings. They were always sparse and unrecognizable, with bold, colorless angular lines. She had just read in *When Children Can't Learn* that *preschoolers' artwork could be very indicative of readiness to learn. The ability to use curved as well as straight lines in their drawings and to include details from their daily lives reveals not only small-muscle development, but also how perceptive they are of the world around them, how much their young brains have processed so far.*

"I'm hungry, Mommy. I need my drink." Rachel ran out of patience as she sat on the floor, watching *Wishbone*. Helsi carried the paper plate of crackers and small glass of grape juice on a child-sized rattan tray, which she placed on the floor in front of Rachel. "Thank you, Mommy," she said without Helsi's having to ask her for the magic word.

That's another thing. To this day, Dylan still has to be reminded to say *please* and *thank you*. More evidence? Helsi could not wait to get back to her book. But it was time now to start dinner.

*

Dinnertime was full of talk about Ian's successful presentation to Dylan's class. The boy was so proud and excited that he could think of nothing else. And Ian had good feelings about the children's attentiveness. He told Helsi that Dr. Fleming had come down to see his talk and was appreciative and complimentary. He kept trying to change the subject in case Robbie was remembering his kindergarten Career Day and feeling slighted, but Robbie did not raise the issue. He seemed too busy enjoying his favorite meal, oven-fried chicken and mashed potatoes.

*

It was not until all five Bradford children were soundly in their beds that Helsi could tell Ian about the informative book she'd found. She told him about her observations of Rachel and her drawings compared to Dylan's at her age, relating them to points the book had made.

"Oh, we have a tentative appointment at Poore Pond next Tuesday." Ian interjected. "Dr. Fleming said she and the teachers have a plan to present to us. She thinks we need to meet and hear the plan before any decisions are made about next year." He put his hand on Helsi's knee. "I told her you would call the school and confirm the time. Or change it. That all right?"

"Yes, of course. And maybe you'll have a chance to read part of this book before we go." She picked it up from the lamp table next to the sofa. "It's easy to read and really hits home." She opened it at its bookmark and began to read. Ian moved to the recliner and switched on the television.

Helsi finished the chapter still wide awake and eager to read further. The title of the next chapter stunned her eyes and resonated in her brain, *Determining Delayed Intelligence.* Her eyes had avoided it when she skimmed the table of contents. She could not ignore it now. Heat rose in her chest. She forced open her dry mouth and reached for the glass of iced tea next to her.

Ian did not notice her sidelong glance his way. Faking a yawn, she stood and stretched.

"Tired, Hon?" His eyes never left the television screen.

"Yes, I'm off to bed." She bent to kiss his cheek, sliding her latest copy of *Home, Health, and Family Magazine* off the table. *When Children Can't Learn* lay on the chair where she had sat.

CHAPTER TWENTY-TWO—HOPE

Bella ushered a tall, gangly boy with downcast eyes into Hope's office. "He has a note for you from Mrs. Klements."

"Thank you, Mrs. Kurowski," Hope said to Bella's exiting back.

"Cliff, sit down please." Hope took the note from his tight fingers. She opened and read it and looked at his shirt. "Cliff, do you know why Mrs. Klements sent you to me?" She sat down opposite him and wondered how long it had been since his last haircut.

No response. Gently lifting his chin, she looked into the boy's deep blue eyes.

"Yes," he said, looking away. Then, in a barely audible voice, "My shirt—it's not allowed." He spread both hands over the front of his black T-shirt, leaving the large, grotesque face and the words *Kill the Man* still visible above *USA Wrestling*.

"That's right, Cliff. Why do you think we do not want shirts like that here at school?" Hope's voice was soft and calm. "What could be the reason?"

"I don't know. My dad bought it for me," Cliff bristled indignantly and jerked his head to clear his overgrown bangs from his eyes.

"I can certainly understand your wanting to wear a shirt your father bought just for you. But please think about why it's not the right shirt for school." She waited for Cliff's response.

"Are you going to call my dad?" His voice was tense.

"Cliff, please help me know that you understand why the shirt is not for school."

"The man looks mean." He dropped his eyes again.

"And?" Hope waited.

"The words are bad." Cliff looked out the window at the courtyard. Two finches skittered noisily in the bird feeder.

"Exactly. *Kill the Man.* Is that how we want children to feel? Do words like that make us feel good about life?" Hope's tone was as kindly as a nun's in church.

"No—they make kids want to fight." Cliff swallowed. He did not look at her.

"You're absolutely right, Cliff. We do not hurt people. And we do not

encourage others to hurt people. You are a boy who understands right and wrong."
Her face riveted on his, she paused. He raised his eyes and met hers.

"As a fifth grader, you are a role model for other students in the school." He
nodded agreement, his face grave. "I know a responsible boy like you wants to be
a proper role model, don't you?" Again he nodded. "Now, there are two choices
for you. You may turn the shirt inside out and wear it that way. Or you may
borrow one of the school shirts in my cupboard. It's up to you."

"I guess I'll wear this one. Inside out," Cliff said with relief.

"All right, Cliff." She smiled at him and he smiled weakly back. "You may
use the clinic lav to do that. And I know I do not have to remind you not to wear
that shirt to school again." She shook his reluctant hand. "You may go. You won't
turn your pants inside out to match, will you?" Cliff gave her a polite little laugh.

Hope smiled to herself, knowing that Cliff with his wrong-side-out shirt would be
simply following a recent trend among elementary students. Inside-out T-shirts: their
first brave venture into unconventional dress. She shuddered to think of the extreme
forms of deviant dress the older students embraced. All that spiked green hair and
pierced body parts she saw on teens at the mall. She had her own theory about that.

Surely, adults' tendency to adopt dress habits of teens, doing everything they
can to avoid looking like the grownups they obviously are, has a bearing. She
firmly believed that as adults mimic teen fads (too-tight jeans, short sweaters that
show a flash of midriff, clumsy platform shoes, pierced eyebrows, backward
baseball caps, etc.), young people are forced to find ever-more grotesque looks to
set them apart. It is one of their rites of passage. *Why does no one want to be a
grownup these days?*

Hope began opening the several sealed envelopes from parents that were in
her in-box. She knew they were likely to be teacher requests for next school year
so would be filed until class lists were being formed next month. She found them
interesting, though, because of points they revealed about parents' personalities as
well as teachers' public relations skills.

She heard her intercom buzz and lifted the phone to her ear. "Your son George
is on line two," Bella's voice, in formal mode, came on crisply.

"Thank you, Bella," she said and pressed the line button.

"Hi, Mom," George said, excitement in his voice. "How's it going?" Without
waiting for her response, he continued, "I'm just about finished loading my worldly
goods, ready to go." She had tried to forget that he was using Michael's company
van to move his things today.

Her heart suddenly racing, she took a deep breath. *He's really moving out, in
with Michael. Michael has won again.* She felt an old weary defeat.

"You're sure you want to do this, Son?" She made a last appeal. "You know
your father's moods."

"Yeah, Mom. I know Dad's jerky side. But he's changed a lot. I told you that."

"That's right, George, you did," she said with deliberate cheer, not wanting to
alienate him. "I will miss you, but I wish you the best." She willed the emotion
out of her voice.

"I'll miss you, too, Mom. And your blueberry pancakes." He laughed. "Seriously, though, I'm excited about the work. Really gotten into polymers and all that. If it works out, Dad's promised to make me a partner in *PolyFlem*. That's the name of his company, remember? Isn't it a great name?" He stopped for air.

"Great name," Hope lied. She waved to Alison's class, congregating in the courtyard and proudly holding up trowels and seed packets for her to notice.

"If I can be a successful businessman, I'll be in a better position to help the homeless cause. People tend to listen to someone who knows how to make money, you know. As if good business sense makes them wise about everything. I can get their cause out there and, hopefully, get them some benefits, shelters and health care, and stuff."

"Maybe you can go back to school as well, get your degree." She noted the pregnant pause and instantly regretted her words. "Later, after you're settled in," she added. "Is there really room enough in that two-bedroom condo for you and your father?" *And his big ego,* she wanted to add.

"Oh yes. The rooms are big. And there are lots of built-ins, so all I need is a bed."

"You don't have a bed?" *That would be just like Michael to find some way to make it tough on the boy.*

"Well, not yet. We're going to get one as soon as I get my stuff in there and we see how much room there is. We'll know what size bed to get then. You know how Dad thinks."

Hope knew very well how Michael thought. And she loathed the idea of George's being on the receiving end of his distorted decisions. Michael's sick way of controlling through his dumb little daily-life inconvenience traps; it made her seethe with anger just to think of it. "George, take the inflatable bed, for heaven's sake. It's in a bag in that basement closet you cleared out for Heather and Jeremy. Has a built-in electrical pump to inflate it. Just press a button."

"Maybe I will, Mom. Thanks."

"The sheets that fit it are in the bag, too. Take one of the pillows on your bed, or several, if you like. There are extra pillowcases in the upstairs linen closet. Take your duvet, too." She could not resist adding, "or Dad will have you using his old overcoat for a blanket."

George laughed. "That he would; that he would, Mom. You know him pretty well."

They said their good-byes and promised each other luncheon dates and phone calls. Hope, her eyes watery, replaced the receiver. She willed herself not to give in to the anger she felt. She did not trust Michael to be fair to George. She did not trust him to treat his son well, not consistently or on a long-term basis. *Now that he has George under his roof, he'll think nothing of trying to sell the Canterbury house out from under me.* She glanced quickly at her watch, then the wall clock, rushing out of the office to post the *Outdoor Recess* sign.

Passing Jan Wheaton's oversized, round thermometer mounted on a tree near an end window in the rear lobby, she noted a temperature of forty-three degrees although the bright sun belied the cold. She included the *Wear Your Jackets* strip on the recess sign and headed to the servery to see the cooks.

The rich smell of beanie wienies and Texas toast seduced Hope as she approached the lunch line. "I'll just have a small bowl of beanie wienies, Helen," she said to the smiling kitchen manager. "They make the granola-yogurt lunch I brought look cold and blah. You have enough, don't you?"

"We sure do, Dr. Fleming," Helen said, scooping a serving into a styrofoam bowl. "Toast?" Hope nodded affirmatively. "Applesauce?"

"I might as well go all the way." They laughed. "How's your daughter doing, Helen? Is she enjoying her new career?"

"Very much. She loves learning all the different medications. She likes working with the customers, too. It was a good choice for her."

"What's the specific program she trained in, again? Was it pharmacy assistant?" Hope took the lunch tray. "Thank you, Helen. I'll enjoy this. I owe you $2.50, right?"

"Yes, $2.50. Bridget's program was pharmacy technician." Helen filled lunch trays with beanie wienies, handing them assembly-line fashion to her colleague, Edie, who added toast and applesauce.

"How long was the training?"

"Six months. Then three months' clinical practice in a pharmacy. There are two tracks: one is nine to three; the other is two in the afternoon to eight in the evening. Bridget took the afternoon track so Bruce could stay with the kids."

"I see. Well, good luck to Bridget. I'll stop back and pay you before you balance. Thanks, Helen." Hope saw the first-lunch classes coming down the hall, so she carried her tray into the lunchroom. She sat down at the first kindergarten table and began to eat hungrily while primary children filed in.

She thought about Bridget Mercer's training and wondered if it would interest Heather Baker. *If she could just acquire a profession that would give her the respect she craved and a decent income, she could have a secure future. With or without a man.*

Every woman should have financial independence. Once she has that, emotional and psychological independence are more attainable. Women today have to have self-reliance. Too many of them are left high and dry.

"Look! We get to have lunch with Dr. Fleming!" Three smiling girls from Mrs. Armstrong's class seated themselves across from their principal and placed colorful cloth lunch bags on the table.

"Well if it isn't the Three Musketeerettes. Hello, Erica, Carly, Ashley." Hope smiled at the excited children. "Are you ready for a weekend?"

"Yesss," they chorused.

"I'm going to an Easter egg hunt," Carly piped.

"It's my birthday and we're going to Chuckie Cheese!" Ashley called out, obviously wanting to one-up Carly.

"You girls are lucky." She looked at Erica's unsmiling face and knew she would be spending the weekend with her grandparents again while her father visited her mother in prison. "And what will you be doing, Erica? Having fun at your gramma's house?" Erica nodded yes, her face more sober than a five-year-old's should be.

"Is your Grampa Bob still teaching you to ride your bike? You told me about that last week." She smiled into Erica's dark eyes until she got a smile back from her. "Maybe you'll be ready for our bike rodeo in June." She reached across the table and patted the child's small hand. More children seated themselves at the table, their faces full of curiosity about the huddle of girls with the principal.

"I'm coming to the bike rodeo," Ashley chirped. "As soon as I learn to ride my bike without training wheels. Can you be in the bike rodeo with training wheels, Dr. Fleming?" Ashley's expression turned serious.

"No, Silly," Carly interjected.

"I'm afraid not, Ashley," Hope smiled at her. "You would not be able to maneuver the turns in the tests. Those tests are designed for riders who are out of training wheels and ready to learn more about safety. But there's always next year's rodeo."

"I'm going to be in this year's bike rodeo," an unsmiling Erica announced to the table.

"Good for you, Erica," Hope validated, privately cheering the child's dignity. Hope gathered the remains of her lunch and stood to leave.

"Are you coming out on the playground, Dr. Fleming?" a husky little blonde boy with big eyes and a round apple face streaked with tomato sauce, asked from the far end of the table.

His charming innocence tugged at her heart. "I just may come out for a little while, Sam," she smiled. "The third graders are on a field trip today, so I won't have a job second lunch." She relished the idea of getting out among the children in the sun. They would keep her so engaged that she would forget the niggling worries that kept distracting her today: George's moving, Michael's threats to sell the house, Heather Baker's future, and the most dire worry of all, Mary Baldwin's estate.

*

Hope soaked up sun and enjoyed watching the children in the playground setting. It was fascinating to see differences between their classroom and playground behaviors, in some cases quite marked. She watched Tommy Halston running the first-grade version of kickball, directing pint-sized boys to their positions and dictating kicking order like a field commander. The other boys deferred to him naturally; not a one challenged his authority. She tried to discern the base of his influence and concluded that it was his athleticism and his take-charge manner. His appearance certainly was not typical of the more popular kids. He did not have the cool clothes the others wore, nor the trendy haircut. Tommy's thick dark hair, always in need of a trim, kept falling in his face. He punctuated every command with a firm jerk of his head to clear his bangs from his eyes. Maybe that was part of his appeal. Or was it the rakish way he wore his frayed chambray shirttails, half tucked in and half blousing out of his waistband? His sturdy little body, muscular though short, looked even shorter in too-large jeans with two-inch wide, rolled-up cuffs which contributed to the total statement that this boy was nothing if not his own person.

"We can jump rope now, Dr. Fleming! Want to watch us?" Two rosy-cheeked girls gripping plastic rope handles appeared.

"Of course," Hope smiled while they started simultaneously. Sort of climbing over the rope one foot at a time rather than jumping with their feet together, nonetheless proud of themselves, the girls managed to keep a rhythm going, their ponytails bobbing with them.

"You're on your way, Mary Kate and Kathy," Hope called as they ran off laughing.

She turned her attention back to the boys and laughed at the comedy of six-year-olds playing kickball. They had their own definition of *foul balls*; foul lines kept changing. Only a handful of them kept their attention on the game while others chatted with teammates or teased girls passing by in pairs. A few engaged in horseplay on the field, attracting attention of playground supervisors who blew their shrill whistles soundly to stop such forbidden behavior.

Hope's thoughts returned to Tommy. The contrast between his ability to be boss of the playground and his floundering academic performance was fascinating. He had serious problems learning to read—indeed, was the poorest reader in Jeff Masters' class—and often did not complete work because of it. But his standing as a low achiever did not diminish the respect his classmates gave him even during class. They were always anxious to help him with directions for seatwork or materials he'd misplaced, couldn't do enough for him. Through it all, Tommy was always pleasant and personable. *That must be a key ingredient.*

Wind carried the high, young voices and Hope overheard Rich Small ask Tommy, "Could I be catcher tomorrow, Tommy, if I get the kickball first?"

"Yeah, but you've got to be first outside with the ball. Don't let Cantrell's class get all the balls, Rich. You know how fast they eat."

Hope glanced at her watch and, still laughing, started toward the building. It was time for the third-lunch group.

*

A post-lunch solitude could be felt throughout the building as Hope completed a door-check round. Hallways were deserted; and Ray was mopping the floor in the cafeteria, soft-rock music sounding faintly from his portable radio. Classrooms were quiet, some with students being read aloud to by teachers, or having whole-class, sustained-silent reading, or watching public television's designed-for-children news programs. This transition time between the stimulating dynamics of outdoor play and the return to the business of learning was essential.

After opening and soundly re-closing every outside door she passed, the welcome feeling of all's right with the world cheered Hope. Gratefully, she savored the sun-drenched corridors, the calls of spring robins drifting through open classroom windows, the responsible teachers and willing students.

Teaching is truly an honorable profession. I feel privileged to work in this school with all these noble people.

Hope knew this was a good time to make her phone call to *McElson-Bourney* and pointedly headed to her office, struggling to ignore the feeling of dread shrouding over her

"I'll take no calls except central office," she said matter-of-factly to Bella who nodded understanding. Hope closed her door firmly and sat down at her desk. The engraved logo on the ivory envelope lay there, menacing. She took a deep breath and reached for a fresh bottle of water. She swallowed. Her hands shook as she unfolded the letter and read the telephone number. She flexed the fingers on her right hand as if checking for control. She dialed the number, pressing each key deliberately with great bravado.

"Good afternoon, McElson-Bourney. How may I help you?" The polished voice with precise diction was just what Hope expected.

"Good afternoon, McElson-Bourney," Hope willed assertion into her voice. "I'm Hope Minster Fleming. I received your letter asking me to contact you regarding the estate of Mary Margarethe Baldwin." She was proud of her control.

"Oh yes, Ms. Fleming. Do you prefer Ms. or Miss? Or is it Mrs.?"

"Actually, it's doctor; but I answer to anything these days."

The precise voice laughed appropriately. "Dr. Fleming, I'll put you through to Mr. McElson. Mr. Bernard McElson, Senior, that is. Thank you for your patience." Her emphasis on senior was not lost on Hope. She felt all confidence washing away.

She swallowed and noted the classical music playing faintly on the line. "Don't be silly," she told herself. "He's just a man. Works for a living the same as I do."

"Dr. Fleming," a deep voice, pleasant and fatherly. "Thank you for getting back to us. Fine day today. Is it a fine day in your neighborhood?"

"Lovely," Hope's control returned. "How may I help you, Mr. McElson?" Her voice did not belie her trepidation.

"It's a matter regarding Mary Baldwin's estate. An important matter, I must say to you." He cleared his throat and Hope's heart sank. "I would ask that you come into my office to discuss it."

"I see. When would you like me to come?" Hope feigned casualness.

"At your earliest convenience, Dr. Fleming. I am sure you will be quite interested in what I have to say." His strictly business tone worried her.

"In that case, I shall come next week." She was proud of herself for slipping *shall* into her words with ease although she no longer used the archaic term. She flipped through the daytimer on her desk. "Would Wednesday afternoon work for you? Say, at 3:30?" *Surely I could manage to leave school immediately after dismissal. Or maybe before. It's a long drive into the city.*

"Wednesday, the third, at 3:30 will work perfectly, Dr. Fleming." *Did a bit of warmth creep into his voice?* "We'll see you then. I look forward to meeting you." *Unmistakable warmth.*

"And I, you, Mr. McElson," Hope said with a smile in her voice.

She replaced the receiver slowly and stared into space. Both relief and dread flooded over her. She was relieved to have finally made the connection and to have mustered the confident response she desired. But the fact that he had given her no indication of the nature of the matter filled her with dread. Should she ring back and pointedly ask? Should she engage an attorney to accompany her? Should she send an attorney in her place?

CHAPTER TWENTY-THREE—RAY

"These daffodils are wonderful, Ray," Hope said as together they surveyed the grounds of Poore Pond. Warm air, unseasonable for April, added to their pleasure in the early morning light. Ray stooped to pick up a large twig resting atop the blossoms.

Ray felt proud of the daffodil gardens he had spent more than five years developing. Now they were in full glory edging the shrubbery across the front of the stately red brick building, accenting lush beds flanking the main entrance drive, and filling the center island in the public parking lot.

"Have you seen the courtyard? They're all over the place, from the pond to the kindergarten windows." They walked to the corner of the building.

"I saw the buds almost ready to flower. Are they open, too? As much as these?"

"Oh yeah, the whole courtyard is bright yellow." Ray held open the service room door. "Come on. I'll show you."

Hope stopped in her office to deposit her briefcase while Ray unlocked and propped open the heavy courtyard door.

"Over there's where the angels will go," Ray pointed with the twig he still carried. "In front of these daffodils, then around the corner in front of the new beds. We'll have Erlicheers—those miniature daffodils—in another six weeks." He walked off the area of the memorial garden. "Then primroses, then asters with late-summer oriental lilies. The kids are doing primroses and asters." Hope followed beside him, nodding and smiling.

Ray grew excited about the memorial garden all over again.

"When are you hoping to have the unveiling, the dedication, Ray?" Hope asked.

"May, I think. That Friday before Memorial Day weekend. The engraved plates to hang on the angels are supposed to be ready by May first." He looked at Hope with eyes shining. "By Memorial Day this courtyard will look like the botanical gardens. Perfect for a dedication ceremony." Ray felt warm with pride just thinking about the finished memorial to Bucky and, of course, the kindergartner.

"I'm going to go ahead and put that date on the school calendar. Friday, May 24, dedication ceremony in the afternoon. We could invite the families of the two children. What do you think? Would Bucky's family be interested?" Hope gave Ray one of her riveting looks.

"I think they would," Ray said, straining to see whose footsteps could be heard tramping down the hall. It was Carmen Ricci and her cast of students with speaking parts in the spring musical, fitting in a rehearsal before the school day started.

"Good morning, Mr. Sellers," they called in unison.

"Good morning yourselves," Ray said, smiling widely. He bent to pick up stray twigs and leaves from the daffodil beds.

"Is that Dr. Fleming in the courtyard?" Carmen asked, heading through the door. "Go on down to the music room, Children. I'll be right there. Start getting out your props."

"Good morning, Dr. Fleming," the children called, poking their heads through the door before diligently walking away.

"Good morning, Performing Artists," Hope returned. "How's it going, Carmen? Are we on schedule?"

"Pretty much," Carmen laughed in that winning way she had when under stress. "But I need to ask you if there are funds to reimburse the parents for some of their costs for costumes." She stepped closer to Hope. "They're not expecting to be reimbursed, but some of them are buying fairly pricey items. Trims and things. And they're buying quantities. Fay Childers paid $4.50 apiece for about eight packets of glass beads for the dancing girls' costumes." She stopped and took a breath.

"We'll take it out of the discretionary fund. Cut a purchase order for a lump sum reimbursement to—is Marge Hatteras the coordinator?"

"Fay Childers is chairing the costume committee. She's phenomenal how she organizes those mothers."

"Will it be more than $150?"

"No. No. Probably about $80 or $85, I think. $12 to one, maybe $15 or $20 to another." Carmen stepped back inside the building.

"As I was saying, we'll cut one purchase order to Fay for the total amount of reimbursements; she can cash the check and pay everyone else. Takes a couple weeks to process through the treasurer's office though. Do you think that will be a problem?"

"Well no. They're not expecting anything. I haven't said a word." She was off down the hall.

"Oh, Carmen," Hope called after her. The music teacher hurried back. "We're planning the memorial garden dedication for May 24th. Remember we talked about it at one of our meetings? Will you give some thought to music for it? The choir or something?"

"You mean hymns? Spiritual music?" Her eyes twinkled mischievously.

"Think about it, please, Carmen. You always come up with just the right music." Ray cupped the collected garden debris in his hands and headed into the building behind Hope. She turned and said, "Thanks, Ray, for your hard work in the courtyard. And on the memorial. It'll be good spiritual nurturing for everyone."

"Think it'll save my neck with Melanie Armstrong?" He laughed.

"Certainly. You'll make many, many points." Hope laughed with him.

Ray found himself whistling down the hall as he pushed the four-wheeler toward the stack of heavy cartons in the lobby. He couldn't wait for the weekend to get here. He was going to Heather's new apartment for dinner, sort of a housewarming. She would do all the cooking; she had insisted because he helped her so much.

Ray stopped at the door to the Latchkey room, and a swarm of children greeted him with anxious cries, "Can I help? Mr. Sellers, Mr. Sellers, Do you need help?" He selected three of the larger students, two boys and a girl, and checked with Nancy, the Latchkey coordinator, for permission to take them. Talking noisily, they pushed the four-wheeler down the hall to the stack of boxes in the lobby.

"Start with the larger boxes," Ray said as the tallest child did just that. "You're way ahead of me, Monica." The children worked quickly with Ray and managed to load all twenty-eight boxes in a matter of minutes.

"Come down to my office with me and I'll give you your pay," he smiled at them. The students gave their all to navigating the four-wheeler expertly down the hall.

Back in the boiler room Ray removed his tin of chocolate-covered caramels from the desk drawer and invited the children to help themselves. They stood there chewing mouthfuls of caramel deliberately and slowly, fully aware of the need to avoid flaunting their treat to the other Latchkey children. "Thanks, Mr. Sellers," they said, each in turn.

"Thank you for your help," Ray smiled at them. You keep doing such good work, I'll have to give you a big raise." They shared a laugh before the children traipsed away.

He had gift-wrapped packages to take to Heather's. Claire had helped him pick out a set of monogrammed towels for her, soft jade with white lettering: H.B. Big, fluffy, thirsty-looking, good quality towels. Claire had suggested the better quality ones, pointing out to him that Heather was probably unused to such nice towels and would really appreciate the luxury. Ray was glad that Claire helped him shop. And for Jeremy, she suggested a set of bright red towels with yellow lettering, Jeremy. He admired Claire's cleverness. He would never have thought of any of that on his own. He'd spent more than he planned to, but he wanted the gift to be just right.

Ray gingerly steered the loaded four-wheeler through the wide doorway and parked it next to the desk. He took out a file of purchase orders and began pulling packing slips from clear-plastic pockets attached to the outsides of the cartons. He matched the slips to the purchase orders and clipped them together.

Anxious to see the contents, he opened the box from *Smalley's Trophy Shop* first. He lifted two small, narrow boxes and brushed the peanut-shaped packing material off them, bits of it sticking to his fingers. He opened the first box, folded back white tissue paper, and saw a lovely bronze plaque engraved in script lettering: *Colin French.* He then opened the second box and found Bucky's plaque. He picked it up and ran his fingers over the engraving. *Bucky Ames.* He held it for a moment, seeing Bucky's spirited face in his mind. He walked to the window and cast his eyes skyward. "This here's for you, Buddy," he whispered, touching his forehead with the plaque in salute.

I wish I had known Colin. But those kindergartners are here such a short time every week. He made a mental note to look him up in the yearbook to see if he would remember his face. Ray rewrapped the plaques carefully and set them aside in their cartons with the paperwork. He would put it in the parents' mailbox later. He began opening other cartons, and his thoughts returned to Heather's dinner.

The best part, the part that filled him with anticipation, was that Jeremy would not be there. Again, Claire had stepped in to help. She suggested that he stay at Caroline's and keep the two of them company. They were going to rent his favorite movie to watch after their pizza dinner. Ray and Heather would be alone together for an evening, the first time.

It had been years since Ray had spent an evening alone with an attractive woman. Just the thought of having the gorgeous Heather all to himself sent electricity surging through his veins. *Hold on, Dude. This is just a thank-you dinner from her, to show appreciation. Don't try to make more of it; you're ten years older than she is, for cripe's sake. She probably sees you as a second father or something."*

Ray knew he would have to restrain his emotions, and he could do that. But that wouldn't stop him from enjoying her company. After all, she was going to all that trouble just for him. And why would she invite him for dinner if she didn't enjoy his company?

*

Saturday finally arrived and Ray awoke early. Normally he would lie in bed for awhile enjoying the luxury of not having to rush to work, but this morning he was eager to get the day going. He went straight to the shower, mentally planning his schedule.

Claire had organized Jeremy. She would stop at Heather's apartment to get the boy at 5:00 and take him with her to the pizzeria and video shop before going on to Caroline's.

Heather was expecting Ray at 6:00. He had to finish all his weekend chores plus wash his van by 4:00.

He came from the bathroom with a towel around his waist and smelled the coffee brewing. *Mom's up already.* He knew she would want to fry eggs and bacon or ham for him, and he relished the idea. He pulled from his small closet, a favorite plaid flannel shirt, worn but clean, and a pair of khaki pants that had been washed so many times the cuffs were frayed into fringe. He put on his old black-and-white athletic shoes, worn down at the soles and creased on the instep, and headed into the kitchen.

"How many eggs do you want, Ray?" Caroline asked from the table where she sat with a mug of steaming coffee. Ray saw she had already taken out the ingredients for his breakfast and had set his place on one of her blue plastic place mats.

"I believe I could eat two, Mom. I'm really hungry today. How about soft boiled? Haven't had those for awhile." He went out to the drive to get the morning newspaper.

Caroline brought him a plate laden with a thick slice of fried ham, two slices of whole-wheat toast, and a bowl of boiled egg already chopped, buttered, and salted. "Just like when I was a kid, eh, Mom?" he smiled at her.

"I always make your breakfast on Saturday, Ray. You know that." She took her own plate to the table and sat down.

"I know. I know," he said. "But I'm perfectly capable of chopping my own egg."

"Of course you are, but why should you? That's why I'm here. You do so much for me." He laughed, drawing her into laughter with him and hoping to change the subject. "Tonight's your big night, isn't it? Yours and Heather's?"

"Jeremy's, too," Ray added. "He brought it up to me every day this week. Wanted to know if Claire was bringing her kids. Seemed disappointed when I told him she didn't have any."

"I'm going to make him a chocolate cake," she gestured toward the box of cake mix on the counter. "Kids love chocolate cake."

"Sure you're up to it, Mom? I can get one at the bakery if you're not."

"No, I want to have a homemade one for Jeremy. But you could get me a can of extra-creamy chocolate frosting. That'll save me having to make my own, and it's even better than mine. I need soda pop for him, too. Do you know what kind he drinks?"

"Any kind, I'm sure. But when you give him a choice, he always takes Dr. Pepper. I'll get some Dr. Pepper." Ray rose and refilled his coffee mug. "More coffee, Mom?" She declined with a nod. "Do you need anything else from the store? I'll go there from the car wash."

"There's a short list on the pad by the phone. Just a few things." She edged scrambled egg onto a piece of toast and maneuvered it carefully to her mouth.

"You really care a lot for Heather, don't you?" she suddenly asked when she had stopped chewing.

Ray, somewhat taken aback, knew he had to be straightforward with his mother. "A lot," he said softly.

"She is a sweet little thing. I can see why you like her."

"She's a good mother, too, Mom. And she tries hard to do the right thing."

"Of course she does. I could see that when you brought her here the first time." Ray reached for the blackberry jam and spread it on his toast.

"Just be careful, Son," Caroline looked at him with soulful eyes. "She's just a youngster. Don't let yourself get hurt."

"I know, Mom. I know." He did not look at her. "I don't kid myself about Heather. She likes me because I help her. I keep that in mind. To her I'm just that older guy who's nice to her boy at school and will drive her places, buy her a hamburger."

He mopped his mouth with a paper napkin and carried his plate to the sink. Caroline rose, plate in hand and laid it on the counter.

"I don't mean to spoil your good time tonight, Ray." She took a large mixing bowl from a lower cupboard.

"You won't, Mom. I can enjoy just being with her, letting her show her appreciation by cooking me a dinner. I don't have false hope." He took the list from the pad and his keys from the hook by the door. "See you later, Mom. Thanks for the breakfast."

But who knows? He eased into the driver's seat. *Stranger things have happened.*

*

It was after 1:00 when Ray pulled into the driveway, delighted to see Aunt Patsy's car parked off to the side. He immediately forgot his irritation with the long lines he had stood in at the wholesale club, car wash, and then the grocery store. He strained to get his arms around all three bulging paper bags at once, admiring the clean van as he kicked the door shut.

Aunt Patsy held the back door open for him. "Hey there, Ray. How's my favorite nephew?" She beamed her doting smile at him. He set the bags down on the table and gave her a proper hug. "Caroline tells me you have a hot date tonight. With that sweet, young thing from school."

"I do. I do." Ray smiled sheepishly. "But I don't know if it's really a date. I mean, I like to think of it as a date. But she probably thinks of it as a payback." He made it a point to smile when he said it. "Payback to an old man who helped her and her son." He forced a chuckle and began removing items from a bag.

"You think of it any way you want to, Ray." Peggy's solemn face cracked into a smile. "Just for tonight."

"Ray's a realist, Peggy. Just like his mom," Caroline chimed in as she polished a skillet with a towel. "Only he learned it sooner than I did. Took me fifty years." She set the can of frosting on the counter and carried the half-gallon milk jug to the refrigerator.

"Hungry, Ray? Peggy and I just finished a tuna-salad sandwich. Want one? I can put it in the toaster oven with cheese. Tuna melt?"

"Sounds great," he said as he watched Peggy fold the empty paper bag into a neat rectangle the same way his mom would do.

"Go sit down in the living room and visit with your Aunt Peggy. I'll bring it in to you." She pulled a plastic-wrap-covered bowl from the refrigerator.

"Aw, Mom. I can make it. You go sit down."

But Caroline insisted, giving Ray that do-as-you're-told look. He followed Peggy over to the sofa.

"Are those the towels, your gifts?" Peggy asked, gesturing toward two large, gift-wrapped boxes on the ottoman. "Caroline told me how nice they were."

"Yeah, they are. Claire's influence, you know." He smiled.

"Claire always had good taste, didn't she?" Peggy returned his smile.

"She's good at spending other people's money." They laughed.

Caroline brought the tuna melt on a tray along with potato chips and a tall glass of orange juice. Ray opened a tray table, and Caroline set the lunch on it. She handed Peggy her cup of coffee to finish.

"Thank you, Caroline. Won't you join us?"

"Soon as I frost that cake. I'll just be a few minutes." She stepped back into the kitchen.

"So she's cooking you dinner in her new apartment?" Peggy sipped coffee from her cup.

"She likes to cook. And now she has her own kitchen to do it in. She's so proud of that apartment." Ray picked up the sandwich and took a large bite, trying to keep tuna salad from overflowing onto his shirt.

"She a good cook?"

"Well, if pumpkin loaf counts, she is." They laughed. "That's the only cooking of hers I've tasted." He used his knife and fork to take the next bite of his sandwich.

"And it was darn good," Caroline called from the kitchen. "Best pumpkin loaf I ever ate."

"Was it the only pumpkin loaf you ever tasted, Ma?" Ray laughed and turned toward the kitchen.

"I can't say that it was."

"But what counts is that she's making the effort." Peggy set her empty cup on the tray table. "And Jeremy's going to be here with Caroline and Claire?"

"You want to join us, Peggy?" Caroline called. "We're going to watch a movie."

"I might do that. What's the movie?"

"You might want to reconsider, Peggy. Jeremy's picking the movie." Ray turned dancing eyes toward hers.

"May I reserve my decision, Caroline, pending what the movie is?" The three of them laughed.

Ray took the last bite of his sandwich; and Peggy handed him the small, cut-glass bowl of wrapped chocolates Caroline kept on the coffee table. He took two. She took one.

"Heather's a lucky young woman," Peggy said, unwrapping the chocolate meticulously.

"You're just biased, Aunt Peggy," Ray protested.

"No, seriously." Her face went solemn again, making Ray uneasy.

"How many women, single moms like her, would kill to have someone nice like you drive them around, help them find an apartment—move—put up with their child, and buy them gifts?" Peggy patted his leg. Ray worried where she was going with this.

"Well, I'm no prize, you know, Aunt Peggy. But she lets me have the pleasure of her company. And her son's company." He felt he needed to make a point. "I enjoy helping them. They're fun to be with." He looked into Peggy's eyes. "They make an old fogey like me feel young." He nodded for emphasis.

"Old fogey? My stars! You're what, thirty-eight years old?"

"I'll be thirty-nine in July, Aunt Peggy. Pushing forty, I am."

"You're not even in your prime till fifty." Peggy spat the words. "How old is this Heather?"

"Twenty-eight," he wheezed out the words. "She's a kid."

"She's a kid with a kid, don't forget. Having a child early makes you grow up fast. I know; I've been there."

Ray wished they would get on another subject. He still felt uneasy about the direction Peggy was going. He looked at his watch. It was 2:10. Less than four hours to go. "Did Claire call, Ma? Is she all set to pick up Jeremy at 5:00?" He stood and walked into the kitchen.

"Think I'll wax the van. It's spick n' span now. Good time to wax it."

As he spread the liquid wax, he thought about Aunt Peggy's remarks. He had to agree with her that Heather was lucky to have his help. *I know she appreciates it. That's exactly why she's making this dinner for me. And I appreciate knowing her. It's a win-win situation.* He borrowed Hope's frequent expression.

Ray took pleasure in spreading the liquid wax over the slick, clean surface of the van's body. The air, though spring-like, had a damp chill to it, which seemed to clear his head. He began buffing the dried wax and felt heat coursing through his body from the exertion. He felt grateful for this task to expend the nervous energy building in him from anticipation of tonight. Of being with Heather. He took deep breaths, rubbing vigorously as he exhaled.

Ray looked up when he heard the back door open. "You leaving now, Aunt Peggy?"

"Yes, Ray. I have errands to run, emails to answer." She came to him and put an arm around his waist. "Have a great time tonight, Sweetie." She murmured in his ear. "And keep your guard up. You've got more on the ball than any of those twenty-somethings out there. Don't think Heather doesn't see that. Just don't get swept away."

He looked at her with eyes full of questions and squeezed her hand at his waist. They said their good-byes, and he watched her get into her car and drive away.

                                          *

Claire was on time and everything went as planned. Ray, gift boxes in hand, rang Heather's doorbell at 6:03 P.M. She came to the door breathless and beautiful in a pink gingham apron, her face flushed. She seemed both perplexed and thrilled with the gifts, placing them on a chair by the sliding-glass doors. Cooking aromas filled the room.

Ray gazed around the spacious kitchen, thinking how bright and homey it looked from Heather's touch. She had grouped several pots of brilliant pink and red begonias and impatiens on the snack-bar countertop. The table was set with pink cloth place mats; white paper napkins with pink floral borders; and drugstore-crystal sugar, creamer, and salt-and-pepper shakers. There were two pink carnations in a matching vase and pale pink candles in clear plastic, star-shaped candleholders. Grey-white china plates stamped with pink flowers were polished to a gleam and flanked by bargain flatware, easily identifiable by its too-shiny finish.

Ray's eyes moved to the counter by the sink where a large, round pineapple-upside-down cake melted onto a pedestal cake plate. "Wheww!" Ray whistled. "Will you look at that." He smiled at Heather. "Did you make that yourself?"

"Yes, I did, thank you. That's our dessert," she said, her voice full of pride.

"I was hoping that was our appetizer," Ray laughed, wanting to prolong the discussion since he wasn't sure, given his nerves, he could think of anything further to say. But he needn't have worried.

"No, Ray. You'll have to wait until after we eat, she said with a voice of surprising authority. "We're having pork chops with milk gravy, mashed potatoes, tossed salad, and buttered carrots." She looked for his reaction. Ray smiled and rubbed his stomach. "Oh, and your choice of dinner rolls or pumpkin loaf." She fussed with the strap of her apron. "Well—not your choice—you can have both if you want." She lifted a pot lid on the stove, emitting a thread of steam into the air. "Are you ready to eat now?"

"Whenever you are. You're the hostess. The hostess with the mostest," he teased.

Gesturing with thumb and forefinger—clearly careful not to point her finger—she directed him to sit across from her.

"Can I help you get anything on the table, Heather?"

"No, you just sit down. I'll take care of it." So he did.

She emptied the contents of a cast-iron skillet into an oval bowl. Pork chops smothered in rich creamy white gravy. Ray could see tiny bits of carrot and onion suspended in the thick gravy. She scooped large spoonfuls of mashed potatoes into a crockery bowl and took a square casserole of bright baby carrots from the oven. Ray helped her guide them onto prearranged wicker and metal trivets on the table.

"Dig in, Ray," she said, peeling plastic wrap off a basket of neat pumpkin-loaf slices and adding miniature, browned rolls from the oven.

"I have ice water on the table," she said, removing her apron and revealing a soft pink, v-neck sweater, the vertex stopping just short of cleavage. "Or would you prefer coffee or coke? I have both." She took a match from a tiny paper box and lit the candles. Then with an "Excuse me," she went to the light switch and darkened the room.

He did not recognize this confident-hostess side of Heather. Her voice sounded unlike the breathless, little-girl voice he knew that instantly melted him on the phone or in person. "I'll just stick with water for now," he murmured, confused.

She sat down across from him. He looked at her and smiled as she handed him the bowl of pork chops. He could not believe he was here with her like this, having a wonderful dinner. Just the two of them.

Eating the surprisingly good food with relish, they fell into easy conversation. They talked about Jeremy's big night with Caroline and Claire and his taste in movies. Ray mentioned that his Aunt Peggy may join them and described how special she was. He tried to convey his devotion to her without gushing.

Ray asked Heather if the landlord had given her any trouble. She said she'd hardly seen him but had met his wife and really liked her.

They had just started dessert and coffee. Ray's first bite of Heather's pineapple cake was even more heavenly than he had anticipated. And the coffee was delicious with half-and-half from the creamer.

A loud, persistent knocking at the door startled them both. "Who could that be?" Heather whispered with furrowed brow. She rose and peeked through the window curtains. Ray saw her face fall. She stood motionless.

The knocking resumed and a male voice called, "Heather! Heather! Open up!" Her face reddened.

Ray tensed. "Who is it?" he whispered.

Her shoulders dropped. Her mouth tightened. "It's Davey," she said, defeated. She walked to the door and opened it a few inches.

Ray could hear Davey's boisterous greeting. Heather stepped outside, closing the door behind her. He sat nervously in his chair, fighting the urge to go out there and introduce himself to Jeremy's father. He heard muffled voices sounding like arguing and thought better of it. He strained his neck to see them through the curtain. Their figures were blurred but obviously tense; it was clear that they were facing off.

"Forget it, Davey!" Heather shouted. "No, you cannot come in. I have a guest. Just go."

Ray found himself standing and striding toward the door. It opened just as he reached for the knob.

"We have a visitor, Ray," Heather said, barely able to speak her teeth were clenched so. Her face was grave. Davey walked in behind her, smiling a tipsy smile and looking rakish in a brown leather blazer and cowboy boots.

"Hey Buddy," he said to Ray, still smiling. Ray introduced himself and offered his hand. They shook hands vigorously. Davey's eyes scoped the room. "Nice place you got, Hon." His eyes fell on the table, the remains of the meal still looking festive. "Did I crash your party?" he asked, his voice kind, insinuating. A chill ran up Ray's neck. He looked at Heather; she looked back with angry eyes.

"I just came to see Jeremy," Davey slurred, looking at Ray. "Got him a light for his new bike. Want to give it to him myself. Where is he?"

Ray could not miss the threatening way he looked at Heather and felt a great need to protect her. Sizing Davey up, he saw that he was about six inches taller than himself with shoulders twice as broad. He had long feet as well to give him a firm foundation. But he was walking at a tilt from drinking while Ray was perfectly in control of his body.

"Jeremy's not here," Heather said, her assertiveness still astounding Ray.

Davey looked with leering eyes from Ray to Heather. "Oh, just a cozy dinner for two?" he mocked.

"Stop that, Davey!" Her face reddened. "Just leave. You can see Jeremy tomorrow if you're still in town."

Ray wanted to grab him from behind by both arms and throw him out the door, but he worried that in his drunkenness he would fall down the outside stairs. He also did not know if the man would fight dirty. Heather had never indicated that he was violent but had referred to him as mean and a bully.

Ray stepped strategically toward Davey who shouted, "I want to see my son dammit!" Ray lunged at his back just as the door opened abruptly, and a curvy brunette in a skimpy red sweater and second-skin black leather pants appeared. Everyone froze.

"What's taking so long, Davey?" She whined through candy-red lips. She looked from Davey to Ray to Heather.

"I'm Desiree, Honey," she said to Heather in a girlfriend voice, stepping toward her.

Heather did not turn toward the woman. "I'm Heather, Desiree; and this is Ray." Ray nodded at her and almost smiled. Heather's polite words belied her distaste, but her body language did not. "Davey's ready to leave; Jeremy's not here," she said to Desiree but looked at Davey.

Ray stood silently, feeling helpless. He felt sorry for Davey, wanting to see his boy. And for Desiree, all got up like a tart and trying to act like a lady.

Desiree moved to Davey and put her arm under his. "Come on, Davey-Dave," she cooed into his face. "Let's be on our way. Our friends are waiting for us at Carl's." She guided him toward the door.

Heather said nothing. She did not move. Ray stepped artfully around her and held the door. He followed them down the stairs, regretting he hadn't led the way so he could break Davey's fall if he slipped. The trio crept slowly down, Desiree pushing Davey along the railing, Ray's hands shadowing his broad back ready to catch him if needed.

Finally, they reached the big, silver town car, once-prestigious but now looking out of date and vulgar. To Ray's horror, Davey weaved toward the driver's side. Ray slipped between them and motioned for Desiree to take the driver's seat. He cupped his hands around Davey's bony elbows and steered him toward the passenger side.

"Desiree's going to drive, Old Buddy," Ray drawled, aiming for casual. Davey, looking as if about to punch Ray, lifted his eyes toward the apartment, then moved to the passenger door. Ray helped fold him into the seat.

"You take care now, Dave. Jeremy will be sorry he missed you. You okay, Desiree?" She rolled her eyes. Ray slammed the door shut, and Desiree gunned the engine backing up. He stood watching until the car pulled into the street.

Ray looked toward the apartment windows and hoped Heather had calmed down. He felt sad. Sad that Davey did not get to see his son. Sad that Heather's lovely dinner had been disrupted. Sad for Desiree, looking like that to attract a man like Davey.

"More coffee, Ray?" Heather asked as a greeting when he returned. She had cleared away the dishes and put fresh napkins, forks, and dessert plates on the table.

She had added a tiny tray of club crackers and cheddar-cheese squares with a small bunch of red grapes on the side. *Where did she learn to be such a good hostess?* "Yes, please. I could use some." He went to the sink and washed his hands, savoring the aroma of fresh coffee brewing.

Heather cut them each a new piece of pineapple-upside-down cake. She was quiet as they began to eat, toying with a bit of cheese and cracker. Not looking at Ray.

Ray noticed that the candles had been snuffed. He tried for eye contact with Heather, but she kept her eyes lowered, her small hands cradling the coffee mug. He wondered why the china cups and saucers were gone.

"Heather? Are you all right?" His voice was tender.

Not looking up, "I'm okay, Ray."

"Could we have the candlelight again? That was really nice before."

She looked directly at him. "You think?" She smiled. She reached for the matchbox and deftly lit the candles. Ray rose and switched off the lights.

"I'm sorry, Ray. Sorry you had to deal with Davey tonight. He has a knack for ruining people's evenings." Her voice was angry, her eyes sad.

"No need to be sorry. He didn't ruin my evening. I had a beautiful dinner with a beautiful woman, and now I'm having a beautiful dessert with her." Heather giggled girlishly, delighting Ray. "Davey was just a tiny blip in this great evening at the Baker's uptown apartment. Davey and Desiree," he mocked. They both laughed.

"Oh Ray." She touched his right hand lightly, electrifying his entire body. "You always make me feel so safe." He put his left hand over hers delicately, afraid to grasp it as he longed to, afraid of going too far. They locked eyes briefly before each turned cautiously away and withdrew their hands.

They finished the coffee and cake, and Ray helped with cleanup. They sat down on the sofa at a polite distance. The evening seemed to be over and Ray knew he should go. "You haven't opened your gift," he said. He brought it to her and sat down next to her again, but just a little closer this time.

"You shouldn't have done this, Ray. You've already done so much." She removed the wrapping meticulously. Ray felt his heart race.

"Oh, Ray!" She covered her mouth with her hand when she saw the elegant towels. She unfolded the hand towel on top and stroked the lovely jade pile, the lettering. "They're beautiful." She reached over and hugged him awkwardly. Ray felt his body temperature explode. "I've never had monogrammed towels before." He could see tears glistening at the corners of her eyes. He wanted to fold her into his arms and hug her properly. He wanted to buy her a roomful of towels.

"The other box is for Jeremy to open." Ray gestured toward the box still on the chair. "Just between you and me, his is towels, too. He may not be thrilled, but they're nice. A house can never have too many towels." Heather laughed. She looked at the clock. Ray knew it was time to leave though his heart hungered to stay. He felt cocooned in the warmth of her.

He stood. "Well, Heather, it's been—"

The telephone rang sharply. "Excuse me, Ray." From his cocoon he heard her answer the phone. "It's for you." She handed the cordless phone to him, a trace of concern on her face.

After a short exchange he handed the phone back to her. "My cousin Millie's been taken to the emergency room. We have to pick up Jeremy, so Mom and Claire can get to the hospital. I'll bring you back here and then go on over there."

He drove too fast, his heart full of love for Heather and fear for Millie. Fear for Ma, too. She may not be strong enough for a crisis like this.

*

After he finished vacuuming Hope's carpet, Ray aimlessly dusted the outer office. He reminded himself to call Heather later to thank her for the nice evening. It was 7:15 and Hope still was not here; that was unusual for her. He left the office and headed back to the boiler room only to hear her call.

"Good morning, Ray. Please wait. I need a word with you." Hope hurried down the hall in her French heels, arms loaded with folders and bags. "What about Millie? Have you had news this morning?" Ray held the glass door open for her; she entered the tiny office and unloaded her things on the table.

Ray explained that Millie had been admitted to the hospital with breathing problems. She'd had a restful night and was to undergo several tests this morning. She was weak and ill, hooked up to oxygen when he'd seen her.

"I didn't think she looked well last week," Hope said, looking sober.

"She told me Thursday she was going to call the doctor cause she kept having shortness of breath. She was worn out." Ray rubbed his elbows and gazed out the window. "Ma talked to her on the phone Thursday night. She said she had an appointment right after school Friday. Ralph—her husband—said the doctor gave her a prescription and scheduled her for tests."

"How did she end up in the hospital?"

"Well, they went home, filled the prescription first. Went home. She took the pills and rested. Felt a little better the next day. But I guess she had a rough time Sunday: coughing, shortness of breath, weak. Finally went to the emergency room about five thirty."

"Can she have visitors, do you know?" Hope asked.

"I'll call the hospital today and ask. Let you know. Wanting to break the tension, he managed a weak smile.

Jeremy passed Ray near the boys' restroom and gave him a shy smile and a wave.

"How are you doing, Sport?" Ray asked, drawing the boy out of his uncharacteristic reserve.

"Okay," he said, dropping his eyes. Ray could see he was troubled. He strode over to him and laid a hand on his shoulder.

"Come help me at lunch time. We'll talk then." Ray looked tenderly down, waiting for him to lift his eyes. Jeremy slowly lifted his chin and looked into Ray's eyes. Ray smiled at him and hugged him against his leg. "Mom's all right, isn't she?"

Jeremy nodded yes, his face blank, making Ray both relieved and concerned.

Ray knew that Jeremy was surely worried about his teacher. Last fall he had told Ray about his fears for her when she was undergoing treatments. Since then Millie had seldom been absent; but on the few occasions when she was, Jeremy, indeed, the entire class tended to look out of sorts when they came down for lunch. Millie was such a vibrant, solid force in their lives at school; they were motherless waifs without her. He was sure Millie's absence was the cause of Jeremy's distress. What else could it be? He did not want to think that Davey may have gone back to Heather's apartment and caused trouble.

Caroline called from the hospital at 10:30, barely able to speak. Millie had lapsed into a coma before all the tests had been completed. She was on life support. Her daughter had been summoned from Los Angeles, her son, from Asheville.

"What are they saying is the cause, Ma?" Ray asked in disbelief. His cousin was only fifty-two years old, for cripe's sake.

"Don't know yet." Caroline's dim voice faded completely.

"Ma, Ma," Ray panicked.

"Ray, your mom can't talk. She's beside herself." Aunt Patsy's soothing voice washed over him.

"You think I should come up there, Aunt Patsy?"

"No, no. There's nothing you can do here except wait and pace. You stay at work. I'll take care of your mom."

"What about Ralph? He could use another guy there, couldn't he?" Ray did not want to go to the hospital but needed to be sure it wasn't expected of him.

"His brother, Donald, is here. And Tucker's coming from Asheville. That'll help Ralph a lot; they're so close, you know." Aunt Patsy chuckled. "Remember how we used to tease Tucker about falling asleep in Ralphs's car, so he wouldn't miss going on his next errand with him? He was about five then."

Ray was only half listening, thinking about the stress on Caroline. She always said Millie was her last link with her late brother. "What's Ma doing now? Is she all right?"

"She's doing fine. Drinking coffee Donald brought her, talking to him. Don't worry, Ray. But there is one thing you can do."

"Just name it,"

"Tell Dr. Fleming about Millie. Ralph said he should call himself, but he isn't up to it. Asked me to see if you would tell her."

"Sure."

*

Bella said Hope was visiting classrooms in A-and B-wings, so Ray headed that way. He found her sitting outside Trudy's room with a small girl who looked spanking clean in aqua pedal pushers and aqua scrunchie on her dark ponytail, listening to her proudly read from pages written in a six-year-old's uneven manuscript.

Ray stood and listened, not wanting to interrupt. Hope held up her index finger, her eyes saying, *be right with you.*

The child read to the end of the page, turned it, and began reading the last page, a half one. She finished and with high praise Hope sent her back to class.

Ray sat down in the empty child-sized chair, angling himself carefully. He told Hope about Millie and watched her carefully made-up face crumble. She closed her eyes and dropped her chin. After a minute, she swallowed and looked at Ray.

"I'm so sorry, Ray. We'll get you a sub. You may have to stay through the lunch periods if the sub doesn't get here."

"No. No. I'll just wait and go this afternoon. Maybe leave a little early. Ma's got her sister with her. There's other family there, too. I won't need a sub yet." They both rose and walked toward the servery together.

Ray saw the gym class lined up to leave the multi-purpose room and looked at his watch. They were leaving ten minutes early. Good. That would give him a head start on setup. He began folding down tables from their wall frames, wondering when he would have a chance to call Heather. That's right; she was supposed to let him know if she could go to the Christian concert with him Friday night. She had acted interested, but Ray wondered if she were just being polite. Of course, with this Millie thing coming up now, he might not be able to go himself. He would just have to wait and see what happens.

The lunchroom was ready ahead of time, so Ray hurried to the boiler room to make his quick phone call. It took the foreman forever to get Heather to the phone. But as soon as he heard her say, "Hi, Ray," in her endearing voice, it was worth the wait.

He said he had only a minute and thanked her for the lovely dinner.

"Have you seen Jeremy today?" she asked, her voice going tense.

"Yeah, he's going to help me with lunch duty."

"Was he okay?" Ray remembered Jeremy's obvious distress and their plans to talk. "Did he say anything?"

"About what?"

"About his dad?" I might as well tell you." Her voice grew hard. "His dad came back Saturday night. After you dropped us off. Made a big stink." Ray felt tense. It was too warm in his office. He looked at the clock.

"I have to go now, Heather. Talk to you later. I'll see if Jeremy needs to talk. Bye for now." His heart sank as he replaced the receiver. He was not sure he wanted to know what stink Davey had made.

He hurried to the cafeteria just in time to monitor the helpers watching for proper placement of empty lunch trays. Jeremy came over, emptied his tray, placed it on the trolley, and reported for duty. Ray put him in charge of garbage, knowing that was his favorite task. He loved to wheel the cart around importantly in front of the kids.

Aggie Fox and Jan Wheaton walked over from the lunch line and told him how sorry they were about Millie. The word is out now.

Most of the first-lunch classes had left the cafeteria; second-lunch students were settled in. Ray and Jeremy took their bag of bird seed and can of fish food to the courtyard. Jeremy wasn't ready to open up but did tell him that Davey was upset about Jeremy's staying at Ray's house and that he had argued with Heather and threatened to take back the money he had given her.

Ray's heart wrenched as he heard the account and watched the shadow come over Jeremy's eyes. He gave him a brusque hug and sent him to class. He wished Jeremy had had time to play outside on such a fine day.

Boris Mathews and Carmen Ricci, carrying lunch trays through to their rooms, expressed concern for Millie, as did Brad Kushner and Annie Klements.

Around two o'clock Taylor Pruett from Ali Cantrell's class brought down a large manila envelope full of hand-made, get-well cards for Millie. Erica Walsh from Millie's class brought down an enormous get-well card on folded four-by-six poster board, all decorated with childish crayon drawings of flowers, hearts, and birds. "It's for Mrs. Blackwell," she said proudly. The whole class signed it." She produced a large envelope crafted from folded newspaper, still oozing white-glue globules. "Put it in this envelope when the glue dries. To keep it clean," she instructed with authority, undaunted by blonde, eye-level bangs obscuring her vision.

Ray prepared to leave at 2:30 as Hope had approved. He had a sick knot in the pit of his stomach; his eyes burned as if he had gone without sleep. He washed his hands and put on his khaki windbreaker in lieu of a fresh shirt. He gathered up the packets of cards and left through the service door, shoulders drooping, feet weighted.

He opened the rear door of the van and piled the cards inside. He walked to the driver's door and thought he saw Heather near the school entrance, waving him down. He climbed in and with motions deliberate, buckled the seatbelt, turned the key in the ignition, and pulled out. Heather's figure in black cropped pants and yellow short-sleeved tee blurred as he drove right past her without looking.

CHAPTER TWENTY-FOUR—IAN AND HELSI

"Good-bye, Mom, Dad," Lucy called as she followed a surly Sean out the side door. The air brakes on the school bus whooshed loudly as it drew to a stop two houses down the street.

"We have to tell him, Ian," Helsi insisted, waving at the door. "Everyone at school will know. He should hear it from us first." She refilled his coffee mug.

"He's done so well with Mrs. Blackwell; he counts on her." Ian spooned sugar into hot coffee. "You know how he bonds with teachers he likes, turns himself inside out to please them." He gazed toward the large front window in the living room. "He's not prepared for this." He looked at Helsi.

"But he knows she's been ill, even told us all about the card he made for her, he was so proud of it. So he's somewhat prepared, wouldn't you say?" The oven timer buzzed; she went to the stove and pressed it off. She picked up plaid potholders and pulled out a tray of blueberry muffins, dropping them into a small basket, which she carried to the table.

"Those look great, Hon." He helped himself. "Being ill and actually dying are two different things, Helsi." He looked at her over a large bite of butter-soaked muffin, his eyes penetrating. "I never thought she'd die, did you? She's only fifty-two years old."

Helsi's face was somber. "And one of the best, if not thee best teacher at Poore Pond. She did a lot to get Sean on track, remember? Tutored him after school for no charge." She shook her head, her eyes misting. "I was hoping Dylan would end up in her class."

Small feet thumped down the stairs. Ian looked at Helsi. "You tell him."

"Better you should tell him. You're his father; you can give him permission to cry if he wants." Suddenly Robbie was in her face.

"Did you get more bananas, Mom?" He pulled an oversized box of Cheerios from a lower cupboard and took a bowl from the stack on the table. Helsi brought a banana from the counter and sliced it into his bowl of dry cereal. Dylan and Rachel could be heard talking loudly upstairs.

Robbie flooded his cereal bowl with milk, maneuvering the gallon jug skillfully, stopping just short of overflowing. He took a bite, his spoon loaded and dripping.

Helsi and Ian watched him eat for a moment. Ian's eyes caught hers, pleading *tell him.*

In the end, Helsi did the telling. Robbie looked to his dad for cues but did not cry although his father told him clearly it would be all right if he did. He surprised them by saying flatly, "I hope she got to read my card."

Dylan came from upstairs and sat at the place where Helsi had put a toasted pop tart.

"Mrs. Blackwell's dead, Dylan," Robbie said without emotion. "She died."

Over a bite of pop tart, Dylan looked at Helsi, his big eyes misty. He put effort into swallowing. Helsi went to him and squeezed his shoulders, lingering while he ate.

Robbie left with Dylan to catch the bus. Rachel nursed a bowl of cereal, her eyes riveted to the living-room television, puppets dancing clumsily on the screen.

"What do you make of that?" Ian asked Helsi.

"Obviously, it hasn't sunk in yet. He'll feel it when he gets to school though. That will be one sad place today." She began to clear the table. "You saw Dylan."

"Robbie's teacher died." Rachel turned from the television to announce.

"That's right, Rachel," Ian said. "We're all sad about it." She turned back to her program. Ian met Helsi's gaze.

"We'll have to go to the wake. I'll call school to see when it is. Probably be at Franklin's; that's where everybody goes, all the prominent ones anyway." She turned toward the ringing telephone.

Ian took his car keys off the hook near the door. He opened his black cloth lunch bag and peered inside. "Can I have a bag of goldfish, Hon?" he asked when she replaced the receiver.

"That was one of the room mothers." Helsi lifted a large basket from atop the refrigerator and took a bag of goldfish from the assorted snacks. "Want some cookies?" Ian took the bag of bite-sized chocolate chip she offered him.

"What did she want?"

"They're getting a meal together for Mrs. Blackwell's family. Wanted me to send dessert or a vegetable. I'll drop it off later today. They want to deliver it right after school." She went to the door to receive his kiss.

"Make your cinnamon bundt cake. Everyone loves it." Ian stooped to kiss Rachel who ran in to say goodbye.

*

Helsi pulled into Poore Pond School parking lot, a cinnamon bundt cake double wrapped in foil on the seat beside her. She had prepared as well, a plate of slices of the same kind of cake to leave for the staff.

Silence seemed to hang over the entire grounds. Classroom windows were open, but there were none of the normal sounds of teachers and children's voices emanating from them. The day, though warm with breaking sun, seemed chill and gloomy.

The outdoor sign bore the message: *Hail and Farewell, Mrs. Blackwell. We love you and miss you.* It took Helsi by surprise. Amazed at the speed with which the sign had been constructed, she felt both offended and comforted.

She gathered her purse, the cakes, and a signed sympathy card she had quickly chosen from a box of assorted greeting cards purchased from the school fund raiser last year. She would have preferred a more expressive card, but it seemed important to include it with the offering of cake and did not want to stop to buy another.

She rang the bell, gave her name on the speaker, and waited to be buzzed in, noting the irony between the secure door and open windows all around the building. The buzzer sounded, and she artfully opened the door around her armload of plates and purse. The door closed automatically behind her, its locking click the only sound she heard. She walked to the office and stood at the window in the glass partition. No one was attending the desk. She coughed a few times.

Dr. Fleming came out of her office on silent feet. "Good morning, Mrs. Bradford," she said with subdued enthusiasm. She opened the glass door and motioned her into her small office. "What can I do for you?"

Helsi gave her the cakes, explaining their destination. Hope taped the card to the Blackwell's cake for her. Helsi expressed sympathy to the principal and asked if there was anything further she could do. Telephones rang in the background. She asked about services.

"Millie—Mrs. Blackwell—wanted to be cremated. So there will be a memorial service Thursday morning at St. Catherine's. Ten thirty." Hope tore off a square of notepaper and wrote details for her.

"I suppose people will go as families." Helsi found her own voice matching the reverential tone of Dr. Fleming's. "Tell me, Dr. Fleming, do you think children should go?"

"I think that depends on the child and the family. I really feel that a memorial service is the best sort of funeral to which to bring a child. It's not as frightening or emotional. And often there are photographs of the deceased displayed, just as there are at wakes these days." Hope smiled warmly, Helsi noting that even her smile was more subdued that usual. "But you must follow your own instincts about that. Most parents have the best instincts where their children are concerned." Telephones continued to ring, then stop as if someone somewhere were answering them.

Helsi could see that Hope was poised to move on and said her good-byes.

"We'll schedule our Dylan meeting with you and Mr. Bradford as soon as we get through these sad days, Mrs. Bradford. Thank you for your kindness and generosity. The cake. We'll enjoy that." She offered her hand.

Helsi tried to guide the automatic door to a quiet closing just as Betsy Peterson approached and caught it.

"Hi, Helsi," she said, not quite smiling. "Terrible news about Mrs. Blackwell, isn't it?" They moved away from the door and continued.

"We're just sick about it," Helsi kept her voice reverently low. "She's done so much for our Robbie. I don't know how he'll make it without—." Her voice cracked and trailed off. She looked away.

"How did he take it? Joey had her last year, wanted to stay home today and make her a special card. For the fune-ral, he said." They allowed themselves a small chuckle.

"Will you take him to the memorial service?" Helsi showed Betsy the note.

"Probably," Betsy said. "Judging from his reaction this morning, he will want to go."

"I wonder if Robbie will want to," Helsi pondered aloud. "That was nice of the PTA moms to call everyone. So we could prepare the kids." Both women cast their eyes about, observing the atypical silence around them.

"It had to be done. I was one of the moms on the phone chain." Betsy looked at her with sad eyes. "Everyone—and we called everyone, not just the parents of kids in her class—was so appreciative of the call. A lot of them were emotional, some said their child never had her; but they had heard what a wonderful teacher she was." Betsy swallowed. "It was amazing." She took a deep breath. "So many asked what they could send, money for flowers? Food? Three moms from her class wanted to come in and just be with the kids today." Betsy looked away. "It was amazing."

Helsi had to get away before she started sobbing uncontrollably. She touched her friend's hand and whispered, "I'll see you later, Betsy."

She saw two mothers from Dylan's class chatting near their cars. She waved broadly but did not join them, although she wanted to. She had to get away from the heartbreaking sorrow before it got the best of her.

*

Of course there was drenching rain on Thursday morning. Sean, who'd never been in Millie's class but had been a drop-out member of the fourth-grade stamp club she had sponsored, surprised his parents by asking to go along to the memorial service. When asked by Ian if he just wanted to get out of school, Sean was indignant. "Well, it is my little brother's teacher, you know. And I had Mrs. Blackwell for stamp club."

Lucy, ever respectful of teachers, wanted to go even though she had not been in Mrs. Blackwell's class; but she had an important Spanish test she dare not miss. Robbie, in the end, decided he had to go. "Nearly the whole class—nearly—was going," he had told Ian. He insisted on wearing a white shirt and necktie for the occasion. His elder brother, of course, wore his customary balloon-legged, draggy-hemmed khaki pants and over-sized, un-ironed oxford shirt, sleeves rolled tightly to the elbows.

Dylan and Rachel would attend their respective classes.

"They must need a whole corps of substitutes," Ian said as the four of them drove to St. Catherine's. "I imagine all the teachers wanted to go to the service." He looked over at Helsi.

"Dr. Fleming said the 'ministrators from the board office are subbing today, even the super-tendent's coming to help." Robbie piped from the rear of the van.

Helsi waited for Sean's sarcastic response, but he said nothing. Concerned, she turned to look at him. He gazed out the window as if what he saw were of great interest. He turned and met his mother's eyes, his face uncharacteristically full of warmth.

"Classes collected money for flowers," Helsi said. "One of the parents owns a florist business. Giving a big discount to the students. So the kids weren't to give more than a quarter apiece for flowers."

"Quarter per student. About 750 students," Ian calculated. "That's more than 175 dollars." He shook his head. "That's a lot of flowers."

"I hope it's a whole room full of flowers," Robbie chimed. "Mrs. Blackwell is the best teacher in the whole world."

"In the universe, Robbo," Sean quipped, to Helsi's great relief.

A long line of cars inched into the nearly full parking lot at St. Catherine's. Robbie waved excitedly at classmates in nearby cars. Ian stopped to let his family out at the door and was waved on by an impatient traffic director in a black trench coat. "Hey, how are you doing, Ian?" the man, instantly transformed, recognized Ian, who had taught him CPR.

"Hi, Forrest," Ian said. "Looks like a big turnout." Helsi and the boys climbed out, protected from the rain by the wide portico.

"One of the biggest," he said, his eye toward approaching vehicles. "Good to see you. Millie Blackwell your kid's teacher?"

"Yes. She's one of a kind." Ian waved and pulled forward. He could hear Forrest Franklin's response behind him.

"That's what I keep hearing from everyone." He located him in the rear-view mirror and waved again.

Helsi found the empty seats were all near the front of the cavernous sanctuary, just behind the rows marked for family. She led her sons to a pew three rows back from the reserved section; they sat near the center aisle, leaving space for Ian at the edge next to Sean. They settled into the gold velour pew cushion.

Helsi strained to see who was playing the organ and realized it was Poore Pond music teacher, Mrs. Ricci.

She looked to her left across the row and waved discreetly back at Mrs. Cooper. Mrs. Armstrong and Miss Fox leaned forward from Trudy Cooper's left and waved, too. *Those teachers look so pale and distraught I didn't recognize them at first. How difficult this must be for them. Losing a beloved colleague. They saw her every day. How many years has Mrs. Blackwell been at Poore Pond? I know it's at least twenty years.*

Robbie poked her arm. "Look, Mom. Look at the flag." He gestured toward the altar where a large U.S. flag hung above a brass urn on a mahogany stand. "It's all flowers, the whole thing."

Sean pointed out the blue banner furling beneath a massive spray of red roses on the altar. White lettering: *We'll miss you, Mrs. Blackwell. Your third-grade class.*

Ian arrived and folded himself into the space at the end of the pew, Helsi, Robbie, and Sean shifting left to give him room. Helsi could hear Sean whispering about the flowers to Ian.

"Hello, Bradford family," whispered a voice from behind. They all turned to see Miss Maher smiling bravely at them. They waved and smiled back.

A choir of young voices burst forth with the hymn, *Coming Home.* The Poore Pond Fifth-Grade Chorus stood thirty-five-strong in the choir loft, singing earnestly to the mourners. Helsi felt her heart stir. She checked in her pocket for the squares of extra-large tissues she'd folded and put there.

Pastor Phelps said kind words about Mrs. Blackwell as a dedicated teacher, active church member, caring volunteer, and all-around pillar of the community.

Millie's brother, Jerry, boyish though grey at the temples, spoke endearingly about his elder sister, how she had made him play school when they were young kids growing up on the farm. He was surprised to find "there were no cats, dogs, dolls, or teddy bears for classmates when he got to real school." Chuckles. "She was born wanting to be a teacher," he said proudly. "Our dad encouraged her to become an administrator to make more money, but she said no, she wanted to stay with the kids."

Millie's genteel daughter gave emotional testimony of her mother's influence on her character, her life, sprinkling it with humorous anecdotes, providing more comic relief to the somber occasion.

Ray Sellers, looking like someone else in his navy blue suit, nervously gave a brief but winning tribute to his cousin, saying how easy it was to work in the same building with her. He never had to worry about overhearing uncomfortable remarks because nobody ever criticized her.

Brian Glover talked about how he and Millie went back thirty years. He had taught across the hall when they were both first-year teachers. He said he admired the way she was secure enough even then to ask a lot of questions. "I didn't want anyone to know I didn't know anything, so I was too embarrassed to ask," he said. "But Millie would always go straight to the office or to veteran teachers to get answers.

"But she really showed what a fine person she was when she bought all those snow boots, lunch boxes, school supplies, even new underwear, school photos, books from the book fair for kids who needed them and had no money. She kept a roll of one-dollar bills on her just to give to kids. When I think about it now, it's unbelievable that a twenty-two-year-old kid, fresh out of college, would know so much about making a difference in the lives of kids. How'd she get so smart so young? Maybe she learned it from all those cat-and-dog students Jerry told us about." More needed laughter.

Then all the teachers lined up at the altar followed by Millie's students who stood in front of the teachers. Robbie excused himself as he tripped over Sean's size-ten athletic shoes. Ian stood to let him out, casting a did-you-know-about-this look at Helsi.

Each teacher and student held a lighted candle and sang *Amazing Grace,* led by Carmen while music teacher Norman Wright accompanied them on the piano.

Some teachers cried as they sang; others had stoic faces, their eyes pools of sorrow. The children's faces were full of earnest love as they sang from their hearts. There wasn't a dry eye in the house.

The mourners filed out past a display of photographs of Millie, with her students, with her family, with her husband on their thirtieth wedding anniversary. Robbie lingered at the photographs until Helsi pulled him on.

Nobody spoke on the ride home.

Ian thought about the impact of Millie's death on so many people. *It's like losing an institution. A teacher like that, a really outstanding one, belongs to all of us. At least, we think she does. How dare she leave us.*

Helsi worried about Robbie and the rest of the class. *Everyone in the class has special problems, insecurities. Millie was able to help them get past those and have the confidence to learn, to succeed. What will those children do now?*

Tears spilled uncontrollably down her cheeks. *Good thing the school year's nearly over.* She mopped her eyes with an extra-large tissue and dug in her purse for her sunglasses.

*

Since the drenching rain continued through Friday and Rachel had a doctor's appointment, Ian picked up Robbie and Dylan after school. He was taken aback by the long, creeping line of parents waiting in cars to pick up their children and was admittedly impatient with the slowness of the process.

I should have opted to take Rachel to her appointment. Helsi has more patience for this sort of thing, always has magazines to read or lists to make. He scoured the van for stray reading matter, finding a bright blue pamphlet tucked into the pocket on the door. He looked at the cover: a face of a young boy whose eyes were full of hopelessness. He opened the fold and saw that it was about ADD and ADHD in children. *Isn't that what Lou Bergant's son has? He told me he has problems paying attention, has to take a drug to concentrate.* Ian read through the pamphlet and slipped it back into the door pocket.

He looked at his watch and wondered where his sons were. He switched on the radio and saw Dylan and Robbie making their way toward him, their shoulders drooping under overloaded book bags. He immediately switched off the radio to avoid listening to their fighting over stations.

The boys climbed into the van, dripping water over the back seat. Ian could barely see Robbie's smiling face behind the hood of his yellow slicker. Dylan's hood was flapping at the back of his neck, his eyes and hair full of water droplets. He handed his father a damp envelope with *Parents of Dylan Bradford* typed on it.

*

"I can get fifty percent off the tuition if I meet these criteria, Hon," Ian spread the paper on his knees so Helsi, sitting next to him on the sofa, could see. He pointed to the printed list. "I need three letters of reference." His index finger underscored each point. "And if I pass their medical proficiency test and psychological screening, well," He looked at Helsi with eager eyes. "Then I would qualify. See here, it's called the National Physician's Assistant Study Grant Program." He wanted her to match his enthusiasm.

"But how would you have time to go to classes? When do they meet?" Ian could feel the tension flowing from her, filling the night quiet of the house.

"Some evenings. Some weekends. I don't know." He stood and looked out the big front window, his back to her. The air was heavy with unspoken feelings. Ian felt let down, unsupported. Helsi felt apprehensive and threatened. Neither spoke. Outside, a dog barked in the distance. Ian cracked his knuckles. Helsi went into the kitchen.

"Want a cup of tea, Ian?" she said, her voice thin.

"I guess so." He followed her into the kitchen and watched her fill the teakettle and put it on the stove to boil. She turned and looked at him with cow eyes. "Do you not want me to pursue this, Helsi? No sense wasting my time trying to get accepted if I'm not going to have your support." His eyes burned into her back as she took teabags, cups and saucers, brown sugar cubes from cupboards.

"It's just that, with the kids and everything. I don't want you to neglect your family for this." She turned and faced him. "That would be pure selfishness, Ian Bradford, and you know it."

"But it would mean something to the kids if I did this. And to you. Can't you see that? A better income, a happier dad and husband." He put his arms around her waist. "You know I've dreamed of being a doctor all my life, Hon."

"I know. I know." She untangled herself from his embrace.

"This would be the closest I could come to that at my age." His eyes pleaded with her. "And you know I'm not going to neglect my kids. Have I ever done that?"

"No, of course not," she had to give him that. The kettle whistled and she poured boiling water over teabags and sugar cubes in the teacups. "Come on, Ian. Tea's ready."

Ian gathered his papers and brought them to the table. He was not going to let this go. He stirred his tea and dunked the teabag several times before placing it on the tiny duck-shaped cup Helsi put out for that purpose. He took a bite from a lumpy oatmeal drop cookie Helsi and Rachel had baked, chewing as he perused the literature.

"It says here, classes run two nights per week and every other Saturday." He looked at her down-turned face. She did not look up.

"We can certainly manage that, can't we?"

"Let's talk about this later, Ian, okay?" She said in a controlled voice. She went to the small CD player on the counter and switched it on, filling the kitchen with Barry Manilow's sweet-sounding voice. *Can't smile without you, can't laugh, can't cry...*

Ian pulled her onto his lap. "That's our song, Helsi, you devil. Does this mean I have your support?" He patted both her arms and nuzzled her neck. She nuzzled back.

"Let's just take one step at a time." She shifted on his lap to face him. "You don't even know if you can get in the program yet." Her palms flew up and she shrugged her shoulders. "You get accepted. Then we'll deal." They kissed through smiles.

*

Ian checked his windbreaker pocket for the envelope and opened the van door. Poore Pond School was ablaze with flag-red azaleas and neon yellow lady slippers lining the grounds. He had to hand it to Ray Sellers, such talent. *Impressive. Looks like the national gardens.* He breathed in the warm, spring air and admired the stately brick building, looking its best in brilliant sunlight. He was overcome with a new appreciation for its hallowed halls.

Ian was buzzed into the main door and greeted by Mrs. Kurowski who sent him into Hope's office.

"Good morning, Doctor," Ian smiled and caught the fragrance of courtyard flowers through her open window.

Hope rose from her desk, knocking a stack of stuffed file folders askew. He helped her retrieve them. "Good morning, Ian," she shook his hand warmly. She invited him to sit down.

"I've just come to pick up the letter," he said, pretending not to notice the envelope bearing his name, ready on the table.

Hope took the envelope and handed it to him. "I gave you two copies, one to keep and one to submit. You must be very excited about this venture."

"I am. I am." He could not stop his smile from widening. "And I want to thank you for your encouragement, for writing this letter and everything."

"I'm sure Helsi and the children are very proud of you." She gave him her direct look. "It won't be easy, you know. But it'll be worth all the sacrifice. And you're setting such a good example. I admire you."

"Thanks again." He offered his hand. "We'll see you Friday for the meeting. Nine thirty?"

"Nine thirty it is," she shook his hand warmly. "But don't forget, the volunteer appreciation breakfast is Friday as well. If you come for the eight o'clock breakfast and stay for the meeting, you'll kill two birds with one stone." They laughed.

*

The upper multi-purpose room was filled with women and quite a few men enjoying a breakfast of mushroom-and-cheese omelet, bacon, muffins and bagels, fresh fruit. Student council members in red-and-white aprons greeted guests, served beverages, and kept tables tidy. Teachers spelled each other dishing food at the buffet tables.

Slides of student activities throughout the school year projected continuously on the north wall. Original posters and drawings mounted on bulletin boards charmingly praised volunteers for working so hard to enrich school life for Poore Pond children.

Helsi and Ian sat across from Joe and Betsy Peterson, making small talk and laughing at Joe's play-by-play account of son Joey's first baseball game of the season.

The large room fairly bristled with a happy sense of having completed another satisfying, productive, sometimes grueling academic year. Teachers and volunteers gave each other credit for the end result of their mutual efforts. They praised the children for their hard work. They expressed appreciation for the wonderful Poore Pond School family who could be counted upon to pull together in good times and in bad.

Fran Flanders was glad school would soon be out, so they would all have a break from the fear of school shootings.

Holly Hapwell thought this year's spring musical was the best ever, and may have stimulated aspirations for the performing arts in her daughter Francine, who had the lead role. A few women at the table rolled their eyes dramatically to chide her.

Andy Tarantino, who lived next door to the Ames family, thought the memorial garden was an excellent idea, had really boosted Ann and Charlie's spirit to a level unseen since their son Bucky's untimely death. And now with the death of Mrs. Blackwell, the garden was even more meaningful. "There's not enough spirituality in public schools," he contended. His tablemates nodded collectively and grew silent.

Ian commended the Conflict Management Program at Poore Pond, citing how it had motivated Robbie to work harder on schoolwork. "He knows he can't be on duty and wear that neon pinny if his work's not done." The table cheered.

Monica Weaver had heard a rumor that Dr. Fleming was being transferred to another school. She hoped it wasn't true. "Even though some of her ideas are weird and out of date, she runs a tight school and keeps everybody on track, including us parents." Not surprisingly, she did not mention the field-trip incident when Hope had chastised her.

Phyllis Egan seconded that, privately recalling her meeting with Dave Myers and Dr. Fleming concerning rough activities in Anthony's gym class.

The 9:05 bell sounded, sending guests to rubbish cans with their litter and out to the parking lot.

Classroom teachers hurried to meet their students at line-point entrance doors. Special teachers swung into clean-up, directing student helpers and Ray Sellers where to put leftover food, serving ware, and the few remaining vases of flowers that had been table decorations but were now unclaimed door prizes.

Hope invited Ian and Helsi to take their coffee to the library and relax while they waited for the team to arrive for their meeting.

*

"I kind of hate to see the school year end, don't you, Ian?" Helsi asked as he navigated the van down tree-lined streets flanked by sunny lawns freshly tended with clean mulch and blooming flowers.

"Sort of," he said, looking pensive.

"We learned a lot this year, wouldn't you say? About our kids. About ourselves." Her eyes sought his.

He looked at her briefly, returning his eyes to the road. "Just what have we learned about ourselves?"

"Well, I've learned I can't always trust my feelings," she paused thoughtfully. "In situations involving my kids' problems, even formal situations."

"What are you trying to say, Helsi?" His brow furrowed. "What situations?"

"I'm saying," she took a deep breath and paused for the right words. "I get emotional over my kids, facing their weaknesses. That first day I volunteered with centers in Dylan's class, I couldn't believe it. I lost total control of my emotions, to the point that Miss Fox noticed and told me to take a lav break."

"I know. It's a hard thing, accepting your kids' failures. You've always been good about seeing it, Helsi, seeing the kids' side." He shook his head in self-disgust. "But me, I take it personally, as if someone's out to get me or something. But then I'm an idiot." He jerked his head upwards. "That's what I learned about myself. I'm an idiot." He laughed robustly and pounded the steering wheel.

"Don't make light of this, Ian." Helsi looked at him, her face somber. "I'm serious. I learned that I can be just like those other ranting parents, fighting like maniacs for their kids. I'm not the master over my emotions I thought I was."

"So what? You're human. What's so bad about that? Anyway, you did okay at the meeting today."

"I guess."

"Tell me, what did we learn about our kids this year?" Ian kept his voice casual.

"That they aren't perfect—"

"Did you ever believe they were?" Ian sounded astonished.

"You didn't let me finish. I learned it's not that they aren't perfect that matters, it's how we handle the whole thing. Our attitudes and all. They can't know what a big deal it is for us, that we're disappointed in them," she said, meaning it.

"That's right. They have to see us just handling it. Taking steps to solve the problem, not holding it against them." He reached for her hand. "They try hard, Hon. They give it all they've got. You're right. We've got to let them know we understand that."

She squeezed his hand. "What do you think about the team's plan for Dylan? Does it make sense to you?"

"You mean test him in August after he turns seven?" Helsi shook her head yes. "Something about he has a better chance of qualifying for a special program if he's older? What was that all about?"

"I guess the older he is and doing poorly makes his problem more significant, something about *norms* being in his favor." She began to chew her knuckle. "We have to prepare ourselves for the worst, Ian." She did not look at him.

"The worst? What?" He grimaced. Still she did not look at him.

"Dylan could end up in a special program for slow kids. You heard Mrs. Davis. She said *learning disabilities* or *developmental delays. Developmental delays,* that's slow learners." She willed herself to turn and face him.

"Then what's *learning disabilities?*"

"That's normal, if I understand it correctly, normal or higher intelligence but not achieving at their level. Mrs. Davis said *expected level for their ability.* Some sort of learning problem."

"Dylan certainly has a learning problem; we all know that." Ian insisted. "But he's no dummy."

"Of course he isn't." Helsi did not want to think about last year's report rating Dylan's IQ below average.

She tried to shake the dark mood that was growing in her mind. *His IQ was only slightly below average, Carol Davis had said in her report. Surely that would not qualify him for a slow learner's class. Why those kids were mentally retarded. They went to another school on a bus with an aide. She saw the bus pass Rachel's preschool lots of times. Some of the kids peering out the bus windows looked— strange—not right, wild-eyed under thick glasses. They didn't seem to know what was going on. More than once she had reprimanded Sean and Robbie for calling them retards. No. Dylan's not one of them*

They drove the rest of the way in silence, each lost in thought.

Ian pulled into the driveway. He helped Helsi gather the small vase of flowers, computer-designed cards thanking them for volunteering, and the cupcake she had taken and not had time to eat. The thick pink frosting leaked through the thin paper napkin covering it, but Rachel would enjoy it nonetheless. Helsi carried it carefully into the house.

I won't think about Dylan's school program until August when we get the new test results. I'll work with him every day this summer. We'll use those workbooks I bought at the wholesale club. Make a game of it. We'll read every day, too. And go to the summer library program.

It has so been a good year.

CHAPTER TWENTY-FIVE—HOPE

Hope stood under an overcast sky facing the newly dedicated memorial garden in the south courtyard. On the verge of weeping, she refused to give in to it. The patch of pink-and-yellow petunias planted by Millie's class winked up at her and made her smile. How lovingly those dear children had planted the seedlings they'd started in the classroom with their teacher before they lost her.

Planting the tiny sprouts in memory of her turned out to be the perfect act for them, a just-right way for children to grieve. Faithful by nature, they were certain the plants would thrive and that their Mrs. Blackwell would look down upon and enjoy them. They talked openly about it as they planted, ever so gently, the baby plants. At the dedication ceremony their faces were full of, not tears but proud smiles as their handiwork was showcased for the entire school.

Hope looked at the three cast-cement angels standing in a semi-circle among the rows of plants. Her eyes scanned the small brass plaques swinging from their necks in the warm wind, and she felt at that moment connected to Bucky Ames and Colin French. Then she noticed a small iron cross, ancient in design, driven into the ground near the skirt of Millie's angel. She wondered who had placed it there and when. She stooped down and examined it closely for identifying marks but found none. "Probably Ray," she murmured and rose and walked into the silent building.

Boxes of textbooks lined the shadowy hallway near the boiler room. Black plastic garbage bags bulging with crumpled colored paper, discarded dioramas, crushed paper sculptures, and the like stood outside the doors of lifeless classrooms.

Hope was filled with relief and melancholy. The burdens of Poore Pond were gone for the summer, but so was the spirit. Now there would be time to rest, reflect, regenerate. *That's what I love about education: everything stops—ready or not—in the spring and begins again in autumn, a brand new start each year.* All summer she would look forward to the excitement of re-opening school while relishing every moment of respite.

She carried a stack of books crudely labeled *need rebinding,* from atop the piano to a box in the office.

"Just in time with those rebinds," Bella barked, positioning a strapping tape dispenser to seal the large carton. "Good thing there's a little space left in here." She inserted the books into the carton and closed the flaps, the dispenser shrieking tape across the opening. "Remember, I'm leaving early today, Hope."

"Yes, at two-fifteen, right?"

Bella nodded and taped the other axis of the closed flaps.

"The new registrations are in the computer?" Hope asked.

Bella raised her eyes. "Yes, and all the class lists are typed."

"Good. Tomorrow we'll finish purchase orders and the kindergarten letters." Hope helped Bella lift the box onto a waiting cart, which she pushed into the lobby. She dusted her hands and awaited the secretary's return.

"Friday's your last day, Bella. Are you free for lunch?"

"Sure am."

"I'd like to treat you. Let's go to The Bistro. Someplace nice. I'll make a reservation." She smiled. "We'll go around eleven thirty. How does that sound?"

Bella rolled her eyes and smiled. Hope watched her walk down the hall and felt guilty for not appreciating her more. She really did have many strengths that Hope, annoyed by her idiosyncrasies, took for granted. She glanced at her watch. There was just enough time to finish signing the rest of the letters before she had to leave for her appointment with Bernard McElson, Senior.

*

Hope found herself gripping the steering wheel desperately on her way to the appointment. *No wonder I'm such a wreck. How many times has this appointment been postponed? First, Bernard himself rescheduled it for "personal reasons." Then I had to change it when Millie died.* She tried to control the uneven pressure her foot was applying to the accelerator. She looked around to see if the jerky driving was attracting attention. Other drivers seemed not to notice.

She patted her jacket pocket for the business card she'd placed there, just in case she needed an attorney. *I may not be able to leave without an attorney. If law enforcement is there when I go in, I'll know right off where I stand.*

But if they have a case against me, why would they wait, why wouldn't they just come and arrest me? She was thankful that school was out for the summer. Her throat was parched and she was without a water bottle. She fumbled in her purse for a lozenge and popped it into her mouth. *They're far too dignified to send an officer to just haul me into custody. And smart. They would want to hear my side first. Especially if they lacked incriminating proof.* She inhaled deeply through her nose; unable to take a complete breath, she opened her mouth widely and took in air. Still, she could not breathe deeply enough. She willed herself to breathe in and out, in and out, in and out, steady though shallow breaths.

All they could possibly have would be the canceled checks I wrote to myself, *which Mary authorized anyway.* Finally, she took a complete breath. *But they* *could have the ledger pages as well, which did not match. Why was I so careless* *with those ledgers?* She found her hands shaking and grasped the wheel more tightly. Should she pull over? No, she was almost there; she could see the office complex just ahead. She turned into the parking lot and slammed her front bumper into the curb as she parked.

She popped into the convenience store on the ground level and bought a bottle of water and a bag of salted cashews. Salt may help her calm down. She stopped in the women's lounge on the first floor. She looked at her watch; she still had ten minutes. She sat in a tapestry-covered wingback chair and opened the cashews, popping a handful into her mouth, feeling salt on her lips. She swigged from the water bottle.

Her stricken face in the mirror frightened her. *What will George think if I am* *charged? Poore Pond, the children? The teachers? The parents? Ray? Bella?* *Helen and all the rest? Michael? Oh, he would relish that. "I told you so."*

She took one last gulp of water and stood. She washed the salt from her hands and freshened her lipstick. *I'll just pay it all back. I'll make a deal to pay it all* *back. That's all they care about, I'm sure.*

*

Hope sat frozen on a smart French chair in the waiting room. She stared at the envelope in her hand as if it were a foreign object. Her brain would not function.

"May I get you something, Dr. Fleming?" The chic receptionist asked, her furrowed brow animating pointy black bangs.

"No. No. I'm—fine." She looked at her, she knew, with glazed eyes. "Just need a moment to collect my thoughts." She rose and zombied herself through the heavy glass door and into the elevator.

In her car at last, she stared at the envelope again. She opened it and removed the deposit voucher. The digits burned her eyes: *$2,500,0000. Two-and-a-half* *million dollars. In my account.*

The nearly empty water bottle and half-eaten packet of cashews mocked her from the passenger seat. Had she held those throughout the meeting with Bernard? How did they get here? She began to laugh, a deep laugh emanating from the soles of her feet, reverberating upwards through her body like soul-shaking, electronic music. Cleansing her.

*

It was lovely on the back terrace. The air was fragrant with lavender. Finches were chirping, and the bird feeder was bustling with robins and chickadees. Hope sipped zinfandel wine from fine Irish crystal. She felt celebratory and wanted to tell someone about her good fortune.

Such a lot of money. I must make precise use of it. Perhaps I'll buy Michael's half of this house so he'll stop badgering me. Or buy George a condo. Take myself and Frances on an exotic sister's trip.

Pangs of hunger broke through her thoughts. She scoured the kitchen for the right supper entrée and finally settled on a veggie-burger patty from the freezer. She popped it into the microwave and placed a halved Kaiser roll in the toaster oven. She put a slice of American cheese on a clean plate along with a few leaves of lettuce and two tomato slices.

I could pay Heather's fees for her pharmacy assistant course if she goes. I could put college money into a trust fund for Jeremy. Buy a new sports car. Have cosmetic surgery.

The microwave sounded and Hope assembled her sandwich, which she carried outside. Clouds had moved away from the sun, making the stone terrace more inviting. Bright shards of light danced off the wine goblet, dazzling her eyes. She went back inside and returned wearing dark glasses. She ate hungrily from the burger, hoping it would erase the knot of anxiety low in her stomach.

It's interesting. Mary Baldwin specified that I not receive this inheritance until after I reached age forty-eight, McElson had said. What was she thinking? Probably knew what was in store for me; she had met Michael. Come to think of it, her words to me at my wedding reception were, "Make your own way, Hope. Above everything, keep your financial independence." Looking aristocratic in head- to- toe grey silk, she had whispered in my ear in the receiving line, Michael not two feet away.

"Why, my entire life has been lived under that principle," she gasped at the revelation. *And at what cost?*

I will take my time deciding this. Make sure I do it right. Please, God, I know this is a test. Help me do the right thing.

The cordless phone rang shrilly, echoing off the metal tabletop.

"Frances," Hope shrieked. "I was just thinking about you. How are you? How's Alec?"

"You can't have. When did he leave?" She laughed robustly.

"Here? You want to come here? I thought you never wanted to set foot in the midwest again. What's changed?"

Hope was silent for minutes, listening intently. Her eyes clouded over; she rubbed her forehead. She shifted her weight. Still she listened.

She gathered empty plate and goblet, balancing them with the phone tucked under her chin, all the way into the house.

"Good-bye then, Frances. Lovely to hear from you. Keep me posted." She fitted the phone into its base and stood staring at nothing at all.

It was good to talk to Frances. They had not spoken since Easter holidays. *Alec is gone, I can't believe it. He was so devoted to Frances. The divorce has gone through. Cancer. Ovarian cancer. She has it. Chemo. Radiation.*

The knot in her stomach turned to sadness.

*

"Good afternoon," Hope greeted Tommy Draco, all in black, at his car door as she made her way toward the stairway to Heather's apartment. His eyes burned the backs of her legs through her white linen cropped pants.

She rang the buzzer at the top of the stairs and heard footsteps and low voices. Jeremy, dressed in khaki camp shorts and red T-shirt, opened the door.

"Hi, Principal," he said shyly.

"Well, hello, Jeremy. May I come in?" He held the door for her.

Hope was surprised to see how attractive and cheerful the kitchen looked.

"Your new home is lovely, Jeremy. Is your mom available?"

"She said she'll be here in a minute. She's brushing her hair. Want to see my room?"

"I would be delighted." She followed him across a short hallway to a small room containing a twin bed, a desk, and a wicker chair. Bookcases made of raw lumber stacked on concrete blocks lined a wall under a window. Books and toys were arranged neatly.

"Sit down," Jeremy patted the blue denim comforter plumped over the bed. "I'll show you my car collection." He walked to the bookcases and spent a few moments selecting cars.

Hope sat down on a red corduroy cushion in the wicker chair. Jeremy dropped five assorted small cars into her lap. She examined each one and commented on the wonder of moveable doors and tiny steering wheels.

Heather came through the doorway. "Hi, Dr. Fleming," she chirped, her face bright and smiling. She wore a pink-and-white apron over jeans and a pink shirt. "Sorry to take so long getting ready. I know you said ten thirty." She removed the apron. "Should we go," she gestured with upturned palm toward the kitchen. "in the other room so we can talk?" She led the way.

Hope thanked Jeremy for sharing and followed Heather. She could feel the cross breeze from open windows throughout the apartment. The kitchen looked sparkling clean in the morning sunlight.

They sat at the table, Heather pushing a wooden bowl of granny smith apples to the side. She emptied the contents of a large manila envelope and spread them in front of Hope.

She ran her finger down the page, "This here's a list of things you need to get into the program." Hope read the list: *birth certificate, social security number, high-school transcript, current physical exam, language proficiency test (administered during registration), drug test, two reference letters from professionals (teacher, pastor, family physician, supervisor, other professional), one personal reference from a responsible long-term friend or a relative, and a one-page essay stating why you want to be a pharmacy assistant.* She looked into Heather's lovely eyes.

"Do you have a problem with any of these, Heather?"

"No—well—maybe some. It seems like a lot of messing around, getting it all together; but, no, I don't think so." She returned Hope's direct look, delighting her.

"Have you thought about who might write references for you? Of course, I'd write one."

"My foreman, Frank Ketchum. He loves my work; he would write one." She smiled broadly. "My doctor—he's been treating my diabetes for years, since I found out I had it when I was just ten years old. He treated Mom, too, until she died." She dropped her eyes. "I know he'd write one."

"And your sister would probably write one for you?"

"Hannah? Oh, yes." She nodded emphatically, mouth down-turned.

Hope asked if taking the language-proficiency test frightened her at all.

"It does, kind of. Can you study for it?" Her face turned serious. "I've always been kind of good with words. But there's a lot I don't know, too."

Hope offered to try to get a sample test from the school and work with her on strategies for passing. "It's worth putting your best effort into getting accepted if," she hesitated for effect, "if you're sure this is what you want to do." She lowered her chin and stared over black-framed glasses at her, straining to read her face as she responded.

"I think it is. It sounds like a career I could do." She scrubbed her small hands together. "How do I know for sure I would like it? How can I know that?" She frowned.

In the end, Hope advised her to start with the essay, which would help her decide if she really wanted to be a pharmacy assistant. Heather agreed. They discussed tuition, Heather maintaining that she could manage the deferred payment plan if she just worked a few extra hours a week. Hope cringed at the idea of her caring for Jeremy, trying to attend class, finding time to study, and working extra hours. She would have to look closely at helping her with that.

Hope rose to leave as Jeremy ran into the room. "Is Dr. Fleming staying for lunch, Mom?" His hand reached out, wanting to touch her. Hope grasped it and modeled a proper firm handshake for the boy.

"Well, sure, she could. If she wants," blushing as pink as her shirt.

"I don't think so," she said on top of Heather's words.

Hope expressed her thanks and good-byes and left after promising to call her once she had the sample test. As she descended the stairs, she could hear sounds of lunch being prepared.

It was a beautiful summer day, a day to enjoy sun shimmering on water. It made her think of her college days, of regattas and beach parties, water skiing and canoeing on cool mountain lakes in the Hamptons. She stopped at a drive-through restaurant for a tuna submarine sandwich with soft drink and drove out Reservoir Road, parking in a lay-by near the water's edge. She pulled an ancient wool stadium blanket from the trunk and spread it over a grassy spot with full view of a sandy inlet and the large lake beyond.

Two fishermen in a small boat silently maneuvered fishing tackle, rumple-brimmed canvas hats obscuring their faces. Soft gurgles and plomps echoed from the water as amphibious creatures moved beneath the surface.

In this perfect lakeside setting, the tuna sandwich and root beer were as elegant and savory as oysters and champagne to Hope. *Life is good.*

She watched a fisherman reel in a small trout with precision and no fanfare from his companion, admiring his skill and envying their obvious oneness with the lake and its inhabitants. *Peace. Comfort. Natural order.*

Peace. I thought I'd never have it. All those years I worried that a knock on the door would someday come. Thank God it never did. And now it never will. It's all behind me, a closed chapter in my life. All that money—I'm a wealthy woman.

She swallowed hard the lump in her throat. She felt suddenly drained, exhausted. Sadness engulfed her. Overhead gulls shrieked as if mocking her. *I'm a wealthy woman but I don't deserve to be. Deceit. I inherited Mary's money out of deceit. She gave me the world and I took all she gave and embezzled more.* She had never before thought of her act as embezzlement. She was shocked by what she'd done. *I'm a criminal. There's no denying it. And I've gotten off scot-free.*

Hope needed to get out of the sun, now high overhead. She gathered her lunch litter and the blanket and made her way through high grass back to the car. She tossed the blanket into the trunk, the litter into a door pouch. She took a last lingering look at the postcard view, inhaled deeply, and climbed into the car seat.

The neat suburban homes and lawns looked painfully upstanding to her as she drove home. She pulled into the driveway on Canterbury trying to recapture a feeling of euphoria. George's red frisbee lay on the lawn as if waiting for him to come back outside, and she was cheered by it.

I wonder how he and his father are getting on in that tiny condo. Perhaps I should buy him a place of his own. Financial security. He'd have some assets. And he'd never again be homeless.

She unlocked the side door and entered the quiet house, as always taking pleasure in the classic rooms and fine furnishings. *I must buy out Michael and protect this wonderful home. Of course, that's not a problem now. Thanks to Mary Baldwin's foresight. If I'd had her money twenty years ago, it would have ended up in Michael's hands. And God only knows what risky scheme he would have squandered it on.*

Hope sat down at the computer in her study and logged onto the internet. She typed the address of the website jotted on the post-it note stuck to the monitor. Frances said it would give all the details of her condition, complete with graphics "whether you want them or not."

She located the paper without difficulty and read the first paragraph. She scrolled to the end and seeing how lengthy it was, clicked *print*. While the printer choked out pages, Hope went to the kitchen for a cold drink. She returned to the study with a short glass of cranberry juice on the rocks.

She read through the article, trying to visualize in her sister the equally harrowing symptoms of the disease and side effects of treatment. She wondered if their sisterly bond, long untended, would emerge strong as ever when Frances arrived. She doubted it. *But how can I turn her away? She wants to be with family during the four-week hiatus from treatment she will have at the close of this series of external radiation doses. No, I cannot turn her away. "If you cannot help me live, Hope; at least, you can help me die."*

"I will help you live, Frances," Hope repeated aloud her response to her sister's morbid appeal. She flipped the page of her desk calendar, still showing May and realized that Frances would be here in eleven days, June 21st. She was flying in from Seattle and would get a cab from the airport, arriving around dinnertime.

Hope made a mental to-do list. She would put Frances in the upstairs guestroom so she would be near her in case she got into trouble during the night.

*

Hope slept fitfully all night despite having exhausted herself rearranging the room for Frances. She had moved the bed for a better view out the double windows. She had pushed the writing table next to the bed, so her sister would have more space for medications, and books. *I must find some really good spiritual books for her. If I were in her shoes, I would be reading those, I know.* She placed the tiny cherry nightstand next to the white silk chaise lounge she'd dragged in from her own bedroom, thinking Frances could rest there as a change from lying in bed. The dainty lines of the lounge blended well with the small nightstand.

She stretched luxuriously, rose, swept to the window and looked out at a brightening morning. The sky was clear and so was her mind. She felt sure the sun would soon rise on a brilliant day.

She knew what she must do. She would give away Mary's bequest to her, every penny of it. She would establish a foundation for the homeless in George's name, and he could live his dream of helping them have better lives. *Such a noble dream. George is a noble young man. Not at all the traumatized misfit I imagined. He's so much more than we deserve, Michael. Thank God.*

No keeping back enough to buy Michael out of this house or to pay Heather's tuition. No. If I'm to make true restitution for my crimes, I must find a way to do those things with my own money, money I have rightfully earned. And I will. George's foundation will have the entire amount.

She stepped into the shower with a feeling of lightness she had never known. Today would be a wonderful day.

Sipping hot tea, she listened to birdcalls and watched redbirds and sparrows at the feeder near the terrace. She breathed deeply of lavender bordering the garden. She soaked herself in the sun's warmth. She appreciated the beauty of a bit of blueberries, strawberry and banana slices, the remains of her breakfast in a creamware bowl.

Positioning the yellow legal pad, she took up the pencil and began a list. It was time to look at new dreams, dreams she would hold fast to from this day forward.

1) Seek advice on how to establish foundation.
   It cannot be all that difficult.
2) Speak to George re: foundation
   It will thrill him.
3) Establish foundation in George's name
   It'll be his design. I'll simply be the catalyst.
4) Forgive self for criminal ignorance
   Ignorance of the law is no excuse, but ignorance in general? This will take work.
5) Arrange 2nd mortgage to buy out Michael
   Back to my original intention.
6) Assist Heather in decision making and enrollment
   If she opts to go through with this training. She has to want it.
7) Poore Pond…

The list came to mind surprisingly easily. Hope rose and stepped to a lavender bed. She picked a stem and brought it to her nose. "Ummmm," she inhaled the fragrance. She thought about her year at Poore Pond. So much had happened in that single year. "I thought I was going to control everything and everyone," she chuckled at her naivete.

She looked again at her list of dreams and saw how different they were from her early ones, the dead dreams. She noticed for the first time that she had listed goals. She thought of them as dreams. *They are dreams, really, only more specific. Goals are specific steps to realizing dreams, a blueprint.*

She erased point seven and began again to write.

7) Continue to learn from Poore Pond family,
   nurturing professional growth and spirituality wherever I can.

She put down the pencil and looked across the lawn, eyes unseeing.

I will take my cue from people and situations.
I will remain open to the possible.
I will balance my life outside Poore Pond, the
better to avoid stress and burnout.
I will celebrate my contributions. And I have
made some.
I might even wear cotton pants when
principals return to school in August.
She chuckled to herself at the idea.

A sharp tat-tat-tat broke the stillness. Hope's entire body snapped toward the stone walk leading to the front of the house. Her heart in her mouth, her eyes riveted on the walk, she expected to see the silver tip of Mary Baldwin's cane. She could almost see her now, her strong presence lending stature to her frail figure, tapping her cane to demand immediate attention.

Tat-tat-tat. Hope's heart pounded. Heat rose in her chest. Her head spun around.

Tat-tat-tat. Tat-tat-tat. Her eyes followed the sound high above. A red-headed woodpecker tapped away in the towering pine tree a few feet from the terrace.

The flat of her hand thumped her chest and she sighed. She knew, at that moment, she would never have the peace she craved. She had not requited her sin.

She stood, resolutely dismissing these destructive thoughts.

There is still much work to do at Poore Pond. She gathered her papers and went inside. *We must work harder to raise test scores; we can do more to help lower-achieving children. And we can give more outreach to single parents who try to do it all on their own.*

"But first I must look after Frances," she announced to the bedside tumbler and carafe she had laid on the table to take later to the guestroom.

Job 27: 16-17 Though he heap up silver as the dust and prepare raiment as the clay: he may prepare it, but the just shall put it on, and the innocent shall divide the silver.

DISCUSSION QUESTIONS

1. In the opening paragraphs, Hope rises on the first day of school *anticipating that this day would mark the beginning of an experience that would change her life, although unaware how profoundly.*
   In what ways was Hope changed by her Poore Pond experience?

2. Hope's personality and behavior show multiple layers of dichotomy.
   a) What is Hope's dominant personality and what story events suggest that?
   b) Give examples of her behaviors (both past and during the story) that conflict with her dominant personality as we see it.

3. Ray Sellers displays ambiguous feelings about working for his first female boss. What elements in his personal life account for those feelings? How common is it for we, as humans, to be predisposed to that type of gender bias? Explain.

4. Ian Bradford harbors deep disappointments and regrets. How do those past experiences get in the way of his relationships at Poore Pond? Is Ian typical of most of us in that regard? Discuss.

5. What unmet needs do Hope, Ray, and Ian have in common? How differently does each character react to those need deficiencies?

6. In the end, did Hope deserve what she got? Explain.

7. Hope cares a great deal about image and dress, as we see in Chapter One. How important is dress for teachers? Principals?

8. Public schools are required to comply with separation-of-church-and-state laws; yet, parent Andy Tarantino comments (Ch. 24, p.256): *There's not enough spirituality in public schools.*
   a) Is total compliance possible in a school full of human beings to whom life happens?
   b) Which other Poore Pond family members appear to agree with Andy? Do you agree?

9. Do people and situations at Poore Pond School accurately reflect:
   a) current lifestyle trends in our society?
   b) constraints on our public schools?
   c) the many levels of human bonding inherent in a school?
   Explain.

10. In Chapter Seven (p.42) Hope laments the *politics* of education, commenting, *It's all politics...Life is just a string of situations, all political.* What political elements are present in Education? Marriage? Parenting? What implications do those political elements have for educators today?

QUICK ORDER FORM

Honor in the Heart is a good choice as a Book Club Selection. It is also a good choice for supplemental reading in teacher-education courses as well as graduate courses in school administration. School life is freshly depicted with emphasis on the many levels of human bonding. The compelling story provides insight in the area of a school's imprint on the lives of its families and the families' imprint on the shape of the school. Discussion questions are included.

Additional copies of *Honor in the Heart* may be ordered using this convenient form.

Hardcover	$23.95
Paperback	$14.95

Add $4.00 shipping for single copies, $2.00 each additional book.

Discounts are available for multiple copies:

6 – 10 copies:	10% discount
10 – 20 copies:	20% discount
More than 20:	**Contact Ambrosia Press**

PH: 440-951-7780
FAX: 440-951-0565
willowhse@yahoo.com

Send check with order form below to:

AMBROSIA PRESS
P.O. BOX B-7226
EASTLAKE, OH 44097-7226

Name: _____

Address: _____

City:_____State:_____Zip _____

____Qty. Hardcover @ $23.95	Total Hardcover	$ _____
____Qty. Paperback @ $14.95	Total Paper.	$ _____
	Total Ship.	$ _____
Honor in the Heart	Total Enclosed	$ _____